Mountain Top

Other books by Robert Whitlow

Life Support

Life Everlasting

The Sacrifice

The Trial

The List

Jimmy

Mountain Top

by

ROBERT
WHITLOW

THOMAS NELSON
Since 1798

NASHVILLE DALLAS MEXICO CITY RIO DE JANEIRO BEIJING

Published in Nashville, TN, by Thomas Nelson. Thomas Nelson is a trademark of Thomas Nelson, Inc.

Thomas Nelson, Inc. titles may be purchased in bulk for educational, business, fund-raising, or sales promotional use. For information, please e-mail SpecialMarkets@ThomasNelson.com.

Scripture quotations are from the HOLY BIBLE, NEW INTERNATIONAL VERSION®. © 1973, 1978, 1984 by International Bible Society. Used by permission of Zondervan Publishing House. All rights reserved.

Publisher's Note: This novel is a work of fiction. Names, characters, places, and incidents are either products of the author's imagination or used fictitiously. All characters are fictional, and any similarity to people living or dead is purely coincidental.

Library of Congress Cataloging-in-Publication Data

Whitlow, Robert, 1954–
    Mountain top / by Robert Whitlow.
      p. cm.
    ISBN-13: 978-1-59554-131-4 (hc)
    ISBN-10: 1-59554-131-4 (hc)
    ISBN-13: 978-1-59554-296-0 (tp)
    ISBN-10: 1-59554-296-5 (tp)
    1. Visions—Fiction. I. Title.
PS3573.H49837M68 2006
813'.54—dc22   2006025328

Printed in the United States of America

07 08 09 10 11 RRD 6 5 4 3 2 1

To people who dream.
You work in the dark,
but your insight helps others live in the light.

When a prophet of the LORD is among you,
I reveal myself to him in visions,
I speak to him in dreams.

Numbers 12:6 NIV

One

"WHAT ARE YOU GOING TO DO ABOUT THE LETTER?" THE VOICE on the phone demanded. "If it fell into the wrong hands, it could cost us millions!"

"I shredded it," the man sitting behind the expensive desk replied without emotion.

"Did anyone on your staff see it?"

"No. I open my own mail."

"But he could still talk."

"Of course, or send a letter to someone else. But I have a plan, and when I'm finished, no one will believe anything he says. It's not going to be an issue."

"You'd better be right. That's why you're in this deal—to make sure everything goes smoothly on the local front. How is our friend in Raleigh doing?"

"Ahead of schedule. But he's low on cash."

"Again? That was quick."

"It doesn't take long when you have his habits. He wants to see you."

"Okay, buy him a plane ticket, but I'm going to lower his limit."

"Not too much, or I'll have to give him a raise on this end."

SAM MILLER DID SOME OF HIS BEST WORK WHILE ASLEEP. SEVERAL nights each week, he had night visions more vivid than movies and spiritual dreams so real he could smell the fragrance of heaven. Muriel never stirred. She had to get her rest so she could fix his breakfast. Sam's lawncare equipment ran

1

on gasoline; he needed eggs, sausage, and biscuits with gravy before facing another day.

Sam rolled over and opened his blue eyes. He ran his hand over his closely cropped white hair and reached for the tattered notebook on the nightstand beside the bed. Some of the pages listed information about customers: the Smiths wanted their grass cut and patio edged before a party on Friday night, the Blevinses had decided to plant day lilies along the back of their property line. Other sheets recorded what Sam had seen and heard during the night: faces of people who lived in Shelton with diverse needs that ranged from salvation for a wayward child to money for an overdue car payment. Several pages contained crude drawings of strange images without easy interpretation. Notes, questions, and Bible verses filled the margins.

Beside the notebook was a picture of Sam and Muriel taken forty-three years earlier. It was their second wedding anniversary. Sam, wearing his Marine Corps dress uniform, stood unsmiling and stern next to his short, curly-haired wife. The soldier in the photo didn't have the large, round belly of the man in the bed nor the twinkle that lit his blue eyes. Those changes came later. Muriel's light brown hair remained curly and her figure trim, but her tanned face was now lined with wrinkles that were the road map to a hundred different ways to smile.

Sam sat up and rested his feet on the threadbare rug that covered part of the bedroom floor. He opened the notebook to a blank page. At the top he wrote the date and the words *Within three months you'll see your son.* He shuffled into the living room. Family photos on the walls recorded the life of Matthew Miller from cradle to manhood.

Tragedy was no stranger to the Miller family. Matthew, an Army medic, had died in Somalia. His pictures stopped with a grainy photo taken at dusk in front of a field hospital. Mountains without trees rose in the background.

Sam went into the kitchen and looked out the window above the sink. Muriel could wash a fifty-cent plastic plate and enjoy a million-dollar view. Their small house rested atop a knoll positioned like a step stool before the Blue Ridge Mountains. In the early light, Sam could see heavy frost on the grass and wispy ice on the trees in the distance. He leaned over and smelled the crisp morning air through a narrow gap at the bottom of the window. Weather ruled his business, and winter's schedule was less rigorous. When spring arrived, daffodils would jump out of the ground in clumps of yellow celebration all across the backyard, and Sam would be out the door to greet them with the first rays of the sun.

Sam always made the morning coffee. He could drink it strong and black, but Muriel liked it so diluted with milk and sugar that it could be served to a child. Sam made the coffee weak. Later, he'd get a strong cup at the Minute Market. The coffee started dripping into the pot, and he returned to the bedroom. Muriel was out of bed and wrapped in her housecoat. Sam leaned over and kissed the top of her head. She responded by patting him on his fuzzy right cheek.

"It's time for my bear to come out of hibernation," she said. "Are you going to shave this morning?"

"Yep, then take tomorrow off before church on Sunday."

SAM SHOWERED AND SCRAPED HIS CHIN FREE OF STUBBLE. Buttoning his shirt, he could smell the sausage in the skillet. Muriel rarely bought sausage at the store; she canned it fresh each fall like her mother and grandmother before her. Sam didn't raise pigs, but he knew a man who did. Homemade sausage seasoned with the perfect blend of sage and pepper couldn't be compared to meat from a factory wrapped in a plastic tube. The smoky smell of sausage in the skillet reminded Sam of boyhood breakfasts cooked on an open fire in the woods. His stomach rumbled in anticipation.

The cupboard at the Miller house didn't look like a grocery store shelf. Mason jars of green beans, tomatoes, okra, squash, and yellow corn cut from the cob filled the narrow space. Sam's garden was legendary. Two acres on the flat spot at the bottom of the driveway produced more than enough to feed the Millers and provided extra income through the sale of fresh produce to Sam's customers. Mrs. Sellers loved to eat Sam's sun-ripened tomatoes like apples.

Sam came into the kitchen, gave Muriel a hug, and rubbed his cheek against hers.

"How's that?" he asked.

"Much better. The biscuits are in the oven."

"I want to take a sausage biscuit to Barry Porter," Sam said. "He's going to deliver two loads of pine bark mulch to a job this morning."

Sam sat at the small kitchen table and watched Muriel's morning routine. Every movement had meaning. She didn't waste energy or ingredients. Sam picked up a jar of molasses and tipped it so the amber liquid rolled to one side.

"How is Barry's boy doing?" Muriel asked.

Sam returned the molasses to its place on the vinyl tablecloth.

"He ran off with a married woman to Florida. He's eating slop and calling it steak, but I saw him turning toward home the other night. I'm going to remind Barry to keep looking down the road and welcome him back when he repents."

Muriel opened the oven door and took out four golden biscuits. When Matthew was a teenager, she baked six to eight biscuits that always disappeared before the male members of the family went out the front door.

"Why don't you take Barry two biscuits?" she suggested. "You eat one, and I'll nibble on the other."

Sam scratched his head. "Only one for me? I don't want to pass out while spreading the mulch around Mrs. Smith's patio. I need all my strength to lift that shovel."

Muriel turned her back to him as she put the sausage on a clean serving plate and sprinkled flour and pepper into the skillet for the gravy.

"I'm thinking about the extra weight these biscuits and sausage are causing around that stomach of yours," she said. "You know your cholesterol is inching up, and Dr. Murray told you to watch your diet."

Sam's mouth dropped open, and he stared at her back for a moment. "Are you serious?"

Muriel turned around with a serious look on her face. "I love babying you, but sometimes I feel guilty fixing what you want all the time."

Sam grinned. "Don't worry. The gravy cuts the calories in half."

"We won't argue about it this morning, but I'm not fixing fried chicken tonight. I found a recipe for broiled chicken that sounds real tasty. It uses some of the herbs I dried last summer."

"Sounds great. The touch of your loving hands is the key to a good meal."

Muriel shook her head. "For a country boy, you're a smooth talker."

After all the food was on the table, she sat down across from him. They bowed their heads.

Sam prayed for Barry's son, moved into his usual blessing over the meal, and concluded with, "And Master, please take all the cholesterol out of this fine breakfast. Amen."

"Your health is not a joke," Muriel said when he finished. "I want to keep you with me as long as possible."

Sam reached across and put his weathered hand on top of hers. "And I don't want either of us to leave a moment before Papa's perfect time."

AFTER BREAKFAST, SAM PUT ON A HEAVY COAT AND WENT OUTSIDE while Muriel washed the dishes. The sun was a large yellow ball in the east, and the frost was in full retreat across the yard, exposing the dead grass. Without any wind blowing, the mountain air would warm up rapidly. The coat, hat, and gloves would keep Sam comfortable until he started working. He filled an orange cooler with water from a back porch sink supplied by pipes prevented from freezing by thick insulation wrapped around them.

Sam kept the utility trailer he used to haul his equipment in a small storage shed. Parked in front of the shed was a dented red pickup truck with the words "Sam Miller – Lawn Maintenance" written on both doors in white paint. Underneath was Sam's phone number. The boy who painted the advertisement on the truck did a neat job. Three years later, the letters and numbers were only chipped in a few places.

Sam unlocked the door of the shed and went inside. The familiar odors of gasoline and dry grass greeted him. Sam owned a large commercial mower, a regular push mower for trimming, and an edger. He did all the maintenance on the equipment himself. The past week, he'd rebuilt the engine in the commercial mower so it would be ready for the spring season. He placed a rake, shovel, mattock, and other hand tools in a rack toward the front of the trailer and secured everything with a strap. He reached into his pocket for the keys to the truck so he could back it up to the trailer. As he stepped away from the building, movement at the bottom of the driveway caught his eye. A Barlow County sheriff's car turned into his driveway. Sam walked around the side of the house. The car pulled up to his front door and stopped. Two deputies got out.

"Morning, Sam," the older of the two men called out. "Cold enough for you?"

It was Lamar Cochran, the chief deputy. Sam and Muriel had known the Cochran family for years. Lamar, a large man with reddish-brown hair, looked almost exactly like his father.

"Howdy, Lamar," Sam said. "Not too bad. Who's your running mate?"

"This is Vic Morris," Cochran replied. "He grew up in Hendersonville and joined us a few months ago."

Sam wiped his right hand on his pants and extended it to Morris.

"Good to meet you," Sam said.

Morris hesitated a moment before shaking Sam's hand.

"Don't have any biscuits to offer you," Sam said to the two men. "Muriel won't make any extras because she knows where they'll end up." Sam patted his stomach.

"Uh, that's all right, Sam," Cochran replied. "I need to talk serious with you."

"Come inside. I'm always here to help."

Sam turned away and climbed the three steps to the front stoop.

Cochran glanced at Morris and sighed. "Okay. I guess it won't hurt. Where is Muriel?"

"Cleaning up after me, of course," Sam replied, opening the door.

The three men entered the small living room. Sam stuck his head in the kitchen.

"Lamar Cochran and a young deputy named Vic Morris are here," he said.

Muriel wrapped her housecoat more tightly around herself and came to the doorway. Cochran nodded to her. Muriel gave him a big smile.

"Hey, Lamar," she said. "How's your mama? I haven't seen her in quite a while."

"Not doing so well. Her sugar is messing her up big-time, and my brother and I had to put her in the nursing home. That way, there is someone to watch her diet and give her the right medicine."

"I'll have to get down to see her—"

"Don't, Muriel," Cochran interrupted, looking at the floor. "This isn't a social call."

Sam tilted his head to the side. "What do you mean?"

Cochran nodded toward Morris, who pulled a sheet of paper from his back pocket.

"Mr. Miller, this is a warrant for your arrest," Morris said. "We're here to take you to jail."

Two

REVEREND MICHAEL JAMES ANDREWS DIDN'T TAKE MONDAYS OFF.

"Why would you need a day to relax?" asked Bobby Lambert, one of Mike's former law partners and an elder at the Little Creek Church. "You only work one hour a week. Every day but Sunday you can tell folks that you're going to pray then slip out the back door to the golf course."

"I can't ignore the eternal peril of my current clients," Mike replied. "Keeping them out of trouble is a twenty-four-hour-a-day job. Take you, for example. Convincing the Almighty to have mercy on your wretched soul is harder than getting Judge Coberg to grant a temporary restraining order in a covenant not to compete lawsuit. Every time I come up with an argument in your favor, you find new and creative ways to sin."

Mike's regular day away from the office was Friday. After almost ten years as a trial lawyer, the brown-haired, broad-shouldered minister continued to view Monday as a normal workday. Not going to the church on Friday, however, created the illusion of a long weekend. By Thursday morning, he'd written and practiced his sermon several times, so there wasn't much to do but wait for Sunday morning at 11:25 a.m. to deliver it.

Mike never felt guilty walking down a broad fairway on Friday afternoons. However, gone were the days when he could lose a dozen balls a round in water hazards without giving it a second thought. Golf was an expensive pastime, and on a minister's salary Mike didn't have the money to pay greens fees and rent a cart whenever he had the urge to play a round of golf. So, while in seminary he took up mountain biking. When his wife, Peg, questioned the change, he told her he'd rather elevate his heart rate

7

pedaling up a steep hill than in frustration over a five-foot putt that rimmed out of the cup.

Little Creek Church was located fifty yards from the small, rocky stream that gave the church its name. For more than 140 years, the congregation of independent Presbyterians averaged 50 to 100 members with the graveyard behind the church being the only part of the church that steadily grew.

During the past ten years, everything had changed. Development of Barlow County's beautiful mountain property had resulted in the construction of hundreds of vacation and retirement homes in the hills surrounding the church. The influx of people caused the church to experience rapid growth.

When Mike decided to leave law practice in Shelton and become a minister, the Little Creek elders followed his progress through seminary in Virginia and issued a call as soon as he graduated. Questions about his lack of experience vanished after doubters heard him preach. In his booming, baritone voice, Mike transferred his oratorical skills as a successful lawyer to the pulpit.

The small white sanctuary couldn't handle the crowds. Some of the older members, not wanting to vacate the well-worn pews occupied by their ancestors, fought the building program, but their efforts proved as futile as a skirmish by Confederate soldiers against advancing Yankee troops in 1865. Within a year and a half, a new sanctuary stood like a big brother next to the old one. The old sanctuary became a wedding chapel and funeral parlor.

Mike's office was at the back corner of an administration wing connected to the new sanctuary. He sold the leather-inlaid, walnut desk from his law office and let Peg decorate his new work space. She selected an effeminate worktable with Queen Anne legs and expensive antique furnishings. Typically, Peg ran over budget, but Mike bit his tongue and didn't complain. He secretly paid the extra expense and viewed it as an investment in convincing Peg to accept the transition from lawyer's spouse to minister's wife.

Mike put down a book about how to be an effective minister in a changing community and looked at the large clock on the wall. It was 11:15 a.m., and he'd only had two phone calls all morning. Compared to the stress of a law office, the pace of church leadership was like floating down a slow-moving eastern North Carolina river. At semiannual ministerial meetings, Mike heard other pastors complain about the hassle and pressure of their jobs, but he kept his mouth shut. Dealing with a church member's concern about the condition of the flower beds in front of the old sanctuary or complaints about the choir director's hymn selections was a lot easier than a four-hour deposition in which the opposing lawyer continuously raised spurious objections and a duplicitous witness refused to tell the truth. There was a light knock on his door.

"Come in," he said.

Delores Killian, the sixty-year-old church secretary, stuck her head into the office. A widow and holdover from the old guard, one of Mike's early triumphs had been winning her support. His strategy was simple. He never asked her to do anything except what she'd always done, and she praised him to all her friends as an excellent administrator.

"Someone is here to see you who didn't have an appointment," Delores whispered in a husky voice that revealed a forty-year love affair with cigarettes.

"Who is it? I'm having lunch in Shelton with Dick Saxby, a man who visited the church on Sunday, and need to leave in a few minutes."

"Muriel Miller. She's not a member of the church. Her husband is in jail, and she wants you to go see him."

"What are the charges?"

Delores raised her eyebrows. "She didn't tell me, and I didn't ask."

Mike waved his hand. "Don't bother. I'll talk to her on my way out."

During his legal career, Mike handled criminal cases and interacted with scores of men wearing orange jumpsuits, handcuffs, and leg irons. Since becoming a minister, he'd not visited the jail and had, in fact, ignored the squat gray building a couple of blocks from the courthouse. He returned to his book. It was an interesting chapter. The author offered several creative suggestions for bringing rural and cosmopolitan church members together. After several minutes, Mike dictated a memo of his findings for the elders. Mike was a hunt-and-peck typist, but Delores was even worse at transcribing dictation.

After checking his hair in a small mirror beside the door, he walked into the reception area where he was startled by the sight of a small, gray-haired woman with a wrinkled face. She sat on the edge of a small sofa and wrung a tissue in her hands. The woman's dress, a plain yellow cotton print, revealed her country roots. She looked up at him anxiously.

"Oh," Mike began. "You're Mrs., uh . . ."

"Miller," Delores said. "Her husband—"

"Is in jail," Mike finished, regaining his bearings. "I'm sorry to hear that."

Muriel stood, and Mike shook her hand. Her fingers were small but her grip firm.

"Reverend Andrews, would you visit my husband? He's been in jail for almost three months."

"Do I know him?"

"His name is Sam Miller. We live off McAfee Road. He has a lawncare business."

Mike thought for a moment but couldn't connect the name with a face. McAfee Road was ten miles on the west side of Shelton, almost twenty miles from the church. No one that far away came to Little Creek Church.

Muriel continued, "He told me you were a good lawyer."

"Not for over six years. I represented a lot of people when I practiced law, but I don't remember your husband."

"Oh, he's never gone to see a lawyer in his life."

"Then why contact me?"

Muriel lowered her eyes and spoke in a soft voice. "He had a dream Saturday night and saw you coming to see him at the jail. When I visited him on Sunday, he told me to get in touch with you here at the church."

Mike's jaw dropped open slightly. Delores leaned forward in her chair.

"Excuse me," Mike said. "Could you explain what you just said?"

Muriel sighed. "Sam has a lot of dreams. The Lord shows him things that are going to happen and stuff about people he's supposed to pray for." Her voice grew stronger. "It's nothing that doesn't happen in the Bible. Jacob had a dream and saw angels on a ladder; Joseph had dreams about himself and interpreted dreams for others—"

"I know the Bible," Mike interrupted.

"Of course you do," Muriel responded quietly. "I just didn't want you to think Sam was a nut."

Mike caught Delores rolling her eyes out of the corner of his vision.

"I'll walk out with you," Mike said to Muriel. "I have a luncheon meeting in Shelton."

They entered a short hall. Mountain landscapes painted by Peg hung on the walls. Mike opened the door for Muriel. It was a warm but pleasant spring day. They walked down a brick sidewalk to the new parking lot. The asphalt sparkled in the sun. Mike had a reserved parking space marked "Senior Pastor."

"Why is your husband in jail?"

"He didn't do anything wrong."

It had been years since Mike heard that familiar line.

"I understand, but he must have been charged with something."

"They claim he took money from the church. But it's either a lie or a big mistake."

"Embezzlement?"

"Yes, that's the word."

"Which church?"

"Craig Valley. It's a little place not far from the house. Sam was filling in as their preacher for a few months while they looked for a new man to take over."

"Is that your home church?"

"Not really. We move from church to church as the Lord directs."

Mike glanced sideways at the strange remark. They reached his car, a Lexus holdover from his days as a lawyer that now had more than 250,000 miles on the odometer. Beside his car sat a red pickup truck with Miller's name on the side. At least that part of this odd woman's story was true. Mike faced her.

"My sympathies are with you, and I'll pray for your husband, but I'm not the man you need. You should hire a practicing lawyer who can request bail. Three months is a long time to sit in jail. If your husband hasn't given a statement to the police, tell him to keep his mouth shut until he talks to an attorney. Confession is good at the church altar, not during a jailhouse interrogation."

Satisfied with his succinct and accurate counsel, Mike opened the door of his car. Muriel didn't move.

"Good luck," Mike said.

"Don't forget the dream," Muriel responded.

Mike slid into the car seat and looked up at her.

"Believe me. I won't."

Three

THE ROAD FROM LITTLE CREEK CHURCH TO SHELTON FOLLOWED the winding course of a valley nestled between two wooded ridges. Three times the road crossed a bold-flowing stream before climbing over one of the ridges and dipping into town. Mike and Peg's house was on a street near the top of a ridge. When the leaves fell from the trees, they could see into the center of town, a picturesque view at Christmas when colored lights along the downtown streets twinkled and large angels with trumpets to their lips perched atop every other lamp pole. Mike liked to bundle up in a blanket, sit outside in a lounge chair, and enjoy the show.

Mike and Peg bought their house when he first started practicing law and were on the verge of purchasing a much larger home when he decided to go to seminary in Virginia. So, instead of moving into a showcase home in the best area of town, they lived in a modest condominium for three years and rented out the house in Shelton. After completing seminary, Mike accepted the call to the Little Creek Church, and they returned home.

Childless, their only house guest was Judge, an eight-year-old Hungarian vizsla. The short-haired, gold-colored hunter/retriever acquired his name the day Mike and Peg picked him out from the litter of a breeder in Highlands.

"Look how that one barks at all the other pups," Peg remarked as they watched the dogs tumbling around in the pen. "I think he's the one."

"He reminds me of Judge Lancaster in Morganton," Mike said.

"Why?"

"He spends all his time barking at the other lawyers."

"Then that's what we'll call him," Peg replied.

12

"Lancaster?"

"No, silly. Judge."

Recently, Mike had suggested they might sell their home and look for a house closer to the church, but Peg cut him off. Her social orbit had the town, not the church, at its center. So, they stayed put. Mike's salary from the church was barely enough to pay the mortgage and their other bills. Mike kept reassuring Peg that the growth of the church would soon justify a significant increase in salary. Her response was a slight twist of her lips that communicated skepticism more effectively than words.

Mike drove down the hill into town. Shelton had twelve traffic lights. Each light had a number on a tiny sign above it that provided a convenient way to give directions—turn left at number six and right at four. The courthouse square was flanked by numbers one through four.

Mike parked on the west side of the courthouse square, across the street from the law firm formerly known as Forrest, Andrews, and Lambert, the most respected law firm in Barlow County. The gold letters over the front door now read Forrest, Lambert, Park, and Arnold. Mr. Forrest claimed it had taken two lawyers to replace Mike.

Mike entered the Ashe Street Café, a long, rectangular room with booths along two sides and tables down the middle. Waitresses brought plates of hot food from the kitchen at the rear of the room. Several men were waiting for a place to sit. He nodded in the direction of Butch Niles, the manager of the trust department for the Bank of Barlow County and a popular young representative in the General Assembly. Standing beside Niles was Jim Postell, the longtime county clerk of court and a savvy local politician.

"Hello, Preacher," said Niles, slapping Mike on the back. "I've been hearing good things about you. What are you going to do next? Run against me for the legislature?"

"The only election I need to win is a majority vote of the church elders," Mike responded. "And there's no way a lawyer turned minister could ever be elected to anything. Half the people in Barlow County are mad because I sued them, and the other half wouldn't vote for me because I'm not part of their denomination."

Niles chuckled. "What if I didn't run and could get Jim to endorse you?"

"Then I could be governor."

A table opened for Postell and Niles.

"Why don't you join us?" the clerk of court asked. "The regulars will be here in a few minutes. We'll argue politics, but it won't amount to anything."

"No, thanks, I have an appointment."

Other members of the legal and business community drifted into the café. There was no sign of Saxby. Mike looked at his watch and inwardly kicked himself for not confirming the appointment. He checked his PDA but hadn't entered a contact number. He then called the church, but Delores had left and turned on the answering machine. He looked at the table where Niles and his cronies were sitting. There weren't any empty seats. Everyone else in the café was preoccupied with lunch and conversation.

Laughter came from the direction of the rear of the restaurant. Mike suddenly wanted to get out of there. After one more glance at his watch, he turned to the blond-haired woman behind the cash register.

"Sue, if a man named Dick Saxby comes in looking for me, tell him I waited as long as I could but had to leave for another appointment."

"Sure thing, Mike. Do you want anything to go?"

"No, thanks."

Mike breathed a sigh of relief. Walking down the sidewalk toward his car, he muttered, "I don't have another appointment."

Blurting out a false excuse as a way to get out of the restaurant didn't make sense. Bogus meetings had never been part of Mike's strategy for managing his day, and he considered a lie an act of cowardice. He stopped at light number four and waited for it to turn green. No one was harmed by his misstatement, but it still made him feel uneasy. It would be awkward to return to the café, but—he stopped.

He could visit the jail and make his statement true.

The light turned green, but Mike didn't cross the street. He glanced in the direction of the jail. Not visible, he knew it stood two blocks away, set back from the street with a small parking lot in front and an exercise yard surrounded by a high fence and razor wire in the rear. He looked again at his watch. He'd set aside more than an hour for lunch and didn't have any reason to return to the church. He began walking slowly down the street toward the jail. Muriel Miller might not deliver his advice to her husband about keeping his mouth shut. It wouldn't hurt to do it himself.

THE VISITORS' WAITING AREA HADN'T CHANGED IN SIX YEARS. Same plastic furniture and light green paint on the walls. Except for the presence of a thick metal door, it looked like the reception room for a cheap insurance agency. Mike knocked on a small glass partition in the wall. A young female deputy slid it open.

"May I help you?" she asked pleasantly.

"I'm Mike Andrews. I'd like to talk with a prisoner named Sam Miller."

The woman pointed to a sign on the wall next to the opening. "Visiting hours are Wednesday evening from 6:00 p.m. to 8:00 p.m., Saturday morning from 9:00 a.m. to noon, and Sunday afternoon from 1:00 p.m. to 4:00 p.m."

"Oh, I'm a minister," Mike said. "Mr. Miller's wife asked me to visit him."

"That doesn't change the rules."

Mike hesitated. "I'm also a lawyer."

The woman's eyes narrowed. "Do you have a picture ID and your attorney card?"

Mike took out his wallet and handed over his driver's license and state bar association card. He'd maintained his law license by paying a small annual fee and attending a yearly seminar at the coast where he took enough classes to satisfy his continuing legal education requirement. Peg liked the beach, and in the afternoons Mike played golf.

The woman disappeared with the items. Mike waited, tapping his finger on the counter. When she didn't return, Mike began to wonder if she was calling Raleigh to find out if anyone had reported a suspicious man traveling across the state impersonating an attorney. Finally, she reappeared, joined by a familiar face.

"Mike Andrews!" bellowed Chief Deputy Lamar Cochran. "What brings you down here?"

"Hey, Lamar, nothing different, still pretending to be a lawyer."

"It's okay," Cochran said to the woman deputy. "Mr. Andrews practiced law before he went to preaching. Let him in."

An electric buzzer sounded, and Mike pulled open the metal door. Cochran waited for him on the other side. The two men shook hands.

"You've kept your law license?" Cochran asked.

"Yeah, once you pass the bar exam, it's hard to give it up. There's not much required to maintain good standing, but I may go inactive in a few years."

Mike followed Cochran into the booking area. A wire-mesh screen on one side of the room overlooked a broad hallway, the holding cell for drunks, and two interview rooms. The cell block lay behind another solid metal door.

"How do you know Sam Miller?" Cochran asked.

"I don't. His wife stopped by the church and asked me to visit him. Is anyone representing him?"

"I don't think so." Cochran shook his head. "I've known Sam and Muriel since I was a kid. He's a bit odd, but I always thought he was harmless."

"Embezzlement?"

"Yeah," Cochran said, lowering his voice. "But I hope it ain't true. Sam is getting up in years and ought to be rocking on the back porch enjoying the mountains, not sitting in a cell block with a bunch of reprobates who broke the law while high on dope."

"What about bond?"

"Too high for him to meet. I gave him the number for a bondsman but don't know if he ever called him."

"Well, let me have a look at him," Mike said. "I'll try to steer him in the right direction."

"I'll get him myself."

Cochran entered the cell block. Mike stepped from the booking area into the hallway. He'd forgotten the smell and feel of the jail. The odor changed depending on the day of the week. Mike had visited the lockup on Saturday nights when there was no escaping the stench of stale sweat and human waste. By Monday afternoon, the foul odors of the weekend had been replaced by lemony disinfectant. Today, the floors were clean, the drunk tank empty. The feel of the jail, however, never changed. Despair clung to its walls. Hopelessness hovered in the air. When he left the correctional center, Mike always celebrated his freedom with a deep breath.

He opened the door to one of the interview rooms. It was empty. Glancing down at the table and chairs, he realized he hadn't brought a legal pad. He thought about asking a booking officer for a sheet of paper but decided not to. He didn't need to take notes. He wasn't even sure why he'd come.

The door to the cell block opened. Cochran returned, followed by a white-haired, rotund man wearing an orange jumpsuit. The older man stepped from behind the chief deputy, saw Mike, and smiled.

"Hello, son," he said, holding out his hand. "I'm Sam Miller. Thanks for coming."

"You can use either room," Cochran said.

"We'll park in number one," Mike replied. "I won't be too long. I need to get back to the church."

Mike held the door open for Sam, who lowered himself into a plastic chair. Mike sat on the opposite side of the table. He got right to the point.

"Why did you want to see me?"

"So we can help each other."

"Help each other?" Mike asked in surprise.

"Yep."

"You're the one in jail, Mr. Miller. How are you going to help me?"

"There are all kinds of jail. One of the worst is the prison of wrong thinking. I spent many years locked up there before I found the key and opened the door."

"Excuse me?"

"Sorry, I'm jumping ahead. We have so much to talk about."

"Don't you want to talk about the reason you're here?"

"Of course," Sam answered, patting his stomach. "You're one reason. But first you can ask me anything you want. I don't want to rush anything."

Mike decided to humor him for a few minutes, then make a quick exit. He could call one of the judicial assistants at the courthouse and find out why an attorney hadn't been appointed to represent the old man. Even if Miller didn't qualify for an appointed lawyer, someone should arrange an evaluation of the older man's mental competency.

"Has a detective asked you questions about the embezzlement charge?" Mike asked.

"Yep. Several times."

"Did you talk to him?"

"Yep, but there wasn't much to say."

"What did you tell him?"

"The truth."

"Did you sign a statement?"

"The last time he came by, he wrote down what I said, and I signed it."

Mike winced. A signed statement never helped the defense.

"What did he ask you?"

"About me and the church. Who took up the offerings? Who counted it? Why so much money turned up in my checking account. Stuff like that."

"How much money turned up in your checking account?"

"Around $100,000. I told him it must have been a bank mistake. I don't keep very much in my personal or business account, and I've never had that kind of money at one time in my life. Cash goes out as soon as it comes in around my house. The detective said he would double-check with the bank and let me know what he found out. He was a nice young fellow, but he never got back with me."

"Do you remember his name?"

"Perkins."

The name wasn't familiar to Mike.

"Are they claiming you stole $100,000 from the church you were serving as a fill-in preacher?"

"I guess so."

"What's the name of the church?"

"Craig Valley Gospel Tabernacle."

"How many people attend?"

"It's been growing. There are about fifty adults and the same number of young-uns."

"How did the church get that much money in the first place?"

Sam shrugged. "I don't know. They've been saving up for a new building. The concrete for the foundation was poured last fall, but I don't know how much they've collected altogether."

Mike sat back in his seat. The old man seemed capable of carrying on a normal conversation when he wanted to.

"Has a magistrate set bail?"

"Yep, it's $100,000, too. That number keeps coming up. I'm not sure what it means."

"It means a felony charge," Mike replied grimly. "Have you tried to post a property bond or called a bondsman?"

"Muriel showed the magistrate the deed for our property, but it wasn't worth enough, so I had to stay put. It's not been easy, but there's been fruit."

"I'm glad they've improved the menu."

"What menu?"

"The food. I'm glad the food is decent."

"I wouldn't say that, especially compared to what my wife puts on the table."

Mike leaned back in his seat. "Mr. Miller, I haven't had lunch today, and I didn't come here to talk about food. Explain in simple terms, with as few words as possible, why you sent your wife to the church to see me."

"Papa told me."

"Your father is alive?"

Sam pointed at the ceiling. "My Papa will never die. He's the Ancient of Days."

Mike stared at the tip of the old man's index finger. "You're telling me God is your father?"

"Yep. Isn't he your father, too?"

"Uh, of course. I thought you meant an earthly father."

"Nope. He's been dead over twenty years. I was just answering your question as simply as I could."

Mike put his hands together beneath his chin. "So, God told you to contact me."

"Yep, so you can be my lawyer."

"Mr. Miller, I used to practice law, but it's been six years since I stepped into a courtroom."

"You could still do it if you wanted to."

"Technically, yes, but as a practical matter, no."

Sam hesitated. "If it's the money, I'm sure we can make arrangements. I don't have much, and Muriel had to dip into our savings to keep the lights on, but I can scrape enough—"

Mike leaned forward and looked directly into the old man's face. "It's not the money. I stopped practicing law because I wanted to obey God, and I'm not going back into the courtroom for any amount of money. You're a minister. You should understand what I'm talking about."

Sam nodded. "You had to count the cost, didn't you?"

"Yes, and I'm making less now in a year than I used to in three months. But I don't believe the size of a person's bank account is the true measure of success."

"That's a good answer. I wouldn't want anyone representing me who believed anything different."

"I'm not going to represent you."

Sam smiled. "Papa knows how to make the most of every situation. I spent a few nights in the brig for fighting years ago, but it was a lot different coming here now. Do you feel the hopelessness in this place?"

Mike tilted his head to the side. "Yes."

"It tried to jump on me, but I sent it packing. The boys in here need help in the worst way, and Papa has let me do some good. There was a young man in the cell block who gave his life to the Master a couple of weeks ago. He'll be a preacher someday. He's not as smart as you, but he'll gather in his share of the harvest."

Mike stared at Sam for a second. "Mr. Miller, I'm glad we've had this talk, but I need to leave. I sympathize with your predicament, but as I told your wife, I'm not the man to help you."

Sam sat silently for a moment. "Then why did you come see me?"

"I was just standing on the sidewalk after a guy stood me up for lunch and decided it wouldn't hurt to come by the jail and meet you."

"Who put that thought in your head?"

"I have no idea, but that's not the sort of thing I'm talking about." Mike stood to his feet. "I hope things work out for you."

Sam didn't budge.

"You were a man of integrity as a lawyer before you became a minister," Sam said. "And I know Papa loves you. Pray about helping me, and see what He tells you."

"Okay, but I'm also going to call the courthouse and ask someone in the judge's office to appoint a lawyer to represent you so you can get out of jail."

"I'd like that a lot. This Saturday, Muriel and I will celebrate our forty-fifth wedding anniversary. She's a jewel of a woman."

"And you should be with her."

"You're right about that."

Mike opened the interview room door and held it as the old man stepped into the hallway. Sam stopped and turned around so he faced Mike.

"Oh, and tell your wife that Isaac is on the way," he said.

Mike didn't respond. Nobody named Isaac was in Mike and Peg's circle of family, friends, or acquaintances; however, Mike had already figured out that Sam Miller was the type of person who could keep a conversation going indefinitely with off-the-wall comments.

Lamar Cochran came forward and gently touched the white-haired man on the arm.

"Sam, you have to return to the cell block," he said.

"You know what I'd like for supper?" Sam asked the chief deputy.

"Some of Muriel's fried chicken."

"Yep."

"If that was on the chow line," Cochran replied, "we'd have people break-ing into this jail."

Cochran looked at Mike and shook his head sadly.

"The guard will push the release for the door," the chief deputy said. "See you around town."

Mike let the metal door close slowly behind him. The female deputy ignored him as he left the building. He didn't look back. Outside, the air was fresh and clean. Mike took a deep breath. He walked away from the jail, as always, glad to be free.

Four

BACK AT THE CHURCH, MIKE HUNG UP THE PHONE. THE WOMAN who handled the assignment of criminal cases to younger lawyers in the circuit told him Sam hadn't requested that an attorney be appointed, but she would send one to the jail. Mike suspected a competent lawyer could quickly get to the bottom of the embezzlement charge and clear it up if it was a clerical error at the bank or arrange a plea bargain if it wasn't. Mike dropped a message from Muriel Miller asking him to call her after he met with Sam into the trash can. He'd fulfilled his civic and religious duty.

Mike returned to studying the book on church growth and didn't take a break for three hours. Several times he caught himself humming a song that had nothing to do with the words on the page. When he finished studying, he decided to take a short walk around the church property and make sure everything was neat and tidy.

"I'll be back in a few minutes," he said to Delores as he passed her desk.

The secretary was working the crossword puzzle that appeared in the local paper and didn't look up.

"Don't forget, I need to leave early for my appointment at the beauty shop," she said.

The grass in front of the new sanctuary had been freshly mowed, but the flower beds looked ragged. He walked behind the old sanctuary. To his right was the church cemetery. Small, weathered headstones streaked with gray filled most of the older section. The newer plots, with larger, more impressive monuments, were over a slight rise in the ground. The old cemetery needed major work.

Just beyond the cemetery lay Little Creek, swollen to springtime levels, but still not much more than a steady stream. During dry spells in summer, the creek dwindled to a trickle, prompting the Baptists down the road to remark that a few drops of water was enough to keep the Little Creek congregation going. That, and the support of a handful of stalwart families, had sustained the church through the generations since its founding shortly after the Civil War.

Trees lined the water, but on the church side, a short path led to an opening that had served as a watering hole for horses and mules when the members of the congregation came to church in wagons. A small spring nourished the creek at the spot, and Mike enjoyed watching the bubbles rise to the surface as the water forced its way past the smooth rocks on the bottom. He dipped his hand into the cold water and rubbed it on his face. He felt doubly refreshed—the water on his cheeks, a tangible sense of blessing in his soul.

Mike stepped away from the creek and looked at the church. It was a beautiful setting with the wooded hills in the background. Joy, like the water below the ground, rose to the surface of his consciousness. Mike's call to ministry had survived the cross-examination of those who doubted. Now, after the upheaval of leaving his law practice and three years of seminary training, it had brought him to a pleasant place.

"Thank You, Lord," he said, then paused before saying, "Thank You, Papa."

Mike smiled and shook his head at Sam Miller's method of addressing the Almighty. Casual familiarity with God might work for an old man who ran a lawncare business, but not for him.

Delores left the church for her hair appointment at 3:00 p.m. Shortly after she left, Nathan Goode stuck his head into Mike's office. The unmarried twenty-five-year-old, part-time choir director and youth minister often stopped by the church on Monday afternoons to see Mike after finishing his regular job as music teacher at the local high school. The young man's black hair crept down his neck, and he had a closely trimmed goatee. Close up, the holes that had once housed multiple earrings could still be seen; however, he'd transitioned from nonconformist to upwardly mobile professional, using his salary from the church to make the payments on a silver BMW.

"Any complaints come in today?" Nathan asked.

"All quiet."

"I wasn't sure about using the alternate tune for the Doxology. It was a pretty big gamble. I watched Mrs. Harcourt. She kept sticking her finger in her ear. I'm not sure if she was trying to clean it out or stop it up."

"The Harcourts left town for Florida after the service and didn't give any feedback. They'll be gone three weeks and won't remember what happened by the time they return. Are you going to try out something new this Sunday?"

"No, I'm going to use a high school flute player for the offertory. That should be tame enough."

"Okay."

"And I have an anthem that dates back a few hundred years. Can you recruit Peg for choir practice this week? This piece has an alto solo made for her voice."

"It might work if I give her a choice between the choir and nursery duty."

In addition to painting classes, Peg had received classical voice training in college and could sing along with the opera CDs she listened to in the car. Mike's taste in music ran more toward Bruce Springsteen.

"Oh, and I enjoyed your sermon," Nathan said.

"You don't have to say that." Mike smiled. "Your job is secure, at least until Mrs. Harcourt gets back into town."

"No, seriously. I'm learning a lot. Your explanation of God's sovereignty put a different spin on some things for me."

"He's the conductor. Our job is to follow."

"Yeah, I appreciated the analogy. I trained under conductors who mixed two doses of terror with three scoops of fear. They were motivated by ego and pride, not love and compassion. I've been thinking about what you said off and on all day."

MIKE ENJOYED THE DRIVE HOME AT THE END OF THE DAY. HE lowered the window of the car and let the breeze blow across his face. He glanced at the ridges running alongside the road. With the arrival of spring, the hills no longer looked like gray-backed porcupines. Budding trees raised green fingers toward the sky. Soon, the gently rising slopes would be thick with summer foliage.

Mike and Peg lived at the end of a dead-end street. He parked on the street in front of the house. For the past hour, his stomach had been growling in protest at the decision to skip lunch. When he got out of the car, he could hear Judge barking inside the house.

A side door opened into the kitchen, a sunny room with a breakfast nook where Mike and Peg ate unless they were entertaining guests. Peg kept the house spotless. Her efforts to train Mike in perpetual neatness had been less successful.

Throughout the house were paintings by Peg. Like many artists, Peg's creativity had gone through phases. The first years after their marriage were filled with Appalachian mountain scenes, perhaps a response to the dramatic change from the upper-class suburb of Philadelphia where Peg grew up. She then entered a long stretch devoted to children. Mike particularly liked a series of watercolors depicting boys playing baseball. The slightly blurred images captured the idyllic world of summer much better than a crisp photograph. Peg then began painting older people sitting in chairs or in front of windows with their eyes closed as the world's activity passed by. This past winter, she'd returned to landscapes and completed several oils of barren trees shaped like giant candelabras. Mike never criticized Peg's work. Unless crafting questions on cross-examination or organizing a sermon could be considered an art form, the creative world wasn't a place he visited.

No smells of supper greeted Mike when he entered the kitchen. The cooktop was bare and the oven cold. A few leftover hors d'oeuvres not eaten by Peg's monthly book club were on the counter. Peg wasn't in sight. Judge wagged his tail, and Mike reached over to rub the dog's slightly wrinkled forehead.

"Did the ladies in the book club tell you how cute you looked?" he asked then raised his voice. "Peg! I'm home and hungry!"

Eating a carrot stick, he went through the great room with its large picture windows and looked up the stairs. Judge pattered after him.

"What's for supper?" he called out.

Peg, fit and trim, appeared at the top of the stairs. Dressed in jeans and a cotton shirt, she had a tissue in her right hand and something Mike couldn't see in the left. Her short blond hair bobbed up and down as she rapidly descended the stairs. Her blue eyes were rimmed in red, but there was a smile on her face, revealing the dimple in her left cheek.

"What's wrong?" Mike asked.

Peg reached the bottom of the stairs and threw herself into his arms. She sniffled then burst out laughing. Mike held her. After fifteen years of marriage, he knew it was wise to let a woman unpack her feelings on her own terms. Peg pulled away and wiped her eyes with the tissue. Mike waited. She held up a thin strip of paper in her right hand. It contained a blue circle.

"Don't you think this would make a beautiful painting?" she asked.

"It's a bit abstract."

"Wrong. It's the most real thing I could ever do."

Mike gave her a perplexed look.

"Do you know what this filled-in circle means?" she asked in a giddy voice.

"Uh, no."

"I'm pregnant!" Peg screamed.

Judge barked. Mike took a step backward.

"Are you sure?"

Peg reached into her pocket and pulled out the instructions from a pregnancy test and held the slip of paper next to a photo on the sheet.

"What does that tell you?"

Mike stared at the images. There was no question about the similarity between the test results and the guidelines provided by the manufacturer.

"Yeah, it looks the same. But don't you think you should go to the doctor?"

"Of course." Peg grabbed him again. "But I know I'm pregnant! I can feel it!"

"You can't feel a baby this early."

"I know that," she said, grabbing his hand and placing it over her heart. "It's a knowing inside here. That's why I bought the test. I'd been feeling odd and wondering if something was wrong. This afternoon while I was out running with Judge it hit me that I should pick up a pregnancy test at the drugstore." She held up the slip in triumph. "And it was positive!"

Peg sat down on the steps and began to laugh. Still in shock, Mike didn't move. Judge nuzzled Peg's leg. Peg reached out, took Mike's hand, and looked up into his face.

"After all these years of doctors, exams, procedures, and giving up, I can't tell you how happy this makes me."

"A baby," Mike murmured. "We're going to have a baby."

THEY CELEBRATED AT THE MOUNTAIN VIEW, THE NICEST restaurant in town. Peg picked at her salad. Famished, Mike didn't leave a crumb of a crouton on his plate.

"I wonder if I'm going to have any strange food cravings," Peg said.

"Right now, nothing would seem strange to me," Mike replied, looking over his shoulder toward the kitchen area.

"You ordered the biggest steak on the menu."

"But it's not here yet. Missing lunch and finding out that I'm going to be a father has increased my appetite."

"Why didn't you eat lunch?"

"I had a glitch in my schedule."

"What happened?"

Mike told her about Muriel Miller's visit to the church, and his encounter with Sam at the jail.

"How did it feel being a lawyer again?" Peg asked, leaning forward.

"It's not my world anymore."

"Are you sure?"

"Of course," Mike scoffed. "The law and the prophets don't mix."

Their meal arrived. Mike savored the thick, juicy steak. On the third bite, he thought about Sam Miller and hoped the old man would get out of jail in time to enjoy fried chicken on his wedding anniversary.

MIKE AND PEG AGREED TO KEEP THEIR NEWS SECRET UNTIL confirmed by the doctor. That night, Peg fell asleep in Mike's arms. In the morning, she didn't lie in bed with her face to the wall but fixed coffee while he shaved and showered.

"Call me as soon as you know anything," Mike said as he kissed her on the cheek.

Peg wrapped her arms around him and placed her head against his chest. Mike didn't know what to think. It had been years since she'd displayed this type of affection before he left for work. He held her for a long time then kissed the top of her head.

"I love you," he said.

"I love you, too." She lifted her head and gave him a lingering kiss on the lips. "Have a good day. I'll call you from the doctor's office."

Mike drove to the church in a daze. If pregnancy could awaken this level of passion and tenderness in a woman, it must be the happiest state known to man.

"GOOD MORNING, DELORES," HE SAID, STOPPING AT THE SEC-
retary's desk.

Delores coughed and cleared her throat. "I took a message off the answering machine from Mrs. Miller, the woman who came to see you yesterday."

Delores handed Mike a pink slip of paper. He suspected the lawyer sent to
interview Sam Miller hadn't made it to the jail yet.

"If Mrs. Miller would be patient and her husband would exercise common
sense, everything could be handled in proper order," Mike replied, crumpling
up the slip of paper and dropping it into Delores's trash can. "But I'll call the
court administrator to make sure everything is on track."

He went into his office and called the courthouse.

"I talked to Greg Freeman and mentioned your concern about the prisoner's competency," the court administrator said. "He promised to go by the
jail yesterday afternoon."

Mike didn't know Greg Freeman, who had come to town after Mike left
for seminary. He looked up the young lawyer's office number. A male voice
answered the phone.

"Greg Freeman, please," Mike said. "Tell him Reverend Mike Andrews is
calling."

"This is Greg."

Freeman's voice sounded more like a member of the church youth group
than an attorney.

"Welcome to Shelton," Mike replied.

"Thanks, I grew up in Wilmington, but I'm enjoying the mountains."

"Great. Listen, I'm calling about a defendant in a criminal case named Sam
Miller. Have you been to the jail—"

"I'm sorry about that," Freeman interrupted. "I met with him yesterday
without realizing that you're representing him."

Mike sat up straighter in his chair. "I'm not representing him. When we
talked at the jail, I made it clear that I wouldn't get involved."

"He claims you're his lawyer. Based on the financial disclosure sheet, he
isn't going to qualify for an appointed lawyer, and I thought he might want
to hire me as a paying client."

"I wish he had," Mike said, looking out a window at the trees along the
creek. "He needs help."

"No doubt, but there wasn't any use talking to him. He's convinced that
you're on the case."

"He's wrong. That's why someone should be appointed to represent him. He may be delusional, and the fact that he thinks I'm his lawyer proves it. I haven't been in a courtroom in over six years."

"I heard you were pretty good."

"Who told you that?" Mike asked in surprise.

"Your name came up last week when I was having lunch with Judge Coberg. He told me about a case in which you cross-examined a witness who confessed on the witness stand. It sounded like something from a TV show."

"Warren Ridley," Mike answered. "It was a white lightning case. A real throwback."

"Yeah, the judge said that's what convinced him you should be a minister. He claimed anyone who could get this Ridley guy to admit his guilt when another man was about to be convicted ought to be in a pulpit urging people to confess their sins. It was hilarious the way the judge told it."

Mike smiled at the memory of the mountain man sputtering and fuming on the witness stand until finally throwing up his hands and acknowledging that he'd secretly built a moonshine still on a neighbor's property.

"That story has been overblown, but if I'm so good, I should have been able to convince Sam Miller that I'm not going to be his lawyer."

"Maybe you should put it in writing."

"Yeah, that's my next step. Sorry to inconvenience you."

"No problem, it's a pleasure meeting you over the phone. Let me know if I can help."

"Thanks, and I'll suggest to Miller that he consider hiring you."

Mike hung up the phone and added Greg Freeman to his list of church prospects. He turned on his computer and quickly typed a letter of nonrepresentation that included a place for Sam Miller to sign.

"Back to the jail," he said to Delores.

"Why?"

"I have to set Mr. Miller straight that I won't be representing him. I don't think the elders or members of this congregation would want me practicing criminal law on the side."

THIS TIME, THE FEMALE DEPUTY ON DUTY DIDN'T OBJECT TO Mike's request for access to the cell block. Lamar Cochran wasn't on duty, and an unfamiliar officer brought out Sam Miller. The older man greeted Mike when he entered the hallway. Mike didn't respond. They went into the same interview room. Mike spoke without sitting down.

"Mr. Miller, I thought I made it clear that I wouldn't be representing you. You don't qualify for an appointed lawyer and need to hire a private attorney. Mr. Freeman is willing to help, but whether you hire him or someone else, you need to act as soon as possible."

Sam looked up at Mike. The old man didn't seem upset at the news.

"Have a seat," Sam said. "I understand."

Mike placed the letter he'd typed on the table.

"This is a letter stating that I'm not your lawyer. Sign it. I have an extra copy for you."

Sam picked up the sheet of paper, looked at it for a few seconds then placed it on the table. Mike held out a pen.

"Do you have any questions?" Mike asked.

"Yep."

"Go ahead."

"Did she laugh?" Sam asked.

"Who?" Mike asked in surprise.

"Your wife."

"Why would she laugh?"

"I told you yesterday that Isaac was on the way."

Mike stared at the old man for several seconds.

"What are you talking about?"

"Your baby. Did your wife laugh when she gave you the news that you're going to be a daddy?"

"Yes," Mike answered slowly. "And cried, too."

Sam patted his stomach. "That's understandable. It's been a long wait. But she's a new woman. A fresh wind from heaven is going to refresh her soul."

Mike sat down in the chair opposite Sam. "How did you know my wife was pregnant? I didn't know it myself until I got home yesterday afternoon."

"I told you Isaac was coming. I figured she'd be laughing since that's what his name means."

Mike's eyes widened in disbelief. "You believe I'm going to have a son?"

"Yep. But I have a fifty-fifty chance of guessing right anyway."

"How did you know my wife was pregnant?" Mike insisted.

Sam grinned. "Papa showed me. It's a sign and a wonder."

"Well, it makes me wonder all right, but you didn't answer my question."

"It was part of the dream," Sam answered patiently. "The one that sent Muriel to the church to fetch you."

"What dream?"

Sam sat back in his chair. "You told me to get right to the point yesterday, so I didn't mention it. Do you want the whole explanation?"

"Yes."

"Okay. Here's what happened. In the dream, my truck broke down on the side of the road in front of your church. A lawyer I know came out of the sanctuary to help me. His wife was with him, and she was laughing and pointing at her stomach. It was obvious that she was pregnant, but she put her finger to her lips, so I knew it was a secret. The lawyer started working on my truck and fixed whatever was wrong with it, then I left." Sam stopped.

"That's it?" Mike asked.

"Yep."

"How do you know it was my church?"

"I don't get over that way much, but I've been by it on the road. Little white building beside a stream that dries up to a trickle in the summer."

"Yeah, but we have a bigger sanctuary now." Mike furrowed his brow. "Who was the lawyer?"

"Jim Somers."

"He's been dead for years!"

"Yep."

"And his wife is close to eighty."

"Yep. That let me know it had been a long wait for you and your wife, like Abraham and Sarah. When the lawyer from the church fixed my truck, it told me that you were the one who was going to help me get out of here and down the road of life."

Mike tapped the letter on the table with his right index finger but didn't look at it.

"But why was Jim Somers in your dream? Neither he nor his wife ever attended Little Creek Church."

"Because I knew him. I used to cut his grass. It's a way Papa uses to speak to me. He shows me a person I know to tell me about someone I don't. You'll learn."

Mike thought for a moment. The unusual man's logic was filled with holes.

"But we have other lawyers in our church," Mike said. "Maybe one of them is supposed to represent you. Do you know Jack Smith? He's a fine lawyer."

"No. You're the one."

Mike shook his head. "Mr. Miller, that is an interesting story, and I can't deny that my wife is pregnant, but your interpretation—"

"Is often the hardest part, I admit," Sam said. "And I've made mistakes. Papa is never wrong, but when things get in my old brain, they can get tangled up and confused."

"Maybe that's what's happened this time, or you were working through a psychological problem you have with lawyers."

"I don't have anything against lawyers. We're all sinners in the hand of the Enemy until the Master sets us free. Papa doesn't pay attention to labels."

Mike digested the unorthodox terminology used by the old man.

"Okay, but you didn't see me in your dream, did you?"

"No, but before I was arrested I knew you were coming in three months, and when I put the two dreams together it all seemed to fit. Where we go from here is around the bend and out of sight, but the first step is for us to get together so you can help me get out of this mess, and I can teach you what I know."

"You had another dream?" Mike asked in dismay.

"Yep. I've had thousands of them. Some are dreams, others are visions."

Mike placed his pen on the letter. He'd heard enough for one day.

"Sign this letter. I know you want to spend time with me, but I don't need to be your attorney for that to happen. Maybe we can talk about your dreams and visions after you make bond and get out of here."

"What's your wife's name?" Sam asked.

Mike was irritated. "You don't know?" he responded with a hint of sarcasm.

"Nope."

"Margaret, but I call her Peg."

"Muriel wants to meet your wife, but I told her to call and check with you first."

"Does your wife have dreams, too?"

"Not like I do."

Mike hesitated. He didn't want to drag Peg into interaction with the Miller family.

"I'll see."

Sam stood. "Thanks for coming."

"What about the letter?" Mike asked, remaining in his chair.

"You and Peg pray about it and let me know."

"And you're going to stay in jail until I get back to you?"

"Yep. I don't want to, but you're not giving me much of a choice."

Mike stiffened and his eyes narrowed. Miller's attempt to manipulate him through guilt was not going to be successful.

"Mr. Miller, I have one piece of advice for you. Hire a lawyer."

Mike left the room without shaking the old man's hand.

Five

MIKE KNEW WHAT TO DO. THERE WAS NO LEGAL REQUIREMENT that he obtain Sam Miller's signature on a piece of paper, and based on their second meeting, it would be easier to ignore the situation than try to address it directly.

When he arrived at the church, Mike saw Peg's SUV parked in front of the administration wing. Beside it was the same red pickup he'd seen the previous day. His irritation returned. He walked quickly through the administration wing. No one was sitting in the waiting area. Delores tilted her head toward his office.

"They're in there," she whispered.

"Peg and the Miller woman?" Mike barked.

"Yes."

Mike burst into the room. Peg was sitting on a small love seat with her shoes off and her legs tucked beneath her. Muriel Miller sat beside her.

"Honey, I think you know Mrs. Miller. She was waiting to see you when I stopped by. Do you remember the painting I did of the woman at the pond?"

"Uh, yes."

"Based on the person you saw in your dream, doesn't Muriel look just like her? When I saw her, it made me wish I'd brought my pencils so I could do a quick sketch."

"Maybe," Mike grunted. "I thought you were going to the doctor."

"I did. Everything is fine. I'm in great shape for a thirty-nine-year-old woman about to have her first baby."

Mike frowned. "We weren't going to say anything to anyone."

34

"Muriel already knew about it. Her husband had a dream about the baby. It's the most amazing thing—"

"I know all about the dream," Mike interrupted. "I've been to the jail and heard the whole story."

"How is Sam?" Muriel asked anxiously. "His heart isn't in the best shape."

"He's okay under the circumstances. He didn't mention any physical problems."

"I hope he's taking his blood pressure medicine."

Mike turned one of the chairs in front of his desk so that it faced the love seat. He sat down and leaned forward.

"Mrs. Miller, I can't get your husband to listen to reason. I keep telling him that I'm a minister, not a lawyer, but he changes the subject. He insists that I'm going to represent him. I know you want him out of jail, and he should have had a bond reduction hearing a couple of months ago, but there's nothing I can do about it."

Muriel reached for her purse and pulled out a tissue. "I'm worried something bad is going to happen to him."

"My sympathies are with you," Mike said. "But talking to me about it is a waste of time for both of you."

Muriel blew her nose. When she began to speak, the words tumbled out. "Sam can be hard to understand when you first meet him, especially when he's talking about the things the Lord shows him. Over the years, we've been asked to leave more than one church, but he has a heart of gold and wouldn't hurt anyone or take anything that didn't belong to him. I know he's not guilty of any crime. After he got over the shock of the arrest, he started looking for what the Lord wanted to do in the situation. He's been witnessing to the men in the jail, but he's convinced one reason this has happened is so he can meet you."

Out of the corner of his eye, Mike saw Peg bite her lower lip.

"I don't have to be his lawyer to talk to him," Mike said.

"That's not the way he sees it."

"But I've turned him down."

"I know, and I'm not trying to make you feel bad for not helping us or talk you into doing something you don't want to do."

"Then why did you come?"

Muriel put her hand on Peg's shoulder.

"For her. Sam says you're going to become more like him, and I wanted to help your wife get ready for it. There wasn't anyone to guide me, and I had it rough, especially in the early years."

Mike could imagine that forty years of marriage to someone like Sam Miller could be stressful. He spoke gently but firmly.

"That's kind of you, Mrs. Miller, but Sam doesn't have the right to decide the path God has for me."

"I know how it sounds to you. Believe me, I do. The revelation about the baby was to help you accept him, but if that doesn't work, I guess I'll have to wait and see where my help comes from."

"Your help comes from the Lord," Mike said.

Muriel managed a slight smile. "Yes, that's always true."

Mike stood to signal the end of the conversation. Muriel rose to her feet, and Mike escorted her to the door.

"Good-bye," she said to both Mike and Peg.

"Bye," Peg responded.

Mike shut the door and leaned against it.

"I'm glad that's over," he said. "Sorry you were dragged into it."

"Sorry?" Peg responded, her voice rising. "You're right about that!"

"What do you mean?"

"I wish I'd had a tape recorder running. Is that the way you used to talk down to your clients?"

"When did you start taking up for uneducated mountain women and their husbands?" Mike shot back.

"Didn't you hear her? She wants to help us. To help *me*. How often does that happen around this church?"

"That's an exaggeration."

"Any examples?"

Mike thought a moment but couldn't quickly retrieve a recent instance.

"Uh, the gifts for the house we received when I took the job."

"That was almost three years ago!"

"That's not the point. Don't tell me you believe that nonsense about me becoming like Mrs. Miller's husband?"

"You have dreams all the time."

"But they don't mean anything."

"Maybe not, but she seemed like a nice old lady, and you treated her like a first-grade child."

"If you thought I was out of line, why didn't you say anything?"

"Would it have done any good?"

Mike hesitated. It was time to cool the rhetoric.

"Probably not."

"That's the most honest, sincere thing you've said in the past fifteen minutes! What a parting platitude—'Your help comes from the Lord,'" Peg mimicked his voice.

"She agreed with me!" Mike protested, his voice getting louder again.

"But God uses people," Peg said, pointing at his chest. "I've heard you say it many times from the pulpit. God initiates—"

"We respond," Mike completed the sentence. "But do you really think I should represent this guy?"

Peg held up her hands. "That's not for me to decide. But the way you cut her off was coldhearted. At supper last night, you made her husband sound like a nut. Why didn't you mention that he told you about the baby? You're still enough of a lawyer to recognize relevant information, aren't you?"

"It didn't cross my mind. As I was leaving the interview room, he made an off-the-wall comment about Isaac coming to visit us. I didn't make the connection."

"Maybe you should have paid more attention."

Mike responded in a softer voice, "There's no easy way to explain some of the things Sam Miller said to me, but the real issue is whether I want to represent him. If I did, there could be consequences. I'd need to get approval from the session."

Peg shrugged. "Tell them it's a pro bono project for an old man who may be mentally unstable but needs guidance through the court system. What are they going to do? Cut your salary?"

Mike couldn't suppress a slight smile.

"Don't you have a meeting with the elders tonight?"

"Yes."

"You can put together a persuasive argument by then. How much time would you spend on a case like this? Didn't you think it might be just an error at the bank?"

"Maybe, but you never know. And every conversation with Sam Miller will be twice as long as necessary."

Peg relaxed against the love seat. "I'm fine with any decision you make so long as you apologize to Muriel Miller the next time you talk to her."

Mike shook his head. "I always knew you would have been a better lawyer than me."

Peg leaned forward and patted him on the cheek. "Don't flatter me. Any woman could do what I do."

THE ELDERS OF LITTLE CREEK CHURCH MET ON THE SECOND Tuesday of each month. Mike always prepared a written report on the state of the church and the items for discussion and action. He'd learned not to include specific recommendations in his report because a few members of the eight-person group opposed any new ideas merely for the sake of argument. So, Mike adopted a simple strategy. He didn't offer an opinion on matters under consideration until after the elders tossed out ideas and criticized one another. Then, when someone made a suggestion close to Mike's opinion, he threw his support behind it and subtly tried to maneuver the final outcome to a desired result. Occasionally, when a better idea came forth, he quickly jettisoned his own idea and praised the person who suggested the better alternative.

Mike usually didn't go home for supper before the 7:00 p.m. meeting. He kept frozen pizzas in the church refrigerator and put one in the oven shortly after Delores left for the day. While he waited for the pizza to cook, Nathan Goode came into the church kitchen.

"What's for supper?" Nathan asked. "Pepperoni or meat lover's?"

"Hawaiian."

"When did you go Polynesian?"

"It's the pineapple. I have fresh pieces to put on when it comes out of the oven."

"Big enough for two? I'll eat fast and help clean the kitchen before anyone gets here."

"Sure."

Nathan rarely came to the session meetings. The music director had a basketful of hassles with the bureaucracy at the high school, and Mike didn't want to add another layer of officialdom to the young man's life.

Mike took the pizza from the oven, sprinkled the pineapple on top, and cut the pizza into large slices.

"Anything you want me to mention to the elders?" he asked as he nibbled a hot bite.

"A twenty-five percent raise and four weeks paid vacation."

"What else?"

Nathan grinned. "Nothing, sir. Working with you is worth more than any amount of money."

"Save that for the school principal."

They ate in silence for a few minutes.

Nathan poured a soft drink into a glass. "There are a couple of kids who told me they're going to visit the youth group."

Not many teenagers attended the church. It was a problem Mike hadn't been able to solve.

"Who are they?"

"One plays electric guitar, the other is a drummer."

Mike reached for another slice of pizza. "You're starting a rock band on Sunday night?"

"Alternative praise music would be more accurate. Nothing too extreme, but different enough to be interesting to the kids. Aren't you the one who told me I would have to take risks in ministry if I wanted to help the people who really need it?"

"Did I say that?"

"Once when you hired me and another time in a staff meeting."

"I'm not sure this plan is going to fly under the radar."

"The drummer is Chaz Gaston, the younger son of Mitchell Gaston. He's a kid on the brink of trouble who could go bad if no one steps in to help him."

Mitchell Gaston had moved to the mountains from Atlanta after selling an Internet start-up at the height of the dot-com boom. All his children except Chaz were grown and out of the impressive house on the crest of a nearby hill. Luring the Gastons to the congregation would appeal to the elders.

"That might work," Mike replied. "Do his parents like the fact that their son plays the drums? I don't want to encourage something the parents don't support."

"They invested five grand in his set."

"I'll bring it up tonight."

MIKE RETURNED TO HIS OFFICE AND INCLUDED "CREATIVE WAYS for increasing interest in the youth group" to the night's agenda. At the end of the list he added "Unique opportunity for outreach to the community." On his own copy he penciled in "Taking risks in ministry to help people on the edge." In Sam Miller's case, that meant the edge of reason.

The session met in a conference room that contained a long wooden table surrounded by twelve burgundy chairs. More chairs lined the walls. On Sunday mornings, the room was used by an adult class known for its coffee. Mike often wandered in before the class started and grabbed a cup.

On session nights, Mike prepared two pitchers of ice water and brewed a pot of decaf coffee. It wasn't unusual for the meetings to last two or three hours, and he didn't want to prolong the time by pumping caffeine into the elders' veins.

There were six men and two women on the session. Used to persuading juries that included all kinds of people, Mike's emphasis was on building consensus regardless of gender.

By 7:00 p.m., the room was ready. Mike placed neat stacks of papers for each elder at the end of the table. With Barbara Harcourt's absence there would be seven in attendance. Bobby Lambert arrived. Bobby spent most of his time poring over contracts and business documents. He researched legal issues for Mr. Forrest but never appeared in court independently. Normally an impeccable dresser, his former law partner's tie was loosened and his hair disheveled.

"What's going on with you?" Mike asked.

"Wishing your name was still over the front door," Bobby replied. "Mr. Forrest has been impossible to deal with for the past couple of weeks."

"Is it his blood pressure?"

"I asked him about his health the other day, and he told me to mind my own business. He's been huddled in meetings and dumped several files on my desk that have taken tons of time to sort through and figure out. I can't double-bill the client for file review, and I have to work overtime to keep my own receipts on track."

"What kind of files?"

"Transactional stuff that Mr. Forrest can do in his sleep. That's what makes it so strange. You know how efficient he is at putting deals together. I've pirated his form books, but each situation requires customization."

His first three years at the firm, Mike served as Maxwell Forrest's associate and learned to appreciate the challenges and rewards of a corporate practice. Creating the right legal framework for each business arrangement could be interesting and the interaction with clients stimulating. Mike shifted into trial

work when the firm's litigation partner retired but remained available as a
backup for Mr. Forrest.

"What about the other guys?"

Bobby lowered his voice. "Park is moving to Charlotte to work for an
insurance defense firm. This is his last week. All his work has been shifted to
Arnold, who is working longer hours than I am."

As the other members of the session arrived, Mike greeted them. When they
were seated, he asked Milton Chesterfield, the oldest member of the group and
the richest man in the church, to pray. Milton's prayer was as predictable as the
opening lines of Genesis. Mike had never heard him utter a modified version.

"Sovereign God, help us to do Thy will in this meeting. Amen."

The elders followed the written agenda. Mike sat back and listened. First,
the financial report. Offerings exceeded the level needed to keep pace with the
budget, but two elders urged fiscal caution and curtailing expenditures. Mike
didn't fret. After thirty minutes of discussion, nothing changed.

The facilities report included a presentation by Libby Gorman on the condition of the church cemetery. Some of the older monuments and markers
needed repair, and she believed family members should bear the expense of
work on their plots, with the church paying for those with no known living
descendants. One of the largest plots in the cemetery was devoted to deceased
members of the Chesterfield family.

"I think the church should take care of the maintenance for everyone,"
Milton said. "I shouldn't be punished because my family stayed loyal to the
church and didn't move away."

"I think it would be a privilege to tidy up our family plots." Libby sniffed.

"What efforts did you make to find relatives?" Milton asked.

"My daughter-in-law spent hours on her computer trying to track folks
down," Libby answered. She held up a sheet of paper. "And I sent out forty
letters."

"This issue is covered by the Equal Protection Clause of the Constitution,"
Bobby said, winking at Mike mischievously. "Everyone who is dead should be
treated the same, especially if the body was transported in interstate com-
merce. Anything less would be a denial of their due process rights—"

"Thanks for sending the letters, Libby," Mike interrupted. "Did you receive
any responses?"

Libby glanced down at a pad she'd placed on the table. "Uh, eight so far, including four from people willing to pay something if the amount is reasonable."

The discussion continued for another half hour. In the end, Bobby was the one who suggested an acceptable compromise. Payment for repairs by descendants was voluntary, but if they did so, the church would place a small marker on the plot indicating that it had been restored through a generous gift from the family.

Most of the argumentative steam in the group had been vented by the time they reached the youth group item. However, Mike didn't try to water down Nathan's proposal. "He wants to allow students to play electric guitars and drums," Mike said.

"In the sanctuary?" Libby asked in dismay.

"No, of course not; I would have stopped that myself. The music will be confined to the youth room and only on Sunday nights."

"It's important to maintain decorum at *all* times," Milton added with emphasis. "Including the Sunday sermon. Mike, you have a lot of good things to say, but at times you get carried away—"

"Let's stay on the issue," Bobby interjected.

"The boy who plays drums is Mitchell Gaston's son," Mike added calmly. "It's a great opportunity to connect the Gaston family with the church."

Milton's eyes opened wide. "Why didn't you say so in the first place?"

After a few minutes of discussion, permission was granted, provided the volume wasn't too loud and no parents complained. Mike didn't push. An open door was all Nathan could ask for. It would be up to him to sell it to the parents.

"The last item on the agenda doesn't require discussion, only your approval," Mike said, straightening his papers in preparation for the end of the meeting. "It involves a fellow minister who needs legal assistance that I'll provide without charge. I wanted to let you know about it before I did anything. Milton, will you pray?"

Before Milton began, Bobby Lambert put down his coffee cup and spoke. "What kind of assistance?" the lawyer asked.

"A misunderstanding about church finances," Mike replied nonchalantly.

"How serious a misunderstanding?" Bobby persisted.

Mike looked at Bobby and tried to send an unspoken signal to leave the issue alone.

"Yeah, give us the details," Rick Weston, another elder, said.

Mike shrugged. "It resulted in a criminal charge but may be the result of a bank error."

"Is it a felony charge?" Bobby asked.

Mike nodded. "Class C."

"Then it involves at least a hundred thousand dollars," the lawyer said, sitting up in his chair. "That's a big error for a bank to make."

"It's just zeros to them," Mike replied. "I haven't investigated anything in detail. His wife contacted the church and asked for help. I met with him at the jail."

"You went to the jail?" Libby asked. "That's not an appropriate place for our minister to be seen."

"The apostle Paul spent a lot of time in jail," Bobby said. "How much time did he build behind bars, Mike? Three or four years?"

"At least," Mike said. "But this man is not the apostle Paul."

"What's his name?" Libby asked.

"Sam Miller."

"The yardman?" Milton asked.

"Yes," Mike said.

"He's no minister," Milton grunted. "He used to cut my neighbor's grass."

"He's a lay preacher," Mike answered. "I doubt he has any theological education or recognized ordination."

"Wouldn't he qualify for an appointed lawyer?" Bobby asked.

"No, he owns a home and runs a small business."

"Then he should hire his own lawyer!" Milton said sharply. "This is a church, not a legal aid society! If you don't have enough to keep you busy, we need to discuss modification of your job description."

Mike started to respond then stopped.

"What's really going on?" Bobby asked. "Why do you want to do this?"

Mike paused before answering. If he wanted to retreat, now would be the time to do so gracefully.

"Because I believe God wants me to help him," he said with more conviction than he felt. "I'm working very hard to be a faithful pastor for this church, and this is not some kind of professional identity crisis. I'm more confident of my call to the ministry than ever and have no interest in returning to the law. This church is where I want to be, and I intend to stay here as long as you'll have me. I'm simply asking you to allow me to help someone in need, and trust me to do it in a way that honors God." There was silence for several seconds. The elders glanced at one another.

"Mike, would you please step out of the room for a few minutes while we talk?" Bobby asked.

Mike hesitated. "Let me make one thing clear," he said. "I want to do this, but if you tell me no, I'll accept your decision and won't mention it again."

Mike stepped into the hallway. The sounds of muffled voices came from the room. He resisted the childish impulse to put his ear to the door and listen. He began pacing up and down the hall, convincing himself that whether or not he helped Sam Miller was an insignificant matter, no more important than how to pay for gravestone maintenance.

By his fifth turn on the carpet, he'd lost the internal debate. He was vulnerable. If his request was approved, there would be whisperings around the church about his actions. If he lost, he would have needlessly expended valuable capital and diminished his stature before the session. He inwardly kicked himself for having a knee-jerk response to Peg's pressure. Time passed. The door opened, and Libby came out.

"Just going to the restroom," she said with a wave of her hand.

Mike didn't walk past the open door. In a few minutes, Libby returned to the conference room without looking at him. He felt as though he were waiting for a jury—only he was the one on trial. He kept pacing up and down the hallway. He thought about Sam Miller. The old man was probably snoring in his bunk, dreaming about gumdrop fairies and cupids. The conference room door opened.

"Come in," Bobby said. "We're ready."

Mike took his seat, but his sense of authority was gone. He quickly scanned the faces around the table. They were inscrutable. Bobby cleared his throat.

"We voted and decided that you can represent Sam Miller."

"It wasn't unanimous," Milton interjected.

"Until he finds another lawyer," Libby added. "Bobby is going to see what he can do to help on that part of it."

"Fair enough," Mike said, trying to regain control. "If any of you have any questions, please feel free to contact me."

"Let's pray and go home," Bobby said, stifling a yawn.

"Before we adjourn," Mike said, "I have one other bit of news and wanted you to be the first in the church to hear it." He paused for dramatic effect. "Peg is pregnant. It was confirmed at the doctor's office this morning. She's fine, and we're looking forward to the arrival of a new member of the Andrews family in about nine months."

Congratulations echoed in Mike's ears as he locked up the church. He'd wanted to announce the news of the baby from the pulpit on Sunday before the entire congregation, but it was necessary to knock the Miller case off the minds of the elders. Nothing worked better than the announcement of a long-awaited baby.

Six

MIKE STIRRED THE CUP OF COFFEE PEG PLACED ON THE BREAK-
fast table in front of him, took a sip, and nibbled a toasted English muffin
covered in melted butter and homemade jam given to them by a woman in
the church.

"Mrs. Ayers gave us this jam," he said.

"I know," Peg answered as she joined him at the table.

"So someone from the church helped us a few months ago."

Peg smiled. "I think the jury has already left the courtroom following yesterday's closing arguments at the church office."

Mike took another bite of muffin. "And you won, but when I tried to
enforce the judgment with the session, I didn't do very well. I could have used
a co-counsel."

Peg sipped her coffee. "I'm supporting you from here."

"Which I appreciate," Mike answered truthfully. "And you don't have to
get up and fix breakfast to prove it. You need more rest, not less."

Peg reached across the table and tapped his wedding ring with her index
finger.

"I want us to practice being a family. For years we've been passing each
other in the process of living separate lives."

"That's an extreme way of putting it."

"It started when you went to work at the law office, and since then we've
never placed a high priority on being together. I had my friends and painting; you had your career and golf. It was easier for both of us not to interact.
Am I right?"

"Yes," Mike admitted.

"Do you want to change or keep the status quo?"

"Change sounds good, but what does it mean to you?"

Peg removed her hand from his. "Didn't you take a counseling course in seminary? What do most women want from their husbands?"

"Quality time."

"To do what?"

"Talk."

"Correct."

Mike looked at his watch. "I need to get going in a minute. When do you want to start having quality time?"

"While you eat your muffin. Ask me a question."

"What kind of question?"

Peg smiled. "You're so smart. That's the perfect question because it lets me tell you what's on my heart. While you were at the session meeting last night, I sat in my reading chair in the bedroom and prayed in a way I've never done before. I put my hand on my stomach and talked to God about our baby, about me, about us. Then I tried to listen. One of the things I realized is that if I want a family in nine months, I'd better start acting like I have one now. And that means being serious about my faith and more committed to loving you."

Mike was speechless. Peg continued.

"I know you've got a soft spot deep down inside, and I promise not to tell anyone about it. You've put up walls of protection because I've been so prickly, but I want to love you enough to convince you to tear down the barriers between us."

"That's great."

"Any other response?"

"I'm not sure what to say."

Peg stood up. "Don't try. An admission of inadequacy is nice from a self-confident male who is always trying to fix everything."

She walked over to the kitchen sink.

"I do have another question," Mike added.

"Go ahead."

"What prompted you to pray last night?"

"Muriel Miller encouraged me to do it. She even wrote some Bible verses on a sheet of paper and suggested I read them. Will you see Sam today?"

"Yes, I'll go to the jail, file a notice of representation at the courthouse, and try to talk to someone at the district attorney's office."

"Is Ken West still the DA?"

"He is, but he's probably assigned something like this to an assistant."

"Who will do your typing?"

"I'll swing by the old office and get Juanita to do it. It won't take her five minutes."

"And don't forget to call Muriel Miller and apologize."

MIKE PHONED THE CHURCH AS HE DROVE DOWN THE HILL TOWARD Shelton. The familiar raspy voice answered the phone.

"Good morning, Delores," Mike said. "I won't be coming in this morning. I have several things to do in town."

"Like buying a baby bed?"

"News travels fast."

"There were twelve messages on the answering machine when I arrived this morning, and someone phoned me before I woke up to make sure it wasn't a false rumor."

"It's true. Peg saw the doctor yesterday. But I'm not picking out pacifiers. I discussed the Sam Miller situation with the session, and I'm going to help him until another lawyer can be hired. I have several stops to make and won't be at the church until this afternoon."

"What should I tell all the callers?"

"Take messages. I'll get back to them before the end of the day. Oh, and I need Muriel Miller's number."

"I put it on a slip and gave it to you."

"Remember, I dropped it in the trash. Check your records."

Mike waited.

"Here it is," she said.

Mike wrote down the number on a pad he kept in the car.

"You're not going to ask me to type any legal papers, are you?" Delores asked.

"No, but I can't think of anyone better able to keep the church running when I have to be away for a few hours."

Delores hung up without responding.

Muriel Miller didn't answer the phone. Mike listened to a brief message about Sam's lawncare business and asked her to call his cell phone number as soon as possible. He hung up as he turned into an empty parking space in front of his old law firm.

None of the law firms in a small town like Shelton had reception rooms filled with expensive antiques and fancy Oriental rugs, but Forrest, Lambert, Park, and Arnold had the nicest waiting area in town. Two leather couches and a pair of leather armchairs gave it an old-club feel. A tightly woven tan carpet covered the floor. In the center of the room rested a low coffee table covered with an assortment of magazines bearing Mr. Forrest's address. Rustic paintings of primitive mountain homesteads by a local artist decorated the walls. The receptionist sat behind a shiny wooden desk at the far end of the room in front of the door leading to the offices. The firm kept the reception room refrigerator cool on even the hottest days. When Mike entered, a new female face greeted him behind the desk. He introduced himself.

"I used to be a partner in the firm," he said. "I need to see Bobby's secretary for a minute."

"Yes, sir. I know who you are. I'll let her know you're here."

The receptionist answered a call and waved him through. Beyond the door, a long hallway extended to the rear of the building. Every room, library, conference area, secretarial suite, law office, and the kitchen opened onto the hall. The first door to the left was the conference room. It was empty. Next, he passed Mr. Forrest's office. The door was closed, and Mike didn't knock. The senior partner only shut his door for a good reason and didn't want to be disturbed except for a matter of life, death, or a visit from Jack Hatcher, the president of the Bank of Barlow County.

Mike's former office was now used by Jeff Park, the lawyer moving to Charlotte. Jeff was on the phone with his back to the door. Juanita Jones, the secretary Mike hired and later shared with Bobby Lambert, worked in the next office.

Despite her first name, the dark-haired, middle-aged secretary had no connection to any Spanish-speaking area of the world. Her family had lived in Barlow County for more than seventy-five years, and she only knew enough Spanish to pronounce the items on the menu at the local Mexican restaurant.

"Are you on break?" Mike asked.

Juanita glanced up at the sound of his voice. "Hey, Mike, I'm so sorry."

"About what?" Mike asked in surprise.

Juanita put her hand over her mouth. "Didn't you hear about Danny Brewster?"

"No."

"He was murdered in prison. Stabbed by another inmate with a homemade knife. It happened a couple of weeks ago."

Mike's face fell. Early in his career he'd represented the mentally limited young man who was charged with multiple counts of burglary. Mike didn't believe Danny knew the difference between being invited into someone's home and breaking and entering, but Judge Lancaster denied an incompetency motion. Ken West offered a plea bargain, but Mike went to trial, confident he could pin responsibility for the crimes on Danny's older brother, the person who sent Danny into the houses. The jury didn't buy Mike's theory and the judge sentenced Danny to ten years in prison. Mike spent two years appealing the conviction but lost.

"He was supposed to get out in a couple of months," Juanita said.

"I thought he was in a special unit," Mike said numbly. "Not with the general prison population."

"I don't know. After you moved to Virginia, nobody kept tabs on him."

"I thought about him the other day but didn't follow up," Mike said, shaking his head. "Is his mother still in the area?"

"Yes, she contacted me looking for you after it happened. I gave her your number at the church and urged her to call you."

"I haven't heard a word."

"Do you know how to reach her?"

"No. She didn't have a phone the last time we talked."

"I'll track her down and let you know. What else can I do for you?"

Mike turned around and shut the door.

"I can't believe I'm doing it, but I've agreed to help an old man who is in some trouble. He runs a lawncare business and preaches on the side. He's a strange person, but I think he's as innocent as Danny and—"

"Sam Miller," Juanita interrupted.

"Do you know him?"

"Oh yeah." The tone of Juanita's voice changed. "But I don't know why you'd want to help him. I think he's either a fraud or a fortune-teller. He told my cousin Lou some things and claimed he was speaking for God, but it was all bogus. I think Lou even gave him some money."

"Did he ask for the money?"

"I don't know the details. Lou is a trusting person who is vulnerable to manipulation. What kind of trouble is Miller having?"

"Criminal charges. He's accused of embezzling money from a church."

Juanita pursed her lips. "That figures. I know the law says the accused is innocent until proven guilty, but I'd be careful. You're wrong about one thing. Sam Miller isn't another Danny Brewster. Danny was a sweet boy abused by that sorry older brother of his. This is different, and I'd hate to see your name linked to Miller in a way that damages your reputation. It's one thing for an ordinary lawyer to represent someone in a criminal case, but you're in another world now. People will assume you believe Miller is innocent, and if he's not, the taint of his guilt will spill onto you."

"You feel that strongly about him?"

"Yes. I've always told you the truth. You could have fired me when I did it before." Juanita smiled slightly. "Now, I'm immune from a pink slip signed by you, but that doesn't change who I am. My cousin's experience with Sam Miller was bad, and I don't want you to get hurt."

Mike was silent for a few seconds. "I appreciate your concern. My main job is to get Miller out on bond so he can hire another lawyer. Bobby is going to work on that part. Is he here?"

"No, he had to leave early this morning for a meeting in Asheville. He's doing a lot of work for Mr. Forrest."

"Yeah, he mentioned that last night at the church."

Juanita lowered her voice. "Did he tell you about Jeff?"

Mike nodded.

"A whole lot of new work is getting dumped on me, too," Juanita continued. "I was here until seven o'clock last night."

Mike made a quick decision. "And I'm not going to add to your load by asking you to type any paperwork for the Miller case."

"Are you sure?" Juanita replied hurriedly. "I wasn't trying to avoid helping you."

"I know, but what you've told me is more valuable than a few pecks on the keyboard. Tell Bobby I'll call him later."

"Okay."

"And thanks for letting me know about Danny." Mike opened the door to leave. "One other thing. What is your cousin's full name?"

"Lou Jasper."

STILL THINKING ABOUT DANNY BREWSTER, MIKE WALKED ACROSS
the street to the courthouse. He would track down Danny's mother and offer
condolences, but he wasn't sure what else to do. He walked up the familiar
steps to the courthouse. The first floor of the building had high ceilings that
helped keep the courthouse cool in summer, but, more importantly, communicated to those who entered the gravity of the business conducted there.

The district attorney's office was on the ground floor next to the main
courtroom. Emblazoned in gold paint over the entrance were the words *Ken
West, District Attorney.* At the rear of the office suite was a door that opened
directly into the courtroom. On trial and arraignment days, the prosecutors
would make a grand entrance beside the bench where the judge sat. It always
looked a little too cozy to Mike, but there was no legal reason to seal the door.
The government lawyers argued that proximity to the courtroom resulted in
increased efficiency.

No one was in the reception area. Mike looked down the hall. He knew
the rotund district attorney's office was the last one on the left. He edged
down the hall.

"Anyone here?" he asked.

When no one appeared, Mike retreated to the reception area. Photographs
of West posing with well-known political figures hung on the wall.

"May I help you?" a female voice asked.

Mike turned and faced a lanky young woman with sandy hair who looked
like a high school intern spending part of her senior year at the courthouse.

"Is Ken West in?" Mike asked.

"No, the rest of the staff is at a training session in Raleigh," she said with
an accent that revealed mountain roots. "I'm Melissa Hall, one of the assistant
district attorneys. Would you like to leave a message?"

Mike introduced himself.

"Maybe you can help me. Are you familiar with the Sam Miller case?"

"Do you have a case number?"

"No, but I know it's an embezzlement charge."

"I'll check his name on the computer."

Hall leaned over the computer at the receptionist's desk.

"Here it is," she said, raising her eyebrows. "The case has been assigned
to me."

"Have you done any investigation?" Mike asked.

Hall looked up. "We don't charge someone with a crime unless there has been an investigation."

Mike managed a smile. "I meant subsequent to any reports from the police."

"Why do you want to know?"

"He's asked me to help him."

"Have you filed a notice of representation?"

"No."

Hall closed the computer screen. "Then I can't give you any information."

Mike kept his voice calm. "I thought Ken might give me an off-the-record perspective on the case. If you don't feel comfortable pulling the file and talking to me, it can wait until he gets back."

"I've only been here six months and would prefer that Mr. West make that decision."

Mike handed her his card. "I understand. This is my number at the church. Ask Ken to give me a call."

Hall took the card and looked at it. "You're a minister?"

"Yes, but I practiced law for ten years. Maxwell Forrest and Bobby Lambert were my partners."

"I'll give Mr. West your card."

Mike left the courthouse satisfied. Hall had given him important information about the case without meaning to. The fact that Ken West had assigned Sam's case to a neophyte lawyer was positive. The weakest and least serious cases flowed downhill to the junior prosecutors.

Mike drove to the jail. He waited in the hallway while an officer brought Sam from the cell block. The older man wasn't smiling. When he came closer, Mike could see a splotchy red mark on the side of Sam's face. They went into an interview room.

"What happened to your face?"

"I turned my back on a new cell mate, and he knocked me down."

"Why?"

"He found something missing from his personal stuff and started swinging. Everyone scattered, but I moved too slow, and he caught me square in the head. I hit the floor and everything went fuzzy. When I came around, some of the other fellows in the cell had grabbed him. The guards got there and dragged him out. He was kicking, screaming, and biting. I didn't think about trying to help him until he was gone."

"What could you have done to help him?"

"I'm not sure, but the Master can still calm a storm."

"Listen, jail is a dangerous place," Mike said, thinking of Danny Brewster. "Don't have some idealistic notion that you're going to save everyone in your cell block. Keep your eyes open, and watch your back. How does your face feel?"

"About like it looks," Sam said with a grimace. "Don't say anything to Muriel. She's worried enough as it is."

"Did you see a doctor?"

"Nope, but it hurts to chew."

"Your jaw could be fractured."

"I don't think so."

"Well, you need to get it checked out. They should take you to the emergency room for an X-ray. I'll speak to the officer on duty before I leave."

"Does that mean you're going to be my lawyer?"

"For now."

Mike placed a blank legal pad on the table and told about his meeting with the elders and their decision.

"Thanks for going to all that trouble," Sam replied. "I know how tough it can be getting Papa's family to agree."

"And you understand this is a temporary situation?"

"Yep. Everything this side of glory is temporary."

Mike stared at Sam for a moment. "Do you believe the Lord has shown you anything about the criminal charge?"

"Nope. Everything has been about helping the men in here and getting to know you. The rest is like the guy who hit me yesterday, a blow out of the blue."

"Do you want me to request a protective transfer to a solitary confinement cell?"

"Nope. I think everything is going to be all right. Most of the guys back there are decent enough. They get into trouble on the outside when they start drinking or drugging."

"Okay, but be on guard against the ones who are crazy all the time."

"Yep."

"And don't try to force religion down anyone's throat. It can be offensive and might be taken the wrong way." Mike shifted the legal pad on the table. "I stopped by the district attorney's office and met the prosecutor assigned to your case."

"What did you find out?"

While Mike related his brief conversation with Melissa Hall, Sam listened closely, nodding several times and patting his stomach twice.

"Make sure she meets the choir director at your church," he said when Mike finished. "That girl is a good singer, and her voice is going to be a key to unlocking his heart to Papa's love and healing her heart from the pain of the past."

"What?" Mike asked in surprise.

"While you talked about her, I could hear a woman singing. Then a big key came down from Glory—"

"And unlocked your jail cell," Mike interrupted. "Are all our conversations going to be like this?"

Sam smiled then winced in pain. "Yep, so long as Papa turns on the spigot. When that's happening, it would be foolish not to drink."

"I'm not thirsty."

"Maybe not, but you have a sharp mind, and you'll remember everything I'm telling you. Papa can't use folks who are lazy. You're a hard worker."

"And I'm going to work my way out of this situation as soon as possible. I'll check the real estate records on your property, then file papers with the court to get your bail reduced to an amount that will let you post a property bond. How much is your mortgage?"

"Nothing. It's paid for. The Bible says to let no debt remain outstanding except continuing debt to love one another. Muriel and I haven't carried any debts for years."

"If the people at the bank find out that's what you believe, they'll never cooperate with me." Mike sat back in his chair. "One last item. Do you know a man named Lou Jasper?"

"Yep. Nice fellow who lives in the western part of the county. I met him a few years ago."

"My former secretary says you took some money from him and lied to him."

"I'm sorry to hear that's what she thinks. Papa has a great call on that boy's life. He's a dreamer, too. I interpreted a few for him, but he was curious, not serious. When he had a dream that meant he had to forgive some people he didn't like, he quit calling me."

"Do you remember the dream?"

"Yep, but it wouldn't be right for me to tell you."

"Okay. Did he give you money?"

"He was real excited at first, and I think he wrote out a check for $150. I used the money to buy a secondhand washing machine for a widow woman who didn't have one."

"Why would his cousin say you're a liar?"

"Maybe I made the mistake of telling him too much, too soon. The call on a person's life may be great, but the path getting there is never smooth. There are lots of tests. It's not automatic. Then, if a true word doesn't happen, folks will blame the messenger when the fault lies closer to home."

"Careful," Mike said. "I believe in predestination."

"I can't argue that stuff. I just know what I've seen. You'll have to figure out if it agrees with what you learned in preacher school. I don't claim to be unfoolable."

"You mean infallible."

"That's what I get for trying to use a fancy word. I've made mistakes."

"But not with your bank account?"

"No. I'm sure about that one."

Seven

MIKE LEFT THE TAX APPRAISER'S OFFICE WITH PROOF THAT SAM Miller's hillside property was worth $65,000. He knew the actual market value was much more. If the eight-acre piece was combined with the parcel next door, it would create a nice tract for a developer who would tear down Sam's house and plant at least a dozen larger homes in its place.

It was too early for lunch so Mike drove home. Peg and Judge were gone, but when he went upstairs he found Peg's Bible open on her chair in the bedroom. A notebook lay facedown beside the Bible. Mike reached over to pick it up then stopped. It would be more fun letting Peg tell him what she discovered than to find out by snooping.

The household computer was in a small downstairs bedroom they'd turned into a study. Mike clicked open the word processing program. It took him fifteen minutes to properly format a one-page pleading notifying the court of his representation in the *State of North Carolina v. Sam Miller*. A Motion to Reduce Bond followed next. As he labored to make everything look professional, he hoped he wouldn't have to type a brief or requests to charge the jury. By the time he'd added a certificate of service upon Melissa Hall and a fill-in-the-blank notice of hearing on the motion to reduce bond, it was almost noon. He printed out several copies of the pleadings.

Bobby's car wasn't in sight at the law firm when Mike returned to town. The trip to Asheville would probably consume most of his friend's day. Mike filed his notice of representation in *State v. Miller* at the clerk's office. He was now officially on the case. He walked upstairs to the office suite used by the superior court judge currently serving Barlow County. Judges rotated across western North Carolina on a circuit designed to lessen the likelihood of favoritism to local lawyers and citizens; however, judges like Harris Coberg still held court in their home districts.

A young man Mike didn't recognize sat behind the clerk's desk in the waiting area for the judge's chambers. Mike introduced himself.

"Who'll be on the bench this week to hear a bond motion in a criminal case?" Mike asked.

"Judge Coberg has started a six-month rotation," the man responded.

"Great. When can you give me a fifteen-minute slot?"

The man glanced at his computer screen. "Tomorrow at nine-thirty."

"Tomorrow?"

"Unless you want to move it to next week."

"No, that's fine. I'll take it. Is the judge in his chambers?"

"No, he's at lunch."

Mike filled in the date and time on the notice and dropped off a copy at the district attorney's office. As he left Shelton and drove to the church, Juanita Jones called him on his cell phone. "Are you on your way to the golf course?" she asked.

"I haven't thought about a golf ball all day," Mike replied. "Did you locate the number for Danny Brewster's mother? I really want to extend my condolences."

"Got it right here."

Mike flipped open his PDA and entered the number while driving with his knees.

"Thanks for letting me know," he said. "And I won't forget your comments about Sam Miller. I want to do the right thing."

"I know. That's the reason I always considered you the best. You had both the will to fight and the desire for truth. I'll be praying for you."

When he reached the church, he phoned Danny's mother. A shaky voice answered the phone.

"Mrs. Brewster, it's Mike Andrews. I just found out about Danny and want you to know how sorry I am."

"I didn't have the money to get him brought home, and they buried him in the prison graveyard," Mrs. Brewster replied. "He didn't have a proper funeral or anything."

"I wish I'd known sooner."

"It's my fault for not calling you."

"No, you've had too much on your mind." Mike paused. "Would you like to have a memorial service here in Shelton?"

"It's been almost two weeks since he died. I guess it's not too late to do something."

"No, it's not. Danny was a fine young man, and those who loved him ought to have a chance to get together to share their sorrow and remember the happier times."

"I've been working on Sundays and haven't been regular at the church down the road. They have a new preacher who doesn't know our family at all—"

"I'd be honored to serve as the minister. I could look for a place on your side of the county to have the service."

"Danny sure did think a lot of you. He saved every one of your letters and read them over and over. They were in his things they sent to me from down yonder."

Mike felt a knot in his throat. He'd corresponded regularly with Danny for several years but slacked off during his time in seminary and had only written twice since returning to Shelton. Danny faithfully replied to every communication. His letters always listed what he'd eaten that day and a Bible verse written with a red pencil. On the back of each letter, he included a crude drawing of something at the prison—his cot, a basketball goal, the guard tower, even the toilet in the corner of his cell. The drawings made Mike both sad and angry.

"I didn't write him enough, Mrs. Brewster," Mike said. "I'd like to do this for him if you'll let me."

"Danny would be glad about that. He was awful proud of you becoming a preacher."

Mike looked at his calendar. "What day of the week is best for you?"

"Wednesday is my day off. We've got kinfolks and neighbors who would come."

"Then we'll do it next Wednesday afternoon. I'll get back to you tomorrow. Do you have an answering machine on your phone?"

"Yes, sir."

MIKE WAS EMOTIONALLY DRAINED WHEN HE WALKED THROUGH the door of the house and plopped down in his chair in the breakfast nook. Peg was cutting up tomatoes for a salad.

"What happened today?" she asked.

"Danny Brewster was murdered in prison two weeks ago," Mike answered in a flat tone of voice.

Peg stopped preparing the salad and gave him a hug. "I'm sorry. Who told you about it?"

"Juanita." Mike shook his head. "He was stabbed by another inmate with a homemade knife. I don't know any details, and I'm not sure I want to find out."

"I know that hurt."

"I called Mrs. Brewster and arranged to have a memorial service on Wednesday."

They sat down to eat. Halfway through the meal, Mike spoke. "You know, Danny was innocent because he didn't know the definition of wrong. I've always blamed the system for failing him because my ego wouldn't let me admit my mistake. It's time to be honest about my responsibility."

"No, Mike. His conviction and death weren't your fault."

"Indirectly they were. My stubbornness forced him to go to trial when he could have received a lesser sentence in a plea bargain and spent less time in jail. It hit me almost as soon as Juanita told me. Back then, all I could think about was winning. It's easier to recognize selfishness and stubbornness with the benefit of hindsight."

Peg turned away.

"What is it?" Mike asked.

"Nothing. Just thinking about the past."

WITHIN MINUTES OF THE TIME MIKE'S HEAD TOUCHED THE pillow, he fell asleep. He rarely woke up until the alarm clock blared in the morning. His nights, however, were filled with unconscious activity. Since childhood, Mike's sleep had been populated by dreams. Most he forgot before dawn, but occasionally one survived the leap from night to day. He had a couple of recurring dreams but never submitted them to an expert for interpretation.

At 3:00 a.m., Mike came roaring out of slumber and sat up in bed. Breathing heavily, he stared into the dark room.

"What is it?" Peg asked sleepily.

"A nightmare," Mike replied. "So bad it woke me up."

Peg leaned on her elbow. "Are you okay?"

"Yes, but I wasn't in the dream."

"Do you want to tell me about it?"

Mike rubbed the side of his face, which was scratchy from an almost twenty-four-hour growth of beard.

"I dreamed Danny, Sam Miller, and I were sitting in an interview room at the jail. Sam was talking his usual nonsense, but Danny seemed to enjoy listening to him. I was frustrated with both of them. Suddenly, the door burst open, and four large men without faces rushed into the room and grabbed Danny and Sam. I was paralyzed. I tried to protest but couldn't think of anything to say. I felt completely helpless. Two of the men dragged Danny away. The other two picked up Sam's chair and started walking out of the room. Sam looked at me and waved good-bye. I had the sense he could easily get away by jumping out of the chair to the floor. I tried to scream a warning, but nothing came out of my mouth. That's when I woke up."

Peg turned on the light on the nightstand.

"I think you're just trying to work through stress," she said. "You had a lot dumped on you yesterday. You were calm at the time but needed to process the tension out of your system."

"Maybe, although it was like watching TV."

Peg reached over and turned off the light. "Ask Sam about it. He's the expert on dreams."

THE FOLLOWING MORNING, MIKE SPENT EXTRA TIME IN FRONT of the mirror adjusting his tie. Peg came up behind him and peeked over his shoulder.

"How are you feeling?" she asked.

"Still tired. I stayed awake for a while because I didn't want to go through the dream again."

"Did it come back?"

"No, but I did wake up with Danny Brewster's face in my mind. Do you remember how toothy he looked when he grinned?"

"Yes. File that in your mental photo album as a happier thought."

Peg smoothed his collar and stroked his hair. "You know, if you really want to create a good impression in the courtroom, you need more gray hair."

Mike shook his head. "I'm going to be a father, not a grandfather."

"We'll probably get those questions anyway."

Mike turned around. Peg looked great in workout clothes from the University of Virginia, their college alma mater and the place they met and fell in love. She leaned up and kissed him.

"I might, but you won't," Mike said. "Visitors to the church often ask if you're my daughter."

Peg shook her head and frowned. "It's a sin to lie."

DOWNSTAIRS, MIKE DRANK A CUP OF COFFEE AND HALFHEART-edly nibbled a slice of wheat toast. Judge sat beside his chair, hoping for a crumb from the table.

"Time to ride into battle," Mike said, looking at the clock on the wall.

"I'll be in the castle with your noble beast when you return."

Mike patted Judge on the head and gave him a sliver of crust. "I wish a human judge would do what I ask in return for a piece of bread."

IT WASN'T A BUSY CRIMINAL ARRAIGNMENT DAY. WHEN THAT happened, the influx of family and friends anxious about the fate of loved ones made it hard to find a parking place near the courthouse. Only a few people were on the sidewalk.

Butterflies fluttered in Mike's stomach. A bond hearing was a perfunctory affair that wouldn't create much tension, but Mike's long absence from the legal arena made him nervous. Sitting in the car, he phoned the jail to confirm that Sam would be present. As he walked up the courthouse steps with a thin folder in his hand, Mike replayed in his mind the legal standard for reducing a bond.

The main courtroom in the Barlow County Courthouse was painted a light cream color. The dark wooden benches had been recently restained, and the faint odor of finishing compound lingered in the air. Half a dozen lawyers were milling around the front of the courtroom. When Mike approached, conversation stopped. Earl Coulter, a veteran criminal defense lawyer, came over and shook his hand.

"Welcome, Preacher. Glad you're here. I could use a character witness in a sentencing hearing for one of the Vinson boys. How much would it cost to get you to vouch for him?"

"It says *Not for hire* on the back of my new business card," Mike replied. "And I don't think you want me giving my opinion of whether your client is a threat to society."

"You know Zane, don't you?"

"Yeah, I got him a deal for two years in and two years on probation when he was about twenty."

"He ran through that and has built more time in prison since. Two years at a work camp would be a blessing from heaven if I could get it today."

Mike pointed up. "You and Zane had better talk to my new boss if you want that kind of help."

Mike stepped through the opening in the wooden railing that ran across the courtroom. Passing into familiar territory, the butterflies in his stomach left. A short young lawyer with dark hair and angular features came over to him.

"I'm Greg Freeman. How is Mr. Miller doing?"

"That's why I'm here," Mike replied. "I filed a motion to reduce his bond, but I'd still like to see him hire an attorney. I'll keep working that angle with him."

Several chairs along the wall opposite the jury box were reserved for the attorneys. Mike sat in the second chair from the end and scribbled a few notes on a legal pad. People began to drift into the courtroom. Bobby Lambert and Maxwell Forrest walked down the aisle and through the gate. Mike stood up.

"Good morning, Mr. Forrest," he said.

Mike never called the gray-haired, distinguished-looking senior partner by his first name and knew few people under fifty who did.

"Good to see you, Mike," Forrest replied with a smile. "Are you testifying as a character witness?"

"No, sir."

"I forgot to tell you," Bobby said to his senior partner. "Mike is representing a man pro bono. When he asked permission from the elders to do it, you'd have thought he wanted to bring a basket of snakes to the Sunday morning service."

"I'm saving the snake request for next month," Mike said.

"That should be easy compared to the other night. Convincing the other members of the session to let you help this man was one of the most difficult jobs of persuasion I've had all year."

"Sorry I missed the argument," Mike said. "I could have learned something, but you kicked me out of the room for the debate."

"I didn't want you to learn all my manipulative tricks. You might use them against me."

Forrest smiled. "If you boys had spent as much time thinking up ways to help our clients as you did upstaging each other, all of us would have made a lot more money."

The back door of the courtroom opened, and a sheriff's deputy brought in a line of four prisoners from the jail. Bringing up the rear and looking around the courtroom with a quizzical look on his face was Sam Miller. There was a visible bruise on his jaw where he'd been struck. The prisoners went into the jury box and sat on the front row. Mike walked toward Sam, but before he reached him, Judge Coberg came into the courtroom.

"All rise!" an elderly bailiff ordered.

Mike gave Sam an encouraging look before returning to the lawyers' side of the courtroom.

"Be seated," the judge said as soon as he positioned himself behind the bench.

It had been many years since Harris Coberg practiced law. His shoulders had started to droop, and his right hand had a slight quiver, but his piercing dark eyes retained the intensity that had made him a successful prosecutor long before Ken West arrived on the scene.

"We'll take up the criminal matters first," the judge said in his deep voice.

The judge glared at the table where the State's attorneys sat. There was no sign of Ken West or anyone else from the district attorney's office.

"What time is it?" the judge barked at no one in particular.

Mr. Forrest was immediately on his feet. "Five minutes after nine, Your Honor."

"Thank you, Mr. Forrest."

The side door leading to the DA's office opened, and Melissa Hall entered with several files crookedly held beneath her arm.

"Glad you could join us," the judge growled. "When I'm presiding, court begins promptly at nine. Is that a problem for you?"

"My apologies, Your Honor," Hall replied. Mike could see the young lawyer's face flush from across the room. "Mr. West was scheduled to handle this morning's docket, but he called in sick."

"Are you ready to proceed?" the judge asked in a voice that dared her to request a postponement.

"Yes, sir."

"Let's have it."

"*State v. Hughes.* Defendant's Motion for Independent Testing of Alleged Controlled Substance," Hall replied.

Partway through the hearing, Judge Coberg glanced over at the lawyers' section and nodded slightly at Mike.

Mike settled into his chair and listened. Assistant DA Hall didn't put up much of a fight to a defense request for independent testing of alleged cocaine found at the defendant's mobile home.

Greg Freeman handled the second hearing, a motion to suppress evidence of stolen merchandise found in the trunk of his client's car. The key issue was the reasonableness of the initial stop of the vehicle. The deputy hadn't figured out the nuances of the Fourth Amendment prohibition against unreasonable searches and seizures, and Freeman roasted him on cross-examination. Hall's attempt to rehabilitate the deputy's testimony only reemphasized his lack of probable cause to stop and search the car. The judge cut into Hall's questioning.

"Deputy, you can't stop a car in Barlow County and pry open the trunk with a crowbar because you heard at a bar the defendant was involved in a burglary."

"But everyone knows he's guilty," the deputy protested. "And I found the stuff to prove it!"

"Not in my courtroom!" The judge's right hand shook as he extended his finger toward the witness. "Next time, do your job right!"

The deputy silently appealed for help to Hall, who looked down at the paperwork on the table.

"Do you understand?" the judge continued.

"Uh, yes, sir."

"I'm not sure you do, Deputy, but by the next time you appear before me, I hope the sheriff's office will have corrected the flaws in your criminal justice education." The judge looked at Hall. "Tell Mr. West that I expect him to do a better job screening searches so the court's time isn't wasted with this kind of sloppy law enforcement."

"Yes, sir."

"Mr. Freeman," the judge continued. "Draw up an appropriate order granting the motion to suppress."

Freeman returned to the lawyers' section and whispered to Mike, "I don't think the judge has granted two defense motions in a row this year."

"I'm next. I hope it's three."

"'*State v. Miller*, Motion to Reduce Bond,'" the judge read from the sheet before him, then glanced up at Mike. "Mr. Andrews, are you representing Mr. Miller?"

"Yes, sir."

Mike moved to the defense table where Sam, still dressed in a jailhouse orange jumpsuit, joined him. The bruise on Sam's cheek had turned from red to purple. The old man smiled at Mike.

"Papa and I say 'Good morning,'" Sam said.

"Keep Papa out of this," Mike replied.

"Proceed," the judge said.

"Yes, sir," Mike answered loudly. He handed certified copies of the real estate records to the judge and Hall. "I tender these records into evidence."

"No objection," Hall responded.

Mike continued. "Judge, this is an embezzlement charge with bond currently set at $100,000. Mr. Miller and his wife own property free and clear in Barlow County, and his residence and the surrounding land have a tax value of $65,000. We'd ask that the bond be reduced to that amount. Mr. Miller has lived in the Shelton area for more than thirty years and operates his own lawncare business. He has no prior criminal record and doesn't pose a serious risk of flight. He's been in jail three months since his arrest."

The judge silently read the documents.

"How is your jaw?" Mike whispered to Sam.

"They sent me to the hospital for an X-ray. It's not broke, but it hurts to chew."

The judge spoke. "Are you going to present testimonial evidence from the defendant?"

"If you think it necessary," Mike answered. "I didn't want to take up too much of the Court's time, and given Mr. Miller's stable background, the records admitted are sufficient to support reduction of the bond."

"That's an issue I'll decide," the judge responded wryly. "Before I do, I have a few questions for Mr. Miller. Ms. Hall may also want to inquire."

Mike turned to Sam. "Go to the witness chair."

Sam ambled to the elevated seat on the right-hand side of the bench. With his rotund belly and white hair, he certainly didn't look like a threat to society.

Mike's concern was that Sam's words would sabotage the motion. The judge administered the oath. Sam looked at Mike.

"I'm ready when you are," he said.

Out of the corner of his eye, Mike saw Bobby Lambert suppress a laugh. Mr. Forrest sat stone-faced beside him.

"Judge, do you want me to go first?" Mike asked.

"Proceed."

"Yes, sir."

Mike faced the witness stand.

"What is your name?" he asked.

"Sam Miller."

"Tell the judge about your background."

"Which part?"

"Your business."

"I cut grass, plant trees and shrubs, fertilize, trim, and do whatever needs to be done to a yard. I've cut the judge's grass a few times when he was out of town and couldn't do it himself."

Mike quickly checked Judge Coberg's expression. His countenance remained inscrutable.

"Do you have a criminal record?" Mike asked.

"Nope."

Mike approached the witness stand and handed Sam a copy of the real estate records.

"Do you and your wife own this property?"

"Yep."

"Any mortgage?"

"Not in a long time."

"If you're released on bond, will you stay in Barlow County until the charges against you have been resolved?"

"Unless the Master sends me elsewhere."

Mike's jaw tightened. "But you'll obey an order by the court instructing you to stay close to home if it's a condition of your bond, won't you?"

Sam shifted in his chair. "I render unto Caesar, but Papa is my boss."

Mike tried to ignore the murmurings that rippled across the courtroom but quickly decided not to dissect Sam's answer in an effort to explain it. The more Sam spoke, the more unstable he would appear.

"Will you be present for all scheduled court dates?"

"Yep, so long as I know about it."

"Subject to any redirect examination, that's all from the defendant."

Mike turned over a fresh sheet on his legal pad and hoped for the best.

"Ms. Hall, you may ask," the judge said.

"No questions."

Mike barely concealed his shock. Even an inexperienced prosecutor could make Sam look ridiculous and perhaps even delusional. The judge stared at Hall for a moment then turned toward Sam.

"Mr. Miller, when was the last time you traveled outside Barlow County?" the judge asked.

"Let's see, Muriel and I drove over to Lake James about a month before I was locked up."

"Did you catch anything?"

"No keepers. I spent most of the time sitting on a stump enjoying the view."

"If you get out on bond, will you have time to plant your garden?"

"Muriel got everything started in the cold frame, but I need to transplant my lettuce, broccoli, and cauliflower."

The judge wrote something on the legal pad in front of him. For all Mike knew, it could have been a reminder to contact Sam Miller for fresh vegetables.

"What happened to your face?" the judge asked.

"A boy at the jail lost his temper and started swinging. I didn't see it coming."

"Who was it?"

"Brinson."

"Was he mad at you?"

"Nope. I think he was mad at you. He mentioned your name along with some other words I heard all the time in the Marine Corps but don't want to repeat today."

"And I've heard enough today," the judge replied. "Motion granted. I find the defendant's real property is sufficient collateral. Mr. Andrews, do you have an Order prepared?"

"No, sir. Will you be in your chambers later today?"

"Until three o'clock."

Mike accompanied Sam back to the jury box.

"You did a good job," Sam said.

Mike spoke in a low voice. "I didn't do anything. He was upset that you got hit." Mike paused. "And probably wants to make sure you get out of jail in time to plant your garden."

The judge called out, "*State v. Garfield.* Mr. Lambert for the defendant."

"He's partial to cauliflower," Sam replied. "But I could tell he respects you."

"I'm not sure *respect* is in his vocabulary when he's thinking about lawyers." Mike pointed across the courtroom. "But did you see Greg Freeman in action? He's a sharp young attorney."

"Yep, but you're the one for me."

"You're harder to convince than Judge Coberg," Mike replied softly. "After the judge signs the Order, I'll come by the jail. You should be home for supper. I'm sure your wife can fix something easy to chew."

Mike left the courtroom. He was halfway down the hall when he heard his name.

"Mike, just a minute!"

It was Mr. Forrest. He was leaning against the wall and breathing heavily. Mike returned to him.

"I'm sorry, I didn't know you wanted to talk to me," Mike said.

The old man caught his breath. "It's about Miller. I don't think it's wise for you to be representing him."

Mike's jaw tightened. Anyone but Maxwell Forrest would have received a curt response. Mike took a deep breath.

"It's temporary, until he can find another attorney," Mike said. "Maybe Greg Freeman could help him. I thought Greg did a good job this morning."

"A much better choice," Forrest said, clearing his throat. "A young lawyer with no reputation to protect."

Mike narrowed his gaze. Forrest continued, "Jack Hatcher at the bank is concerned about this situation. There was a lot of money involved."

"I planned on contacting someone at the bank about the account. If the charges are the result of a data entry error, I wouldn't do anything to cause public embarrassment for the bank."

"There's no mistake, Mike," Forrest said soberly. "I've seen the documentation. It's embezzlement, although not a very artful attempt."

Mike shrugged. "If that's the case, it will probably be a matter of working out a guilty plea. Could you call Mr. Hatcher and arrange access for me to the bank's records?"

"I'd rather not."

"Why?"

"Your involvement creates an awkward situation."

"How?"

"You're no longer with the firm, of course, but our names remain linked in the minds of many people, and a possible conflict with the bank would be an undesirable scenario. As a minister, you hold a position of respect in the community that is above the unpleasantness of involvement in a criminal case. Trust me. I'm only trying to protect you."

Mike was puzzled. "Is there more to this than I know?"

"Not really, except recognizing the wisdom of disengaging yourself from this matter so you can return to what the good Lord called you to do."

Mike spoke slowly, "Mr. Forrest, I really appreciate your concern. It gives me a new perspective."

Forrest patted Mike on the shoulder. "Good. You were always a quick learner."

"Why would Andrews get involved in the first place?" Jack Hatcher asked.

Maxwell Forrest shifted the phone receiver against his ear and made a note about the call on his time and billing slip.

"He's always had a touch of crusader in him, but it doesn't matter who handles the case. The evidence is ironclad."

"Could Andrews delay the case?"

"Of course. No defendant wants speedy justice."

"The board of the bank wants a conviction, the sooner the better."

"I can encourage the process to move along."

"Do it."

Eight

MIKE WENT HOME AND PREPARED THE ORDER REDUCING SAM'S bond then returned to the courthouse. Two lawyers were vigorously arguing a motion for summary judgment in a civil case. With no spectators present, the attorneys were like gladiators fighting in an empty arena. Mike sat in the front row and listened.

After the attorneys packed up their briefcases, Judge Coberg spoke to Mike. "Mr. Andrews, you may approach."

Mike came forward and stood in front of the judge.

"I prepared the Order in the Miller case. Do you have time to review it before lunch?"

"So long as you didn't write it in Hebrew or Greek."

"Your Honor, my familiarity with ancient languages proved as fleeting as my understanding of the Rule against Perpetuities."

"Let me see what you have," the judge said.

Mike handed a single sheet of paper to the judge, who quickly scanned and signed it. The judge sat back in his chair.

"I've missed seeing you in my courtroom. How's the four-legged Judge doing?"

"Still barking at anyone who doesn't agree with him."

"I ought to name my new pointer Preacher," the judge responded.

"Only if he points in the right direction."

Judge Coberg rewarded Mike with a rare smile.

"Are you enjoying the ministry?"

"Yes, sir."

"Still have an itch to practice law?"

"No, sir. My involvement in this case is not the sign of a trend."

The judge nodded. "Nonetheless, I'm glad you're helping Sam Miller. He's a unique individual. I've known him a long time and was surprised to see him on the criminal calendar. Do you think I should recuse myself?"

Mike stepped back in surprise. "Why?"

"Because I like his cauliflower."

"He mentioned that to me, but I don't have any objection to you sitting on the case."

"The DA might. I'm going to send you and Ken West a disclosure memo about my prior contact with Mr. Miller."

"You've rubbed shoulders with a significant percentage of the people who live in Barlow County," Mike protested.

"How many of them are like Sam Miller?"

Mike studied the judge's face. The dark eyes revealed nothing.

"We're all different," Mike replied slowly. "How is Mr. Miller unique?"

A slight smile again lifted the corners of the judge's mouth. "You don't have me on the witness stand or kneeling at the altar, Reverend Andrews. If you have to ask that question, you don't know your client."

MIKE MADE SEVERAL COPIES OF THE ORDER, FILED THE ORIGINAL in the clerk's office, and dropped a copy by the DA's office. He left the courthouse and walked to the jail. Mike took off his jacket and threw it over his shoulder. At the jail, he handed the Order to the officer on duty.

"I'll send word around to the back," the deputy said. "They'll bring him up."

While he waited, Mike called Muriel Miller and gave her the good news. Her voice cracked with emotion as she thanked him, and he could imagine the tears rolling down her wrinkled cheeks.

"How long will it take you to get here?" Mike asked her.

"I don't know. I left the truck's lights on last night, and it has a dead battery. I'm still waiting for someone to come by and give me a jump start."

"Don't worry about it," Mike said. "I can bring Sam to your house."

"But that's out of your way."

"It's not a problem. I don't have to be anywhere else, and I only have one client."

In a few minutes, Sam came out wearing blue jeans and a denim shirt.

"I'm taking you home," Mike said. "Muriel knows you're coming but couldn't pick you up because the battery in your truck is dead."

"That's happened before. She doesn't like walking up to a dark house."

Outside, Sam looked up at the sky.

"The grass has been growing, and so have I," he said. "Ninety-six days in jail is a long time. It was tough, but I can see why so many of Papa's children have been locked up. It forced me to think seriously about some things."

Mike didn't take the bait. "I'm parked at the courthouse," he said. "Can you walk that far?"

"My legs are fine," Sam replied. "It's my jaw that hurts."

Sam set a surprisingly brisk pace. Mike fell in beside him.

"You're a fast walker," Mike said.

"When you make your living walking behind a lawn mower, you can't be a slowpoke. Muriel is worried about my heart, but I get more exercise than most men half my age."

"I didn't say anything to her about your jaw."

"Thanks. They took away the boy who hit me, and he didn't come back. I was sorry to see him go."

"Why?"

"After someone hurts you is often the best time to help them. They're invulnerable."

"You mean vulnerable."

"That, too." Sam shook his head. "I'm going to have to stop trying to impress you with my vocabulary."

They passed the local drugstore where Mike enjoyed ice cream cones when he was a boy. No longer dressed in jailhouse garb, Sam looked even less like a criminal. The old man glanced around as they walked and seemed to study each person they encountered on the sidewalk.

"Tell me about Judge Coberg," Mike said. "He seemed to know more about you than just the fact that you cut grass and grow vegetables."

"I never worked for him regular, but when I did, he always paid me on time."

"There must be more to it than that. He's going to notify the DA's office that his relationship with you may justify his removal from the case. He didn't give me any details, but I suspect you've had conversations with him similar to what you've told me."

"He's not one of my sons. We never talked too much, and he was always at the courthouse or out of town when I worked at his house."

"He said you were a different type of person."

Sam smiled. "That could be said about him, too."

They reached Mike's car and got in. Sam settled in the leather seat and sighed.

"This sure is comfortable. I've missed my recliner at home."

Sam gave directions to his house then immediately closed his eyes. Mike wasn't sure if his client was awake or asleep.

After they passed the west edge of commercial development for Shelton, fewer and fewer houses dotted the countryside. There weren't many farms in the rocky soil of Barlow County. Most of the people who lived outside the city limits did so because land was cheaper and neighbors more distant. Like Sam, they drove into the more populated areas to work. When they came to a stop sign, Sam opened his eyes and looked at Mike.

"You know one thing I learned in jail?" Sam asked.

"I guess you're going to tell me whether I want to hear it or not."

"It's something you'll agree with. You bringing up Lou Jasper the other day got me thinking. Papa showed me that sometimes I run my mouth when I ought to keep quiet. Even after all these years, I get excited when He shows me something and look for the first chance to tell it."

"If the Lord really reveals something to you, it's understandable that you would be excited."

"But it's not an excuse for loose lips. The right word in the wrong time is as bad as the wrong word in the right time. I need to call Lou and apologize."

Mike, temporarily caught in the convoluted web of Sam's logic, didn't immediately respond.

"Uh, I'm not sure I follow you, but I don't see why an apology is necessary. You said Lou Jasper didn't follow through on what you shared with him."

"That's his problem. I have to deal with mine."

They turned onto McAfee Road.

"Which house is yours?" Mike asked.

"A half mile on the left," Sam said. "It's yellow with blue shutters and sits on top of a little hill. You can't miss it."

They passed a mailbox resting on a car tire painted white and partially buried in the ground. A few stodgy Angus cattle glanced up from a field on the right-hand side of the road. They drove up a steep driveway to a small frame dwelling.

"Could you park in front of my truck so you can give me a jump before you leave?" Sam asked.

They got out of the car. Muriel came onto the small front stoop. Mike held back while Sam walked quickly across the grass and climbed three concrete steps to greet her. They embraced. Mike could tell that Muriel was crying. He looked away. When Sam turned around, his eyes were red, too.

"Toss me the keys to your truck, and I'll hook up the jumper cables," Mike said, backing away. "You need to spend time together without me interfering."

"Don't be silly," Muriel said with a wave of her hand. "Come in the house. You can mess with that old truck later."

"She's right," Sam added. "We won't keep you long."

The interior of the small house looked surprisingly normal. Mike wasn't sure what he'd expected, but Sam Miller didn't live in a cave. He glanced around the modestly furnished yet meticulously clean room. Muriel went into the kitchen and returned to the living room with two glasses of iced tea. Sam, sitting in a fat recliner, squeezed a thick slice of lemon in his glass and took a deep drink.

"Thank you, sweetheart," he said. "This is delicious."

Mike positioned himself on a plaid sofa and took a sip.

"Yes, ma'am. It's very good."

Muriel, a glass of water in her hand, looked at Sam. Mike saw her expression change to one of alarm and concern.

"What happened to your face?"

She kept her lips pressed tightly together while Sam related the story of the attack.

"It wasn't near as bad as some of the licks I took when we first got married," Sam said. "Getting hit by four drunk sailors who thought they could whip two Marines was a lot worse."

"And you were a lot younger," Muriel said. "I'm just glad you're out of that jail." She turned to Mike. "Thanks again for helping us."

"You're welcome."

Mike relaxed on the sofa and listened while Muriel brought Sam up to date on their household news. Sam had lightbulbs at the edge of the roof to change and a leaky faucet to fix. Hearing the couple talk about everyday issues made

Sam seem more normal. Mike drained his tea glass of the last drop. Muriel took it to the kitchen for a refill.

"Preacher," Sam said, "I have a question."

"What?"

"Will there be sweet tea in heaven?"

"Only in the Southern part."

Sam laughed. "That's where I want my mansion."

Muriel returned to the room.

"You should have seen Mike in court," Sam said to her. "He was smooth as your egg custard. Judge Coberg thinks highly of him."

"And he thinks highly of you," Mike responded. "Especially your vegetables. However, everyone doesn't agree with the judge. My former boss was in the courtroom this morning. He caught me in the hallway after the hearing and told me it would be an embarrassment to both of us if I continued to represent you."

"What's his name?" Sam asked.

"Maxwell Forrest."

"Oh, yeah, I've heard of him."

"He also mentioned that Jack Hatcher, the president of the bank, was very interested in your case."

"Is he the man you wrote the letter to?" Muriel asked Sam.

Sam put his fingers to his lips and shook his head.

"What letter?" Mike asked sharply.

"Mike, I told you I can't go running my mouth about everything."

"And you can't expect me to represent you if I don't know the facts." Mike placed his glass on a coaster. "Mr. Forrest told me the bank records clearly show how you embezzled the money. Why shouldn't I believe him?"

"I passed the money test many years ago. It doesn't have a hold on me."

Mike looked at Muriel. "Why is he making this so hard for me? Ever since we met he's been dumping a lot of stuff on me that I don't understand or want to hear. Now, he won't answer a simple question."

"Sam, you've got to tell your lawyer what he needs to know so he can represent you. I'm glad you're home, but this isn't over. The thought that you might be sent off for a much longer time—" Muriel stopped.

Sam went to her chair and kissed the top of her head. "I'm here now, and we're going to start praying about the future."

"What about the letter?" Mike persisted.

Sam returned to his recliner. "I don't have a copy and can't see how it could have anything to do with what's happening now."

"You should let me make that decision. Do you have any notes?"

"Check in one of your notebooks," Muriel suggested.

"Yeah, a written notation may refresh your memory," Mike said.

Sam sighed. "Okay. You seem determined to find out one way or the other."

Sam left the room. Muriel spoke. "He writes things down in a notebook that he keeps beside the bed. He has stacks of them in boxes on the floor of our closet, so it may take him a while to fetch it."

"How long ago did he write the letter to Mr. Hatcher?"

"Maybe six months ago."

"Did he show it to you?"

"No, but I remember he thought it was unusual."

"If he thought it was unusual, I'm sure it was different," Mike said. "Does he know Mr. Hatcher?"

"I don't think so, but he's written lots of notes and letters to people he doesn't know. He writes the president a couple of times a year."

"President?"

"Of the United States. He sends it directly to the White House. He never hears back, but that doesn't seem to discourage him."

Mike guessed the FBI couldn't check out every eccentric individual who regularly wrote the president.

"What about Judge Coberg? Does he write him?"

"Not that I know of, but it could have happened."

"Has he ever had any dreams about the judge?"

"Not so fast," Sam said as he entered the room. "Don't use your lawyer tricks on Muriel." He held up a tattered notebook. "I think what you want to see is in here."

Sam sat in his recliner and began turning the pages. Mike leaned forward on the couch so he could get a better view. It was impossible to decipher the meaning of the words, numbers, and drawings scrawled on the pages.

"Here are the verses Papa gave me to share with Myra Cordell," Sam said to Muriel. "She was thinking about killing herself. How is she doing?"

"Better. Her daughter has moved back from St. Louis to stay with her for a while."

"Get back to your notebook," Mike said.

While Mike sipped his tea, Sam kept turning the pages.

"Tell me about the photos on the wall," Mike asked Muriel.

Muriel gave him a brief family history.

"Matthew dying overseas was a hard blow," she said. "Losing a young-un is one of those things you never get over. Now we're praying for Anne Marie, one of my great-nieces. She's battling leukemia."

"I'll put her on the prayer list at my church."

Mike entered her name in his PDA.

"Ah, take a look at this," Sam said. "Down at the bottom of the page."

He handed the notebook to Mike, who examined the heavily stained and wrinkled sheet of paper for a few seconds.

"I can't read it. What's that brown stuff?"

"Coffee, I guess. I must have spilled a cup on it while I was writing the letter at the kitchen table."

"Can you make it out?" Mike asked.

Sam squinted at the paper. "Some of it. What I do in the night is write down a few words that remind me of other things in the morning. Have you started keeping a notebook by your bed?"

"No."

"You should."

"Let's see," Sam said. "I remember it was nighttime in the dream. There was a hatchet, a box of finishing nails, a baseball bat, and a tree. They were all standing up and talking like men. I could see Cohulla Creek behind them. The baseball bat gave a man I know named Larry Pasley a string of glass beads. They were pretty, but I knew they were worthless. Larry seemed happy, but I knew he was being duped. They didn't know I was watching because they didn't believe I could see in the dark. But day and night are the same to Papa. And here in the margin are the verses I sent, Ephesians 5:11–14."

Sam looked up at Muriel. "What does that passage say?"

"It's about the deeds of darkness. I'll get the Bible."

Muriel left the room and returned with a black Bible that showed signs of heavy use. She touched her index finger to her tongue as she flipped through the pages.

"Here it is," she said. She read slowly and deliberately. " *'Have nothing to do with the fruitless deeds of darkness, but rather expose them. For it is shameful even to mention what the disobedient do in secret. But everything exposed by the light becomes visible, for it is the light that makes everything visible."*

"Yep," Sam said. "That's it."

"What does that mean?" Mike asked.

"Exactly what it says. Papa always tells it like it is."

"I know, but why would you send those verses to Jack Hatcher at the bank?"

"'Cause he was in the dream. Papa often uses pictures to speak to me."

Mike stared at the sheet of paper.

"Jack Hatcher was the hatchet."

"Yep."

"Who are the other people?"

"I'm not sure."

Mike continued to stare. "Maxwell Forrest."

"Yep, that might be right, but there was only one tree. A forest has a bunch of trees."

"I'm doing the best I can," Mike answered. "Who is a box of nails and a baseball bat?"

"I don't have a clue."

"How did you know it was Cohulla Creek?"

"They were standing near a spot along the creek where I like to pray when the weather is nice. There is a rock that sits out in the stream. I can sit on the rock and enjoy the view in both directions. Praying by a creek, listening to the voice of the Lord in the waters—it restores my soul."

"Did you put all the symbolism in the letter?"

"What?"

"The pictures. Did you tell Jack Hatcher that you saw him as a hatchet in a dream?"

"No, he would have thought I was crazy. That part was for me, not him."

"The crazy part makes sense. How can you interpret this stuff and claim God is communicating to you?"

"After you eat a lot of peaches, you know what a good one tastes like."

Mike gave Sam a puzzled look.

"Check the fruit—the change in a person's life or things turning out exactly like Papa showed you. Have you counted how many dreams are in the Bible?"

"No."

"Me either. But there are hundreds of them."

Mike's face remained skeptical. "So what did you write?"

"I don't remember exactly, but I think I warned him not to take advantage of Larry, who owns property along the creek. It looked like Larry was getting the bad end of a land deal."

"How did you know that?"

"Because they were meeting at night, handing him some worthless beads. And it fit with the verses about the deeds of darkness. Do you understand?"

"Land deeds."

Sam smiled in satisfaction. "Yep. You're going to do just fine. And I told Mr. Hatcher that the Lord saw what he was doing and would bring it into the light."

"It's a far-fetched theory. Did you mention other people being involved?"

"Not by name, since it wasn't clear, but I told him I saw a group of people. It's not as important that I understand what I see as the person receiving it. They're the ones who have to ignore it or act on it. Since they were all together, I figured he could tell them himself."

"What about Larry Pasley? Did you contact him?"

"Yep. I went by his place. He lives in an old shack that his grandpa built, and his family has owned property up that valley for a long time. Larry dropped out of school when he was a boy and can't read and write very well. He said he'd been paid enough money to buy a new hot water heater and a color TV and in a few months might get enough to buy a trailer for his son and daughter-in-law. I told him it might not be a good deal, but he told me I didn't know what I was talking about. He'd had a lawyer check everything out for him."

"Who was the lawyer?"

"I didn't ask, and he didn't say."

"Was he selling his home place?"

"I doubt it, because he bought a new hot water heater."

"Is that all?"

"No, there was something else. I remember ending the letter with a little poem. I've never done that before."

Sam turned the page in his notebook. "Here it is. I put it on the next page."

"Let's hear it."

"Don't laugh at me. I barely graduated from high school, and I'm not much of a poet."

"Go ahead."

Sam cleared his throat like a schoolboy about to recite before the class.

> *Deeds of darkness produce only tares.*
> *Those who sow for gold will reap despair.*

He looked up at Mike. "It's not much, but at least it rhymes."

Nine

MIKE AND SAM WENT OUTSIDE TO JUMP-START SAM'S TRUCK.

"I had a troubling dream last night about you and Danny Brewster," Mike said as they walked across the yard. "I didn't want to bring it up in front of Muriel."

"I'm listening."

Mike told him the dream about the interview room at the jail and dark figures who carried Danny and Sam from the room. Sam leaned against the side of the truck and listened.

"I woke up in a sweat," Mike concluded. "What do you think?"

"We're in a fight, and it's not just against flesh and blood. You helped Danny in his case and now you're helping me. Some of our enemies have faces; others are in the spiritual world. I've seen the faceless ones myself. They are pure evil."

Mike shuddered slightly. "Why didn't you get out of the chair?"

"Because I was at rest in the battle."

"You were in danger."

"I know. And with your help, I won't mess up."

"I was paralyzed and couldn't think of anything to say."

"Words with power come from your spirit, not your mind," Sam replied with a smile. "Keep loving Papa, walking with the Master, leaning on the Helper, and eating the Word. After a while, you'll learn how to fight the Enemy in the right way."

Sam attached the cables to the dead battery. Mike raised the hood of his car.

"Hook up your end of the cables," Sam said. "Make sure the ground is on black."

Mike attached the cables to the battery of his car and turned on the engine. He joined Sam while they waited for the dead battery to build up a charge. Sam got in the truck and turned the key. The truck engine sputtered to life. Mike unhooked the jumper cables from both batteries and coiled them up.

"I'll let it run awhile," Sam said. "It'd better start tomorrow because I need to be out of here at the crack of dawn. There's no telling how much business I've lost."

"Was there anything in the paper about your arrest?"

"Just one line, but you know how people are. That could really hurt me."

Mike thought a moment. "Would you be willing to put in a bid to cut the grass at Little Creek Church? It's a long way across the county, but it might be worth the drive. The cemetery alone would take a full day."

"That's mighty nice of you," Sam said appreciatively. "I'll try to get over there and take a look at it."

It was almost 1:30 p.m. by the time Mike returned to Shelton. He pulled into a parking space near traffic light seven and made notes on a legal pad about his conversation with Sam Miller. The information in Sam's notebook was too speculative to serve as a cogent defense in the case. Mike's stomach growled. He'd missed lunch, and the sweet tea provided by Muriel Miller wasn't a substitute for a meal. Mike called the church. Delores answered.

"Any problems?" he asked.

"No, it's been real quiet. I've been reading one of my magazines."

Delores loved gossip magazines and kept close tabs on the real and imagined scandals of movie and soap opera stars.

"Anything I need to know that's going on in Hollywood?"

"Not really, but if I see a good sermon illustration, I'll mark it."

A concrete-block building on the outskirts of town was home to the world's greatest hamburger. Owned by identical twin brothers, the Brooks Brothers Sandwich House had been serving up hamburgers topped with homemade chili and sweet onions since Mike attended high school. He pulled into the gravel parking lot.

Next to a pale yellow building was a long wooden table under a tin roof that provided open-air eating. The building itself was too small for a dining room, so all the brothers' business was either take-out or eaten by customers alfresco style at the communal table. Between noon and one o'clock, the line of construction workers and businesspeople stretched out the door.

The kitchen was open to public view, and one of the brothers was busy flattening round balls of fresh meat on a grill top. In a pan on a single-coil electric unit rested a smoking pot of chili. Orders were written on the white bags used to hold each order. The Brooks brother at the grill looked up when Mike entered the restaurant.

"Hey, Mike! How you doing?"

"Pretty good."

Mike had known the Brooks brothers for more than twenty years. He'd watched their hair turn gray and their waistlines grow, but he'd never been able to tell them apart. In middle age, they remained carbon copies of each other. While one brother cooked, the other filled Styrofoam cups with tea and lined up orders of thick-cut french fries.

A rough-looking man named Dusty with the sleeves cut out of a biker T-shirt took the orders. Scowling, and with a pen in his hand, he stood behind the counter and waited for Mike.

"I recommend the fried liver mush," Dusty said. "It's fresh and crisp."

Mike would occasionally eat the square patties of liver, but if Peg found out, she made him brush his teeth twice and gargle with mouthwash before getting close to him.

"No, my wife has been extra nice to me the past few days, and I don't want to ruin it. I'll have two cheeseburgers all the way."

He moved down the counter toward the cash register. Hamburgers sizzled on the black grill. Above the cash register hung a small bell that Dusty rang every time a first-time customer came into the shop.

"Been on any cruises lately?" Mike asked Dusty.

The counterman saved his money so he could book a cheap three- or four-day cruise every year.

"It's coming up in a month."

"Where are you going?"

"Aruba, Grand Cayman, and St. Thomas."

The brother pouring tea laughed. "Don't believe him, Mike. It's the same thing he always does. They fly him to Miami, drop him in a dingy, and tow him to the Bahamas where he drinks beer for forty-eight hours before coming home."

Dusty patted his belly with a grin. "I know what they mean by all-inclusive—it's all the boiled shrimp and beer I can put down from the time the boat leaves Miami until it gets back to the dock."

The door opened and Braxton Hodges, a reporter with the Shelton paper, entered. Braxton, a balding man with glasses and rumpled white shirt, reported on everything from livestock winners at the county fair to the annual black-tie fund-raiser for the local hospital.

"Heard you were in court this morning," the reporter said to Mike after he ordered.

"That's not news."

"It is in Shelton. Getting bored with the pulpit?"

"No, just trying to help someone out of a jam."

Dusty handed Mike his sack of food. "The liver mush makes a tasty dessert."

"Talk Braxton into it," Mike said. "He can write an article about what it does to his digestive tract."

Mike went outside with his food. He bowed his head for a silent blessing, then pulled out a burger and took a bite. Like the Brooks brothers' physical appearances, the hamburgers were always the same and uniformly excellent. Braxton Hodges joined him.

"Admit it," Hodges said. "You wanted a thick slab of liver mush between two pieces of white bread."

"If a loaf of mush had been hanging on the forbidden tree in the Garden of Eden, I don't think Adam and Eve would have sinned."

Hodges smiled. "Years ago I started to write a story about the history of liver mush. I didn't go back to Genesis, but like many regional dishes, I discovered it was created by poor folks who couldn't afford to get rid of anything remotely edible. I finished the prep work but couldn't get past the third paragraph of the article. I dreamed about pig livers for weeks."

Mike took a large bite from his burger. The combination of onions and chili with the slightly crispy meat was superb.

"Have you had any dreams worth reporting lately?" Hodges asked.

Mike looked sideways as he chewed his food. "What kind of newspaper reporter question is that?"

"If you're hanging around Sam Miller, I figure you've been talking to him about dreams."

Mike wiped his mouth with a thin napkin. "Until I started representing him, I didn't realize how famous the old guy is around here."

"Who else mentioned him to you?"

"Can't say. It's an ongoing case."

Hodges shrugged. "You probably couldn't tell me much I haven't heard. He's been writing letters to the paper for years. Most of them land on my desk then transition to the round metal file I keep on the floor."

"What does he write about?"

"Nothing for the editorial page. Mostly about his dreams mixed in with Bible verses. For a man who cuts grass for a living, he has a very vivid imagination. I guess that's what happens when you walk behind a lawn mower for thirty years. If I could come up with some of the stuff he writes, I'd quit reporting the facts and start writing the world's greatest science fiction novel. In the meantime, I'm waiting on his prediction for the end of the world. Once that's in, I'm running a full story on him."

"Do you always throw away the letters?"

"All except one."

"Why?"

Hodges turned toward Mike. "Because he wrote it to me."

"Tell me."

Hodges dipped a french fry in ketchup. "Now you're the one in confidential territory. The only thing I'll say is, whether from looking in a crystal ball or reading his Bible, Sam Miller knew a few things about me that no one else knows. It got my attention."

"It wouldn't be hard to guess your sins," Mike said.

"It wasn't like that," Hodges answered seriously. "It was encouraging—in a religious sort of way. And ever since, I've always had a soft spot for him. I was sorry when he got into trouble."

"He's worried the report of his arrest in the paper is going to hurt his business."

"I buried the crime blotter for that issue at the bottom of the fourth page. As a felony, I couldn't keep it out; however, the negative publicity could have been worse. The publisher in Asheville got a call from Jack Hatcher asking us to write an investigative piece. I put him off and haven't heard anything since."

Mike stopped unwrapping his second burger and put it down.

"Jack Hatcher called the owner of the paper?"

"Yes, which I found strange. Hatcher should want to keep the situation quiet, not publicize it. The bank wasn't at fault, but no one likes to think their money is going to end up in the wrong account."

"How do you know the bank wasn't in the wrong?" Mike asked. "That was the first possibility I considered when I met with Sam."

"A bank error that made it all the way to a criminal prosecution? That's a stretch. Even a sloppy investigation would uncover that type of problem."

"You've got more faith in the criminal justice system than I do." Mike shrugged. "A few wrong keystrokes, and anyone could be a millionaire. The more I've talked with Sam, the less I think he would embezzle a hundred thousand dollars."

Hodges shrugged. "I've seen him around town but never met him. He could be a wife-beater who grows marijuana in an abandoned chicken house."

"I've been to his place and met his wife a couple of times. That's not happening. Do you know if he writes letters to anyone else?"

"No one has ever mentioned it to me, but I wouldn't be surprised."

Mike paused and decided to make a calculated gamble.

"Last year he wrote a letter to Jack Hatcher."

Hodges looked up. "Really? What did it say?"

"I haven't seen it, but I believe it was inflammatory and would like to find out more about it. It could definitely shed light on Hatcher's personal interest in the case." Mike took another bite of hamburger and chewed it thoughtfully. "Could you revisit the idea of an investigative article about Sam and see if you could uncover anything?"

"If a one-liner hurt Miller's business, what do you think an article is going to do? He'd starve or leave town."

"Liver mush," Mike responded simply.

"Sam Miller likes liver mush?"

"Probably eats it three times a week for breakfast, but that's not what I had in mind. Just because you research an article doesn't mean you have to print it."

Hodges grinned. "I see, but I couldn't spend a lot of time working on something that wasn't going to run."

"It might be a quick dead end, but then again—it might be the piece of journalism that wins you a Pulitzer prize."

MIKE FELT ENERGIZED DURING HIS DRIVE TO THE CHURCH. Appearing in court was stimulating, but the investigative part of the law, whether researching a legal issue or uncovering a factual matter, had always been his favorite part of the practice. He could happily sit for hours in front of a computer screen, analyzing a tricky point of the law and enjoyed tracking down and interviewing hard-to-locate witnesses in out-of-the-way places.

Most clients he'd represented in criminal matters had been so obviously guilty that a jury trial wasn't the prudent path to follow. In those cases, he usually worked out a plea bargain. The Danny Brewster burglary and Ridley moonshine cases were different. Because there was doubt in his own mind, the desire to find the truth about the charges against his clients motivated him to work harder. In the Ridley matter, the result was a stunning victory. Danny Brewster's story had a tragic conclusion. Mike wasn't sure where Sam Miller's future lay.

When he entered the administration wing of the church, Delores put down her magazine and stifled a yawn.

"You have a big stack of congratulatory phone messages on your desk."

"Congratulating me for what?"

"The baby, of course. Have you forgotten that you're going to be a father?"

"No, I'll get right on it."

Mike settled in behind his desk and began returning phone calls. The wholesale excitement about the baby was touching. Several wanted to talk at length, offering advice about everything from safely designed nursery room furniture to the wisdom of using a pacifier. It was almost five o'clock before he reached the bottom of the stack. He stood up, stretched, and stuck his head out the door.

"That's it," he told Delores. "I'm up to date."

"Not quite," she replied, holding up a thinner stack. "These came in while you were on the phone."

"Should I return them now or tomorrow?" Mike asked.

Delores flipped through the names. "I'll pull out the ones who will be upset if they don't hear from you today."

AN HOUR LATER, MIKE LEFT THE CHURCH. WHEN HE ARRIVED home, Peg was in the kitchen stirring a pot of soup. He came over to the stove and sniffed. She greeted him with a kiss. Judge, who lay in his bed in the corner, raised his head and gave a short woof.

"What did you have for lunch?" Peg asked.

"Brooks Brothers."

"I thought I tasted a hint of onion. Something light would be good for supper. Will you stir while I put together the salad?"

Mike took the spoon. Peg opened the refrigerator.

"What happened in court?" she asked.

Mike told her about his day. She listened without comment until he reached the part about his encounter in the hallway with Mr. Forrest.

"Maxwell Forrest squeezed all he could from you when you worked for him," Peg said matter-of-factly. "Now that you're no longer under his control, he'll treat you differently."

"I thought you loved it when I was part of the firm."

Peg placed two large salad bowls on the table. "I did. But you're in a different place now. If Mr. Forrest thinks you're going to hurt his business, he'll cause problems for you."

As they ate, Mike related the private courtroom conversation with Judge Coberg about Sam.

"I know what happened," Peg said, pouring more dressing on her salad. "Sam has told him things about court cases."

Mike put down his fork. The idea that the judge may have received information about a legal dispute from a totally independent source like Sam Miller was unnerving. Peg continued, "I don't know, of course, but it fits what we know about him. He could have had a dream or something."

"I tried to talk to Sam about it, but he wouldn't open up. He has notebooks filled with information about dreams and visions he's had. Some of them are symbolic and so vague it's impossible to figure out. I went behind his back to Muriel about the judge, but—Sam cut me off."

"I could ask her."

"When are you going to see her again?" Mike asked in surprise.

"I don't know, but it wouldn't hurt me to take on a new friend."

"I doubt Muriel Miller owns a tennis racket or a pair of running shoes."

"Are you telling me not to see her?"

"Of course not. It just seems odd."

"No more than you taking Sam's case."

"But—" Mike stopped. "Anyway, I ran into Braxton Hodges at Brooks and asked him to see what he can find out about some of the issues."

"His wife was at the country club this morning. She has a regular doubles game on Thursday."

"It's Thursday?" Mike asked.

"All day."

Mike let out a groan. "And I haven't started my sermon. The Miller case has thrown off my whole routine."

"That's not supposed to happen until after the baby is born."

"Well, I'm practicing. I wanted to relax tonight, but I'd better get to work after supper. I'm not even sure what I want to talk about."

"You'll think of something." Peg carried her empty soup and salad bowls to the sink. "That's the most I've eaten all day. My food choices are already changing. You know how much I love apples? I had to force myself to eat one for lunch."

"I've had an unusual food craving, too," Mike said. "It's probably a sympathetic reaction."

"What did you want to eat?"

"Liver mush. I talked about it with Braxton. If you really loved me, you'd fry a couple of patties to go with my grits in the morning."

Peg threw a wet dishrag at him. Mike caught it with his right hand.

"That's not a preference; it's a perversion. But it gives me an idea for your sermon. Preach about the clean and unclean animals."

Mike shook his head. "No way. That might split the church. We have too many barbecue lovers who would revolt if I condemned them for eating pork."

Ten

MIKE AWOKE EARLY ON SUNDAY MORNING AND SLIPPED OUT OF
bed. Peg was sound asleep and didn't stir. Putting on a pair of old shoes, he
took Judge into the backyard and walked across the wet grass. There was a
light fog in the air.

Mike enjoyed early mornings, especially Sunday. He spent time praying
while most members of his congregation were still in bed. The ritual helped
him feel like the shepherd of his flock, watching over them from a hillside as
he asked God to bless them.

He sat on a small cast-iron and wood bench near the edge of the hardwood
trees that bordered their lot. In a few weeks, the bench would be surrounded
by flowers. Judge left his side and explored the smells in the nearby woods.
Mike closed his eyes and ran through the main points of the sermon he'd written on Thursday night. The words had flowed rapidly through his fingers
onto the computer screen. He couldn't deny Sam Miller's subtle influence on
his thinking. Phrases the old man used stuck stubbornly in his mind until he
was forced to extract and examine them.

A robin flew to the ground near his feet and plunged its beak into the soil
to capture a wiggling worm. The truth, like the worm, didn't always come in
a pretty package, but that didn't make it any less vital for life.

"YOU LOOK NICE," MIKE SAID TO PEG AS THEY PULLED OUT OF
the driveway. "*Glowing* might even be a more accurate word. The blue in your
dress really sets off your eyes and hair."

"Thank you," she said. "I'd kiss your cheek, but that would mess up my lipstick and raise questions at church."

They saw few cars on the valley road until they neared the church.

"Are you ready for the onslaught of people?" Mike asked. "If the number of phone calls I received is any indication, this pregnancy is being viewed as a church-wide event."

"I'll smile sweetly and keep my mouth shut."

"I'm not trying to squelch you," Mike began, "It's just—"

Peg reached over and patted his hand. "Don't worry. I'll be good."

THEY PULLED INTO THE CHURCH PARKING LOT. SUNDAY SCHOOL attendance lagged behind the growth in the main worship service. Persuading the congregation to get out of bed and come early to church, even with the temptation of good coffee and fresh donuts, was a challenge.

"I'm going to Nathan Goode's class this morning," Peg announced when Mike turned off the car engine.

"Why? What do you have in common with teenagers?"

"Our child will be a teenager someday. If it's as bad as some people say, I'd better start early."

"Take notes. Oh, and I forgot to tell you. Nathan has an alto part he really wants you to sing."

"A solo?"

"I'm not sure. There's also going to be a flute solo by a high school student."

Mike saw Peg receive three congratulatory hugs before she crossed the parking lot. As an expectant mother, her acceptance by the church was bound to go up. Mike retreated to his office where, for the next forty-five minutes, he alternately reviewed his notes and paced back and forth across the room practicing his delivery. As time drew near to go to the sanctuary, he stopped and looked out a window that gave a partial view of the parking lot. He spotted several first-time visitors, the best sign of a healthy church and a radical departure from the norm prior to Mike's arrival at Little Creek. He slipped on his black robe and checked his appearance in the mirror.

Mike and the choir crowded into an anteroom adjacent to the front of the sanctuary for a brief prayer. Peg was lovely in a burgundy choir robe trimmed in gold. The same robe made Nathan Goode look like a fugitive from *Alice in*

Wonderland. For the minister and choir members, wearing robes was a non-negotiable tradition. They all entered the sanctuary to the stately sound of an organ prelude. Mike stepped into the pulpit area.

From the first time he sat in the high-backed chair behind the pulpit, it felt right. During the ensuing three years, he'd never tired of steering the service like the captain of a ship.

It was close to a full house, more than three hundred and fifty people. Mike scanned the crowd until his gaze fastened on an older couple sitting on the far left side of the sanctuary in the second pew from the front. The man turned his head from side to side then looked up at the ceiling for several seconds as if closely inspecting the rafters. Mike looked up, too, but saw nothing except wood. The woman beside the man stared straight ahead with a slight smile on her wrinkled face.

It was Sam and Muriel Miller.

After the opening prayer and a congregational hymn, the flutist played her song. Mike tried to interpret his client's expressions as the service progressed. The first time their eyes met, Sam smiled broadly. Mike nodded in greeting but remembered Muriel's comment that she and Sam moved from church to church "as the Lord" led them. It was one thing to spend time with Sam Miller at the jail or in the privacy of his living room. Having him in the Little Creek congregation where he might say something bizarre to one of the members of the church made Mike's stomach tighten in a knot.

The choir performed a baroque anthem that sounded familiar. Peg sang a brief solo. Her clear, mellow voice moved perfectly from note to note. Mike listened with pride.

Mike delivered a pastoral prayer that followed an outline familiar to the congregation. He requested divine help for the world, the nation, the state, Barlow County, the church, and anyone who had been sick enough during the week to require a night in the hospital. When he said "Amen" and opened his eyes, he saw that Sam still had his head bowed.

The announcements for the week were printed in the bulletin; however, Mike had learned not to trust the congregation's ability to take note of them and dutifully read the list. He reached the end and paused to allow silent consideration of the money contributed the previous Sunday. To read aloud the numbers would be in bad taste.

"The last announcement isn't in the bulletin," he said. "Peg and I are thrilled to announce that she is expecting our first child. She's been to the doctor and everything looks fine."

There was a splattering of applause. Mike looked at Peg, who was beaming. Out of the corner of his eye, he saw Sam Miller with his left hand raised in the air like a schoolchild wanting to attract the teacher's attention. Mike quickly looked away as the clapping died down. An impromptu speech by Sam definitely wasn't in the morning bulletin. "Thank you very much," Mike said. "You can't imagine how grateful Peg and I are for the love and support of this congregation."

During the offering, Mike avoided looking in Sam's direction. As the offering plates left the sanctuary, Mike stood up and stepped forward to the pulpit. He kept his notes folded in his Bible and slipped them out to preach. His mouth suddenly dry, he took a quick sip of water from a glass he kept on a shelf in the pulpit.

"Our scripture lesson this morning is a single verse from the words of Jesus in John 10:27. *My sheep listen to my voice; I know them, and they follow me.* Recently, these words have come to have a new meaning for me."

Mike paused and distinctly heard Sam say, "Yep."

Mike hurriedly continued, "We're God's sheep if we've submitted to Him as the shepherd of our souls, and personal communication with Jesus is the birthright of every Christian. This morning, I'm going to discuss ways to recognize the voice of God and how to respond to what He says.

"Some of you may wonder how God can carry on multiple conversations at once. We become easily confused in a four-way conference call; however, God can talk with everyone on earth at the same time. It's one of the great advantages of being omniscient and omnipresent. And the reason I'm in this pulpit is because I heard the voice of God calling me to leave my happy life as a lawyer and become a minister."

There were a few laughs from the congregation. Mike noticed that Bobby Lambert's expression didn't change.

"As many of you know, I like to go mountain biking," Mike said. "Often, my dog, Judge, goes with me. About six years ago, Judge and I took off one Saturday morning and went to the base of Jefferson's Ridge so I could ride the abandoned logging roads. I took a small backpack containing snacks for me, dog treats for Judge, and extra water bottles for both of us. I also had a copy of the New Testament. We left the car at Hank's Grocery and started up the road that begins behind the store. It switches back and forth as it climbs the ridge and is washed out in a lot of places. Judge is built for rugged terrain, but even with the bike in low gear, it's a strenuous workout for me. It took almost an hour to reach Stratton Bald, the highest point on the ridge. It's one of my favorite places in Barlow County because I can see all the way from Shelton to the Blue Ridge Mountains."

Mike, a faraway look in his eyes, could see the ridge in his mind's eye and hoped the congregation was joining him.

"I love mountain tops because they are places of perspective. The higher I go, the more connected I am to the vantage point of God. When Judge and I reached the highest point, we sat down to enjoy the sun and the light breeze that always blows across the crest of the ridge. I'd been thinking and praying about going into the ministry for over a year but couldn't decide what to do. I'd asked people for advice and received so many opinions that it would take a pack of index cards to keep them straight. Opening my New Testament, I started reading in Galatians. The first verse got my attention."

Mike turned the pages of his Bible. "*'Paul, an apostle—sent not from men nor by man, but by Jesus Christ.'* My heart began beating a little faster, not from the ride on the bike, but in anticipation that something important was about to happen. I read verses 15 through 17: *'But when God, who set me apart from birth and called me by his grace, was pleased to reveal his Son in me so that I might preach him among the Gentiles, I did not consult any man, nor did I go up to Jerusalem to see those who were apostles before I was, but I went immediately into Arabia and later returned to Damascus.'*"

Mike looked up at the congregation. "At that moment, those verses became the voice of Jesus to my life. I knew without a doubt that I should preach the gospel. I no longer needed the opinions of others, even people I respected. I knew what to do. I didn't go to Arabia, but to seminary in Virginia, and ended up at the Little Creek Church, not Damascus. However, the application of those verses to me as the guidance of the Lord couldn't have been clearer. The term 'called to preach' has been used so often that we accept stories like mine as orthodox Christianity. Ministers are expected to hear from God. It should be part of their spiritual résumé."

Mike stepped from behind the pulpit and made sure he had everyone's attention before he continued. He raised his voice.

"But what about you? Do you have the same right to receive guidance from the Lord as a person considering a career-altering switch into full-time ministry? Is there a distinction between God's children that gives access to some but not to others? Can all the followers of Jesus have the hope of hearing His voice? Was my experience on the mountain top six years ago a once-in-a-lifetime event? After that, did God become mute and abandon me to my own devices? I think not. As one of God's sheep, I want to continue to hear His voice, and I believe with all my heart that each of us has the same opportunity. Let me tell you why."

Mike launched into the main body of his sermon with enthusiasm. Time passed quickly as he gave the congregation examples of the ways in which God communicates, using several biblical stories to make his points. When he glanced at his watch, he realized that he'd run almost ten minutes over the normal time limit. He quickly jumped to his conclusion.

"Don't you think it would be worthwhile to calm down the frantic activity of our minds and listen? Perhaps we'll revisit this topic in a future sermon. Amen."

Mike gave Nathan the sign to sing a single verse of the final hymn. After announcing the benediction, Mike took his place at the main front door in the narthex and shook hands with the people as they left. He braced for negative comments about the length of the message but, except for a few references that he was really fired up that morning, none came. Milton Chesterfield wasn't present. Bobby Lambert approached.

"Mr. Forrest said he talked with you after the hearing," Bobby said.

"Yes."

"Good. He appreciates your altruistic motives toward the downtrodden but cares more about your reputation in the community. Listen to him."

Bobby moved past Mike and out the door before he could respond. The crowd thinned; Peg joined him.

"You were awesome this morning," she whispered in his ear. "Your sermon was a lot better than the one I suggested."

Mike shook the last person's hand, and they were left alone in the narthex. He realized he'd not seen Sam and Muriel Miller leave the sanctuary.

"Did you talk to the Millers?" he asked Peg.

"No, I came around the side of the church after leaving the choir room."

He stepped back into the sanctuary. Sam was still sitting in the pew with Muriel beside him.

"Come on," Mike said to Peg.

They walked down the aisle and approached the couple from the side.

"Good morning," Mike said.

"Yep, it is," Sam said.

"Is everything okay?" Mike asked.

"It will be."

"The service is over," Mike said.

Sam tilted his head to the side. "Not for me. I've been sitting here doing what you told us to do—calm down and listen to Papa. You were so right. The cares of the world have dulled my senses. I need to be more like the boy Samuel. When you read those verses about the Lord speaking to him at Shiloh, it made tears come to my eyes. None of his words fell to the ground, but so many of mine have ended up in the dust."

Mike reached over and put his hand on Sam's shoulder.

"Don't be too hard on yourself," he said. "It was your influence that inspired the sermon."

Sam smiled. "That's good, but it doesn't change what I need to do. Like you on the mountain top, I can't let man interfere with what Papa wants to do with me. You may have stopped preaching, but there are still words bouncing all around this room. If it's okay, I'd like to stay a while and listen."

Mike paused for a moment but heard nothing except the sound of his own breathing.

"Okay. Peg and I will wait for you at the door."

"How long do you think Sam will stay in there?" Peg asked as they walked back up the aisle.

"I don't have a clue. But I can't complain. He's the only person who took my message seriously enough to do something about it."

They waited in silence for several minutes in the narthex. Peg sat in a chair for a while, then stood and stretched.

"Ever since I found out about the pregnancy, I've enjoyed sitting quietly in the chair in our bedroom and reading my Bible. I'm trying to listen to God."

"I know. I thought about you and Sam when I was preparing the sermon."

Mike stepped toward the sanctuary to check on the Millers. When he reached the open door, an invisible presence suddenly rested on him. It was much stronger than the pleasant sensation he experienced beside the creek. He leaned his hand against the wall.

"Are you okay?" Peg asked.

Mike stepped back, and the weight lifted. He stepped forward. The invisible weight returned. He retreated, and it left. He repeated the sequence a few times with the same result.

"What in the world are you doing?" Peg asked. "It looks like a new dance step."

"I felt something when I crossed the threshold into the sanctuary," Mike responded. "It left when I stepped back."

Before Peg could ask another question, Sam and Muriel came from the sanctuary.

"Thanks for waiting," Sam said. "It's been a good day in church."

They went outside. Peg and Muriel walked ahead; Mike and Sam lagged behind. Mike mentioned what he'd felt.

"Papa is letting you know that He's in the house. The weight you felt is the glory. Look it up in your concordance. I had to search that one out myself."

"Did you feel it?" Mike asked.

"No, but it happens to me a lot."

"I wanted to go back into the sanctuary and stay there," Mike said.

Sam smiled. "Yep. What did King David say? 'Better is one day in the house of the Lord than a thousand in the tents of the wicked.'"

They reached Sam's red pickup at the far end of the parking lot.

"Are you still interested in giving the church a quote on cutting the grass?" Mike asked.

"Yep, but before I name a price, I'd like to cut it once and see how long it takes."

"Okay."

"Would you like to have lunch with us?" Peg asked.

"No, thanks," Sam replied. "I'm still chewing on what your husband said this morning. I think that's all I'll be eating for the rest of the day."

Muriel stepped forward and gave Peg a hug. "You look lovely."

"I've been doing what you suggested," Peg replied.

Muriel rewarded her with a wrinkled smile. "I can see it in your face. It's showing a lot quicker than the baby."

Sam and Muriel drove out of the parking lot. Mike took Peg's hand as they turned toward their car.

"What do you think about the Millers?" Mike asked.

Peg was silent for few steps. "They're simple, yet complicated. Harmless, but a little scary."

Eleven

MIKE WAS AT HIS DESK MID-MORNING ON MONDAY WHEN Delores brought in the mail.

"I hope you're not in trouble," she said. "You have a letter from Judge Coberg."

She'd placed the envelope from the superior court judge on top of the stack. Mike picked it up.

"No, it's something I expected."

Delores stood in front of his desk while Mike opened the envelope. He stopped and looked at her.

"Is there anything else?" he asked.

"Where do you want me to file the things you get from the court?"

"Uh, since we're not running a law firm here, I'll keep the correspondence and letters at home. I have to protect the attorney-client privilege with Sam Miller."

Delores sniffed as she turned to leave the room.

"Unless it's something that's part of the public record," Mike called after her.

Delores closed the door without further comment. Mike realized she'd been somewhat aloof all morning, but the reason for her coolness would have to wait. He turned his attention to the letter addressed to him and Ken West with a copy to Melissa Hall. Referencing the *State v. Miller* case, the judge briefly wrote:

> Counsel for the State and the defense are hereby notified that on several occasions the defendant, Sam Miller, has provided information to the Court about pending cases. Should the State or the defense desire to schedule a hearing regarding specific information, please notify me.

Mike put the letter in his briefcase. He picked up the phone, not to dial the judge's office, which would be an improper ex parte communication, but to contact the district attorney.

"Ken West, please," he said. "It's Mike Andrews."

Mike waited. In a few seconds the familiar, booming voice of the veteran prosecutor came on the line.

"Mike, why would the minister of the church beat up my newest assistant in court on Thursday?"

"You've mixed me up with Greg Freeman. Have you read your mail this morning?"

"No, I'm still working on last Thursday."

"Pull out a thin envelope that came today from Judge Coberg and open it."

Ken West weighed almost three hundred pounds, and Mike could hear the prosecutor's chair squeak in protest as he swiveled it.

"That's not it," the veteran prosecutor muttered. "Okay, here it is. I assume you mean the one regarding the Miller case."

"It's the only case I have."

"Humph," West grunted after a minute. "What is this supposed to mean?"

"That's why I called you. I wanted to find out your position."

"I don't know enough to have one. You're not going to waive your client's right to a jury trial and let the judge decide the case, are you?"

"No."

"Then the jury will determine the facts, assuming we don't work out a plea bargain."

"Correct. Do you want to meet with the judge?"

"Probably, but let me talk with Ms. Hall so she can be involved in the decision. I'm not going to jerk this case away from her. It will be good experience for her to respond to the different strategies you'll use in an effort to manipulate her."

Mike ignored the dig. "Did your office perform any independent investigation of the factual basis for the charges against Miller? Ms. Hall wouldn't let me manipulate that information out of her."

"Good for her. I've been knee-deep in the Anson murder case and trying to rework our budget proposal for the next fiscal year. I don't recall much about this file except that it involved a church and met the $100,000 felony threshold."

"Could you take a look at it and get back to me? The judge is going to expect a response from us."

"I have a case review meeting with my assistants later this week. I'll put it on the agenda and get back with you."

SEVERAL VISITORS HAD ATTENDED THE CHURCH ON SUNDAY. Part of Mike's Monday morning routine was to work through the visitor cards and thank the people for coming. Sometimes routine calls uncovered immediate needs in the lives of people desperate for someone to talk to. Today, one woman spoke with him for thirty minutes about her teenage daughter. Mike promised to ask Nathan to make a special effort to reach out to the young woman. When he crossed off the last name, Mike stood up, stretched, and went to Delores's desk.

"I had quite a few calls to visitors this morning," he said.

"I've been getting a lot of calls, too," Delores replied.

"What kind of calls?"

"About your sermon on Sunday."

"I know I went longer than usual, but I didn't get any negative feedback from folks as they left the church."

"Well, my phone rang quite a bit Sunday afternoon."

"Who called?"

"Different people."

Mike didn't pressure Delores for names. Eventually, she always revealed her sources of information.

"What was the complaint?" he asked.

"That you didn't sound like yourself, and the stories you told were weird."

"Anything else?"

"One person was upset when she found out that Mr. and Mrs. Miller were in the sanctuary."

"Why do you think it's called a sanctuary?" Mike asked testily.

"Don't get mad at me. If you don't want to know—"

"Was it a member of the session?"

Delores didn't respond, but Mike easily interpreted her expression as a yes.

"Well, Libby Gorman made her wishes known at the meeting," he said. "And Sam Miller had a business reason to be here. I asked him to look at our property and submit a bid to cut the grass. Our current service does a sloppy job, especially in the cemetery."

"But they don't have any criminals working for them."

Mike stared at her for a moment, decided not to remind her of the presumption of innocence until proven guilty, and returned to his office. He didn't come out until Delores left for lunch.

After she had gone, Mike fielded a phone call from a church member wanting to know the charge for a nonmember to rent the old sanctuary for a wedding. A few minutes later, the phone rang again.

"Little Creek Church," Mike said.

"I didn't know the pope answered his own phone," Braxton Hodges responded.

"I don't think I'm qualified for the job."

"You don't seem afraid to multitask," the newspaperman replied. "Preacher on Sunday, lawyer for the people on Monday. Do you have a few minutes to talk?"

"Sure. The answering machine will pick up the calls."

"I'm working on an article about your client, Sam Miller."

"Good. What have you found out?"

"That when I left a message for Jack Hatcher this morning, he didn't immediately return my call."

"He's a busy bank president. Even if he wants you to write an article, he's not going to drop everything to talk to a reporter."

"But Maxwell Forrest did. He phoned me ten minutes after I told Hatcher's assistant that I wanted to ask a few questions about the Miller embezzlement case."

"That makes sense. After all, it is a legal matter. What did Mr. Forrest say?"

"Nothing worth printing. He rolled out a nebulous comment or two that the pertinent information had been turned over to the proper authorities. I could tell he was processing me toward a quick end to the conversation until I asked him if there had been any correspondence between Miller and Jack Hatcher."

"What did he say?"

"Do you want to listen?"

"You recorded the conversation?"

"Yes."

"Did you tell him?"

"Do I have to?"

"No, so long as you're a party to the conversation."

"I already knew that, so don't send me a bill for your opinion."

"Are you recording this conversation?"

"Not unless you change your mind about running for pope."

"No chance. Turn on the tape of Mr. Forrest."

"Actually, it's digital, which makes it a lot clearer. I'll start at the beginning."

Mike pressed the receiver close to his ear, but it wasn't necessary. The voices were clear. He could easily recognize Hodges's nasal tone and Forrest's carefully modulated Southern drawl. In every conversation, Maxwell Forrest chose his words with skill.

"I think you're doing the community a service," Forrest said. "Many people don't follow the results of the criminal docket, and an article might deter someone thinking about mismanaging church money in the future."

"Let's hope so," Hodges replied. "One other thing. Did Mr. Hatcher receive any correspondence from Miller prior to the filing of the embezzlement charge?"

"I'd have to check with Mr. Hatcher about that."

"Could you do that and let me know?"

"Mr. Hatcher gets a lot of correspondence."

"People who get a letter from Sam Miller usually remember it."

There was a long silence on the phone.

"Mr. Forrest? Are you still there?"

"Yes. Any newspaper article should focus on the circumstances surrounding the criminal charges, not the bank."

"Which it will. But are you aware that Mr. Miller writes letters to people he doesn't know? I received a note from him myself a few years ago and still keep it in my desk."

"Are you going to include your note in this article?"

"No."

"Have you met Mr. Miller?" Forrest asked.

"No."

"Does Mr. Miller contend that he wrote a letter to Mr. Hatcher?"

"You're asking a lot of questions, Mr. Forrest. Could we go back a few steps? Would you check with Mr. Hatcher and find out if he received a letter from Sam Miller?"

"I'll run it by him, but I still don't see what it has to do with your article."

"Embezzling money from a local church is a serious charge. That alone is newsworthy. When combined with Miller's odd personality, I think I have a story a lot of people will be interested in reading. When should I expect to hear from you?"

"In due time. I'm late for an appointment. Good-bye."

Mike heard a click.

"You know Maxwell Forrest," Hodges said. "What did you think?"

"He'll vigorously protect the bank's reputation. It's the firm's biggest client."

"Do you think a letter exists?"

"If it hasn't ended up in the landfill with the ones Sam sent the newspaper."

"Did Forrest know more than he told me?"

"Maybe, but he'd be naturally cautious. When faced with an unexpected problem, he slows down and reconnoiters before moving forward."

"I'm not going to write an article, but from what I've seen from Sam Miller over the years, trying to interpret one of his weird, Bible-verse-filled letters wouldn't qualify as serious journalism."

"It depends on what it says. Let me know if Mr. Forrest gets back in touch with you."

"I'll record every word."

MIKE SPENT PART OF THE AFTERNOON TYPING STANDARD MOTIONS to file in the Miller case: a request for a list of potential witnesses, a copy of the statement given by Sam to interrogating officers, and the disclosure of any exculpatory evidence that might assist in establishing Sam's innocence. Mike felt especially uneasy about the signed statement taken by Detective Perkins. Few items of evidence were more damaging to a defendant than a written confession the prosecutor could wave in front of a jury during closing arguments. Mike hoped Sam's persistent obfuscation of reality flowed over into the statement.

There was a knock on the door. Nathan Goode entered.

"Good job on the anthem," Mike said. "And thanks for cutting the final hymn short. I ran way over."

"I check my watch as you come in for landing."

"What about the youth group last night? Nobody called complaining, so I assume there weren't any problems."

"Not a hitch. The Gaston boy showed up with his buddy who plays guitar. The kids liked it. I enjoyed it, too."

"What are you planning for this week's Sunday morning service?"

Nathan outlined his idea. "The anthem has a soprano solo. I thought I'd invite a guest soloist."

"A high school student would be fine. The girl on the flute did a beautiful job."

"I've been spending time with someone recently who could be for the soprano section what Peg is to the altos."

"What does *spending time* mean? Are you giving her voice lessons?"

"She's way beyond me. She was a voice major in college then decided to go to law school."

"Who is it?" Mike asked, sitting up straighter in his chair.

"Melissa Hall. She works for the district attorney's office. She grew up way back in the mountains just over the line in Tennessee. You'd never guess her interest in classical music by talking to her, but she can sight-read like a pro and hit the high notes without a problem."

Mike visualized the young prosecutor with a microphone in her hand serenading a crowd. It was a radically different venue from the Barlow County Courthouse.

"Where did you meet her?"

"At the Shelton community theater tryouts. We're going to perform *Oklahoma!* at the end of the summer. Nobody could touch Melissa's voice for the female lead."

"Hmm," Mike responded. "Does she know I'm the pastor of the church?"

"No."

"You should let her know. She's prosecuting a man I'm representing pro bono in a criminal case, and she might feel uncomfortable at the church."

"If she's willing to sing, do you have a problem with her coming?"

"Me? Of course not. The church is open to everyone."

PEG, DRESSED IN HER RUNNING GEAR, ENTERED THE GARAGE with Judge on a retractable leash as Mike pulled into the driveway.

"Are you going to keep running?" he asked when he stopped the car and got out.

Peg brushed a few stray strands of blond hair from her eyes. "Until the day before delivery. Judge and I both need regular exercise, and I can't imagine taking a total break from running for nine months."

"Did you ask the doctor about it?"

"Yes, she told me it would be fine for the first two trimesters so long as I felt okay. After that, we'll have to discuss it, but Jodie Wheeler ran five miles less than a week before her daughter was born."

"Jodie Wheeler ran the Boston Marathon a few years ago. Be careful."

Peg kissed him on the cheek and patted her abdomen. "Our baby is going to be in shape from day one."

They entered the house. The mail was jumbled on the counter in the kitchen.

"There's a small roast with potatoes and carrots in the Crock-Pot," she said.

Mike stood at the counter and began sorting. The bill pile was disturbingly high. Peg picked up the lid. Judge, who was standing beside her, barked.

"Yes, it smells good," she said to the dog.

Mike reached the bottom of the stack. The last item was an envelope from Forrest, Lambert, Park, and Arnold.

"Something from the old firm," Mike said.

Peg glanced at him. "I saw, but since it was addressed to you, I didn't open it."

Mike tore off the end of the envelope. Inside was a letter from Maxwell Forrest. Mike read it, furrowed his brow, and then examined it more slowly. Peg came over to him.

"What is it?" she asked.

"Mr. Forrest is ordering me not to come to the office or discuss the Miller case with anyone at the firm. I talked with Juanita last week, and she must have mentioned it to him."

"Can he do that?"

"Partly. I don't have the right to go beyond the reception area. That would be trespassing. But a private gag order as to firm personnel is way out of bounds. I wouldn't expect anyone to violate the attorney-client relationship with the bank, but my duty to Sam involves investigating the facts, no matter who has the information."

Twelve

MIKE'S PREOCCUPATION WITH THE MILLER CASE DIDN'T KEEP him from eating the fork-tender roast. While they ate, Judge lay underneath the table, occasionally giving a slight groan that communicated his deep desire to lick a plate or gulp down a less-than-perfect piece of meat. Mike responded to Peg's attempts at conversation with grunts that were first cousins to Judge's groans.

"Are you enjoying your food or just filling up your stomach?" Peg asked as Mike speared the last carrot on his plate.

"Oh, it's great. The meat almost melted in my mouth. And the carrots are just right."

"Still thinking about the letter?"

"Yes."

"Have you figured out what's going on?"

"No, but my focus for the case has been off. I've been thinking about the end, not the beginning. I need to interview the leaders of the church where Sam was preaching. It's their money that was allegedly embezzled."

"What's the name of the church?"

"Craig Valley something. I'll call Sam and find out who to talk to."

Mike took their plates to the sink. Judge followed him and looked up with such longing that Mike put one of the plates on the floor so he could lick it.

"When are you going to talk to him?" Peg asked.

"Tonight. He works during the day."

"Before or after you eat a bowl of the apple cobbler I bought from the little lady who sells them from the back of her car at light number nine?"

"Do we have ice cream?"

"Of course. But you shouldn't have more than one scoop. If you keep eating like you did tonight, you're going to get big around the middle faster than I am."

Mike's stomach had always been solid from daily sit-ups. He touched his shirt and felt a slight pudginess.

"Skipping a meal then gorging isn't the best," he admitted. "But tomorrow would be a better day to begin cutting back than tonight."

After dessert, Mike helped clean the kitchen. Peg went upstairs, and Mike phoned Sam Miller. "Do you have time to talk business?" he asked.

"Did you buy a notebook yet to put beside your bed?" Sam responded. "You're going to need it."

"No."

"Don't put it off."

"If I promise to get one, will you agree to answer a few questions without getting off track?"

"Go ahead."

Mike told Sam about the conversation between Braxton Hodges and Mr. Forrest.

"If it still exists, getting a copy of the letter you sent Jack Hatcher is going to be difficult," Mike concluded.

"Why do you need a copy?"

"Your testimony about the letter wouldn't prove that it existed or was delivered to Jack Hatcher. He could deny any written communication from you, and there wouldn't be anything I could do about it. Without verification, your story about hatchets, baseball bats, and glass beads would sound ridiculous. And there may be something in the letter you've forgotten. You've had lots of dreams and visions since that night."

"True," Sam agreed. "Can't you file one of those subpoena things?"

"Yes. There is a procedure to request documents held by a third party in criminal cases. I'll do that at the proper time and see what turns up. But first I need to interview some folks from the Craig Valley church. What's it called?"

"Craig Valley Gospel Tabernacle."

"Have you had any contact with them since the charges were filed?"

"Nope. The young detective who met with me at the jail told me not to talk to anyone from the church. He said it would look like I was trying to harass them, and they might charge me with something else."

Mike felt a spurt of anger at the detective's intimidation tactic. He would like to teach Perkins a lesson, but nothing allowed by the law or his faith immediately came to mind.

"That's not true. You'd have to actually threaten someone to cross the line. Do you think any of the church leaders would talk to me about the case?"

"Yep."

"Who would be the one most likely to cooperate?"

"Larry Fletchall is the head deacon. His daddy was a preacher and a friend of mine."

"Do you have his phone number?"

"Yep, but I think it would be best to meet with the other deacons, too."

"How many are there?"

"Four."

"That's a manageable group. Set it up for any evening this week except Wednesday. I have a memorial service for Danny Brewster, the former client I told you about who died in prison. The service is in the afternoon but might run late."

"I know some Brewsters who live on the west side, but I don't recall Danny."

"Same family. Call me after you contact the folks at Craig Valley."

"Okay. And I'll come to your church before the end of the week to cut the grass so everything will look nice on Sunday. I could really use the business. Several folks have called and canceled on me. This should be one of my busiest times of the year, but I didn't have anything to do this afternoon except work on my equipment."

"Are people giving you a reason?"

"Nope, but you know there's been talk. People are nervous about having someone who's been in trouble with the law on their property."

AFTER MIKE HUNG UP THE PHONE, HE TURNED ON A BASEBALL game, but his thoughts returned to Danny Brewster. Mike's memories of most clients he'd represented had faded, replaced by people who needed his help in the present. But his memories of Danny endured. Mike could still recall details of his investigation, conversations with Danny, questions to the witnesses at the trial, even a few lines from his closing argument to the jury. Anger without an outlet rose up in him. He could try to convince Braxton Hodges to write an article for the paper about Danny, but he doubted the prison death of a young man convicted of multiple counts of burglary would warrant public interest.

Mike continued to stew until another vivid memory of Danny, an antidote for anger, rose to the surface and forced him to smile. While in the local jail, Danny made a large cross from toothpicks in a craft class, painted it with bright colors, and gave it to him. Mike still had the cross in his desk drawer at the church. The colors had faded, but the love behind the gift remained.

Judge pattered into the room and sat beside the chair with his head on the armrest so Mike could rub the area of wrinkled skin on the dog's forehead. Mike put his hand on the dog's head and started scratching. A few minutes later, Peg, wearing her pajamas and a painting in her hand, joined them.

"Remember this?" she said, turning the painting so he could see it. "Don't you think she looks like Muriel?"

It was an oil painting of an older woman wearing the type of plain dress worn by Muriel Miller and standing in a field of wildflowers. The area where the woman stood was filled with light, but she teetered at the edge of total darkness that covered a third of the painting. Peg portrayed the woman in profile with hair the same length and color as Sam's wife's.

"It could be her."

"But in your dream she doesn't stay in the sunlight."

"No." Mike involuntarily shuddered.

Several times since he'd married Peg, Mike had watched the old woman leave the light and walk into the darkness until it enveloped her. Each time he witnessed the sequence of events, he tried to force the woman back to shore by the strength of his will but without success. When she failed to reappear, he always woke to a deep sense of sadness and regret, as if the loss was as great for him as for her.

The phone rang. It was Sam. Mike shook his head to clear the troubling images prompted by the painting and dream.

"Thursday night at seven o'clock at the church," Sam said. "All the deacons will be there. Come by my house about six-thirty, and we'll ride together."

"I'll be there."

"What's going on?" Peg asked when Mike hung up.

"I want to interview the leaders of the church where Sam was preaching and find out what they know about the embezzlement charge. I'll need to leave here about six o'clock on Thursday so I can pick up Sam."

Peg yawned. "Anything else going on that you can tell me about?"

Mike pointed at the television. "Unless Cincinnati gets more than four innings a game from their starting pitchers, it's going to be a long season along the Ohio River."

Peg was asleep before the Reds came to bat in the seventh. Judge lay on the floor in front of the couch. Judge liked Mike, but he loved Peg. The dog had spent many miles in tandem with her as they jogged Peg's favorite routes.

Peg's nose twitched. Mike enjoyed watching her sleep. He reached over and turned the painting so he couldn't see it. Watching Peg was much more pleasant. At rest, she reminded him of a picture on the wall of her old bedroom at her parents' home. In the photo, Peg, a little blond-haired girl wearing pajamas, lay with her head on a pillow while holding a stuffed rabbit wrapped tightly in her arms. Mike muted the volume on the TV for the remainder of the game. After the last out, he picked Peg up in his arms. She awoke but pretended to remain asleep as she rested her head against his shoulder.

Carrying Peg to bed had been one of Mike's favorite rituals during the first year of their marriage. The top sheet and comforter had already been pulled down. Mike smiled, kissed the top of her head, and covered her up.

"DID YOU FLOAT UP TO BED LAST NIGHT?" HE ASKED WHEN PEG came into the kitchen in the morning.

"No, I dreamed Prince Charming picked me up in a golden carriage drawn by rust-colored horses and took me to his castle on a hill above the town."

Mike smiled. "At least the hill-above-town part is real."

Peg ground some coffee beans and brewed a pot while Mike released Judge to run around in the backyard. Mike returned to the smell of dark liquid in the pot. He poured a cup and took a sip. Peg knew how to unlock the secret of the coffee bean.

"This is the best," he said.

Peg sat across from him.

"Aren't you going to have a cup?" he asked.

"I'm cutting back on caffeine."

Mike studied her face as he raised the cup to his lips.

"You're a beautiful woman," he said.

Peg gave him a puzzled look. "Without makeup or doing more than running a brush twice through my hair?"

"Yes."

MIKE PARKED IN THE GRAVEL DRIVEWAY OF THE BREWSTER HOUSE and walked across the yard that was more weeds than grass. Rose Brewster came onto the front porch that was flanked by two cracked and discolored concrete fountains with no water in them. She'd aged more than the years since he'd seen her. She was in her late fifties but looked closer to seventy.

"Come on in," she beckoned. "Everyone should be here in a little while."

Mike shook her hand, weathered from contact with chemicals at the metal processing plant where she worked. She opened the screen door, and they stepped into a living room filled with about twenty folding metal chairs.

"We moved out all the furniture and borrowed chairs from the church my sister attends. They have to be back for Wednesday night family supper."

"This will be fine. Who's coming?"

Mike braced himself for her answer. All day long, he'd been trying to get ready to face Danny's older brother Quentin, the one who duped Danny into breaking into the houses.

"I'm not exactly sure. Some folks are working. Others are sick. My mother and her sisters are riding over together from Boomer."

"What about Quentin?"

Rose shook her head. "Didn't you know? He's got the HIV and moved to Asheville so he could get free treatment. He don't come around too much."

Mike winced. "I'm sorry, Rose. You've had more dumped on you than a human being could be expected to stand."

"Sometimes I feel like that man in the Bible who had so much trouble."

"Job."

"Yeah. And I'm still a-waiting for things to get better. Do you want to see the letters you sent Danny? I put them in a box so you could take them with you."

Mike followed Rose into the kitchen. Dishes of food wrapped in aluminum foil rested on the table.

"The neighbors have chipped in nice," she said, pointing at the table. "A few of them are going to come."

"That's good."

"Danny was my baby," Rose said as she opened the drawer of a small plastic filing cabinet. "And he thought the world of you."

She handed Mike a cardboard shoe box. He lifted the lid. A stack of letters was bound together by a thick rubber band. The box also contained copies of pleadings Mike had filed in Danny's case along with the brief to the Court of Appeals and the Court's decision denying a new trial.

"As far as I know, he saved everything you ever sent him, even the legal stuff that he couldn't read or understand."

There was a loud knock at the front door.

"I'd better get that," Rose said. "Make yourself at home."

Mike flipped through the papers, not sure what to do with them. With the box under his arm, he walked down the short hall to the living room. Passing a bedroom, he saw Danny's picture in a frame beside Rose's bed. It was a high school photo featuring Danny's unique grin. The service was scheduled to start at 4:00 p.m., but people straggled in for another twenty minutes. Mike waited.

At 4:30 p.m., Rose looked at him and announced, "I guess that's about it."

Mike stood before the group. Even with the front door open it was stuffy in the little house. He left the notes he'd prepared in the pocket of his jacket beside the toothpick cross.

"One of the things we like to do at memorial services is remember the person who has passed on. I remember Danny as a young man with a big smile, simple faith, and generous spirit. When he found out I was a Christian he always wanted to pray after we had a meeting about his case. No one I represented left a deeper impression on me than Danny. In fact, knowing him influenced me to go into the ministry so I could focus on people's spiritual, not just legal, needs."

Mike took out the cross and showed it to the group then handed it to Rose.

"It was a privilege serving as Danny's lawyer, and losing his case was the worst experience of my career. I'll never forget the moment of the verdict." Mike paused and let a wave of emotion pass. "After the jury foreman spoke, Danny turned to me and asked me what had happened. When I told him the bad news, he patted me on the back and told me it would be okay."

Mike lowered his head for a moment before continuing with more intensity. "But it wasn't okay. Our court system failed, I failed, and the prison system failed. And now Danny is gone. There's a part of me that wants to scream at the injustice of it all. But Danny never cursed the darkness that exists in this world. His answer was to let his light shine."

Mike looked at Rose. "Do you remember how much he liked the little song many of us learned as kids about letting our light shine all over the neighborhood?"

Rose nodded. "He loved that song."

"That song has kept me from anger and despair over Danny's death. His light never went out, and I guarantee you, at this moment, it's blazing like a bonfire. Danny won't be coming home to us, but as King David said after one of his sons died, *'I will go to him, but he will not return to me.'* If we're one of God's children, we'll one day join him in a place where no evil dwells. Grieve. It's healthy. But also remember the goodness that came through knowing a wonderful young man."

Mike scanned the faces of the mourners. "Now it's your turn. Like Danny, we're not in a hurry. Let's hear from you. It's time for you to remember."

Mike sat down. There was a long, awkward silence, and Mike wondered if anyone would speak. Then, one of Danny's aunts stood up.

"I got a story," she said. "When Danny was about twelve years old, he and his mama came over to our house to eat one Friday night. I'd worked all day and was beat, but I knew how much Danny liked potatoes fried in a skillet with onions, so I was in the kitchen peeling potatoes. He came in to see me, stood right beside me at the sink, and watched for the longest time without saying a word. Finally, he spoke up. 'Aunt Betty, you make the best potatoes in the world. I love to put ketchup on them and eat a whole plate. When I eat one of your potatoes, it makes me feel good all over my insides, not just in my stomach.'"

Betty looked at Rose. "You raised that boy right, and don't you ever believe anything else."

Several others spoke. One story made Mike laugh; another brought him to the edge of tears.

Finally, Rose wiped her eyes with a tissue and spoke.

"Thank you for coming." She turned to Mike. "I appreciate you telling me to do this. I hadn't seen Danny for several months before he got killed, and listening to y'all makes him seem more alive to me."

Later, Mike and Rose were standing beside each other in the kitchen.

"You know," Rose said, "Danny didn't believe me at first when I told him you was going to school to be a preacher. He said Mr. Andrews didn't have to go to school to be a good preacher. He already was one."

"And I want to be a better one."

"You did a good job today."

"It's not hard when it's about someone like Danny."

Mike lingered until everyone except Rose's sisters had left. He gave Rose a hug, took the shoe box from her, and put it in the passenger seat of the car.

"Can I give you the cross?" he asked.

"No, but thanks for showing it to me. He meant it for you."

Rose put the cross in the top of the box.

WHEN MIKE ARRIVED HOME PEG MET HIM IN THE KITCHEN.

"How was it?" she asked.

"I hope Rose felt loved and comforted. For me, it was like stepping back in time."

"What did you find when you went back?"

Mike set the shoe box on the kitchen counter. "This."

While Peg leafed through the letters and legal paperwork, Mike spoke.

"As a lawyer I met people from all across Barlow County. That doesn't happen anymore. Our church congregation is a lot more homogeneous than I'd realized."

"Do you miss it?"

"A little," Mike admitted, "but not enough to go back." He smiled slightly. "Maybe that's the reason I'm representing Sam Miller. He should be different enough to satisfy my itch for the peculiar for a long time."

THAT NIGHT MIKE DIDN'T KNOW WHAT TIME IT WAS WHEN HE awoke. He glanced at the clock. The numbers were blurred, and he blinked his eyes several times. It was 3:18 a.m. There was no notebook or PDA on the nightstand, but the dream was so vivid that he could easily remember it until morning. He yawned and closed his eyes before waking up again. It was 3:38 a.m. Trying to make it through the rest of the night in twenty-minute intervals wasn't going to work. Mike rolled out of bed and walked barefoot downstairs. Judge rose from his bed in the kitchen and greeted him with a loud woof.

"Quiet!" Mike said. "Don't you know what time it is?"

Mike opened the back door so Judge could go outside then retrieved his PDA from its place in the kitchen beneath where he hung his car keys. Returning to his chair in the living room, Mike opened a blank screen and entered the date. Judge scratched at the door, and Mike let him in. The dog always received a treat when he went out in the morning.

"Remember this in a few hours," Mike said as he deposited a large dog biscuit between Judge's teeth. "If I only get one scoop of ice cream, you only get one dog biscuit."

Finally settling down in the chair, Mike started to record what he'd heard and seen, but the sequence of events and words spoken in the dream was hazy. It had been as vivid as the dream about Danny, but he couldn't recall it as clearly. He could remember talking to a group of men. He didn't recognize any of them, but knew they were affiliated with the Craig Valley Gospel Tabernacle. Sam Miller was also present.

"What was it?" Mike muttered.

It had something to do with finding out information about Sam's case. Everyone was sitting in a dimly lit room. The atmosphere was very tense and no one spoke. Then something happened that changed everything, and the light in the room increased. However, in the midst of waking up, dozing a few minutes, going downstairs, and taking care of Judge, the details of the dream now escaped him. Mike furrowed his brow until it wrinkled like Judge's forehead, but all he could muster was a general sense of the scene. Closing the PDA, he returned to bed.

And slept the rest of the night.

Thirteen

"I HAD A DREAM," HE TOLD PEG IN THE MORNING. "BUT I LOST the details before I could write it down."

"What do you remember?"

Mike told her what he could recall. Peg poured him a cup of coffee.

"Maybe it will come back to you later in the day," she said.

"If anything can help, it's this coffee," Mike replied, taking a sip. "It should wake up my lazy brain cells."

SEVERAL TIMES DURING THE DAY, MIKE TRIED TO REMEMBER additional details of his dream, but nothing came. He arrived home to a message from Peg that she'd gone shopping with a friend and wouldn't be back before he left for his meeting at the Craig Valley church. Mike fixed a salad before leaving to pick up Sam. He put on a coat and silk tie so he would look like a lawyer.

The sun was barely above the tree line when Mike turned onto the driveway to the Miller house. Sam stepped onto the front stoop and waved as he approached.

"Did Papa send you a letter last night?" the old man asked as soon as he sat down in the passenger seat of the car.

Mike had heard so many of Sam's off-the-wall comments that he responded without thinking the old man was crazy.

"Is that what you saw?" Mike asked.

"Yep. It had your name on it in big print."

"Did you open it?"

"Nope. It wasn't addressed to me, but the return address was *Craig Valley Gospel Tabernacle.*"

Mike told about his dream in the night as he drove down McAfee Road.

"It was so vivid, I didn't think there was a chance I would forget any part of it."

"You're like a little baby that has to be told the same thing over and over before it understands. Papa is teaching you a lesson. You should have listened to me about the notebook. As you get more mature, you'll get better at remembering. Then the hard part is interpreting what Papa shows you."

"I'll use my PDA."

"What's that?" Sam asked.

Mike took the device from his pocket and showed it to Sam.

"Oh, yeah, but that thing is no good if your batteries are dead. My notebooks don't need batteries."

"I keep it charged. If I start having dreams with meanings, they are going to be high-tech."

Mike told Sam about Danny Brewster's memorial service.

"That's good," Sam said when he finished. "It makes me look forward to meeting Danny myself." Sam paused. "And it makes me feel better about you being my lawyer."

"Why? I lost Danny's case, and he went to prison where he was murdered."

"Yep, but there's no condemnation from Papa. That's the important thing."

They rode in silence for several miles.

"What kind of reception are we going to get from the deacons?" Mike asked.

"Larry is one of my sons, so everything should be fine. He was in a hurry when I called him, and we didn't have a long conversation."

"I didn't know members of your family attended the church."

"Yep. Including you, I have ten sons," Sam answered. "Papa has bunches of sons, and sometimes He lets me help raise them."

"Spiritual sons."

"Yep, isn't that the most important part of being an earthly papa?"

They made several turns. The Craig Valley area contained several clusters of houses.

"Is the church near the Rea home place?" Mike asked, referring to the oldest house in Barlow County.

"Yep. Less than a mile past it on a side road."

They passed the Rea home, a weathered log cabin built in 1758. A marker along the road gave a brief history of the site where Scottish immigrants first settled in the county.

"Turn at the next right," Sam said.

It was a paved road. The church, a small, rectangular, concrete-block building painted lime green, was a short distance on the left. A wooden sign with black letters on a white background proclaimed the name of the church. Underneath the name was a place to identify the pastor. It was painted over with new white paint. Two pickup trucks and an older-model car were parked out front. To the side of the building, a large flat place had been cleared and trenches for concrete footings had been dug. Wooden stakes with strings surrounded the work area.

"That's where they're going to build," Sam said.

Mike parked beside one of the pickup trucks. They went to the front door of the church, a double brown door that looked too flimsy to withstand a hard kick.

"You take the lead and introduce me," Mike said.

Sam pushed open the door. The inside of the church was as plain as the outside. Rows of wooden pews rested on a floor covered with thin, cheap carpet. A raised platform with two steps leading to it contained a single chair and a wooden pulpit. There was a piano to the left of the platform, but no area for a choir.

"They use one of the adult Sunday school rooms for deacon meetings," Sam said. "It's behind the sanctuary."

They walked down the aisle, through a door to the right of the platform, and entered a short hall. No one was in sight. Sam opened a door. Mike followed. Inside, he saw four African-American men on their knees around a table. They stopped praying and stood. The tallest of the men stepped forward and extended his hand to Mike.

"I'm Larry Fletchall," he said.

After he shook Mike's hand, Larry turned to Sam.

"We got here early so we could pray for you."

Mike couldn't help staring. The room was similar to the one in his dream, but the men he saw in the night were white, not black.

"Are you okay?" Sam asked him.

"Huh? Yeah."

Sam spoke to the other men. "Jesse Lavare, Bob Gordon, John Franklin. Good to see you again."

"Don't, Sam," Larry said. "We've been trying to pray through on this situation for over an hour. We agreed to meet with you and your lawyer, but you betrayed our trust. We can't pretend nothing happened."

"But I didn't do anything," Sam started, then stopped. "I'd better let Mike speak for me."

The men rose from their knees, their faces serious. They were working-class men dressed in clean pants and open-collared shirts.

"Could we all sit down?" Mike asked.

They sat around the table. As in Mike's dream, the lights in the room were dim. One of the bulbs in the overhead fixture must have burned out.

"Thank you for agreeing to meet with me," Mike began. "Part of my job is to find out what happened."

He put a legal pad on the table.

"No notes," the oldest of the men said. "We don't want you trying to twist our words if this thing goes to court."

Mike placed his pen on the pad. "All right. I won't write down anything unless you give me permission; however, it might be helpful to record a name or phone number if that comes up."

Larry nodded. "We'll see."

Mike continued. "First, I'm a minister who used to be a lawyer. I don't want to do anything that would embarrass you or hurt your church. My job is simply to investigate the charges against Sam. To do that, I need to ask you some questions. I'm not going to try to trick you, and if you don't want to answer, that's fine."

Mike gave a reassuring smile, but no one reciprocated. He suspected his natural charm wasn't going to create an atmosphere of trust.

"I'll get right to the point. How many bank accounts does the church have?"

"Two," Larry answered. "An operating account and a building fund."

"Who has access to the accounts? Who can sign checks?"

"All the deacons are on the operating account," Larry answered. "Jesse, Bob, and I signed the card for the building fund account."

"What about former deacons?"

"They're removed from all accounts when they stop serving on the board."

"How long have you been without a pastor?"

"About a year."

"Was your former pastor on either bank account?"

Larry looked at the older man. "Bob, was Brother Mark able to sign checks?"

"No," Bob replied. "It hasn't been that way since Brother Tyner was here."

"How long ago was that?" Mike asked.

"Over twenty years," Bob answered.

"Was Sam given authority to sign checks?"

"No," Larry replied. "But when we went to the bank, the man showed us the checks Sam filled out and put in his account."

"Who did you talk to at the bank?"

Larry reached into his pocket and took out a business card.

"Brian Dressler and another man who didn't give us his card."

Mike knew Dressler, a vice president at the bank.

"How many checks were there and for what amounts?" Mike asked.

"Two, one for $10,000 and another for $95,000."

"Who signed the checks?"

"They had Jesse's signature on the bottom, but they went into Sam's account."

Mike turned toward Jesse. "Did you sign checks in those amounts?"

Jesse, a large man with powerful arms and a deep voice, jumped up from his seat. "No! And don't you come in here accusing me—"

"Wait, calm down," Mike interrupted. "I only meant, did you sign checks in that amount for a legitimate building fund purpose? Did you have construction bills to pay?"

Jesse continued to glare at Mike.

"No," Larry responded. "There weren't any bills to pay."

"Do you recall the dates on the checks?"

Larry looked at Jesse. "Do you remember?"

Jesse sat down, but there was still anger in his voice. "They were two days apart. It was during the time Sam was preaching for us. He forged my signature on the first one, and when it went through decided to do another one. It was most of the money we'd saved over the past five years for our building fund."

Mike saw Sam out of the corner of his eye. The old man was sitting with his eyes closed, patting his stomach.

"Did you pay Sam when he was preaching here?" Mike asked.

"Yes," Larry said. "A hundred dollars a Sunday."

"Did you pay him by check?"

"Yes."

"From the operating account?"

"Yes."

"Did he know about the building fund?"

"Yes," Larry said, shaking his head with obvious regret. "He told us five years ago that a greater harvest was coming, and we needed to build a bigger barn to hold it."

"Was he right? Has the church grown?"

"Yes. Sam knows what has happened."

Jesse grunted. "Don't come in here with that soothsayer stuff."

"No, Jesse," Larry said. "We agreed that I would do the talking."

Jesse stood and stretched out a meaty hand clenched in a fist at Sam. Raising his voice, he thundered, "He came in here like a fortune-teller and fooled everybody! I warned them, but they wouldn't listen to me! Then he tried to make it look like I was the one who done wrong!"

Jesse took a step toward Sam. Larry jumped to his feet and reached out, but Jesse pushed him aside. Mike stood and stepped between Jesse and Sam, who pushed his chair against the wall.

"Don't! You'll be sorry!" Mike yelled.

Jesse came directly into Mike's face. "And have to hire some dirty lawyer turned preacher!"

Mike felt a hand on his back.

"Now," Sam said softly.

Mike stared into Jesse's face and knew the threat of harm wasn't a bluff. Suddenly, involuntary tears filled Mike's eyes. The room blurred, and if Mike had wanted to block a blow from Jesse, he couldn't have seen clearly enough to do so.

No blow came.

Mike rubbed his eyes with his hands, but the tears continued. He couldn't remember the last time he'd cried in public or private. The emotion he felt at Danny Brewster's memorial service was the closest he'd come to tears in public since he was a teenager. Mike groaned. The tears continued to flow. He sobbed with an agonizing groan that embarrassed him even more. He heard Larry's voice.

"Sit down, Jesse."

Mike held his sleeve against his eyes. After several moments, he took a deep breath.

Sam spoke. "Papa's heart breaks when His children hate. Those were His tears for us."

Mike looked up. Jesse had returned to his chair. The large man sat with his head down, staring at the floor.

"It's the Spirit of the Lord," Bob said simply.

Mike could feel the tears drying on his cheeks. Larry turned to Bob. "What are we supposed to do?"

"Quit talking and go back to praying," Bob replied.

Larry motioned toward Mike and Sam. "With them?"

"Yes."

Jesse stood up and quickly moved toward the door. "I don't want any part of this! A lying spirit has come on all of you!"

Larry reached toward Jesse.

"Let him go," Bob said.

Jesse left the room, leaving the door open behind him. Without another word, Bob slipped to his knees in front of his chair. The other men and Sam did the same. Mike hadn't prayed in a kneeling position for years, but he joined them. The room was silent for several minutes. Then, Mike felt the heaviness he'd experienced the previous Sunday in the Little Creek sanctuary.

"Oh, God; oh, God," Larry began.

For the next hour, Mike listened as the men cried out to the Lord in a way he'd only imagined. Mike didn't believe emotion moved God's heart, but he suspected the three deacons didn't agree with him. They acted as if the future of the Almighty's will for Sam Miller and the Craig Valley Gospel Tabernacle depended upon their zeal. Sam didn't speak, and Mike wondered if the old man prayed the same way. The deacons' words built to a zenith and ebbed several times before Larry said, "Amen and amen."

Mike opened his eyes. Everyone rose from the floor.

"Thanks for meeting with us," Sam said. "The time will come when we will break bread together."

"The light will come; the truth will be known," Larry said. "My heart is clear."

"Amen," the other two men echoed.

"Who should I contact if I have other questions?" Mike asked.

"Me," Larry replied.

MIKE AND SAM WALKED THROUGH THE SANCTUARY. SAM TURNED and faced the pulpit.

"I'll be back," he said then turned to Mike. "You, too."

When they sat down in the car, Mike took a deep breath and exhaled.

"I didn't know what to expect, but that was different," he said.

"Yep."

"Were you surprised by Jesse's reaction to you?"

"He's shaken my hand many times, and I've prayed for him and his family. I don't know all that lives in a man's heart. Sometimes, a good heart lets a bad guest come for a visit. I hope that's the situation with Jesse."

Mike put the car in reverse and drove away from the church. They passed the Rea homestead.

"I have a theory about what happened at the bank," Mike said. "And Jesse is at the heart of it."

"How?"

"It's not complicated and eliminates the existence of proving a bank error. Jesse wrote the checks from the building fund and put them in your account to discredit you and eliminate your influence in the church. He'd be taking a tremendous risk, but it would explain the financial transactions. Finding out the number of your bank account wouldn't be too difficult. He then simply presented the checks for deposit to your account."

"But he said his name was forged on the checks."

"He could have modified his normal signature so it would look like a forgery. We can have the checks examined by an expert. It might not turn up anything, but it would be worth a try. Getting Jesse to admit a criminal act would be next to impossible; however, there are three credible witnesses who will testify about Jesse's attitude toward you this evening. It might be enough to create a reasonable doubt."

"What would happen to Jesse?"

"Nothing, unless the DA decided to prosecute him. If the charges against you are dropped or a jury finds you not guilty, I suspect the whole matter would all go away. It's not the kind of case Ken West, the district attorney, likes to take all the way."

They rode in silence. Mike turned onto another road.

"But do you think Jesse wrote those two checks?" Sam asked.

"It was a stupid thing to do, but if he's as mad at you as he showed at the church, anything is possible. Now, he's probably scared that he'll get caught."

"Did you see anything about Jesse in your dream?"

Mike shook his head and smiled. "I'm not sure about my dream. All the men in my dream were white. Why didn't you tell me it was a black church?"

"Would it have made a difference?"

"Of course not, but it makes me question my dream."

"Does Papa see in color?" Sam asked with a grin.

"Don't mess with me," Mike responded.

"It doesn't make me doubt your dream," Sam continued. "Papa likes variety. All creation shows it."

"Well, whatever happened at my house around 3:18 a.m. didn't seem to have much relevance to that meeting."

"Is that when you woke up?"

"Yes, it's one of the few things I remember."

"Do you have a Bible in the car?" Sam asked.

"Check the backseat."

Sam reached behind him. While Mike drove, Sam flipped through the pages.

"What are you looking for?" Mike asked.

"A clue to understanding your dream."

Sam turned several more pages. "Here's something. Listen to this. '*As I have often told you before and now say again even with tears, many live as enemies of the cross of Christ.*' That's Philippians 3:18. Your tears came when you looked at Jesse. The time of a dream is often important."

Mike didn't look at Sam. "You can believe there is a connection if you want to, but I think plugging a verse into an alarm clock and concluding it's a message from God is speculation."

"Just consider it. I'm trying to help you get smarter about the things you're moving into."

Mike turned onto McAfee Road.

"I'm not sure about the tears or the time of night," he said. "My goal is to move you safely through the criminal justice system and out the other side without any more tears for Muriel or jail time for you."

Fourteen

THE FOLLOWING DAY, MIKE FILED A FLURRY OF MOTIONS IN
Sam's case, including a request for scientific evaluation of the checks deposited
to Sam's bank account. Late in the afternoon, he received a call from
Melissa Hall.

"I went over your motions with Ken," the assistant DA said. "There isn't
much in the file, but we'll let you copy what you want."

"Is there a statement from Miller?"

"Signed after receiving his Miranda rights."

"And the checks?"

"Yes, copies along with other bank records."

"Okay. When will the file be available?"

"Whenever you want to review it. The secretary knows you have permission. Also, Ken wants to have an informal meeting with Judge Coberg about
the letter the judge sent. Would you have any objection to meeting with the
judge in chambers before bringing in an outside judge for a hearing?"

"That's fine."

"What is your availability?"

"Any time except Sunday morning."

Mike waited for an acknowledgment of his attempt at humor but none
came. He looked at the calendar on his computer. "Actually, I would prefer to
do it next week, either Tuesday or Wednesday afternoon."

"Both of those times work for Ken. I'll check with the judge's clerk and
confirm via e-mail."

THAT EVENING MIKE TOOK PEG OUT TO EAT. ON THE WAY HOME, they passed a road that led away from town and deeper into the mountains.

"How is your energy level?" Mike asked.

"Mostly good."

"Do you have any plans on Friday?" Mike asked.

"Just my usual date with Judge for a run. I might call Elizabeth Lambert for lunch."

"Would you like to climb Jefferson's Ridge? I've been thinking about it since my sermon."

"I thought you and Bobby were going to play eighteen holes."

"I'd rather spend time with you."

Peg turned sideways in her seat. Mike stared straight ahead and fought off a guilty smile.

"Bobby canceled on you," she said.

Mike nodded. "Yes. Sam Miller thinks he sees the past and the future, but he's no match for you. Bobby is still swamped at work and can't break away for a few hours. But I'd still rather be with you than playing golf with Bobby."

"Are you going to ride your bike while Judge and I run along beside you?"

"No. We'll all be on foot."

Peg was silent for a moment then sighed. "Okay. It's time."

"For what?"

"To go with you to the top of the mountain."

THURSDAY MORNING, DELORES BUZZED MIKE.

"The lawn man is here," she said curtly.

Mike made a final note for a finance committee meeting and came out of his office. Sam, dressed in blue overalls and wearing a cap from a local feed and seed store on his head, stood in the waiting area. Delores had scooted her chair as far away from her desk as possible and eyed the older man suspiciously.

"Glad the church is still standing," Sam said.

"What do you mean?" Mike asked.

"In a dream last night, you and I were sitting in the sanctuary of your church when Bud Putnam came running in."

"The fire chief?"

"Yep. The building was on fire. We had to leave and went outside to the parking lot. When I looked up, the roof of the church was covered in flames. At first, I wasn't sure about the meaning. Papa often uses fire to represent good things, like His presence in a place, but the more I watched, the more I knew this was not a good fire. It was a fire from hell."

Out of the corner of his eye, Mike could see a shocked expression on Delores's face.

"Let's go outside," he suggested. "I'll show you what to cut."

The two men walked down the hallway.

"It wasn't an actual fire, was it?" Mike asked.

"I don't think so."

"Why would you see a church on fire?"

"Fighting. When I see a church on fire in a bad way, it's usually because there has been a lot of friction caused by fussing. Have you ever started a fire with a flint rock?"

"No, and friction isn't a problem here. We have a unified, growing congregation."

The two men walked out of the building. Mike helped Sam lift his push mower from the back of his truck and unload a couple of old metal gas cans. Sam quickly set a ramp and rolled off his riding mower.

"Make sure you have plenty of smoke detectors," Sam said.

"We do. The insurance policy requires it. The custodian checks the batteries the first of every month."

"I'm talking about the kind that can detect a foul spirit from the pit."

Mike rolled his eyes. "The cemetery is the only tricky part of the property to cut. Everywhere else is clear enough that you should be able to use your big mower; however, the cemetery has some very old, partially missing markers. Be careful not to break a mower blade on a piece of marble or cause any damage. Families take the resting place of their ancestors seriously."

Sam leaned over and checked the oil in his riding mower.

"I'll be careful. It's the hidden dangers that can cause the biggest problems."

Mike returned to the administration wing.

"I can't believe you invited that man to cut our grass," Delores sniffed when he reached her desk. "He's a criminal—"

"Wait a minute," Mike interrupted. "He may have been tried in the court of public opinion, but in the eyes of the law, he's innocent until proven guilty."

"You know what I mean," Delores retorted. "Coming in here talking about setting fire to the church!"

"It was a dream, not a literal event. And he didn't mention anything about burning down the church. God speaks to men and women like him through pictures and symbols. Don't let it bother you. I'll be here until he finishes working."

The phone rang, and Delores picked it up. Mike went into his office. Over the next few hours, he occasionally glanced out a window to check on Sam's progress. The old man was a steady worker, but once, Mike saw him kneeling at the water hole where the spring bubbled up through the rocks. At noon, Mike let Delores leave for lunch and went outside. Sam was finishing up the far side of the cemetery. Mike waved him over. Sam turned off the push mower and walked across the graveyard.

"Do you want anything to eat or drink?" Mike asked.

Sam mopped his forehead with a yellow bandanna he took from the front of his overalls.

"I brought a plate of cold fried chicken, green beans, and black-eyed peas left over from supper last night."

"Want to heat it up in the microwave?"

"It's good cold, but better hot. What are you going to eat?"

"A cup of yogurt."

Sam scoffed. "Not unless you have a chicken leg first."

Sam retrieved a small cooler from the front seat of his truck and followed Mike into the church kitchen. After a couple of minutes in the microwave, the fragrance of the chicken seeped into the room. Mike sniffed.

"You should have tasted it last night," Sam said, patting his stomach. "Since I got out of jail, Muriel has been spoiling me rotten."

When the beeper sounded, Mike opened the door of the microwave. It was an impressive amount of food.

"Get yourself a plate," Sam said. "I'm going to share Papa's bounty with you. It's the least I can do, seeing that you're not charging me to be my lawyer."

Mike handed the old man a plate, and before he could protest, Sam scraped half the meal onto the second plate.

"Pray and eat up," Sam said, handing it to him. "If you're still hungry, you can eat all the yogurt you want."

They sat on folding metal chairs at a rectangular table. Mike prayed and took a bite of chicken.

"What did she put in this batter?" he asked.

Sam held up a drumstick. "A secret recipe Colonel Sanders didn't know about."

The meal reminded Mike of dinners at his aunt Sue's house. Twice a year, Christmas and the Fourth of July, his family gathered at the large white home of his father's sister in an older section of Raleigh to visit and eat, not necessarily in that order.

"What will I tell Peg when she asks me about lunch?" Mike asked as he collected the final bite of black-eyed peas. "I've been trying to cut back."

"Pray she doesn't ask," Sam replied. "If she does, tell her you ate organic."

"Organic?"

"That's a word, isn't it?" Sam replied. "For food that's homegrown without using bag fertilizer."

"Yes. I can believe that about the vegetables, but did you raise this chicken?"

"No, but I know the man who did. Muriel likes him because he kills and cleans them, too."

"Tell Muriel it was good. Sorry I can't offer you dessert."

"I skip the sweets if I can have the rest."

Mike rinsed the empty plates in the sink and put them in the dishwasher.

"How is the work progressing?"

"You were right about the cemetery. It's slow going, but once I finish I should move faster with the big mower. Do you know about the spring at the edge of the creek?"

"Yes, I like to go there. It used to be a watering hole for horses."

Sam nodded. "I splashed some of the water on my face and got refreshed. There have been some praying people in this church. It would be good if a few new ones came to the surface to put out the fire."

Mike didn't respond. He liked it better when Sam talked about Muriel's fried chicken.

FRIDAY MORNING, MIKE LIFTED HIS DAY PACK FROM ITS HOOK on the wall of the garage and brought it into the house. Judge saw the pack and began barking.

"Settle down. You're included," Mike reassured him.

He loaded the pack with water, snacks, a jacket for Peg, and an old quilt.

He was lacing up his boots when Peg entered the kitchen. She was dressed in jeans and a yellow T-shirt with her hair in a ponytail sticking out the back of a ball cap.

"How do I look?"

"Perfect," Mike answered. "I saw your hiking boots in the corner of the garage. Do they still fit?"

Peg propped her left foot on his leg. "Are my feet swelling yet?"

Mike tickled the bottom of her foot. Peg didn't flinch.

"No, and I see you haven't lost your willpower. Don't fix the coffee. I thought we would stop for breakfast on the way."

They went outside. It was a cool morning but without any clouds in the sky. "Do I need a jacket?" Peg asked.

"Probably not, but I put one in the pack."

"And my pillow in case I want to lie down in the grass and take a nap?"

Mike pointed to his chest. "This is your pillow."

They took Mike's car. Peg didn't like to get her car dusty, and the parking lot behind Hank's Grocery wasn't paved. Judge jumped into the backseat and lay down peacefully. Mike drove to the bottom of the ridge and through Shelton to the west side of town. He and Peg didn't have to debate where to eat breakfast. He pulled into the parking lot for Traci's Restaurant, a low-slung brown building with plate-glass windows along the front and one side. Calico curtains hung in at the edges of the windows. Mike cracked the back window for Judge, who sat up and sniffed the morning air.

"I'll bring you a bite of sausage biscuit," Peg promised the dog as they left the car.

A single door opened to a small waiting area beside the cash register. The restaurant was an L shape with bench seating along the walls and a row of tables down the middle. Within a few seconds of entering, Mike heard a female voice call his name.

"Mike! Get over here!"

Across the room, a skinny waitress in her late fifties motioned with her hand and pointed to an empty table. Mike and Peg came over to her.

"How are you, Judy?" Mike asked.

"Better now that you're here."

Judy turned to Peg and patted her on the arm. "I used to see him all the time when he was practicing law. Now that he's a preacher, he's quit eating breakfast."

Judy had raised three children with no help from their father. For many years, she reported to work at 5:00 a.m. and worked through the lunch shift, arriving home in time to greet the school bus and begin her second job as a mother.

"Don't tell me what you want," Judy said to Mike. "Let me take care of you."

Peg gave her order. The waitress returned with coffee: black for Mike, sugar and extra cream for Peg.

"Fill me in on the family," Mike said.

"I have a new grandbaby, a little boy who is already sleeping through the night. But the funny thing is my younger daughter Margie. She's been working out at the gym and is almost as buff as I used to be."

When in her twenties, Judy had been a serious weight lifter. She still retained enough wiry strength to beat unsuspecting bus boys in arm wrestling.

"Peg and I are going to have a baby," Mike said. "We just found out."

Judy lifted her hands in the air. "Hallelujah. You get all that lawyer pressure off and get pregnant."

"I thought that applied to women," Mike replied.

"No, honey. It's always the man."

Judy hustled away to take care of another table.

"What did she mean?" Peg asked.

Mike shook his head. "I'm not sure. Until I met Sam Miller, Judy was the most difficult person to understand I knew."

The waitress returned with two eggs over easy for Mike, crisp bacon, and dry toast. Peg's plate held two scrambled eggs with a sausage biscuit along with a large glass of orange juice.

"I looked out the window and saw that dog of yours in the car," Judy said.

"We're going for a hike up Jefferson's Ridge."

"That's good. Your baby will be an early walker. I did a lot of walking when I was pregnant. It paid off until I had to start chasing them around the house."

Judy moved on at a rapid clip. Peg sipped her orange juice.

"In her mind, everything is connected," Peg said. "If I like orange juice, our child will want me to buy bags of oranges."

"Are you going to swim this summer?" Mike asked.

"Probably."

"Good. When you combine swimming with your running and my bike riding, we're going to produce a future triathlon champion."

When they finished, Mike left a generous tip on the table. Peg offered part of her sausage biscuit to Judge in her open palm. The dog scooped it up with a swift flick of his tongue.

Mike drove away from town. Within a half mile, the number of older houses along the road dropped off, and they began to climb higher. New asphalt roads to the side signaled points of access to housing developments in the hill. Land that farmers once considered less desirable because it was rocky and hilly now commanded good prices.

After driving almost ten miles, they reached Hank's Grocery, a seventy-year-old country store and center of the local economy. The fourth-generation owners of the store stocked general merchandise even though most people now treated it like a convenience mart. Hunters and fishermen appreciated the availability of shotgun shells and fish hooks, and it was also possible to buy a connector hose for a clothes washer. A large graveled area behind the store had once served as a feed lot for cattle. Mike parked the car.

"I'll be right back," he said to Peg. "I'm going to let someone in the store know we're here."

Mike walked past a Mercedes and opened the screen door. The store was dark and the layout chaotic. A well-dressed woman placed a head of lettuce, several tomatoes, a cucumber, and a jar of salad dressing on the counter.

"Good morning, Mike!" called out Buzz Carrier, the thirty-five-year-old owner of the store.

"Good morning. I have Peg and Judge with me. We'll be gone till early afternoon."

"Have a good time."

Mike held the door open for the woman as she left with her purchases. He turned back to the man at the cash register.

"Do you have a set of small Allen wrenches?" he asked. "I need to work on my bike."

Buzz motioned toward the rear of the store, a close-packed array of shelves and boxes. "I'll find them before you get back."

Mike walked past a large propane tank to the parking lot. Peg was holding the end of Judge's leash as the dog sniffed the woods at the edge of the lot. When he saw Mike, Judge barked and strained in his direction.

"Ready?" he called out to Peg.

"Or not," Peg replied. "Judge is about to jerk my arm off. I need to let him go or start running myself."

"Turn him loose."

Peg pulled the dog in and unhooked the leash. Judge took off toward the opening in the woods that served as the entryway to the old roadbed and disappeared from sight. Mike didn't worry. He'd trained the dog to come on a whistle. He and Peg passed into the splattered shade cast by the young leaves on the trees beside the trail. He took Peg's hand in his.

"That feels much better than a pitching wedge," Mike said, squeezing her hand.

Peg squeezed back. "You're so romantic, comparing my hand to a golf grip. Did you read that in one of your marriage counseling books?"

Mike laughed. "No."

He whistled, and in a few seconds, Judge tumbled down the bank to their right. Mike scratched the dog's neck and released him to continue exploring.

They climbed gradually yet steadily. The woods had encroached on the old roadbed, but it remained a gently sloping, broad trail. Mike marveled at the ingenuity of the men who had determined the path up a mountain. Contours that could be seen from the air were much more difficult to gauge on the ground. The loggers who constructed the roadway didn't punish those who climbed but rather wooed them. The switchbacks were interspersed with flat runs across the face of the hill to places where the climb resumed at the best gradient available. After his initial burst of explosive energy, Judge returned and stayed closer to them.

"Don't try to race your pregnant wife to the top of a mountain," Peg said, catching her breath.

"Sorry."

Peg sat on a large rock to the side of the trail. Mike opened his backpack and handed her a water bottle. Before drinking from his own, he poured water in a plastic dish he'd brought for Judge. Mike held the dish steady so the dog wouldn't tip it over with his vigorous lapping.

"How do you keep Judge from going too fast on your runs?" Mike asked.

"After we get started, he understands the leash a lot better than most men do. A quick jerk and he heels."

"Is that what you want from me?"

Peg stood up and patted Mike's cheek. "No. That would be boring."

They continued up the trail and turned a corner onto a flatter section.

"You surprised me the other day when you told me you had no regrets about my leaving the law firm."

"I'm not sure that's what I said, but I'm full of surprises. My nesting urge is getting stronger, and for the past few days, I've been studying the home furnishing catalogs we get in the mail. Don't you think it's time to make some major changes in the house?"

"How much is this going to cost?"

"I don't have a clue, but don't worry." Peg paused. "Yet."

As they trudged onward, Mike thought about the hit to their savings a major overhaul of the house would cause.

"I told you not to worry," Peg said, cutting into his reverie, "but there is something I want to tell you when we reach the top of the hill."

"Why wait until the top?"

"Because I can't climb, breathe, talk, and grow our baby at the same time."

They could see clear sky above the trees that marched up the hillside, but several switchbacks remained before they broke into the open. Mike enjoyed watching Judge. Vizslas could be trained as both trackers and pointers. The dog moved from side to side as his sensitive nose appreciated the entire palate of scents on display in the wild.

The top of the hill was crowned with a canopy of trees. The trail ran beneath the trees along the ridgeline for a hundred yards before ending at the edge of a small mountain meadow. It was still early spring at this altitude, and only a few green strands of grass were beginning to sprout from the brown stalks of the previous year. Mike dropped the backpack on the ground and served water all around. Peg rubbed her forehead with a red kerchief she took from a hip pocket of her jeans. A slight breeze stirred the warm air.

"Didn't need my jacket," she said.

"I know, but I brought it anyway."

"And I felt cherished and cared for."

"Are you going to tell me now?"

Peg smiled. "Show me your holy spot."

"What holy spot?"

"The place where God spoke to you from the burning bush and ordered you to ignore your wife's advice, leave the successful practice of law, and lead His people out of bondage."

Mike pointed to the west side of the meadow.

"Over there."

Judge was rolling back and forth on his back in the grass. He jumped up when Mike and Peg moved away. The meadow was small, about three hundred feet across and five hundred feet long, but from its exposed position on top of the hill it seemed larger. The dead grass crunched beneath their feet as they walked. Judge joined them. On the west edge of the meadow, a row of exposed rocks had broken free into the sunlight. One jutted from the ground about three feet.

Mike pointed. "There. That's where I was sitting when I read the verses in Galatians."

Peg took Mike by the hand and led him over to the rock.

"Sit," she said.

A puzzled look on his face, Mike sat on the rock. Peg knelt down in the grass at his feet and stared away in the distance for several seconds before looking up at him.

"I need to ask your forgiveness," she said.

"Why?" Mike shifted his weight on the rock. "I'm the one who forgot our anniversary two years ago."

"No, I'm serious. Please listen."

Mike grew still.

"I've put you through a lot the past six years," she said. "A few times I kicked and screamed out loud and did it a lot more than that on the inside. I wasn't with you in the transition to the ministry, and when you continued in that direction, I decided you didn't care about me. Our marriage wasn't as important as your lofty notions of saving the world. Last November, I came close to leaving you."

Mike's eyes widened in shock. He'd known there was tension, but chalked it up to the stress of major changes, not a potential end to the marriage.

"I never—," he began.

"Let me finish," Peg interrupted. "I paid a deposit on an apartment in Asheville and talked with a divorce lawyer." She looked down at the ground. "I even signed the verification page on a divorce petition."

Mike felt as if he'd been punched in the stomach. A spark of hurt and anger flared up inside him. Peg looked at his face.

"You have a right to be upset," she continued. "I was wrong, and not telling you about this has eaten at me. I thought it would go away, but after listening to your sermon last week, I knew I had to be honest and ask you to forgive me."

"Was there anyone else?"

"No, just selfish me."

Mike's mind was spinning.

"Why did you stay?"

Peg reached into the front pocket of her jeans and pulled out a well-creased sheet of notebook paper and held it up in her hand.

"In part because of this. The day after I met with the lawyer, I received a letter in the mail that described exactly how I felt. It got behind my defenses then warned me that a decision I was considering would not bring the joy and happiness I wanted. I threw the letter in the trash but couldn't get it out of my mind. I pulled it out, and, during the next few days, read it over and over. It was just enough to make me reconsider. I called the lawyer, stopped the divorce, and forfeited the deposit on the apartment."

"Who sent the letter?"

"It wasn't signed, so I never knew." Peg paused. "Until you met Sam Miller."

Mike's jaw dropped. "Sam Miller wrote you a letter?"

"Yes. After you told me about the letter he sent Jack Hatcher, I remembered what happened with me. I called Muriel and went over to their house. Sam looked at the letter and said, 'Yep. I wrote it. But only Papa knew our paths would cross someday.'"

Mike smiled slightly. "That sounds like Sam."

"He'd forgotten about it. Muriel says he writes lots of letters, but doesn't keep any copies."

"So I've learned."

Peg touched Mike's knee. "But this isn't about Sam Miller. It's about us. I'm the one who walled off my heart, who abandoned you, who forgot something a lot more important than our anniversary—the vows we made on our wedding day. I put out the fire of my love, and I've been wrong, terribly wrong."

Mike saw tears in Peg's eyes as she continued, "We agreed to walk together through life no matter what. Now, I want to remove everything that would be a wedge between us and build the right kind of marriage for us and our child. Will you forgive me?"

"Of course."

"No." Peg shook her head. "That's too quick. I want you to know how deeply, terribly sorry I am for being so selfish. I haven't supported you in the way I promised when we married or the way God wanted me to. I said I loved you, but I've been rotten."

Mike slid off the rock onto the grass beside her. He took her in his arms, brought her close, and kissed the top of her head.

"I don't feel worthy to say I forgive you," he said.

"But do you?"

Mike took a deep breath. "Yes."

"Think about it. Are you sure?"

Mike held her tightly and spoke softly into her ear.

"With all my heart."

 *Fifteen*

Staring at the blue sky, Mike lay still so he wouldn't wake Peg. Her secret burden lifted, she'd rested her head on Mike's chest and dozed. The old quilt cushioned them from the scratchy grass. There wasn't a cloud in the sky. Mike could hear Judge crashing through the grass off to the left.

Reeling from Peg's revelation, Mike couldn't take a nap. He couldn't believe he'd been so oblivious to the mortal danger threatening his marriage. He'd always considered himself an astute judge of people but failed miserably at discerning what his own wife was considering.

God, using Sam Miller, intervened.

Before falling asleep, Peg let him read the letter from Sam. It was a simple message of warning and encouragement but had done the job. Peg could be tough to convince, and the power of a few words scrawled on a sheet of notebook paper was stunning. That the lawncare man took the time to write a letter to a total stranger was unfathomable. Mike cared about people, but Sam Miller took the concept of loving your neighbor to another stratosphere.

Peg's nose twitched. Mike kept his breathing regular so his chest rose and fell in rhythm. Peg moved her head slightly and snuggled closer to his chin.

"I love you," she said.

Mike stroked her hair. "I love you, too," he managed.

"How long have I been dozing?"

"Not long."

Judge suddenly appeared over Mike's face and licked his nose.

"That's a wet alarm clock," Mike said, pushing the dog away.

Peg looked up. "Remind me not to kiss that spot until you wash your face."

139

They sat up. The breeze across the top of the mountain had picked up while they rested. It felt clean and fresh. Peg stretched her hands in the air then threw her arms around Mike's neck and gave him a long kiss on the lips.

"You were holding back," she said when their lips parted. "Do I need to ask you to forgive me again? I'll do it five times a day until you're convinced I mean it."

"I know you meant it. It's just going to take time for me to adjust to how close I came to losing you."

Peg took his hand and placed it on her abdomen. "Any time doubts come to your mind, think about the child inside me, and remember that I'm committed to you—completely."

Mike looked into her eyes. There was an honest clarity present that gave no room for deceit.

"Even if I'm not perfect?" he asked.

"You're perfect for me."

Peg stood and brushed a few pieces of dried grass from her shirt.

"I'm ready to go," she announced. "We have lots to talk about on the way down."

"What else?" Mike asked apprehensively.

"Redecorating the house. We need to get a nursery ready and make the whole house safe for a baby. Now, I can really put my heart into it."

They held opposite ends of the blanket and shook it before folding it up. Judge came running over, and Mike poured water into the plastic dish for the dog to drink.

"That's amazing about Sam Miller," he said to Peg as Judge lapped up the water. "Every town doesn't have a yardman who writes letters to save marriages."

"It should."

Peg was filled with carefree chatter on the return trip down the mountain. Mike tried to match her mood but couldn't. Peg carried the knowledge about how close they'd come to divorce to the top of the mountain. He bore it down. Several times, he started to say something, but Peg's reminder of the child growing within her stopped him. Never had such a tiny person exerted such great influence over him.

"How did you manage to keep your secret?" he asked finally. "Except for confidential information in my cases, I've never been able to keep anything important from you for more than a few days."

Peg slowed her steps. "After I changed my mind, I was ashamed but still angry with you. If I'd said anything, it might have caused a huge fight that would have driven us farther apart."

"What's different now?"

"Sam and Muriel told me what I needed to do."

Mike stopped. "That's amazing."

"Am I that hardheaded? Can't you tell that I'm changing?"

"Yes," Mike replied and started walking again.

"Do you like it?"

"Yes. But it's—"

Peg glanced sideways as they rounded a bend in the trail.

"A challenge relating to the new me?"

"Just different. I'm a minister who is supposed to believe God transforms people for the better, but when my own wife tells me it's happening to her, I wonder if I can handle it."

"At least you won't be bored."

Peg took a few quick steps ahead down the trail. Judge ran along beside her. Mike plodded along in the rear.

They reached the parking lot. Mike went into the store. The Allen wrenches were waiting for him on the counter.

"Beautiful day, isn't it?" the store owner said as he rang up the purchase. "How was your hike?"

"Not what I expected. You can always see farther from the top of the ridge." Mike paused. "Today, I saw the past."

Buzz tilted his head to the side. "Don't mess with me, Mike. I have enough strange people from other parts of the country coming in here. I don't need any of the local folks getting squirrelly."

THAT NIGHT AFTER PEG WENT TO SLEEP, MIKE LAY IN BED WITH his eyes open. During the drive home, he'd decided his ignorance had been a disguised blessing. He'd not known his marriage was stalled on the train tracks until it moved out of danger. As his eyes adjusted to the darkness, he turned on his side so he could see Peg. A pale sliver of moonlight crept into the room and faintly illuminated her golden hair. He hadn't admitted it to Peg, but his pride was deeply wounded by her secret rejection. He tossed and turned for a long time. He hoped the hurt would soon find healing in the hospital of his soul. Instead, he revisited the dream of the old woman who passed into darkness. She looked familiar, like Muriel, but distinctly different. He woke up wishing Peg hadn't brought out the painting.

THE FOLLOWING DAY, HE SPENT SEVERAL HOURS WORKING OUT-side. Late morning, Peg joined him and together they planted flowers. Peg had a knack for landscape design, and their yard moved with grace from one season of the year to the next. Daffodils and tulips in later winter, day lilies in the spring, and mums in the fall. Kneeling beside each other, their hands frequently touched as they worked the soil. Once, Mike glanced up and saw Peg wipe her sleeve across her eyes.

"Why are you crying?" he asked.

"I'm happy. I know we're dirty, but I've never felt so clean on the inside. Is this what it means to be forgiven?"

"Yes."

Peg sat sideways on the grass. "And doing this with you is special. Do I need to ask you to forgive me today?"

Mike smoothed the soil around the flower he'd deposited into the ground and sat with his legs stretched out in front of him.

"No. I'm not going to be petty, but it may take a while for me to be healed. When I counsel people, I tell them forgiveness forgets."

"That's impossible."

"I know," Mike admitted. "And I won't be so glib to toss it out in the future until I've done it myself and can explain it better."

"What would you say?"

Mike thought while they continued working. He put down the bulb planter.

"That the memory of a wrong isn't stronger than the grace to forgive and go on."

Peg smiled. "That would make a good sermon."

SUNDAY MORNING ARRIVED. MIKE ENTERED THE PULPIT AREA. To his delight, Sam and Muriel Miller had returned.

The topic of forgiveness wasn't in Mike's notes, but he mentioned it a few times with Peg in his line of sight. The radiant look on her face caused him to smile. The power of forgiveness he expressed to the congregation welled up in his own heart.

After the service, the last two people in the narthex were Sam and Muriel.

"Peg showed me the letter you sent her," Mike said as he shook Sam's hand. "Thanks."

Sam smiled. "Papa holds the whole world in His hands, doesn't He?"

"And I'm going to stick by you," Mike replied. "Don't worry any more about it."

"Yep. I knew you would help." Sam patted Muriel's hand. "She wasn't so sure until Peg came by the house. Then all the pieces of the puzzle fell into place."

Mike followed Sam and Muriel out the front door of the church. Peg and Bobby Lambert were talking in the parking lot near Bobby's car.

Mike went over to them.

"Do you have a minute?" Bobby asked.

"Sure."

"It's about the Miller case," Bobby added then stopped.

"Is that my cue to find something appropriate for the minister's wife to do?" Peg asked. "I'll look for someone who needs a tuna casserole this week and set up a time to deliver it."

"Go easy on me, Peg," Bobby said. "Why don't you catch up with Elizabeth? She's getting the kids from the nursery. I think she brought you a card congratulating you on your pregnancy."

Peg departed with a smile. Bobby shook his head and turned to Mike.

"How do you handle her tongue? It's sharper than a razor."

"She reserves her soft side for me. What did you want to tell me?"

"Have you found anyone to take the Miller case?"

"No one has come forward."

"Your client saw Greg Freeman in court the other day. For a young lawyer, he handled himself well. Miller should be glad Freeman is interested in taking him on."

"That's not going to happen," Mike said bluntly. "Sam has made up his mind that I'm going to be his lawyer, and I'm on board. I've begun my investigation."

"But Mr. Forrest—"

"Is a man I greatly respect, but he isn't my boss. According to him, I shouldn't even talk about the case with you."

"What?" Bobby replied with a surprised look on his face.

Mike told him about the letter. Bobby swore softly then immediately apologized.

"He's been bugging me about your involvement in the deal all week," Bobby said, "but I had no idea he'd ordered you to stay off the premises."

"Or talk to anyone from the firm."

"He can't do that."

Mike shrugged. "It removed any question I might have about how strongly he disagrees with what I'm doing, and any hope of cooperation from the bank went out the window, too."

"What have you found out on your own?"

Mike placed his hand on the top of Bobby's new car. "I'm sorry, but I don't think I should discuss details of the case with you. We're not law partners anymore."

Bobby looked away for a second before responding. "From now on, my interest will be as an elder of this church, not a lawyer."

"That's right."

Bobby looked Mike directly in the eyes. "And as an elder, I urge you to find someone else to help Mr. Miller. I went to bat for you before the session, but our approval was contingent on you taking steps to disengage from representation as soon as possible. If you don't get out soon, we'll have to bring it up for discussion."

"I understand. All I ask is notice. Ecclesiastical due process, you know."

"Mike, this isn't a joke. Consider this conversation your notice."

Mike set his jaw. "Okay, but I think I can explain to the satisfaction of a majority of the session why I believe I should remain involved."

TUESDAY AFTERNOON, MIKE ARRIVED A FEW MINUTES EARLY TO Judge Coberg's chambers. The judge's secretary, a middle-aged woman Mike didn't recognize, phoned the DA's office.

"Tell Mr. West and Ms. Hall that Mr. Andrews is here," she said. "The judge wants to get started as soon as possible."

Mike waited for the prosecutors to arrive. When Ken West walked in, he shook Mike's hand as vigorously as he had at election time. They went into the judge's office. Melissa Hall followed her boss but didn't come out from his shadow. Mike stepped to the side and greeted her.

Judge Coberg's chambers contained personal items collected during his long career. Along with the usual pictures of politicians and other judges, a corner was devoted to baseball memorabilia. The judge only collected items from before the 1960s. It had been several years since Mike had seen the baseball collection, and he noticed a number 9 Boston Red Sox jersey hanging behind a glass frame.

"Who wore it?" he asked the judge, pointing to the frame.

"Ted Williams. My wife bought it for me a couple of years ago."

On the front corner of the judge's desk, Mike saw one of the judge's trial notebooks containing his personal analyses of the decisions by the appellate courts. Many times during a trial or a motion hearing, Mike had seen the judge reach for one of his notebooks, flip to a handwritten notation, and issue a ruling from which he wouldn't retreat.

There were three chairs positioned in front of the judge's desk.

"Ken," the judge said, "do you remember the Debary case? You tried it."

"How long ago and what was the charge?"

"Eighteen years ago, an assault and battery by a stepfather against his six-year-old daughter."

"Yes, sir. The little girl suffered a broken arm when the man hit her. A lawyer came all the way from Charlotte to defend it and went back with his tail between his legs."

"As he should have. During a pretrial hearing, I asked if any neighbors were going to testify."

"I don't recall that coming up."

"Well, it did. And I suggested that someone should interview a man named Hopkins who had moved to Missouri after the charges were filed. I even mentioned the town where Mr. Hopkins lived. The defense lawyer wanted to object but didn't know what to say. After all, it's the duty of the Court to determine the truth. When the case came to trial, the little girl was unable to testify, but the Hopkins fellow saw exactly what happened."

"Yes, sir. It's coming back to me."

The judge sat back in his chair. "Sam Miller wrote me a letter about the Debary case. He'd read about the charges in the paper, told me the name and address of Mr. Hopkins, and claimed Hopkins was an eyewitness."

"What was Miller's connection?" West asked.

Mike wasn't surprised by the judge's answer.

"None. He didn't know anyone. He claimed he got the information in a dream and wrote it down."

West was silent for a moment before he spoke. Mike was almost surprised Ken West hadn't received a letter from Sam. The DA's ego would have been wounded if he realized he'd not been included in the group with the president of the United States, Judge Coberg, Jack Hatcher, and Peg Andrews. West spoke.

"That's odd, but it could have been a way for Miller to tell what he knew without admitting personal knowledge."

"I would agree, except that it's happened more than once. On three other occasions, Miller has either written or called me with information about a case. What he passes along is sometimes hard to interpret, but in every instance, it's proven reliable."

"Did he give you any information about the charges against him in this case?" West asked sharply.

"No," the judge responded dryly. "If that had happened, I would already have recused myself, and we wouldn't be having this conversation. He's cut my grass a few times, and I buy vegetables from him in the summer, but I have no personal relationship with him. However, I believe the unique aspect of some of our previous interaction should be disclosed."

West glanced at Melissa Hall. "What do you think? You're the one who is going to try this case."

Hall turned toward Mike. "Are you going to waive a jury trial?"

"I'm considering all options," he replied.

Hall faced the judge. "Your Honor, if Mr. Andrews requests a bench trial, I would ask you to recuse yourself; however, if a jury will determine the facts and credibility of the witnesses, I have no objection to your continued involvement."

"How about you, Mr. West?" the judge asked. "I'd like to hear from you, too."

West grunted. "Miller's crystal ball must have gotten a bit cloudy if he thought he could get away with embezzling a hundred thousand dollars from a church. However, just because he claims to be psychic doesn't mean you can't preside in the case. I agree with Ms. Hall, and as a safeguard, I would ask Mr. Andrews to instruct his client not to attempt to contact the Court about his case or any other matter while the charges are pending."

"That's appropriate," Mike responded.

"Does your client object to me presiding in the case?" the judge asked Mike.

"I haven't asked him," Mike answered.

"Do so. Then decide whether you want a jury trial and notify Ms. Hall and me."

"Yes, sir."

The judge shuffled through the papers on his desk. "Mr. Andrews has filed several motions. Any need to have a court reporter present to record testimony for or against his requests?"

"No, sir," Hall said. "We have no objection to the standard pretrial disclosure motions and have agreed to open our file to Mr. Andrews so he can copy any documents he wants an expert to examine."

"When is that going to happen?" the judge asked.

"Today, if possible," Mike replied.

Hall nodded. "That's agreeable. We'll provide everything else he wants by tomorrow. The case will be on the trial calendar in a few weeks."

"That's rushing it, don't you think?" Mike responded quickly.

"Delay for the sake of delay isn't an option."

"But I won't know what else I need until you furnish answers to my requests."

"That's enough, counselors," the judge barked. "Mr. Andrews, if you want a continuance, file a motion."

THE LAWYERS LEFT THE JUDGE'S CHAMBERS, AND MIKE FOL-lowed the prosecuting attorneys downstairs to their office. The DA's office controlled the appearance of cases on the criminal docket, and there wasn't much Mike could do to delay the Miller case.

"I'll have the file pulled, and you can review it in our conference room," Hall said.

Mike went into the small, plainly furnished room and sat at the old conference table. The prosecutors had no clients to impress with fancy surroundings. Mike tapped his fingers against the scratched wooden surface of the table. On several occasions, he'd been ushered into the room and seen it covered with evidence: sawed-off shotguns, burglary tools, and stacks of documents needed to prove larceny.

A secretary brought him the file. Mike quickly flipped past copies of the checks signed by Jesse, the bank records for Sam's account, and the bill of indictment charging Sam with the crime. Mike wanted to see the signed statement taken from Sam by Detective Perkins. It was the last item in the file.

> *I, Sam Miller, make this statement of my own free will after having been told of my right to remain silent and have an attorney present to represent me. During the time I served as temporary pastor of the Craig Valley Gospel Tabernacle, money was illegally taken from the church building fund and put in my bank account. I did not have the right to sign checks for the church or transfer church money into my account.*
>
> —Sam Miller

Mike frowned. Perkins was a crafty interrogator who had transformed a nonincriminating statement into a document that could be used against Sam at trial. On its face, Sam's statement admitted nothing criminal, but it could still be valuable to the prosecution. Sam accepted as true the detective's conclusion that money had been taken illegally from the church building fund. That mistake allowed Perkins to construct a statement removing every legitimate reason Sam might have for church money ending up in his bank account.

At trial, the detective would read the statement and make it sound like a wholesale admission of guilt obtained after a grueling interrogation. Mike could point out the precise language of the statement, but that would result in courtroom sparring with the detective, which always had a negative impact on one or two jurors who believed law enforcement officers were exempt from original sin. It was a thin file, a simple charge, the perfect case for Melissa Hall to cut her prosecutorial teeth.

Mike took the file to the front desk and asked for copies. Hall came to the door of the reception area.

"Finished?" she asked.

"Yes, waiting for copies. Why the rush?"

"This case has been pending for three months. Ken wants it on the docket, and I have no reason to argue with him."

"Is the bank pushing for a speedy trial?"

"I have work to do."

"Do you have a few minutes to talk?"

Hall looked at her watch. "A few. I'll be in my office."

The secretary handed Mike the documents. He cross-checked them with the ones in the file to make sure everything was included. As he did, he compared Sam's signature at the bottom of the statement with the endorsement on the reverse of the two checks. It looked the same. There was an unusual extra loop at the bottom of the *S* that appeared in all three signatures. Mike put the copies in his briefcase.

The door to Hall's office was open, and she was on the phone. Mike knocked on the door frame. She motioned for him to come in and sit down.

"That's not going to be a problem," she said into the receiver. "Get back to me on Monday."

She hung up the phone.

"Any surprises?" she asked Mike.

"Not really."

"What did you think of the statement taken by Detective Perkins?"

"It is what it is."

Hall smiled slightly. "Mr. Andrews, I'm new at the legal business, but I made it through law school and passed the bar exam. There's no criminal admission in your client's statement; however, we believe the bank records are enough to convict Mr. Miller under the embezzlement statute. Ken talked to me about the case while you were reviewing the file, and I'd like to make an offer."

"What is it?"

"Because all the money was recovered, I can offer six months probation on the lesser included misdemeanor of illegally lending the money of a charitable organization without its consent. No jail time. No fine."

It was a good offer. If Sam had admitted committing the crime, Mike would have recommended it without reservation. Even so, an opportunity to spare Sam the dangers of prison was tempting.

"I'll discuss it with him."

"We'll leave it open for ten days. After that, it's withdrawn, and we go to trial."

Mike studied the young DA's face for a moment.

"What did you think of the judge's revelation regarding his prior contact with Miller?"

"It was the appropriate thing to do, so we can decide whether to file a motion for recusal."

"No, I mean the information my client has given the judge over the years. What do you think about that?"

"I have a personal opinion."

"What is it? Do you believe that sort of thing is real?"

Hall hesitated. "My grandmother had dreams in which she saw things before they happened."

"And you believed in her gift?"

"Yes."

Hall turned in her chair, picked up a photograph on a small table behind her desk, and handed it to Mike. A large number of people that included little children, teenagers, and adults surrounded an old woman sitting in a chair. A small white church building, not unlike the old sanctuary at Little Creek, could be seen in the background.

"My grandmother is in the center of the picture, and I'm standing beside her," Hall continued. "It was her ninetieth birthday. She lived two more years. Now, she's in heaven."

All the people in the photo were plainly dressed. Hall's grandmother wore a print dress and old-fashioned black shoes. She had a bouquet of flowers in her hand and a sweet smile on her face. A younger, gangly version of Melissa Hall stood behind the old woman's right shoulder. Mike returned the snapshot.

Hall stared at the picture that remained in her hand for a few seconds before looking up. "I'm no saint, either, but listening to your client talk about the Lord and call Him 'Papa' made me think about my grandmother. She didn't use that term, but it was the same kind of familiarity. I asked Mr. West to let me offer you a favorable plea bargain."

"And I appreciate it. Sam is odd, but all he wants to do is help other people. The more I've been around him, the less I believe he tried to steal money from the Craig Valley church."

"I disagree. My grandmother said spiritual people don't always have the character to match the gift."

"But what if Miller isn't guilty?"

Hall's face hardened. "Then you'd better convince Ken and me within the next ten days. After that, it's up to a judge or jury."

Sixteen

MIKE LEFT THE COURTHOUSE AND CALLED THE MILLER HOME. Muriel answered.

"Where is Sam this afternoon?" he asked.

"At the Bowen house."

"On Polk Street?"

"Yes. He's worked for them since before Mr. Bowen died."

Polk Street was a block from traffic light eleven. Mr. Bowen, an insurance broker, was a client of Forrest, Andrews, and Lambert for many years, and Mike had encountered him at the office several times. He didn't know his widow.

The houses on Polk Street were built in the 1920s. Most had been remodeled and updated. Mrs. Bowen lived at the end of a street in a brick home with broad holly bushes and a small, neatly manicured front yard. Large shade trees stood along the edges of the lot. Mike pulled in behind Sam's truck, which was parked beside Mrs. Bowen's older-model Cadillac. Sam wasn't in sight.

Mike walked up a driveway made of cobblestones covered by bits of moss. The backyard was enclosed in a fence. He could hear a small dog barking as he approached the white wooden gate. Mike looked into the yard, which was surprisingly large and sunny, with islands of flower beds in several places and two outdoor fountains. Near the house was an artificial pond surrounded by vines and exotic-looking plants. Mike could see why Sam would need to spend a lot of time in the yard. The yardman and a small, slender woman were standing at the rear of the lot.

"Sam!" Mike called out.

Sam and the woman turned around.

"Come in!" Sam yelled.

Mike unlatched the gate. The little brown dog nervously sniffed his ankles for a few seconds before running across the yard toward the woman. Mrs. Bowen faced him. Her gray hair was pulled back tightly in a bun, and she was wearing a dark skirt, blouse, and sweater. Sam stepped forward as Mike approached.

"Mike, do you know Mrs. Bowen?"

Mike extended his hand. Mrs. Bowen must have been at least eighty. Her fingers were slightly gnarled by arthritis, but she gripped his hand firmly. Diamonds glistened on several fingers.

"No, but I met your husband several times when I worked with Maxwell Forrest."

"Humph," Mrs. Bowen sniffed. "I still get letters from him wanting me to come in for a chat. Why should I do that? If I do, he'll ask a few questions about my bulbs then send me a bill for estate planning!"

"It's good to have your will reviewed from time to time," Mike offered.

Mrs. Bowen narrowed her eyes. "Did Maxwell Forrest send you here? I'd better not get a bill in the mail for a house call!"

"No, ma'am. I'm a minister now, not a lawyer."

Mrs. Bowen turned toward Sam. "Is that right?"

"Yep. He's one of my boys."

Mike started to protest but stopped when he saw Mrs. Bowen relax.

"Then the Lord surely is in the miracle business!" the old woman exclaimed. "A lawyer turned minister must make the angels scratch their wings in amazement!"

"Yes, ma'am," Mike agreed and turned toward Sam. "Will you have time to talk before you go home?"

"Yep. I'm finished here. Mrs. Bowen and I were visiting for a few minutes."

Sam reached into his pocket and handed the old woman a piece of paper. "Here's my bill and a word of encouragement about one of your grandsons."

"Billy?" the old woman asked.

"Yep."

Mrs. Bowen blinked her eyelids behind her glasses. They walked toward the gate.

"You have a beautiful yard," Mike said.

"I couldn't do it without Sam. We're growing old together, but I'm ahead on the race to the finish line."

"I'll be back toward the end of next week," Sam said. "The grass is beginning its spring growth spurt but won't need to be cut until then."

The old woman went into the house. Mike and Sam stepped onto the driveway.

"So, I'm one of your boys," Mike said.

"Which puts you on her prayer list," Sam replied. "It's a good place to be."

"She ought to put Maxwell Forrest on it."

Sam chuckled. "Do you think she's bitter toward him?"

"Maybe. Or mad at lawyers in general."

"I have no complaints about my lawyer. Papa picked him."

"We had our meeting with Judge Coberg this afternoon," Mike said.

Sam leaned against the side of the truck while Mike told him about the conference in the judge's chambers.

"Yep," Sam said when he finished. "The judge and I have also had a few talks when he gets his cauliflower. Did you know he's studied all the verses in the Bible about being a judge?"

"No. I need to tell the judge and DA if you want a jury trial."

"What do you think?"

"In almost all criminal cases, I recommend a jury trial."

"Okay, that's what I want."

Sam moved toward the front of the truck.

"That's not all," Mike said. "The case will be on the trial calendar in a few weeks."

The news of an impending court date stopped Sam in his tracks. He turned toward Mike.

"Then we'd better get ready. I'll try to do my part and leave the lawyering up to you."

"That's what I'm doing. I went to the DA's office and reviewed your file. I have copies of everything in my car."

After retrieving his briefcase, Mike laid out the documents on the hood of Sam's truck. "Here's the statement you gave to Detective Perkins."

Mike waited while Sam read it.

"Do you remember signing this?" Mike asked, pointing to the signature.

"Yep."

"Didn't you realize how the words could be twisted to make it look like you knew about misappropriation of funds from the checking account?"

"What?"

"That money was wrongfully transferred."

"The detective told me what happened. He wasn't lying."

"But—," Mike began then decided not to argue. "Anyway, the statement could give us trouble at trial."

He took out the checks.

"What about the signature endorsement on the back of these checks?" he asked. "It looks the same as the one at the bottom of your statement."

Sam held up the checks and squinted at them. "Yep. It looks like my handwriting."

"Is that your account number?"

"I don't have the whole thing memorized, but the last four numbers are right."

Mike waited. Sam put down the check copies but didn't say anything else.

"Well?" Mike asked.

"What?"

"How are we going to explain your apparent signature on the checks?"

"I didn't do it."

"Okay, I hope the handwriting expert agrees." Mike put the papers in his briefcase, clicked it shut, and put his hands on top of it. He spoke in measured tones. "After I reviewed the file, I talked with Melissa Hall. If you agree to plead guilty to a misdemeanor charge of illegally borrowing money from a nonprofit organization, you would receive six months on probation with no jail time or monetary fine. The offer will remain open for ten days then it will be withdrawn, and we go to trial."

"Say again?"

Mike repeated the basis and terms of the plea bargain.

"Do people do that?" Sam asked.

"What?"

"Plead guilty when they didn't do anything wrong?"

"It happens, and there are court cases that allow it. The fear of going to jail is a strong motivator. Sometimes it's easier to take something certain and avoid the possibility of a harsh sentence." Mike paused. "There is also the danger of prison. You saw what happened to you at the local jail. A state facility can be a hundred times worse."

"What are you trying to tell me? I hear fear in your voice."

"Aren't you afraid?"

Sam managed a weak smile. "I've been in tight spots in the past and always saw Papa come through in the end. Sometimes I suffered before help arrived; other times I escaped from the mouth of the lion. I'm not sure which kind of situation I'm facing. Have you ever told an innocent client to plead guilty?"

"I've had a few who told me they were innocent, but when the DA put an offer on the table they jumped on it. They were probably guilty but wouldn't admit it." Mike continued more slowly, "I've never advised an innocent client to plead guilty, but I wish I'd encouraged Danny Brewster to do so. He trusted me and would have done anything I suggested. There was an offer on the table prior to trial that would have given him twelve months in jail and the rest of his time on probation. If he'd taken a deal, he might be alive today."

"Papa kept that boy in His hand and—"

"I know," Mike interrupted. "But I can't ignore what happened when he went to prison."

Sam reached out and put his hand on Mike's shoulder. "And you wouldn't be a true pastor if you did."

Mike looked into Sam's eyes. "Do you want to consider the offer and talk it over with Muriel?"

"I'd best not mention it to Muriel. She's so worried about me going to jail, she can't rest at night. Most nights I wake up several times, but she's always been able to sleep through anything. Now, she's often awake when I come out of a dream."

"So what should I tell Melissa Hall?"

Sam looked past Mike's shoulder for a moment before answering. "Tell her Papa is going to turn her mourning into dancing and restore the song she thought she'd lost."

"And after I deliver that message, do I turn down the plea deal?"

"I don't see the apostles telling lies to get out of jail, and I don't intend to start either. How could I lose in court? I've got the best lawyer in the world."

"Don't say that about me," Mike replied.

Sam shook his head "If you think I meant you, think again."

IT WAS TOO LATE IN THE AFTERNOON TO RETURN TO THE church, so Mike drove home. Peg and Judge weren't there. Mike leafed through the mail then noticed the blinking light on the answering machine in the kitchen. He pressed the Play button.

"I know you're recording this message, which is fine with me," a voice said. "I like to record conversations, too. I'll be at the office until six o'clock. Give me a call to set up a meeting."

Mike dialed the direct number for Braxton Hodges's desk. The reporter answered on the second ring.

"Where are you?" the reporter asked.

"At home."

"What were you doing at the courthouse this afternoon?"

"Meeting with the judge on the Miller case. I didn't see you."

"I was driving by and saw you come out the front door. Are you in the mood for a hamburger tomorrow?"

"I don't have to be in the mood."

"Meet me at Brooks at noon."

"Can't you talk to me now?" Mike asked.

"No."

The phone clicked before Mike could ask another question.

THAT NIGHT, MIKE LAY AWAKE WHILE PEG SLEPT PEACEFULLY beside him. He'd been able to get his mind off Sam's case during supper and a quiet evening, but once he turned off the lights, various courtroom scenarios began flashing across his mind. He wasn't sure of the best approach to take in defending the case, and trial strategy without focus was the grist of nightmares. So, he stayed awake, not wanting to process in an unconscious state what he couldn't sort out while alert. It had been so many years since a criminal case kept him up at night that he'd forgotten the churning feeling produced by responsibility for the freedom of another human being.

And he'd never represented someone like Sam Miller. He and Muriel shared one primary goal—they didn't want Sam to go to prison.

MIKE SPENT A BUSY MORNING AT THE CHURCH. TIME WORKING on the Miller case required more efficient performance of his duties as pastor.

"Delores, write the announcements for the bulletin after contacting the chairpersons for the finance, worship, and building and grounds committees."

"I've never done that in the past," she protested.

"You're smart enough to handle it. I'll proofread the text before we send it to the printer." Mike checked his watch. "I'm late for a meeting in town at noon. Don't forget to include notice of the session meeting on Tuesday."

Mike heard Delores grumbling under her breath as he passed her desk but didn't take time to slow down and unruffle her feathers.

BRAXTON HODGES WAS STANDING AT THE OUTDOOR TABLE unwrapping his food when Mike pulled into the parking lot.

"I'll be there in a minute," Mike called out.

"Take your time. I don't like to talk with my mouth full of hamburger and onions."

Mike entered the restaurant. It was packed with customers. He waited at the counter behind a large bearded man with "Paul" embroidered on his blue work shirt.

"Three hamburgers all the way, an order of fries, and tea," Paul said.

"Not hungry today?" asked Dusty.

Paul pulled at his beard. "I had a snack a couple of hours ago."

Mike placed his order and waited. One of the twins was manning the grill while the other cooked fries and poured tea. After paying for his food, Mike went outside. Hodges was on the last bite of his hamburger. Several other men, including Paul, stood along the long wooden table. Eating rather than talking was the priority, and the table was quiet.

"Eat," Hodges said. "We'll sit in my car for a few minutes after you finish."

Hodges tossed his empty bag into a fifty-five-gallon metal drum. Mike ate as fast as he could and still enjoy his food. Hodges gave him a status report about the high school baseball team.

"They have two strong pitchers," the reporter said, "but no middle relief, and once they get into the play-offs and need a third starter, there isn't much there. The shortstop, a scrawny kid named Charlie Martin, will be the leadoff batter. I wouldn't be surprised if he bats over .400. He's impossible to strike out. The younger Hinshaw boy will get his share of home runs. His older brother was a brute, and he's about the same size."

"Who have you been talking to?"

"Coach Gott. I'm going to do a big feature on him since he's retiring after this season."

Mike ate his last french fry and took a sip of tea.

"I'm ready," Mike said.

Hodges pointed toward his car.

"This is kind of a reverse of Woodward and Bernstein, isn't it?" Mike asked as they walked across the gravel parking lot. "You're the source; I'm the one needing information."

"If you want to play that game, my code name is 'Hamburger Chili.'"

Mike opened the passenger door of the plain-looking Pontiac and pushed aside a stack of old newspapers so he could sit down. The backseat was cluttered with notepads, envelopes, empty coffee cups, and individual scraps of paper.

"Sorry about the mess," Hodges said. "In my world, deadlines come before either cleanliness or godliness."

The reporter reached into the backseat and retrieved a brown envelope.

"What do you know about the Cohulla Creek watershed?" he asked.

"Uh, it's one of the most beautiful areas this side of the Blue Ridge and a good place to catch trout on Thursday if the State Game and Fish warden stocks it on Wednesday."

"Who owns it?"

"Part utility company, part state, with a little in the hands of private investors."

"Did you know that in the 1930s there was a plan to dam the creek and create a lake at Horseshoe Bottoms to generate hydroelectric power?"

"No, I wasn't born then."

"Me either. But all those plans were scrapped when it became cheaper and easier to make electricity by burning coal than by harnessing water."

"Which is good for fishing but doesn't do a lot for the economy in general."

"You're ahead of me. Over the past three years, there has been a huge change in the percentage of ownership between utility, private, and state."

"What kind of change?"

"Utility company ownership is down to a couple hundred acres on the south side. Private owners now hold options on two thousand acres, and the state controls about six thousand acres, including Horseshoe Bottoms. There has been discussion in the legislature about selling the state's remaining share of the watershed to open the entire area for private companies that could create a deepwater lake surrounded by residential development."

Mike opened his eyes wider. "That would be one of the biggest things that ever hit this county."

"Yes. And a lot of money could be made by people in the right place at the right time. The options controlling access to Horseshoe Bottoms are already in place."

"Who holds the options?"

Hodges held up the envelope. "Companies in Nevada and New York."

"Who are the local contacts?"

"That's where it gets fuzzy, but I have an opinion. I believe the initiative for this whole project came from within Barlow County." Hodges paused. "Have you seen the new house Representative Niles is building?"

"No."

"It's a monster. Some would say a monstrosity. I've heard rumors of Italian marble, gold-plated fixtures in the bathrooms, and a bunch of other stuff a man who works in the trust department of a bank couldn't afford. He's telling everyone he hit a home run on an investment, some new stock offering he bought for pennies and sold a year later for dollars. But I'm skeptical."

"Butch Niles is getting a cut for getting this through the legislature?"

"If I printed that, it would fall in the category of unsubstantiated allegations and would result in a lawsuit putting our puny newspaper out of business. However, if my guess is true, there has been a high level of coordination between people wanting to make a lot of money, those holding political influence, and politicians with enough inside information to let the group get ahead of the curve."

"What about environmental concerns? I always thought Cohulla Creek would end up as a state park, not a huge subdivision."

"You're behind on that one. The developers' plan includes dedication of a tract for public use, a nice little picnic and camping area, but without boat access for the unwashed masses. Only landowners get to ski on the pristine waters."

"How do you know about this?"

"Through the inadvertent help of a former bank employee who now heads the accounting department at the paper. His cubicle is near mine, and I didn't want him to hear me talking to you the other night."

"He told you about this?"

Hodges shook his head. "Not exactly. I have my sources."

"Braxton, are you rummaging through the trash again?" Mike asked with a smile. "I hope you washed your hands before you ate your hamburger."

"Trash? You're in the dark ages before computers."

"You snooped on someone's computer?"

"Are you my lawyer?" the reporter asked. "This has to be confidential."

"Yes, I can handle two clients."

"His laptop. He'd brought one from home until we got him up and running on our system. Last week, he left it on when he went to the restroom, and I couldn't help but see what was on his screen. I sent the information in the file to my computer and printed it out after he left." Hodges held up the envelope. "It's in here."

"Who are you talking about?"

"Brian Dressler."

"From the Bank of Barlow County? He's one of Jack Hatcher's chief assistants."

"Not anymore."

"Why did he leave the bank?"

"I'm not sure, but it wasn't a friendly divorce. I didn't participate in his interview at the paper, but he needed a job as soon as possible and took a huge pay cut. His wife has cancer, and he needed health insurance. That's about the only employee benefit we have that's first rate."

Mike remembered Sam's dream about the hatchet, deeds of darkness, and Cohulla Creek.

"This is all juicy local gossip that I wouldn't hear sitting in my office at the church," Mike replied lightly, "but what does it have to do with Sam Miller?"

"Miller is mentioned in a memo in the file."

Mike sat up straighter in the seat. "Let me see the memo."

Hodges opened the envelope and handed a single sheet of paper to Mike, who quickly read it. It was a memo from Dressler to Hatcher about the meeting with the deacons from the Craig Valley church. It listed the check numbers, the amount of the checks, and the deposits to Sam's account. It contained no new information.

"I met with the leaders of the Craig Valley church and already know all this," Mike said.

"That doesn't surprise me, but why would that memo be in this file? Everything else has to do with the Cohulla Creek project: companies holding the options, the acreage involved, and preliminary plans for development of the property."

Mike shook his head.

Hodges leaned closer to him. "Read the last line of the memo."

Mike held up the sheet of paper and read, "*This should take care of the Miller problem. Will keep you advised.*"

"Doesn't that sound strange?" Hodges asked.

Mike shrugged. "Yes, but it's ambiguous and subject to various interpretations. Just like the statement Sam gave Detective Perkins. What expands this case beyond a routine embezzlement charge is the degree of interest Maxwell Forrest and Jack Hatcher have in what's going on, including my involvement."

"Admit it. They know you're one of the best investigative attorneys in this circuit. Ken West once told me you drove him nuts with all the time and energy you put into even little cases."

Mike grinned. "If God hadn't taken away my ego, that sort of compliment would make my head swell."

"Then use what's left of your brain. Sam Miller wrote one of his crazy letters to the president of the bank and made Hatcher think he knew there was something shady about the acquisition of the Cohulla Creek property. Hatcher tells Dressler to frame Sam on an embezzlement charge so anything the old man says, especially about the bank, will be automatically discredited."

Mike was impressed by the reporter's deductive abilities but knew that without Sam's consent he had to keep his own information private.

"If you print that story it will definitely be libelous," he said.

"I know, but you're a defense lawyer. You can say anything you want in court and get away with it. Isn't your strategy in a criminal case to put everyone on trial you can think of except your client?"

"Yes, it can be an effective way to go on the attack."

"Which is what I want to do. If you stir this thing up enough, something may break for me. A little light can dispel a lot of darkness, and a story like this would be the opportunity of a lifetime."

"Have you considered going directly to Dressler?"

Hodges shook his head. "I thought I'd leave that to you."

Seventeen

MIKE LEFT BROOKS SANDWICH HOUSE WITH A FULL STOMACH and a computer disc containing the information Braxton Hodges had obtained from Brian Dressler's computer. While driving back to the church, he debated when to call Dressler and how to bring up the subject of the memo. He decided the best approach would be to set up a face-to-face meeting as soon as possible. Delores didn't speak when he greeted her as he passed her desk.

Mike went into his office and shut the door. There were two stacks of phone messages on top of the announcements for the bulletin. Delores's work on the bulletin was accurate but without the embellishments Mike normally added to make the upcoming events more appealing. He took out his red pen to make changes then stopped. Better to leave it alone than to raise her ire. He went to the door.

"Delores, the wording of the announcements was fine. No corrections needed. However, next week I'll make sure I allocate the time to take care of it myself."

"That's better," she replied. "You've been acting more like a lawyer than a minister. Ordering me around like a twenty-year-old clerical worker, staying out of the office half the time, thinking more about one man who committed a crime than the three hundred law-abiding people depending on you here."

Mike withdrew before his face revealed his irritation at the secretary's attitude. He didn't want to see her the rest of the day, but a sudden idea drew him back to the office door.

"How is your sister?" he asked.

"Not good. We had a long talk this morning. Her husband filed for divorce and hired a sleazy lawyer who got a crooked judge to sign an order kicking her out of the house. She's checking into a motel this afternoon but has no place to go."

"Could she come up here and stay with you?"

"That wouldn't work. She's allergic to cigarette smoke."

"What about Jo Ellen Caldwell? Doesn't she have extra space?"

"Do you know her?"

"Not well. She visited the church about a year ago."

"I hadn't thought about her," Delores said thoughtfully. "That's a great idea. She has an extra room available since her granddaughter moved out. I'll call her right now."

Delores had the receiver in her hand before Mike closed the door. Impressed with his insightful suggestion, Mike began returning phone messages and included an appropriate apology for his tardiness in returning the call. After he finished the last one, he called the paper and asked for Brian Dressler.

"He left a few minutes ago," the receptionist said. "Would you like to leave a voice mail?"

"No, I don't want to leave a message," Mike said. "I'll check back tomorrow."

Mike pushed aside an unfinished financial report and inserted the Dressler disc into the computer. He scrolled through the file. Except for the memo about Sam, the data looked like benign corporate records. Mike felt slightly uneasy reading what was obviously considered confidential information by the companies furnishing it to the bank. The bank's exact role wasn't clear. Nothing in the records indicated the source for funding.

High dollar options to purchase land along the Cohulla Creek watershed had been in place for several years. Real estate options held a high degree of risk since all the earnest money, which amounted to several hundred thousand dollars, would be forfeited by the prospective buyers if the sale wasn't completed. The option contracts didn't make finalization of the sale contingent on legislative action authorizing the sale of Horseshoe Bottoms. In fact, they contained no contingencies. Thus, the original owners probably thought they were getting a great deal from out-of-town speculators. Even if Braxton Hodges didn't write a massive exposé of local corruption, the current owners' anger when they realized what the developers intended would be newsworthy.

The more recent documents confirmed the project was as big as Mike imagined. The pro forma financial data had eye-popping projections for revenue in the tens of millions. Mike didn't recognize the names of any of the people connected with the business entities; however, the last folder he opened caught his attention. It contained a letter from his old law firm as local counsel for Delvie, LLC, a Nevada limited liability company. The letter was signed by Bobby Lambert. In the letter, Bobby provided Dressler information about the credit worthiness of Delvie, LLC. However, the supporting documents mentioned in his former partner's letter weren't included on the disc. Mike shut down his computer without printing anything. The information in the files didn't span the canyon between the charges against Sam and the bank's involvement in the Cohulla Creek project.

THE FOLLOWING DAY, MIKE PHONED THE NEWSPAPER SEVERAL times but never caught Dressler at the office. He began to wonder how the new head of accounting at the paper could hold a job when he didn't show up. Finally, he called Braxton Hodges.

"Where is Dressler? He's never there, or he's avoiding my phone calls."

"It's his wife. She's taken a turn for the worse and is at the hospital receiving treatment. He won't be back in the office until next week. I should have let you know."

"Any other news on your end?"

"Plenty. It's going to be a late spring, so you'd better not plant your Silver Queen corn for another week or two. I interviewed the county extension agent, and we'll have a suggested schedule for planting all your garden vegetables in this week's paper. Don't miss it."

Mike chuckled. "I'll take that as a negative about matters of interest to me."

"Imagine the world without Silver Queen corn. Oh, Maxwell Forrest never called me back about any correspondence from Miller and Hatcher."

"Which doesn't mean much."

"Except that he doesn't want to talk to me, a sure sign of something to hide."

"Talk about media bias. Have you considered that some people are afraid to talk to reporters?"

"And lawyers. But does that apply to your old boss?"

"No," Mike admitted. "Mr. Forrest isn't intimidated by anyone."

MIKE DELAYED LETTING MELISSA HALL KNOW ABOUT SAM'S decision rejecting the plea bargain and desire for a jury trial. It was a week before the deal would expire, and in spite of Sam's clear instructions to nix any offer, Mike didn't want to eliminate any option prematurely.

The following morning, he woke up later than usual. He'd stayed up working on his sermon, and while it wasn't yet up to his usual standards, he was satisfied that all the main points were properly organized. Peg wasn't in bed when he opened his eyes. He went downstairs in his pajamas and bare feet and found Peg in the kitchen with a coffee cup and an open notebook on the table in front of her. She put down her pen when he entered the room.

"What are you working on?" he asked.

"Writing down a dream I had last night."

"You never remember your dreams except bits and pieces that don't make sense."

"I remembered this one. It was so vivid."

"Tell me."

Peg hesitated. "Not until I have time to think about what it might mean. It may be important in a religious way."

"I'm a minister. I've been dreaming for years. Trust my experience and training."

Peg smiled. "How many classes in dream interpretation did you take in seminary?"

"None."

"That's what I thought. If you had, I'm sure you would have made an A, but I may call Sam Miller and ask him about it. He has a lot of experience."

"Wait a minute. I'm Sam's protégé, and he didn't say anything about God giving you dreams."

"Jealous?"

Mike poured a cup of coffee and took a sip.

"I'm not in danger of violating the tenth-commandment prohibition against jealousy when it comes to my wife," he teased, "but don't make me wait six months before you let me know what you really think."

As soon as he said the words, Mike wished he could take them back. Peg's face fell. She closed her notebook.

"Were the words in your sermon the other day about forgiveness just a minister talking down to his congregation?" she asked.

"No, it came straight from wrestling with our situation. I meant every word."

"It's a new day. Do I need to ask you to forgive me?"

"No. I'm sorry," Mike responded quickly. "I shouldn't have said that. I know what you said on the mountain was from your heart, and I received it that way. Seeing the glow on your face Sunday was worth the pain."

"Is that what you really think?" Peg asked.

"Yes, and I respect your right to keep the dreams to yourself until you feel comfortable sharing them. Call Sam Miller if you like. I'm sure he'll be glad to help if he can."

Judge, as if knowing Peg needed to be comforted, came over to her. She patted the dog on the head.

"I was thinking about going over to Cohulla Creek today," Mike said. "Would you like to go with me?"

"No. My energy level isn't very high this morning. I'd better stay here and take it easy."

"You're not sick, are you?"

"No, pregnant. Are you going to park and ride your bike?"

"Yes."

"Then take Judge with you; he'll enjoy it."

PEG WASN'T IN SIGHT WHEN MIKE PREPARED TO LEAVE. JUDGE, sensing an outing, paced back and forth across the kitchen floor.

"Peg!" Mike yelled up the staircase.

"Bye!" she called back.

Mike climbed several steps of the stairs. He wanted to clear the air between them. Judge barked and scratched at the door. Not sure what to say, Mike retreated down the stairs.

WITH JUDGE ON THE SEAT BEHIND HIM AND HIS BIKE IN A RACK on the roof, Mike drove west of Shelton. The main access road to Cohulla Creek was about a mile from Sam Miller's house. Mike turned onto a gravel road. Within a few hundred yards, he began to notice red and orange survey ribbons tied to the lower limbs of trees. The color had faded from some of the ribbons, but others appeared fresh. Survey ribbons marked more than boundaries; they were the first sign of permanent change coming to the woods.

The road crossed the creek on a one-lane bridge. A fisherman wearing hip waders stood at the edge of the water below the bridge. Focused on his line, he didn't look up when Mike drove by. The emerging leaves shaded the road as it skirted a small hill then emptied into a parking area where fishermen left their vehicles. Mike parked beside a white pickup truck. From this point forward, the road remained passable for vehicles but received less maintenance and became more dirt than gravel.

Judge bounded out the door and immediately put his nose to the ground. Mike unhooked his bike and lifted it from the roof rack. He slipped on a small backpack and whistled for Judge, who had ventured down the road.

To Mike, a mountain bike earned its name if used to climb hills and mountains. Hopping curbs in Shelton didn't count. The red paint on his bike was nicked from contact with rocks and trees. Only once had he hurtled over the handlebars. During a ride in Virginia, his wheel had slipped into a deep rut, causing him to become airborne. His helmet slammed against an exposed tree root. Stunned for a few seconds, Mike recovered and continued.

He'd ridden along Cohulla Creek shortly after they moved back to Shelton, but because it was relatively flat, and he wasn't a fisherman, the route dropped off his list. Mike enjoyed the physical workout required in a climb followed by the exhilaration of reaching a high place of perspective above the world below. The Cohulla Creek watershed didn't offer any thigh-burning challenges.

He pedaled upstream. The dirt road stayed close to the creek for several hundred yards then rose slightly until the stream lay thirty or forty feet below on the right. Mike pedaled at an easy rate. Judge loped alongside him. The dog could maintain his pace as long as Mike's legs could pedal the bike. More survey ribbons appeared at various intervals then stopped when they passed onto land owned by the state. Two vehicles containing fishermen passed them on the road. The ground rose sharply on the opposite side of the creek, but on the roadside, Mike could easily envision areas for housing development. The road dipped down and rejoined the creek, which slowed and broadened in a flat, wooded area. They'd reached Horseshoe Bottoms.

Mike stopped and looked behind him. He wondered how far upstream the lake would extend. Without a doubt, it would be a magnificent setting—a mountain finger-lake filled with clear, cool water surrounded by gentle hills. Mike would enjoy stepping onto the front porch of a home on one of the hills to inhale a view.

Mike remounted his bike. The road split in two, climbing into the hills to the left and continuing near the stream on the right. He'd not remembered the fork in the road.

"Which way, boy?" he asked Judge, who was sniffing the air.

The dog padded onto the road into the hills. It looked like a newer cut.

"That's the way I wanted to go," Mike said, slipping his feet into his toe clips and shifting into a lower gear.

Sure enough, it was a new track that ascended the hill in a series of short switchbacks. Large rock gravel spread on the road made the ride bumpy. Mike had to hold the handlebars tightly. He came around the corner into a cleared area. A new silver SUV was parked beneath a large oak tree. Mike slowed to a stop beside a large poplar tree. The front doors of the SUV opened.

Maxwell Forrest and Jack Hatcher got out.

Even on a Saturday far back in the woods, Mr. Forrest was wearing a starched shirt and silk tie. Hatcher, his brown hair closely cropped in military fashion, was dressed casually. The back doors of the SUV opened, and two men Mike didn't recognize stepped onto the ground. Mr. Forrest raised his hand in greeting. Mike resisted the urge to jump on his bike and ride down the hill. His flight response was immediately replaced by anger at the thought of the letter Mr. Forrest had written him. Mike leaned the bike against a tree. Judge, his tongue hanging out as he panted, stood beside him.

"You've come a long way to see me," Forrest said. "It would be a lot easier to catch me in town."

"I thought I was banned from the office," Mike replied.

Hatcher cut in. "Good to see you, Mike. What are you doing out here?"

"Just going for a ride in the woods with my dog. Sorry to disturb you."

"You're not disturbing anything," Hatcher replied. "Meet Dick Bunt and Troy Linden."

Two men in their fifties, one bald and the other with a thick head of salt-and-pepper hair, stepped closer and shook his hand. Mike tried to remember if he'd seen their names while reviewing the information supplied by Braxton Hodges. Linden sounded familiar, but he couldn't be sure.

"Nice dog," said Bunt, the bald man. "I have a friend in San Bernardino who has a vizsla. What's your dog's name?"

"Judge," Mike replied.

Bunt laughed. "I've seen a few judges I considered dogs. Does he have a last name?"

"No, that might get me into trouble."

"Mike is a lawyer who used to work with Maxwell," Hatcher said. "Now he's gone into the ministry."

"Except for one case," Forrest grunted.

"How long have you been the pastor at the church?" Hatcher continued.

"Almost three years."

"The bank financed their new sanctuary," Hatcher said to the other men. "As soon as Mike came on the scene, the congregation began to grow by leaps and bounds."

"What brings you gentlemen so far into the woods?" Mike asked.

"Showing Dick and Troy around."

"Beautiful area," Bunt added.

"Yes," Mike said, nodding. "But it looks as though things are about to change. Someone used several rolls of survey ribbons along the road. If I had to guess, I'd say these hills are about to be carved for residential development."

Hatcher spoke. "That's happening all over this part of the country."

"Yes, it's one of the reasons we've had so much growth at the church," Mike said as he turned toward the two strangers. "Are you gentlemen real estate developers?"

"I've dabbled in it," Bunt replied. "Troy and I are always looking for business opportunities, but most of our work has been in the commercial real estate area."

"What part of the country?" Mike asked.

"All over. We're not limited."

"Anything in Las Vegas?" Mike asked.

"Why do you ask about Las Vegas?"

"Maybe it's your accent," Mike replied. "It sounds western, but not Texas."

Bunt stared at Mike. Forrest cut in, "Mike, could we have a private chat?"

"So long as we don't go to your office."

Forrest walked away from the vehicle toward the edge of the clearing. The other three men moved in the opposite direction. Judge, his breathing returned to normal, sniffed the ground around the SUV.

"Don't lose your salvation over the letter I sent you," Forrest said. "Look at the situation from my side. The bank has an interest in the successful prosecution of an individual who embezzled money from one of its customers. I can't give you access to our building where bank files are kept until this matter is dealt with, one way or another."

"Is there anything in your files that would impact my client's case?"

"I don't see how there could be, but that isn't the point. I can't compromise the confidentiality of the firm's attorney-client relationship with the bank." Forrest paused. "Even for one of the best lawyers I've known since opening my office in this county forty years ago."

"A phone call before you sent the letter would have been nice."

"I probably should have done that, but I've been very busy. Too busy. The firm is undergoing changes. Park is leaving. Arnold is smart and has a great future, but he's not ready to assume primary responsibility for major clients."

"Any replacements on the horizon?"

"Not yet, and until that happens, Bobby and I will be spending most of our time chained to our desks."

"Except Saturdays along Cohulla Creek."

"With businessmen who have a right to keep their plans private," Forrest responded. "Where were you going with your cross-examination of Mr. Bunt?"

"Who knows? You stopped me."

"Don't play that game. I trained you to know the answers to questions before you asked them. You're right about the survey ribbons. It's no secret. There are options on record at the courthouse, although I have no idea why you would care. You're not a trout fisherman or an environmentalist."

"Just a bike-riding preacher who still doesn't understand why a busy, important lawyer like you is so interested in Sam Miller."

"I told you. I'm looking out for the bank's reputation."

"I hear you, Mr. Forrest, but that's not enough. My client has been offered a sweet deal to plead guilty, but I can't advise him what to do without access to the bank's records. That's the only way I can properly evaluate the charges against him."

"If he's guilty, let him plead. I'm sure the district attorney's office has the pertinent information. Have you filed a motion—"

"They've allowed me to copy the entire file."

"What was in it?"

"Not much. Copies of two checks along with records for the accounts involved."

"What else do you want? That's all the bank would have in its records."

"There must have been an internal investigation before the matter was referred to the sheriff's office. And I'd also like to know about any communication between the bank and my client."

"Your client should have copies of anything the bank sent him, and he'd be aware of anything coming from his end."

"Miller cuts grass for a living. His filing system is a shoe box in the bottom of a closet."

"His lack of organization isn't the bank's problem."

"I know, but it will become the bank's problem when I file a subpoena dragging a bank officer into court so I can take a look at what they have. I don't want to do that, and it shouldn't be necessary."

Forrest glanced over at the other men. "I'll talk to Hatcher about it," he replied. "But not today. This meeting doesn't have anything to do with your client. And my advice to you the other day still stands. You have no business practicing law as a hobby."

"When will I hear from you?" Mike asked.

"Don't give me a deadline," Forrest replied, his jaw set. "I'll get to it. You can count on it."

They started walking toward the other men. Bunt and Linden got into the SUV.

"Good to see you, Mike," Hatcher said as he opened the driver's-side door. "We need to be on our way. Be careful on your ride. I bet the gravel on this road makes it hard to maneuver on a bicycle."

"I'm used to it," Mike answered. "Maneuvering in tough places is part of the fun."

Hatcher backed out of the parking area and started down the hill. Mike didn't want to inhale a cloud of dust by following too closely behind them and waited several minutes. He poured some water into a plastic bowl and set it on the ground in front of Judge, who greedily lapped it up.

"What did you think about those men?" Mike asked the dog.

Judge didn't respond. His focus in life didn't extend beyond the liquid at the end of his nose.

MIKE CAREFULLY COASTED DOWN THE HILL TO HORSESHOE Bottoms. By the time he reached the main road, there wasn't any dust in the air caused by the departure of the SUV. Mike retraced his route along the creek road.

Just before the road began to climb to its vantage point above the stream, he veered toward the water and stopped at a creek-side campsite. A well-used fire ring made from rocks taken from the streambed lay in the middle of the clearing. Judge began a circular reconnaissance and quickly unearthed a candy wrapper. While the dog investigated the smells left by campers, Mike walked down to the creek. The water rushed along at a rapid clip. Mike sat on a large rock, watched the water swirl by, and listened to the sounds of the stream. He wondered if this was the spot Sam Miller liked to visit.

Taking off his shoes, Mike dipped his feet into the water. Spring might be in the air, but the water in Cohulla Creek hadn't received the news. It felt ice cold. Mike left his feet in the water until they became slightly numb, then put on his socks and shoes. He returned to the campsite. In search of fresh scents, Judge had ventured farther into the woods. Mike unzipped his backpack to get a snack bar and saw the message light flashing on his phone. Maintaining an adequate service signal in the woods was difficult, but he had a single bar. Mike pressed the button to retrieve his message and waited. It was Peg.

"Please call me! I'm at the emergency room. I'm bleeding, and the doctor is going to order an ultrasound!"

Eighteen

PEG DIDN'T ANSWER WHEN HE HIT THE SPEED-DIAL NUMBER for her cell phone. Mike left a voice mail that he was on the way then mounted his bike. Pedaling furiously, he tore along the road. Mike had read in a pregnancy brochure that prenatal bleeding often occurred during the first trimester of a pregnancy. But that didn't lessen his concern. Peg wouldn't have gone to the doctor unless she thought the situation might be serious. Judge gamely tried to keep up but began to lag behind. Mike came around a corner and waited for the dog to rejoin him and continued at a pace the dog could manage. There was no use sprinting ahead; he'd have to wait for Judge at the end of the ride anyway.

Mike rounded a corner and skidded into the parking area. He quickly locked his bike onto the rack. Judge hopped into the car and lay down in the backseat. Skidding around corners, Mike didn't encounter any other vehicles on the way out of the wilderness area. He reached the main highway and tried Peg's number again, but there was no answer.

The Barlow County Hospital was outside the Shelton city limits on the south side of town. Mike reached the parking lot for the emergency room and saw Peg's car. He dashed through the sliding doors, rushed up to the desk, and introduced himself.

"Your wife is in zone three," the attendant told him. "I'll have someone take you to her."

Mike waited impatiently until a nurse's aide appeared and led him into the treatment area. Peg lay in a bed in a room divided by a white curtain. Her eyes were closed. Mike leaned over her.

"Peg," he whispered intensely. "It's me."

She opened her eyes. They looked listless.

"The pain," she said, touching her abdomen. "It was horrible."

"What's wrong?"

"I don't know. They did an ultrasound, but Dr. Hester hasn't talked to me."

"Do you still hurt?"

"Not as much. They gave me something to stop the pain. I didn't want anything, but they said it wouldn't hurt the baby."

"Is the baby okay?"

"I don't know. The technician who did the test wouldn't tell me anything."

Mike pulled a chair to the edge of the bed and held Peg's hand. It was shocking how quickly she'd gone from vibrant energy to lethargy. He heard footsteps. A short, dark-haired man entered and introduced himself as Dr. Hester. A female nurse accompanied him.

"The baby appears fine on the ultrasound," the doctor began.

Mike exhaled in relief. Peg nodded slightly.

"Thank God," she said.

"How are your cramps?" the doctor asked.

"Better, but I'm afraid it's because of the medication."

"It's safe. That's why we gave it to you."

"What's causing this?" Mike asked.

"Bleeding and cramps this severe can be the precursor to a miscarriage, but fortunately the placenta appears intact. I want her to stay in the ER until we're sure the bleeding has stopped, then I'll let her go home to bed rest."

"Total bed rest?"

"Until she sees her obstetrician. I called Dr. Crawford, and she concurs. Make an appointment with her the first of the week."

"Can she walk up steps?"

"Do you have a downstairs bedroom?"

"Yes."

"Put her there. The next few days are about avoiding unnecessary strain of any type."

The doctor left, and Peg closed her eyes. Seconds later they popped open.

"Where's Judge?" she asked.

"In the car with the windows cracked. He's passed out in the backseat, as worn out as you are."

"Take him home, then come back for me."

"I'm not going anywhere."

Peg didn't argue. She closed her eyes. Two hours later, an orderly rolled her to the curb. Mike held the door open so she could get in the car. Judge, his tail wagging, watched.

"What about my car?" she asked.

"Why did you drive in the first place? You could have called Marla or Elizabeth."

"Marla wasn't home, and I thought it would be quicker to come myself."

"We'll figure out how to get your car later. First, I want to get you home and into bed."

Peg was more alert during the ride home.

"I don't need to ask Sam Miller about my dream," she said as they reached traffic light six.

"Why not?"

"Because I think I know what it meant."

"Do you want to tell me?"

Peg paused before responding. "Yes. I was sitting in a lounge chair on the top deck of a huge cruise ship. I was alone, which was odd because you know how they're always jammed with people. If I wanted something, all I had to do was ring a little bell, and a waiter would bring it to me. I ate the best fruit you can imagine. I thought about getting up but decided there was no better place to be on the boat than resting in the chair."

"Were you pregnant?"

"Not that I remember."

"Why did you think it was a religious dream?"

"Because in addition to the crew assigned to take care of me, there were angels present."

"How did you know they were angels? Did they have wings?"

"No."

"Then how did you know?"

"I'm not sure. I just did. That's one of the things I still want to ask Sam."

Mike's face was troubled. A dream about angels, especially before a trip to the hospital, worried him.

They arrived home. Judge, revived by his long nap in the car, ran around the corner of the house. Mike tried to help steady Peg as she got out of the car, but she shooed him away.

"I'm not an invalid. I can walk to the downstairs bedroom. Just get me into bed so I can dream about my cruise ship."

Mike opened the door of the house for her.

"Was I on the cruise?"

Peg stepped up into the kitchen. "I'm not sure. If you put on a waiter's uniform it might come back to me."

Mike managed a slight smile. The return of Peg's wit was a sign of health.

THE DOWNSTAIRS BEDROOM WAS AT THE REAR OF THE HOUSE next to the computer room. For years, Peg had used it as her art studio and emergency dumping ground for items that needed to be quickly removed from sight when guests arrived. Mike opened the door. To his surprise, it was as neat and tidy as a photograph in a home decorating magazine.

"What happened in here?" he asked.

"Nesting urge. I cleaned it out last week without any idea I'd be using it myself."

Mike pulled back the covers. Peg slipped off her shoes and climbed into bed.

"I'll put on my pajamas later," she said. "The medication is making me tired."

Mike tucked her in and kissed her on the forehead.

"I'll put on my ship waiter's uniform while you sleep," he said, trying to be more lighthearted than he felt. "I want to be a part of both your conscious and unconscious lives. Should I close the door?"

"Open is fine. Judge might want to lie on the floor beside the bed."

An hour later, Peg woke up hungry. Mike opened a can of soup. While it was heating up on the stove, he called Sam Miller. Muriel answered the phone, and Mike told her what had happened.

"Is her mother coming?" Muriel asked.

"She lives in Philadelphia and has severe arthritis. She needs daily assistance herself."

"Then I'd like to come over and help out."

"Uh, let me check with Peg."

When Mike turned around, Peg was standing in the doorway.

"What are you doing out of bed?"

"I had to go to the bathroom. Who are you talking to?"

Mike kept his hand over the receiver. "Muriel Miller. She wants to come over and help. I wasn't sure if you wanted one of your friends or someone from the church—"

"Tell her yes," Peg said, turning toward the bedroom.

Mike lifted the receiver. "We don't want to impose on you, but that would be great."

"Sam should be home in a few minutes. I'll get him to bring me."

MIKE WAS IN THE COMPUTER ROOM REVISING HIS SERMON when the doorbell rang. Sam and Muriel Miller stood on the front landing. Muriel stepped into the front hall. Mike led the way.

"Peg is in a bedroom behind the stairs."

Peg was sitting up in bed reading a book. Her face lit up when she saw the older woman.

"Thanks for coming," she said.

Muriel came to the side of the bed and took Peg's hand in hers.

"Tell me what happened."

Mike left the bedroom and returned to the front door. Sam remained outside, staring up at the edge of the roof. Mike joined him and looked up as well.

"Is there a problem?" Mike asked.

"Nope, this is a Passover house. The angel of death isn't going to stop here."

"How can you tell?"

"By the blood."

"You see blood on my house?"

"Yep."

"Sam, that's gross."

"You wouldn't think so if you knew it meant your firstborn son is going to live and not die."

Mike stared hard at Sam. "And Peg will be all right, too?"

"She's going to have the boy. Beyond that, I can't say. The two of you may have to go through Pharaoh's testing."

"Pharaoh's testing?"

"To prove what is in your heart."

"You're mixing your metaphors. The plagues were for the Egyptians, not the Israelites, and the Passover came after the plagues, not before."

"It did, but Papa works in circles, not lines. He'll give the promise then let our circumstances take us around the back side of the mountain before fulfilling it. The blood on your house will work, but its power isn't proven until your faith and obedience overcome the challenges against it."

"I'm not sure what that means, but you must have been reading in Exodus this week."

"Nope. I'm in Lamentations."

Mike hesitated a moment then told him about Peg's dream. "The angels worried me. That's why I asked you if she was going to be all right."

"There are plenty of messengers around here, not just in heaven. I'll think on it, but don't be too quick to believe it's bad. Even a dream with warning often has a way of escape."

"What should I do?"

"Take care of her. Your part is easy."

"Okay," Mike said. "Come inside. We also need to talk about your case."

The two men went into the kitchen.

"Do you know what I see in here?" Sam asked.

"No idea."

Sam pointed at a fruit bowl on the counter next to the refrigerator.

"A bunch of perfectly ripe bananas."

"Would you like one?"

"Yep."

Mike handed Sam a banana.

"Make sure Peg eats one tonight," Sam said. "She needs plenty of potassium."

"Yes, Doc," Mike replied.

Sam peeled the banana. They sat at the kitchen table while Mike told him about the information obtained from Dressler's computer.

"Do you know Dressler?" Mike asked.

"Nope."

"I want to talk to him, but he hasn't returned my phone calls. His wife is—" Mike stopped.

"What?" Sam asked.

"Dressler's wife is in the hospital receiving treatment for cancer. Peg's car is in the parking lot at the emergency room, and I need to pick it up. Could you give me a ride over there? Maybe we can talk to Dressler."

During the drive to the hospital, Mike told Sam about his bike ride along Cohulla Creek and the encounter with Mr. Forrest and Jack Hatcher near Horseshoe Bottoms. Sam listened without interrupting.

"What do you think?" Mike asked when he finished. "If this was a movie, it would be a good place for the Lord to tell you something specific that will help me defend you."

Sam shrugged. "Believe me, I'd like more light myself. Cohulla Creek is a pretty spot. Years ago, I would go for long walks far back into those woods. I'd hate to see it ruined."

They parked beside Peg's car and walked around to the hospital's main entrance. Babies were born in Shelton, broken bones set, and minor surgery performed, but serious cases were whisked to Asheville or beyond. It puzzled Mike that Dressler's wife was receiving care at the local hospital. There were only two floors to the facility. They approached the information desk.

"Mrs. Dressler's room, please," Mike said.

An older woman serving as the volunteer on duty punched a few keys and looked at her computer screen.

"Room 237."

They walked down a spotless hallway to the elevator area. Mike pushed the Up button. The elevators at the Barlow County Hospital were nursing-home slow. It took an incredibly long time to travel up one floor. Mike fidgeted while they waited for the elevator door to open.

"If Dressler is here, let me do the talking," Mike said.

"Are you going to tell me that every time we go somewhere?"

"Yes, until further notice. Keep all your blood-on-the-doorpost comments to yourself."

The elevator door opened, and an orderly rolled out an old woman on a gurney so Mike and Sam could enter. At the second level, Mike impatiently waited for the door to open then walked quickly down the hall. Sam lagged behind.

"Come on," Mike called over his shoulder.

Sam didn't respond. Mike reached room 237 as a nurse exited.

"Is Mr. Dressler here?" Mike asked.

"No, I think he left to get something to eat."

"Did he say when he'd be back?"

"No, but he's never gone for long."

Mike turned to Sam.

"We could wait in the lobby and catch him on the way in. I don't want to intrude into his time with his wife—"

While Mike talked, Sam pushed open the door to the room.

"Where are you going?" Mike asked sharply. "We don't know these people."

Sam didn't respond but continued into the room. Mike looked up and down the hallway. No one seemed to be paying attention. He followed Sam into the room.

The woman in the bed was a bony silhouette beneath the sheets with a single IV tube attached to her left hand. She looked old, but after a closer look, Mike suspected she was in her mid-fifties.

It didn't take medical training to see she was near death. Four times since becoming a minister, Mike had been present when someone died, and on two occasions he'd heard the telltale breathing pattern that signaled the end. He stopped just inside the door. Sam walked directly up to the bed, held the woman's hand for a second, and gently touched her on the cheek.

"Marie," Sam said. "Papa sent me to you."

"No," Mike began, then stopped.

The ragged breathing continued. Mike stepped to the end of the bed and watched.

Sam leaned over and began speaking into the dying woman's ear. Mike couldn't hear what he said. Mike nervously glanced at the door. There could be an ugly scene if Brian Dressler walked in while two strange men hovered around his helpless wife. Sam touched two of his fingers to his tongue and placed them on the woman's forehead. He sighed loudly several times and blew into the woman's face. He seemed to be watching something closely then straightened up and turned to Mike.

"We can go now."

Relieved, Mike moved toward the door. In a few seconds, they would be in the hallway where they could either leave or wait for Dressler. He glanced back to make sure Sam was in tow. When he stepped forward, he collided with the wooden door as it opened into the room. Stunned, Mike staggered backward.

"What the—," Dressler said.

Mike put out his hand and touched the wall.

"Sorry," he said as his head cleared. "We were stepping out of the room to wait for you."

Dressler stared at Mike but didn't move out of the way.

"Andrews, isn't it?" he asked.

"That's right, Mike Andrews."

Dressler extended his hand. "I remember you from Maxwell Forrest's office. I heard you went into the ministry. Thanks for coming. Marie and I don't have a pastor to help us and haven't attended church in years."

"That's okay," Mike managed. "And this is my friend, Sam."

Dressler shook Sam's hand.

"We should have waited in the hall," Mike began.

"No problem. You just startled me. I've been here by myself for a couple of days. No one has visited." Dressler paused. "You may not have heard, but I'm no longer with the bank."

"I know," Mike replied. "Braxton Hodges is the one who told me about your wife."

"I see. Please, sit down."

There were two wooden chairs in front of the air-conditioning unit and a comfortable chair that could be converted into a nighttime couch. Mike and Sam sat in the wooden chairs.

"Hospice nurses were coming to the house," Dressler continued, "but she reached the point that I couldn't handle the in-between times."

"Braxton told me she was receiving treatment for the cancer," Mike said.

"No, we're finished with all that." Dressler looked at the floor. "There's nothing to do but wait. She's been unconscious for three days. The doctor said she might go anytime."

"Her eyes are open," Sam said.

Sure enough, Marie Dressler's eyes were open, and she was staring at the ceiling.

"Marie!" Dressler said.

When Dressler spoke, his wife's eyes moved in the direction of his voice. The dying woman began moving her lips and making sounds, but Mike couldn't distinguish the words. Dressler immediately leaned over with his ear close to her mouth. Mike caught a few words but had no idea what she was saying. He glanced at Sam, who was sitting with his eyes closed, a slight smile on his face, and his hands clasped in front of his stomach. Mike looked back at Dressler. As his wife continued whispering to him, the former banker's left cheek revealed the trail of a tear. Dressler remained riveted in front of his wife's face.

In a few moments, he kissed his wife on the forehead near the spot Sam had touched with his fingers. Then, he leaned over and spoke into her right ear. The woman's eyes remained open but revealed no emotion. When Dressler withdrew, she closed her eyes and continued breathing with a steady pace that didn't sound like the harbinger of death. Dressler sat down with a thud and closed his eyes.

The three men sat in silence for several minutes. In most circumstances, the enforced quiet would have felt awkward, but at the time it seemed the natural thing to do. Finally, Dressler looked up.

"I shouldn't have ignored you—," he began.

"Is everything okay now?" Sam asked.

Dressler nodded.

"Including what happened in Mobile?"

"She was speaking so softly, how could you hear?" Dressler responded in surprise. "Did you read her lips?"

"That's not important. What matters is that she can run free into the arms of the Master. She needed His forgiveness and yours."

"But she was more in the right than I was." Dressler shook his head. "It made me mad at God when she became sick. I should have been the one to suffer."

"But Papa is good enough to let both of you make amends."

Sam turned to Mike. "I'm finished here. Why don't you pray together while I step into the hallway?"

Before Mike could respond, Sam rose from his seat and left the room. Mike watched the door shut behind him then turned to Dressler, who had a puzzled look on his face. Mike wasn't prepared to explain Sam's actions and didn't want any questions.

"May I pray for you?" he asked quickly.

Dressler nodded.

Mike bowed his head and closed his eyes. He spoke hesitantly at first but in a few moments gained confidence. Words started coming easily. As soon as he finished one sentence, the next one stood ready to take its place. Several times, words of familiar Bible verses prompted his requests for Brian and Marie Dressler. He didn't rush, but let the pace of the prayer form as his inward impressions set the tempo. He continued until nothing remained to say except "Amen."

He glanced up into Brian Dressler's face. Marie's eyes remained closed, but the banker's eyes were at peace. He reached across and shook Mike's hand.

"Thank you, thank you," he said warmly. "While you were praying, it seemed the weight of the world rolled off my shoulders. The past few months have been unbelievably difficult."

"You're welcome."

Mike stood.

"Tell the other man from your church how much I appreciate you coming," Dressler said.

Mike tried to think of a smooth segue into legal matters, but when he saw Marie Dressler's serene face over her husband's shoulder, he didn't have the heart to bring it up. He took a step backward toward the door.

"I will. Call if I can help you."

MIKE RETURNED TO THE HALLWAY; SAM WASN'T IN SIGHT. MIKE approached the nurses' station and handed his card to the woman behind the counter.

"I'm a minister helping the Dressler family. Can I be placed on the list to obtain information about her condition?"

The woman took the card. "I'll clear it with her husband."

"Of course." Mike glanced down the hall, but there was still no sight of Sam. "Did you see a heavyset, white-haired man come out of Mrs. Dressler's room?" he asked the nurse.

"No, but I just returned from break."

Mike walked slowly down the hallway, peering into rooms with open doors, half expecting to see Sam leaning over someone he'd never met. But there was no sign of him. Mike returned to the elevator and downstairs to the main lobby. Sam was sitting in a chair reading the newspaper.

"What are you doing?" Mike asked.

"Not what we thought when we came here tonight."

"Yes, that's true," Mike admitted. "After I prayed, I couldn't bring myself to ask Dressler any questions about your case. I'll have to find another time to bring it up."

"That's okay. Have you noticed how most people thought the Master should be doing one thing, but He was often interested in doing something else?"

"Yes."

"Why is that?"

Mike thought a moment. "Because He only did what He saw His Father doing."

"Yep. And living that way is what this life is all about. Tonight did more for my case than a bunch of those motions you filed at the courthouse."

They walked out into the night air. With the setting of the sun, air from the mountains drifted down on Shelton. Even in the middle of summer, evenings were often cool. Mike shivered slightly.

"Where did you meet Marie Dressler?" he asked Sam as they stepped from the sidewalk to the parking lot.

"In that hospital room."

"I mean before tonight."

"Never."

"Then how did you know her name?"

Sam grinned. "It's on the plastic bracelet they wrap around your wrist when you come into the hospital."

Mike chuckled. "Okay. But it didn't say anything about Mobile on the bracelet, did it?"

"No, Papa shared that with me."

"Are you going to tell me about it?"

"Nope. That stuff is washed from the record books of heaven."

They neared the cars.

"Is she going to live?" Mike asked.

"Yep. I believe she'll live forever. I threw her a lifeline, and she grabbed hold of it with all her might. Her flesh is weak, but her spirit is willing."

"But what about here on earth? Is she going to get well? I've never seen a miraculous recovery from terminal cancer."

"Oh, it can happen. But I don't want to be presumable."

"You mean, presumptuous."

"That, too."

Nineteen

Monday morning, Peg was examined by Dr. Crawford, her obstetrician, who kept her homebound and on bed rest until her next appointment. Peg tried to protest, but the doctor wouldn't entertain debate.

"Peg, at your age it's not the time to take chances. We'll monitor the baby with monthly ultrasounds during the rest of the pregnancy. If everything looks fine, I'll let you get up during the third trimester. Maybe earlier, but no promises."

Peg was glum when Mike opened the car door for her.

"Do you feel like stopping by the hospital for a few minutes?" he asked as they left the doctor's office. "I'd like to check on Marie Dressler, the woman Sam and I visited on Friday evening."

"I don't see how I can protest. According to Dr. Crawford, I'm at your mercy for the next eight months."

"No, according to your cruise ship dream, it's the other way around."

Mike drove to the hospital and parked in a clergy spot.

"I'll be right back," he said. "I won't be long."

"Don't rush. I'm not going to run away."

There was more activity on the ward than there had been Friday evening. Several people joined him in the slow-motion ride to the second floor. Mike walked past the nurses' station to Marie Dressler's room. The door was shut. Mike knocked and waited, but there was no answer. He pushed open the door and looked inside.

The room was empty, the bed neatly made.

Mike's heart skipped at the possibility the sick woman had gone home. He opened the closet. No personal belongings remained in the room.

He returned to the nurses' station and introduced himself.

"Did Marie Dressler go home?" he asked.

"No, she expired Saturday morning."

"Expired?"

"Yes, she died at 5:46 a.m."

Mike deflated. "Where was the body taken?"

"It was picked up by Lingerhalter's Funeral Home."

Mike returned to the car.

"How is she?" Peg asked.

"Dead," Mike answered flatly.

"Oh."

Mike phoned Braxton Hodges at the newspaper.

"I met with Dressler at the hospital on Friday, but we didn't talk about the case," Mike said. "When I came back this morning, I found out his wife died on Saturday. Do you know anything about the arrangements?"

"We received a group e-mail this morning that the funeral service and burial will be in Mobile."

"Any idea when Dressler will return?"

"I'm not sure. I'd be surprised if he hangs around the newspaper. A guy like him can relocate and find a higher paying job at a bank."

"Let me know when he shows up."

"Sure. I want to get to the bottom of this as much as you do."

"I thought she might recover," Mike said to Peg when he hung up the phone. "I've never had a hospital visit like the one Friday night."

"Tell me about it."

Mike gave her the details. Peg listened without comment until the end.

"How old was she?"

"I'm guessing in her mid-fifties, but she looked older."

"Did they have children?"

"I don't know. It didn't come up."

Judge bounded past them and around to the backyard when they opened the garage door.

"With me out of commission, how is he going to get his exercise?" Peg asked. "He needs a good run every day."

"That will fall on me."

The next morning, Mike rolled out of the smaller bed he shared with Peg in the downstairs bedroom and stumbled into a jogging suit. He disdained skintight cycling gear and forbade Peg from buying him formfitting black shorts or aerodynamic nylon shirts for Christmas. "Don't be too hard on him," Peg mumbled as Mike tied his shoelaces.

"Are you talking to me or Judge?"

Peg rolled over and snuggled deeper into her pillow.

It was still dark when Mike and Judge went down the street to the entrance of a nature trail that skirted their neighborhood. The trail ran along the back of the subdivision and descended to the bottom of the hill not far from traffic light eight. It was a quick five minutes to reach the bottom and a strenuous ten-minute climb to the top of the ridge beyond Mike and Peg's house. Mike listened with satisfaction as Judge panted when they strained toward the crest of the hill and turned around for another descent. Two circuits were enough to give both man and dog a vigorous morning workout. When Mike returned to the house, Peg was in the kitchen with the coffee dripping into the pot.

"What are you doing out of bed?" he asked sharply.

"Making a slight detour from the bathroom to fix your coffee."

"Don't make me handcuff you to the bedpost."

Peg poured a cup of coffee and started toward the downstairs bedroom. "Surveillance cameras would be more humane. Or you could ask Judge to keep a log of my activities."

"Judge would be cheaper. We'll give him a try first, but I'm warning you in advance that I might make a surprise visit home to check on you."

"Visit any time."

Mike sat on the edge of the bed. "Are we okay with each other?"

"Yes."

Mike took a breath and exhaled. "Good."

After Mike cleaned up in the master bathroom and dressed for work, he went to the downstairs bedroom. Peg was sitting up in bed with her Bible open.

"Did you know Sam and Muriel pray together every morning at the kitchen table?" she asked.

"She also fixes homemade biscuits and gravy."

"Which explains the size of Sam's belly. We don't have to do everything like the Millers; however, praying together would be a low-fat thing to do before you leave for work." Peg stretched out her hands. "They hold hands."

Mike joined his hands with hers. "Anything else?"

"Not that I remember."

"Does Muriel pray?"

"I'm not sure, but since she prayed for me the other night, I haven't felt any pain. That's another reason I wanted to argue with Dr. Crawford about the need for bed rest, but I guess that wouldn't have made any difference in her recommendations."

"No, but we can still pray."

Mike closed his eyes. He started to speak, but the same inner nudge that had prompted him to pray at the hospital now restrained him. Other than blessing a meal, he and Peg hadn't prayed together more than a handful of times in their marriage. Finally, Peg spoke.

"Jesus," she said in a soft voice, "we love You this morning."

Mike pressed his lips together. The Name, spoken by his wife, touched a tender spot in his heart. Peg continued, and Mike listened in amazement as she talked to God with a familiarity that made him slightly jealous. His wife, who for years had been resistant to his brand of faith, had leaped over him into the arms of Jesus.

"Thank you for being close to us today," she said. "Amen."

Mike looked within his heart for something to add, but everything that came to mind seemed petty. He squeezed her hand.

"Amen," he said.

Peg opened her eyes.

"Why didn't you pray?" she asked.

Mike stood, came over, and kissed her on the cheek.

"Because there wasn't anything to add."

He kissed her again.

"Call me if you need anything. I'll be home before the session meeting to check on you."

"I'll be good. I promise."

WHEN MIKE ARRIVED AT THE CHURCH, DELORES WAS TYPING the weekly report of church statistics. Mike documented every change in attendance at church meetings, Sunday school classes, and the size of offerings. Having the data at his fingertips had been handy at session meetings, and so far, all the important numbers since his arrival at the church had been up.

"Giving has been down the past three weeks," Delores quipped as he came by her desk. "I don't recall that happening in quite a while."

"But attendance has been up. Don't fret the weekly numbers. Monthly totals are more significant."

"Then why do you want me to keep a weekly record?"

"Because it helps me stay more current," Mike responded patiently.

Delores sniffed. "I just don't want to be doing busywork."

"It's helpful. You know there are elders who love to see the latest data. Any calls this morning?"

"No complaints, if that's what you mean."

MIKE WENT INTO HIS OFFICE. THE FIRST ITEM ON HIS TO-DO list was to locate a handwriting expert. In normal circumstances, he would have called Bobby Lambert for a referral. He tapped a finger against his desk and considered his options. An Internet search would yield results but no guarantee of competency. Experts for hire could be nothing more than pretenders with bogus diplomas and spurious pedigrees. He dialed Greg Freeman. This time a secretary answered the phone and put him through.

"Good morning," Mike said. "Is this the number to call for free legal advice?"

Freeman laughed. "A lot of people believe so. What can I do for you?"

"I need a handwriting expert. Any recommendations?"

Freeman was silent for a moment. "About a year ago, I deposed a handwriting expert in a will contest case. He testified against my client's position, so I tried to discredit him. The more questions I asked, the more convincing he became. I couldn't shake his research and opinion."

"Sounds like my man. Can you locate his contact info?"

"Just a minute."

Mike waited. Freeman came back on the line.

"Darius York. He doesn't have a PhD, but that's not how they learn the craft. York is a former FBI agent who retired to the mountains near Blowing Rock. He supplements his income by providing handwriting analysis. The first ten minutes of the deposition were a recitation of his qualifications and experience. I thought he would never stop talking about how much he knew."

"Is he expensive?"

"Yes, but he's close by."

Mike frowned. "I need something fast. West has put the Miller case on a fast track."

"Why?"

"I suspect it's political, but that doesn't do me any good. I've got to get ready."

"Here's the number for York, and you can mention me as a referral. It will flatter his ego."

"Is he arrogant?"

"A little, but he can back it up."

Mike jotted down the number.

"Thanks."

"Sure. If you need anything else, let me know."

Mike hung up the phone and immediately punched in the numbers for York. An answering machine picked up the call, and he left a detailed message.

Mike made copies of the checks, Sam's written statement, and the estimate for cutting the grass at the church. He hoped the documents would provide enough comparison samples of Sam's handwriting for York to render an opinion.

MID-AFTERNOON, MIKE WENT HOME TO CHECK ON PEG AND found her napping on the couch in the great room with an open notebook turned upside down on the floor beside her. She woke up, stretched up her arms, and held him tightly around the neck when he leaned over to kiss her.

"How are you surviving?" he asked.

"Wishing I really was on the deck of a cruise ship. One day of inactivity is not too bad, but when I think about months with nothing to do except travel between the bed and the couch, it gets depressing. Both Judge and I started getting restless when it was time for our run."

"Are you feeling okay?"

"Yes, but it would have been nice if you'd come home for lunch."

"I worked on the Miller case part of the morning and spent lunch in a counseling session. I've been putting people off who want to come see me, but there was a husband and wife who really needed emergency help."

"Did you help them?"

"I don't know. The husband is hardheaded and resistant to my suggestions.

Sometimes I think my opinion carried more weight as a lawyer than it does as a minister. If he files for divorce, he'll find out that no one gets his way one hundred percent of the time."

Peg scooted away from the edge of the couch and patted it with her hand. Mike sat down.

"I'm glad we didn't go that route."

"Me, too."

"Are you ready for the session meeting?"

"Mostly. I have to print copies of the agenda and get the room ready."

"Can't Delores do it?"

Mike put his hand on Peg's forehead. "Do you have a fever? You sound delusional. I made the mistake the other day of asking her to do something new, and she went into a funk."

"Can I ask you to do something?" Peg asked.

Mike withdrew his hand. "I'm open to reasonable negotiation."

"Where's the trust?"

Mike saluted. "I'm wearing my waiter's uniform, and your every wish is my command."

"Pick up my notebook."

Mike leaned over and retrieved the notebook.

"Go into the office, find a blank page, and write me a short letter. Make it something you'd like me to read while you're gone tonight."

"What kind of letter?"

"A friendly one," Peg answered.

"That shouldn't be too hard."

"Okay."

"And when you finish, put a load of white clothes in the washer, pick up and vacuum the upstairs bedroom, and clean the master bathroom."

"Dr. Crawford told you to stay off the steps," Mike responded sharply. "Have you been upstairs?"

"No, but you have, and I have a mental image of our bedroom and bath that needs to be erased. After you finish, we'll plan an early supper so you can get back to the church."

Mike took the notebook into the office and sat at the desk. Handwritten personal notes had never been a big part of his relationship with Peg, but he was smart enough to realize she wanted to include them in their future. He started to write something sentimental, but his ideas, though nice, didn't feel right. He leaned back in the chair.

And remembered the letter Sam wrote Peg.

That letter needed a bookend, a written resolution for any doubts lingering in Peg's mind that he was ready to forgive the past and go on. Turning to a blank page in the notebook, he began to write.

He intended to fill, at most, a single page, but it quickly stretched to four sheets. Thoughts and emotions he hadn't expressed in person flowed out. And he also discovered his need to ask Peg's forgiveness. She was his wife, but he'd been selfish, too—hiding behind a few Bible verses in Galatians as justification for unilateral action that fundamentally altered their lives. In part, he'd used the Bible as an excuse to impose his will, not as guidance for a future to be shared with the one God joined to walk with him.

Having acknowledged his failings and asked for forgiveness, he concluded with words of hope for what lay ahead. At the bottom of the page, he wrote in large letters "All my love, Mike."

"I'm done!" he called out from the office when he finished.

"Was it that hard finding something nice to write?" Peg responded from the couch. "You've been in there forever!"

Mike returned to the great room and handed her the folded letter.

"No, I just wanted to put off starting my chores."

Twenty

MIKE FINISHED HIS PREPARATIONS FOR THE SESSION MEETING with plenty of time to spare. He'd put on a fresh shirt and tie before returning to the church. He wanted to look his best for the meeting.

After every agenda was neatly in place and the decaf coffee was dripping into the pot, he walked around the room, praying silently as he placed his hand on each chair. While making his second circuit, a voice interrupted him.

"What are you doing?" Bobby asked.

Mike turned quickly toward the door. His former partner's shirt might have been starched twelve hours before, but it was thoroughly wrinkled now. His yellow tie was loosened.

"Waiting for you," Mike said. "How's it going?"

Bobby plopped down in the nearest chair. "Have you ever felt like you have too many irons in the fire?"

"A thousand times."

"That's the way I feel, and I'm worried that a couple of them are about to be taken out to brand me."

"Avoid that if possible."

"How's Peg?"

"On bed rest."

"I wish the doctor would tell me to lie around the house and do nothing except press the remote control for a few weeks. Park cleaned out his office and left yesterday. At least eighty percent of his remaining caseload has landed in my office."

Mike poured Bobby a cup of coffee.

"I'll try not to keep you here too late tonight," he said. "We have a light agenda."

Bobby took a sip of coffee. "How's business?"

"What do you mean?"

"Your caseload. Since I haven't heard from you, I assume you're still handling the Miller case."

"Yes, but it's moving along at a fast clip. Ken West is bumping it up on the trial calendar."

Mike studied Bobby's face for any response, but his former partner stared past him across the room. Bobby picked up the agenda and took a sip of coffee.

"I'm glad to see you have the Miller case on the agenda for discussion. If the case is jumping up the calendar, I look forward to hearing about your exit strategy."

Mike glanced down at the packet in front of him. "That's not about the criminal case. Miller cut the grass this week. If you come out in the daytime, you can see what a neat job he did."

Before Bobby responded, Libby Gorman and Barbara Harcourt came in together and were immediately followed by Milton Chesterfield, along with the other four members of the session.

"Did you ride together?" Mike asked in surprise.

"Everyone but Libby and Bobby had supper with Barbara," Milton responded.

"Did you show them any new photos of the Florida grandkids?" Mike asked Barbara.

"Only a few," the older woman responded crisply.

"Let's get started," Mike said to the group. "I've promised Bobby that I'll get him home at a decent hour."

When everyone was seated, Mike continued. "The first item on the agenda is the quarterly report of the finance committee."

Rick Weston, the credit manager at a local car dealership, served as the chairperson of the committee. A quiet man, Rick rarely expressed an opinion. He read the report in a monotone voice. Mike was relieved when no one pointed out the slight downturn in giving.

"On the other side of Rick's report are the attendance figures," Mike said. "We continue to attract new visitors almost every Sunday."

They plodded through the remaining committee reports. It had all the marks of a lethargic meeting. Mike had placed Sam's bid to cut the grass as the last item and labeled it "Grounds Maintenance Bid from Miller Lawn Care." As the elders moved through the agenda with no more than minor discussion, Mike inwardly debated whether to present Sam's bid or table it until another meeting. Bobby had yawned several times, but they were ahead of schedule.

"The last item is a bid from a new company to cut the grass and maintain the shrubs and flower beds. Does anyone have an opinion about our current service?"

"It's not good," Libby responded immediately. "A few weeks ago, I noticed that the grass on one side of the church had been cut, but the other side looked ragged. It reminded me of my grandson's hair after his older sister gave him a haircut."

Milton coughed. "Is this a bid from Sam Miller, the man you're representing in the criminal case?"

"Yes, but this doesn't have anything to do with that," Mike answered. "Miller's bid is fifteen percent cheaper than our current service, and I believe he'll do a better job."

"Does he need the money to pay your fee?" Milton asked.

"No, I'm handling the case pro bono. I thought I made that clear when I asked permission to help him."

"And it doesn't concern you that he's charged with stealing money from a church?" Milton persisted.

"Yes, but he won't have access to our bank accounts or records."

"The church would pay him with a check," Rick said softly. "Then he would have our account information."

At Rick's comment, Mike quickly examined the faces around the table. Everyone except Libby Gorman looked grim. Libby appeared perplexed.

"You haven't found another attorney to represent Miller?" Milton asked.

"No, he wants me to help him, and I'm willing to see it through. The case will come up for trial in a couple of weeks. After that, my involvement will end."

Bobby pulled the knot in his tie closer to his neck. "Unless it isn't called for trial, or you request a continuance, or Miller is convicted and you file an appeal."

"Of course, those are possibilities. Trial work is always unpredictable."

Barbara Harcourt spoke, her voice strained and imperious. "I wasn't here when the session discussed this matter, but in my opinion, it is totally improper for our minister to represent a criminal. There are plenty of lawyers around, and this man should have hired one of them."

"I understand," Mike answered, keeping his voice calm. "But this is a unique—"

"There's only one thing to consider," Milton interrupted, pointing his finger at Mike. "We've gone over this matter in detail on two occasions, and we want a commitment from you to withdraw immediately from the case. We didn't get a chance to talk to Libby before the meeting, but the rest of us are unanimous in our decision."

"And I voted against it in the first place," Libby said.

"Was that the reason for your joint supper before this meeting?" Mike asked, his voice hardening. "Don't you think it would have been appropriate to allow me to offer my perspective before ambushing me at this meeting?"

Milton cleared his throat.

"We're aware of your position. It would have been pointless to rehash it."

Mike turned to Bobby. "Are you part of this?"

"I made my position clear two weeks ago," Bobby answered. "None of us enjoy putting this kind of pressure on you, but it's the only way to make you wake up and realize that what you're doing is inconsistent with your calling as the senior minister of this church."

"Really? Doesn't the Bible say that God is interested in justice? What do the prophets say about acquitting the guilty and convicting the innocent?"

"We're not here to debate," Milton responded. "We need your answer."

Mike waited until everyone in the room looked at him then slowly scanned the room. Only Rick and another elder didn't hold his gaze.

"And if I decide to honor my commitment to Sam Miller," Mike said slowly, "what then?"

"Get out of the case or leave the church. Is that clear enough?" Milton shot back.

Mike hesitated. Political prudence would dictate a request for time to consider his options, but he didn't feel either political or prudent. He wanted to call the elders' bluff. The church had grown and become much stronger since his arrival. Many of the new members were linked to him as leader. Any harsh action taken against him would split the congregation. He turned to Bobby.

"I need to know your position," he said.

Bobby looked at Milton and nodded his head. The exchange between the two men pierced Mike's heart. He'd hoped Bobby was a reluctant, not willing, participant in the assault against him.

Milton took a sheet of paper from his pocket. "We've made arrangements for an interim pastor to fill the pulpit."

"You've already lined up someone to replace me?"

"On a temporary basis. He's a retired minister from Shelby. You would be given a sabbatical."

"Sounds more like a permanent suspension than a sabbatical."

Bobby spoke. "That's not what we would tell the congregation. In fact, our hope is that we could present this action in a positive light. Peg is experiencing a high-risk pregnancy and needs your help at home. We would announce the sabbatical as a gesture from the session to accommodate your family situation. Then, if things work out, you could return to the pulpit without any stigma of disciplinary action."

Mike couldn't believe what he was hearing.

"The sabbatical would be with full pay and benefits for three months," Rick added. "One month for each year of service."

"Thanks, that's generous," Mike replied with thinly veiled sarcasm.

Milton Chesterfield's eyes flashed. "You better believe it is! And if you want to lose it, keep talking! Just because you used to be a hotshot lawyer in Shelton doesn't mean you can come out here and run over those of us who have been in this church longer than you've been alive!"

"If I recall, you were on the committee that interviewed me and voted unanimously for me to come," Mike responded coldly.

"Stop it!" Bobby held up his hands. "This isn't easy for any of us, and we don't need to end up in an argument. I move we ask for a written response from Mike by the end of the week. If he withdraws from the Miller case, this discussion will have served its purpose. If not, we have a plan to move the church forward and allow Mike to do what he wants to do."

"Second," Barbara responded quickly.

"All in favor," Milton said.

Mike watched seven hands rise into the air, and with a sinking feeling in his heart, knew his days as pastor of the Little Creek Church had come to an end.

Normally, Mike stayed after a meeting until everyone departed the premises. Tonight, he couldn't wait to get away. Abandoning all pretense of civility, he left the conference room and walked directly to his car. He heard Bobby call his name, but he didn't turn around. Bobby had been right about one thing—any additional words would only fuel a fight.

During the drive home, Mike's mind raced in a hundred directions. He'd never been threatened with firing in his life. The thought of posting his résumé on the seminary Web site in an effort to locate another pastorate made him feel slightly nauseous. Returning to law practice in Shelton in the face of open animosity from his former firm was not an option. He pulled into his driveway. Ever loyal, Judge greeted him at the kitchen door.

"Peg!" Mike called out. "Where are you?"

"Lifting weights in the bedroom!" she responded. "Please bring me a glass of ice water."

Mike took longer than necessary to fix the glass of water. He stopped to let Judge go out to the backyard.

"You sure are a slow waiter!" Peg yelled. "In my dream you were always at my elbow!"

Mike took the glass of water into the bedroom. Peg was leaning against a couple of pillows with a sketch pad in her lap.

"What are you drawing?"

"A concept. I'd like to paint some watercolors for the baby's room."

"Maybe you can do a few extras to sell."

Peg laughed. "Don't be silly. I'm not interested in going commercial."

"In a few months we could use the money."

"What do you mean?"

"It's serious."

Peg's face fell. Mike sat on the edge of the bed.

"The elders told me to get out of Sam's case or leave the church."

"What? That's crazy!"

Mike told her what had happened at the meeting. When he reached the part about the sabbatical and the reason for it, she began to cry. He handed her a box of tissue.

"Do you want me to stop?" he asked.

Peg blew her nose. "No, it just hurts so badly. I'm more mad than sad. To use my pregnancy as an excuse to the congregation is so dishonest and unfair."

"Yeah, it's cowardly."

His voice growing more despondent as the adrenaline released during the meeting drained from his system, Mike finished his account of the night's events.

"I've prided myself on staying ahead of the curve on the political activity taking place at the church, but this caught me off guard. Bobby should have tipped me off to a mutiny of this magnitude, but he may have been the one who came up with the sabbatical idea in the first place."

"Elizabeth Lambert hasn't returned my calls for almost two weeks."

Mike grunted. "She didn't have the courage to face you, knowing what was in the works."

Peg shook her head. "It doesn't make any sense. Such a mean attitude. If they knew more about Sam—"

"It wouldn't make any difference. He's already a convicted felon in the minds of some members of the session. And Milton was just looking for an excuse to vent his animosity toward me. To him, Sam is irrelevant."

"Who agrees with Milton?"

Mike shrugged. "I'm not sure how many people believe the church would be better off going backward than forward. I've worked hard for three years to communicate a vision for the future—tonight it came crashing down in a few minutes. The support I thought I had among the leadership of the church was an illusion."

"That may not be true."

"I have to assume the worst. Part of my failure has been in believing what people said to my face and trusting it as their true opinion."

"Mike, that's awful. It makes the church sound like a charade."

"It's made up of imperfect people."

"Who are supposed to be getting better."

Mike smiled slightly. "Like you are. I'd like to think you're the result of my ministry, but Sam Miller has had more to do with what God is doing in your life than I have."

"That's not true. You've been so steady and faithful. Even when I was angry with you or wanted to ignore you, it wasn't possible. And you've helped a lot of people."

Mike kissed her forehead. "That's sweet, but can't you let me wallow in self-pity and doubt for a few minutes?"

"We'll schedule your pity party later. When are you going to tell Sam about this?"

"I'm not sure I should. He's facing enough pressure without taking on my problems. I don't like being coerced into doing—"

"What you don't want to do," Peg said, finishing his sentence. "That's your pride and ego talking."

"So? It's still about doing the right thing."

"And when you're upset isn't the best time to make an important decision. You've told me that plenty of times when I was in an emotional upheaval. Sam needs to be brought into the loop. He'll find out anyway if he and Muriel visit the church."

"It'll be all over town," Mike added gloomily. "There's no way the spin Bobby wants to put on this is going to stand up to the scrutiny of the rumor mill. One of the elders will crack, and the real reason will leak out. The fight within the church will begin, and the whole community can enjoy the latest gossip about the big blowup at Little Creek Church."

"Don't make your final decision until you talk to Sam. I've supported you on this from the beginning, but you should talk to him and give it some time. You don't have to respond until the end of the week. When you figure out the right decision, you'll make it."

"Are you worried about what will happen to us?"

Peg pointed to Mike's letter that lay open on the nightstand. It seemed a week since he'd penned it, and he'd forgotten all about it.

"Of course, but a woman can trust her future to a man who would write a letter like that."

Twenty-one

MIKE SPENT A RESTLESS NIGHT TOSSING AND TURNING IN BED. Shortly before dawn, he gave up on sleep and went downstairs to the kitchen. He tried to pray and read the Bible, but couldn't concentrate. He looked at the clock. It was early, but he suspected Sam Miller didn't linger in bed. He picked up the phone.

"Did I wake you up?" he asked when Sam answered the phone.

"Nope. I've been listening to you all night."

"What?"

"In my dreams."

"I hope I made sense. Can you meet me for breakfast?"

"Sure. Muriel will enjoy sleeping in."

"How about Traci's in thirty minutes?"

"Yep."

Mike put on a pair of sweatpants and a T-shirt. When he arrived at the restaurant, the sun had turned the sky a dull gray. In a few minutes, it would rise above the clouds to dispel the remaining darkness. The restaurant did a brisk morning business from customers anxious to get a two-cups-of-coffee start on the day. Sam's truck was parked at the side of the building. Mike entered and saw Sam sitting alone in a booth. Judy brought over coffee. Sam hadn't shaved for a couple of days, and Mike rubbed his own bristly chin.

"Judy, do you know Sam Miller?" Mike asked after the waitress greeted him.

Judy smiled. "Yeah, Sam and Muriel have been there a few times when I needed them."

Judy took their order.

Mike glanced around the restaurant. He wished he didn't have any worries greater than whether to order his eggs scrambled or over easy.

"Do you know why I wanted to talk to you?" he asked.

Sam didn't hesitate. "The fire started."

"Yes. I got out of an elders' meeting last night without being fired on the spot, but I didn't hear the sound of any sirens coming to the rescue."

Mike told Sam about the meeting. In the middle, Judy brought the food. Mike managed a few bites between sentences. Sam's remained untouched.

"Aren't you going to eat?" he asked. "There's nothing worse than cold grits."

Mike saw a deep sadness in the older man's eyes that made them look more gray than blue.

"How can I eat when I hear about Papa's children devouring one of their own? Go ahead."

Mike continued his story.

"It was rough," he concluded. "I didn't want to burden you with this, but Peg insisted I talk it over with you."

"She was right. And it helps me understand a dream I had last night."

"About the church?"

"Nope. You and I were in the courtroom. Judge Coberg was there along with the young woman district attorney, Miss Hall. Four people who have been my longtime enemies were in the jury box."

"Who? I want to make sure I strike them if they turn up in the jury pool."

Sam shook his head. "You don't need to know. Not yet. One is dead and another moved away a long time ago. The other two are still in the area. Anyway, when I saw the jurors, I knew I didn't have a chance in court. I went into the hallway. Muriel was there, and when I told her about the four people in the jury box, she got scared. I hugged her, and we went back into the courtroom. The judge banged his gavel, and we left."

"What happened next?"

"That's it."

"Did you go to jail?"

"No."

Mike poked his eggs with his fork. His breakfast had also grown cold.

"Do you think you accepted the plea bargain?"

"Is that how it would work?"

"Maybe. Although, the judge would want to talk to you, so you could explain that you were taking the DA's offer because you didn't want to go to jail, not because you committed the crime."

"If I did that, what would happen at your church?"

"The reason given for suspending me would go away, but I'd still have to deal with the opposition of one or more of the elders." Mike leaned forward and spoke with all the earnestness he could muster. "But I want to make one thing clear—you're not going to plead guilty to a crime so I can keep my position at the church."

"That's what I have to decide, isn't it?"

MIKE LEFT THE RESTAURANT, NOT SURE WHETHER TO GO HOME or to the church. Driving through town, he concluded hiding out at home would be an act of retreat. Even if his days at the church were numbered, he was determined to hold his head up high until the end. He called Peg on his cell phone and told her about his breakfast with Sam.

"At this point, I don't believe I could trust his decision to take the plea bargain," Mike said.

"But he's the client. He can decide for himself."

"That's how the conversation ended. When I first met him, I questioned Sam's competency. If he pleads guilty just to help me, I'll know he's crazy."

"It's not right for an innocent man to plead guilty, but Muriel may not want to risk him going to jail. Are you on your way home?"

"No, I'm going to the church."

"Why?"

"To take your advice and carry on as normally as possible."

Mike felt a surge of confidence as he turned into the church parking lot. It reminded him of the calm before the start of a big jury trial. The challenge was at hand; the preparation complete; ignoring the battle ahead not an option; he was going to war. In those moments, he'd experienced the euphoria reserved for happy warriors. He marched through the front door of the administration building.

"Good morning, Delores," he said cheerily. "I've been up early and ready for the day."

"I hope it gets better," she responded. "How was the session meeting?"

Mike quickly studied the church secretary's face. Delores couldn't conceal knowledge of information as inflammatory as the previous night's action by the elders. Her countenance was clear. Libby Gorman had kept her mouth shut—at least for the first twelve hours.

"Brisk and businesslike," Mike answered. "Any calls?"

"Uh, yes, I put a note on your desk from a man named York. He said he was a former FBI agent."

"Good. Hold my calls for a few minutes."

Mike phoned the number for Darius York. A man with a Midwestern accent answered the phone.

"York, here."

Mike introduced himself and the reason for the contact.

"How many documents do you have?" York asked.

"Two checks and an interrogation statement that can serve as a sample of my client's handwriting."

"Do you have the documents in front of you?"

"Yes."

"Did he sign the statement?"

"Yes."

"Are the checks originals?"

"No, everything is a copy."

"Does the signature on the two checks look the same to you?"

Mike studied the checks for a moment. "Yes."

"How similar?"

Mike looked more carefully. The shape of every letter, the location of the dot on the *i* in Miller, the curve in the *S* in Sam all matched exactly.

"Identical."

"Can you make the original checks available for analysis?"

"Maybe. The case has been fast-tracked, and I'm not sure who has custody of the original checks. They weren't in the DA's file, so I assume they're at the bank."

"Without the originals, I'm not sure I can help you."

"Why not?"

"Technology. It's not hard to electronically collect a signature and imprint it on a check so that it looks genuine. A copy of the original check masks the transfer process. If the signature appears legit on the copy and that's all I have to work with, I'll have to testify it's a match. I can offer an explanation of the process for lifting a signature and transferring it onto the checks, but you'll have to decide if that type of information helps you or hurts you."

Mike stared at the checks. His theory about Jesse Lavare as the instigator of the charges against Sam was evaporating. "What would the originals show?" he asked.

"I could examine the signatures under a microscope and identify the transfer process, if any."

"And if I can't get the originals?"

"I could still microscopically examine the signatures. If they are identical at the microscopic level, it would give you an argument that the checks are forged, because no one can exactly duplicate a signature. They would be too perfect. I've testified that way in other cases."

"Successfully or unsuccessfully?"

"Both. Juries don't always trust expert witnesses, even former FBI agents."

"You're not trying very hard to market your services."

"I do what I do because I enjoy it. The government sends me three checks every month whether I go outside the door or not."

"Will you examine my copies while I try to locate the originals?"

"Yes. Did the lawyer who referred you have a copy of my fee schedule?"

"No."

"And I can give you the open dates on my calendar."

Mike made notes on a sheet of paper. York was expensive but available.

"Agreed," he said when York finished. "I'll overnight everything to you today."

Mike hung up and wrote down the amount of money he'd need from Sam Miller. With his own job in jeopardy, Mike couldn't finance the case. That check would need Sam's original signature. There was a knock on the door.

"Come in!"

Delores stuck her head inside. "Bobby Lambert called twice while you were on the phone, and you received a fax from your old law firm."

"Did Bobby leave a message?"

"No, I asked if it was an emergency, and he wouldn't tell me."

"Let me see the fax."

Delores handed him several sheets of paper. The cover sheet was from Maxwell Forrest's office. Delores remained standing in front of his desk.

"Anything else?" Mike asked.

"I'm not sure what to say," the secretary said. "I had no idea."

The knowledge absent from her eyes when Mike arrived at the church was now present.

"Libby called you?"

"I got so mad at her that I almost hung up the phone. You've been out of the office a lot, but you do more in half a day than the last two pastors did in half a week. I know what's going on at the church better than any member of the session!"

"Did she tell you about the sabbatical?"

"Yes, and nobody is going to buy that story." Delores's eyes flashed. "I'm going to war on this. In two hours, I can get a phone campaign started that will make the elders wish they'd—"

Mike held up his hand. "Don't. Please. Not yet. Maybe never."

"You can't leave us," Delores shot back. "This church has a chance to be something more than a place where people are married and buried."

Mike couldn't hide his shock at her perspective.

"Don't look so surprised," she continued. "I've seen the good you're doing."

She quickly listed five individuals and three families significantly helped by Mike's ministry.

"There's no way to avoid a big church split if you leave now. The feuding and fussing will be ten times worse than the fight over whether or not to build the new sanctuary."

"Which is why I'm asking you to take it easy. What happens now is more important than my—"

"Don't even start with that stuff," Delores interrupted with a snort. "Giving up and leaving would be the worst thing that you could do for this church. There are plenty of weak preachers who would run at the first sign of trouble, but you've got the backbone to fight. Milton Chesterfield and his family have tried to run this place forever. I thought those days were over, but I guess I was wrong."

"Did Libby tell you they've already contacted an interim pastor who would serve if I'm kicked out on sabbatical?"

"No. Who is it?"

"I'm not sure. Someone from Shelby."

"I'll call Libby and find out more information. I was too mad to listen before."

"Leave her alone. I don't want either one of us to react in a wrong way."

"I can't just sit here and do nothing!"

"Yes, you can. Do you remember Sam Miller and me talking about the church being on fire?"

"Yes. I don't think he should be hanging around here. The man is dangerous and is a threat to—"

"Don't take his words literally. The fire he saw in a dream represented conflict. I didn't see it coming, but now that it's here, I don't want either one of us to pour gas on it. That's not the way this is going to be worked out."

"What do you mean? I've never believed you were a quitter."

"I'm not. Peg and I will pray until we get direction."

Delores sniffed and shook her head. "Prayer is fine, but I'm going outside to smoke a cigarette."

Delores left the office. Mike stood at the window and watched her walk resolutely to the edge of the old cemetery. In a few seconds, she blew out a billow of smoke that showed the vigor she brought to her habit.

Mike returned to his desk and picked up the fax from Mr. Forrest. The cover sheet stated that the attached records constituted the complete Bank of Barlow County investigation into the misappropriation of funds from the Craig Valley Gospel Tabernacle construction account. The papers contained no new information, and Mike knew without a doubt the records were incomplete—the memo from Brian Dressler to Jack Hatcher wasn't included.

He glanced at the two slips indicating the times of Bobby's calls. Still mad at Bobby, Mike dialed the number for Braxton Hodges.

"Any word from Dressler?" he asked.

"No. He's still in Alabama with his family."

"Do you know when he'll get back?"

"No. What have you found out?"

Mike read from the sheets forwarded by Maxwell Forrest.

"At least he responded to you," Hodges said. "He's never returned my calls. I've had my finger on the Record button so long that it's starting to cramp."

"Ken West has his finger on the trigger of the Miller case. It'll appear on the next term of criminal court."

"Whew, you just got involved. Can they do that?"

"Probably. It would be hard for me to argue that my caseload is so heavy I can't be ready for trial. Dressler needs to be questioned and available to testify if needed."

"I'll let you know as soon as he shows up. Any other leads?"

Mike debated whether to mention the encounter with Hatcher, Forrest, and the developers at Cohulla Creek.

"That's a newspaper term," Mike answered, dodging the question. "What have you found out?"

"Not much, unless you consider it important that one of the men mentioned in Dressler's file has a criminal record."

Mike sat up straighter in his seat. "Which one?"

"A guy named Troy Linden from New Jersey. He entered a no contest plea in state court in New Jersey about ten years ago. Got a slap on the wrist and paid a fine of a few thousand dollars."

"What was the charge?" Mike asked, making notes on a legal pad.

"Improper lobbying."

"Bribing a public official?"

"That's what I would guess."

"How did you find this?"

"We're a tiny paper, but we're part of one of the best proprietary databases in the country. It's a great equalizer. When it comes to background information, I can find out as much as a reporter in New York or Los Angeles. Give me a name, and I can give you a history. I punched in everyone mentioned in the files. The info on Troy Linden was a one-paragraph blurb in a local rag that included a quote from his lawyer that his client didn't admit any wrongdoing."

"What did Linden do?"

"No details given."

"Anything interesting on anyone else?"

"No."

"Are you going to follow up on Linden?"

"As soon as I finish an article about the good health benefits of herbs and spices. Did you know a teaspoon of cinnamon a day is great for your heart?"

"I should be chewing a stick right now."

"Me, too. It's a lot better than the cigarettes I used to smoke. Amid all the crazy claims out there, at least no one still believes inhaling the burning residue produced by the leaves of a dried tobacco plant is good for you."

"My secretary at the church might disagree with you."

Mike hung up the phone and called his old law office. Waiting on hold, Mike's anger at his former partner's betrayal began to grow. Until the past twenty-four hours, their friendship had transcended every competing influence. When Bobby answered the phone, Mike spit out his opening comment.

"How did it feel stabbing me in the back last night? It hurt on my end."

Bobby didn't immediately answer.

"Did you hear me?" Mike repeated.

"Yes, but I'm not going to talk to you now."

"Then why did you call?"

"Meet me in the deed room at the courthouse at one-thirty."

"Why do you want to do that?" Mike asked, then listened to the silence of a dead phone.

Mike glared at the receiver for a few seconds before slamming it down. He checked his calendar. He had an appointment at 1:30 p.m. and couldn't go to town in the early afternoon. He didn't call Bobby back to let him know.

A few minutes later, Delores knocked on the doorjamb. Mike glanced up.

"Did you call Bobby Lambert?" she asked. "Libby claimed he was the one who came up with the idea for the sabbatical."

"We talked briefly. He wants to meet me in town after lunch, but I have an appointment."

"Not anymore. It's rescheduled for tomorrow morning at ten."

Mike grunted. "It doesn't matter. I'm still not ready to talk to Bobby. I couldn't keep from getting angry in a one-minute phone conversation."

"Maybe that's what he needs to hear from you. It might make him think."

Mike shook his head. "He's never listened to me, and I doubt he's going to start now."

MIKE WENT HOME TO CHECK ON PEG. THE CHURCH HAD ALWAYS been a place of peace for Mike. Now, his home felt more like a refuge. Peg was lying on the couch in the great room. Mike kissed her on the forehead.

"Can't you do better than that?" Peg responded. "I'm not sick."

Mike kissed her on the lips.

"Thanks," Peg replied. "I didn't have much to look forward to all morning."

Mike sat on the couch beside her feet. "You're one person I can please and be glad doing it," he said. "Did Muriel come by to see you?"

"Yes, she brought supper. It's in the refrigerator. All I have to do is put it in the oven about five o'clock."

"Chitlins?"

"No, but you guessed the right animal. It's a pork loin basted in a special sauce she came up with. There are also lima beans, creamed corn, homemade biscuits, and a pecan pie for dessert."

"I hope Sam won't go hungry."

"And Muriel already knew about the DA's offer to Sam. She brought it up and asked me what I thought about it."

"What did you say?"

"That I don't know the ins and outs of criminal law and never liked criminal cases because you became so focused on your clients that you forgot about me."

"But you think Sam's case is different?"

"You're still one hundred percent focused on it. However, I think he deserves the attention. Did anything happen at the church?"

Mike told her about Delores's strong negative reaction to the session's actions and willingness to heed his advice.

"Can you trust her?" Peg asked when he finished.

"She seemed with me one hundred percent."

"You've tiptoed around her feelings for three years. Why would she suddenly have a less-self-centered attitude?"

Mike thought for a moment. "She considers herself the mother hen of the church. By delivering an ultimatum to me, the elders invaded her turf without asking her permission. And you know that she and Milton have been in competition for years."

"Just be careful. You can be too quick to trust someone who claims to be doing the right thing when in fact they have a secondary agenda."

"What would be Delores's agenda? She was ready to go on the warpath for me and burn her bridges."

"I'm not sure. I've always thought she was the type of person who could be friendly one day and turn into an enemy the next."

"I already have one of those."

He told her about the call from Bobby Lambert. Peg sat up and listened, her eyes wide.

"Eat a snack for lunch and meet Bobby at the courthouse," she said when he finished.

"What? And punch him in the nose?"

"He called you twice and tried to set up a meeting. Didn't he try to pull you aside after the session meeting last night?"

"Yes."

"He's reaching out to you for a reason."

"If he wants me to grant absolution and relieve his guilt, he's looking to the wrong person."

"Why? You're the one he wronged."

Mike stared at Peg. "Are you serious?"

Peg picked up her Bible from the low table beside the couch.

"Muriel and I talked about what we're going through. She suggested I read a verse in Colossians."

Mike's jaw dropped open. Peg, turning the pages, didn't notice.

"Here it is. *'Bear with each other and forgive whatever grievances you may have against one another. Forgive as the Lord forgave you.'* Muriel and Sam have been attacked in a bunch of different churches, and she said the only way to survive is to forgive. I've been thinking about the last sentence of that verse ever since she left."

Mike shook his head. "I hate it when a layperson like you gets spiritual."

Peg grinned. "Don't give me too much credit. I'm not ready to invite the Chesterfields and Harcourts over for supper, but give Bobby a chance. He's been your friend almost as long as we've been married."

"You have too much time to lie around and think," Mike answered.

Peg handed her Bible to him. "It's your decision. You know a lot more about the Bible than I do. And Muriel may have been wrong or taken the verse out of context."

Mike went into the kitchen and fixed a large sandwich for himself and a smaller one for Peg. He left the Bible on the counter unopened. He didn't have to read it. He knew what it said. He put the food on two plastic plates, cut up some fresh fruit, and returned to the great room where he arranged everything on a pair of TV trays.

"I'm going into town for a few minutes after lunch," he said as he speared a piece of cantaloupe with his fork. "It's been a while since I went by the deed room at the courthouse to make sure no one has tried to sell the house out from under us."

"Wouldn't selling it without our permission be hard to do?" Peg asked with a smile.

"Impossible. Just like forgiving people who've wronged me in the same way Jesus forgave me."

Twenty-two

AT 1:45 P.M., MIKE WALKED UP THE SIDEWALK AND INTO THE courthouse. If Bobby Lambert wanted to show remorse, there was no harm in letting him stew in his guilt a few extra minutes. The deed room was in the windowless basement of the building. Mike had searched a few real estate titles in his career but pitied the lawyers and paralegals who spent the majority of their time, mole-like, on the lowest level of the courthouse.

Bound in large, leather-covered folios, some of the older deeds were beautifully handwritten documents dating back to the 1830s. More recent records were kept in computer files that could be accessed in seconds. Mike walked down a flight of stairs to an opaque glass door marked "Register of Deeds" and opened it. A few men and women glanced up in curiosity when he entered. Mike nodded to an elderly lawyer named Rex Bumgardner, who had spent his entire career in the deed room and achieved status as a living oracle of the history of land ownership in Barlow County. Written recitals of real estate transfers would survive his death, but his stories describing how and why the land changed hands would be buried in the ground with him.

There was no sign of Bobby. Perhaps he'd not bothered to wait when Mike didn't show up on time. Mike approached Mr. Bumgardner.

"How are you, Mr. Bumgardner?" he asked in the soft voice that deed room etiquette required.

"Fine, except for my arthritis. Don't get old, Mike. It's no fun."

"I don't plan on it. Has Bobby Lambert been down here today?"

Mr. Bumgardner glanced over his shoulder. "He was here a few minutes ago."

Mike walked past the shelves of deed books and looked down the aisles. He didn't spot Bobby until he reached the far corner of the room. His former partner was standing with his back to him and held a leather deed book in his hand. He turned as Mike approached and closed the deed book.

"What do you want?" Mike asked.

"Did you ever read the old handwritten deeds?"

"Not unless I had to. What is this all—"

"Take a look in here," Bobby said, handing the book to Mike. "There is something in it you might find helpful. Read it, then forget you saw me here."

Bobby stepped past Mike, who grabbed him by the arm.

"Why are you doing this to me?" Mike asked sharply.

Bobby jerked his arm free. "Because whether you believe it or not, I'm your friend."

"That's not much of an apology."

Bobby turned his back on Mike and left the aisle. Mike glared after him. He turned the heavy book over in his hand. It was one of the oldest volumes, the red leather cracked and worn. Mike placed the book on a nearby stand and opened it. It covered a nine-month period of land transfers in the 1850s. He flipped through the pages without seeing any mention of Cohulla Creek and wondering why such an old book would have any current relevance. He was about to close it and return it to its place when a loose sheet of paper, folded in half and placed between the sheets, caught his attention. Mike opened it. The script was barely legible. His eyes went to the bottom of the page where in a familiar scrawl Maxwell Forrest had written "Minutes from JH."

It was from Jack Hatcher.

Mike spread open the paper and examined it more closely. Dated the previous year, it appeared to be informal notes Hatcher had made at a meeting. Hatcher mentioned the "CCP," which Mike interpreted as the Cohulla Creek project, as well as references to "TG, DB, and BN"—Troy Linden, Dick Bunt, and Butch Niles. Linden and Bunt participated in the conference via speaker phone. Halfway down the sheet, Mike's eyes stopped when he saw the name "Miller." Beside the name Hatcher had written "How?" and underlined it twice. On the next line, he'd written "BD will handle." Brian Dressler. The remainder of the memo contained action steps related to the CCP and the dates by which they were to be completed. A circle was drawn around a day in May only a few weeks away. Mike tried to figure out the significance of the May date, but there wasn't enough information to do so. There was no reference to anyone else.

Except for the handwritten notation at the bottom of the sheet, nothing linked the document to Maxwell Forrest.

Mike folded the sheet and stuck it in his pocket then returned the volume to the stacks. He reentered the open area of the deed room and approached Mr. Bumgardner.

"Did you find Bobby?" Bumgardner asked.

"Yes, sir."

"I don't see him down here too much. Did you hear that Park is moving to Charlotte?"

"Yes." Mike paused. "Mr. Bumgardner, are you aware of the activity associated with the Cohulla Creek watershed?"

"Sure. Some of the local landowners have called me with questions, but I've not done any work for the companies buying the options. That's being handled by outsiders probably charging three times as much as I would."

"What's going on?"

"The usual. It's one of the prettiest stretches in the area, and developers would understandably be interested."

"But what about the tracts owned by the state?"

"That will probably end up in a state park. It's a great little trout stream."

"No rumors otherwise?"

Bumgardner shook his head and looked at Mike more closely. "If you know one, I'm listening. The folks seeking my advice wanted my opinion about the fair market value of the options. I gave it based on the available land and how it could be developed."

"If the options are already sold, my information wouldn't make any difference."

"Except that a few of the options expire soon, including the main ingress and egress route to the area. A key parcel is tied up in the estate of a man who died last summer. If that option isn't exercised, it will be tough for the developers to get all the heirs to agree on anything."

ON THE WAY OUT OF THE COURTHOUSE, MIKE MET MELISSA HALL near the district attorney's office.

"Did you get my fax?" Hall asked. "I sent it to the church before lunch."

"No, I've been away from the church for a few hours."

"Ken instructed me to withdraw the plea offer in the Miller case and notify you in writing."

Mike's eyes narrowed. "The ten days aren't up."

"I know, but you didn't accept the deal while it was still on the table."

"Why renege on the offer?" he asked testily. "That's not very professional. The integrity of the system depends on lawyers keeping their word to one another."

Mike saw Hall's face flush.

"I'm following orders."

"Is Ken still pushing the case up the calendar?"

"Yes, and I'll be the one handling it."

"Good." Mike paused. "By the way, how many cases have you tried?"

"Two misdemeanors. This will be my first felony. Have you tried a lot of criminal cases?"

"Plenty, but this will be my last."

MIKE LEFT THE COURTHOUSE. HIS PHONE BEEPED, INDICATING that he had a voice message. It was from Sam.

"Tell Miss Hall I'll accept the plea deal. I believe my dream was a warning that my enemies will be in the jury box, and if I go to trial, I'll be convicted. Papa was looking out for me, and even though it doesn't make sense, I'd be foolish to ignore the message."

Mike hit the Redial button. The phone at the Miller house rang, but no one answered. He was about to click off when Muriel answered.

"Is Sam there?"

"No, he's on a job."

"Did you know he called me?"

"Yes. He doesn't want to have a trial. He's going to tell the judge that he didn't do anything wrong but will plead guilty to the charge you mentioned, so he won't have to go to jail."

"Where can I reach him?"

"Let me check his work schedule."

Mike waited.

"He has several places to go on the east side."

Muriel gave Mike the addresses. Mike made notes on a legal pad.

"I have got to talk to him," Mike said. "There have been some new developments."

MIKE DROVE TO THREE PLACES BEFORE HE SAW THE FAMILIAR TRUCK and trailer parked alongside the street. Sam was on his riding mower, cutting a large flat yard that had a single maple tree in the middle. The tree was covered in young leaves that would turn brilliant yellow and orange in autumn. Mike parked behind the truck and stood beside his car while Sam made another loop around the yard before cutting off the mower's engine.

"Did you get my message?" Sam asked as he approached and wiped his hands on his overalls. "My decision doesn't have anything to do with your situation at the church, and I know what I said the other day about the apostles, but there are times when I have to do things that seem wrong at the time. Later, it turns out right because Papa had another plan in—"

"The DA's office withdrew the offer a few hours ago," Mike interrupted. "Taking a deal to end the case is no longer an option."

For the first time since he'd known Sam, the older man looked shocked.

"But why? I thought we had ten days to decide."

"It should have been left open. Usually, the DA's office honors its commitments to make sure the system runs smoothly. But with me, there's no incentive. They can renege without worrying that I'll do something to them in another case."

Sam wiped his forehead with a red bandanna he took from his back pocket.

"What is Papa up to?"

"I don't know, but I've been busy. As of now, we need to assume that we're going to trial."

Mike told Sam about his conversation with Darius York. Sam didn't seem encouraged by the strong likelihood that his signature was lifted from a real check and imprinted on two forged ones. When Mike reached the part about York's fee, the look on the old man's face stopped Mike from asking him for money.

"The handwriting evidence will give the jury a scientific reason to believe in your innocence. But that's not all I have to show them."

Mike reached into his pocket and pulled out the paper Bobby had left in the deed book.

"I have a copy of the minutes of a meeting Jack Hatcher had a year ago with some of the people involved in the Cohulla Creek land development. Your name is mentioned along with Brian Dressler's."

Mike placed the sheet on the hood of his car.

"It looks like something from one of your notebooks, but with what I already know, I can make some sense of it." He went over the minutes in detail and concluded by saying, "This should give you hope. I can drag all these people into court and sequester them. They won't know what hit them until I start my questions."

He waited for Sam's response.

"I appreciate what you're doing," Sam said slowly. "If this trial was about who has the best lawyer, I'm sure we'd win. But the important thing for me to figure out is Papa's plan. Without that, all the lawyer skill in the world won't help me in the way I need it most."

"Sam, this isn't a religious game; it's real. You're charged with a criminal felony, and if you're convicted, you could go to prison for a long time. I believe God will help us if we ask Him, but that doesn't mean He's going to tell us everything in advance. We may have to walk blind and trust Him to keep us from falling in the ditch."

Sam's face softened. "I see what you're saying. We're all little children who don't see everything perfectly, and Papa looks out for us in a million ways we never realize. There are many times I've had to trust Him with the future when I didn't understand the past." Sam paused and continued with more intensity. "But doing what the Master wants is all I care about. In something as big as this, I have to know His will so I can obey it."

"I'll leave that up to you. But I'm clear about my obligation. I'm going to represent you in this case and do everything in my power to prove your innocence. I will not abandon you."

Mike knew it was the only decision his conscience would allow, and speaking the words with conviction empowered him. He might end up as lonely as the solitary maple tree, but at least he'd stand up for what was right without yielding to intimidation.

Sam put his hand on Mike's shoulder and looked him in the eye.

"Thank you. What happens next?"

"I'm going to track down Brian Dressler. He could be the key to the whole case."

WHEN MIKE LEFT SAM, HE PHONED BRAXTON HODGES.

"Any word on Dressler?"

"No, what about your end?"

"Just pursuing leads," Mike answered noncommittally.

"You're holding back on me," Hodges said. "I can hear you sniffing like a bloodhound on the scent."

"A legitimate defense for the case is coming together, but there's nothing I can reveal—yet. Mr. Forrest claimed Sam was an inept criminal. I could say the same thing about the people trying to frame him."

"At least tell me if you've gotten a copy of Miller's letter to Hatcher. You don't have to read it to me, just tell me it exists. I want to print a facsimile in the paper when I break my story."

"I wish I had the letter, but I don't."

"But I can hear it in your voice. You've found something good."

"Maybe better. Talking to Dressler is my number one priority."

"I'm staring into his empty cubicle as we speak. Nothing has been touched since the day he left for Alabama."

"Let me know as soon as he shows up."

"Will do. You'll owe me a hamburger when this is over."

MIKE RETURNED TO THE CHURCH. DELORES WASN'T AT HER DESK. The fax from Melissa Hall had been slipped into Mike's in-box. Even if Delores could be trusted, it disturbed him that she knew an offer had been extended then withdrawn in the Miller case. Mike checked his phone messages. None of the other elders had phoned. No cracks appeared in the unity of those seeking to bring disunity to the congregation.

An hour later, Nathan Goode came in and sat down while Mike finished a phone conversation about vacation Bible school with the children's ministries coordinator.

"Have you heard the rumors?" Mike asked when he hung up the phone.

"It's not true," Nathan replied. "I admit to four earrings in my right ear, but I never broke the law except for a few traffic tickets when I owned an old car that was unsafe at any speed."

"No, I'm serious," Mike answered. "I need to tell you about last night's session meeting. If I continue to represent Sam Miller in the criminal case I mentioned to you, I'm going to have to leave the church."

Nathan's jaw dropped open. "If you're kidding, this is the worst joke of the year."

"It's not a joke. I'm sticking with Miller, which means I'm out by the end of the week. They're calling it a three-month sabbatical, but there's no guarantee that I'll return."

"Are you sure about this? Can't someone else help this guy?"

"They could, but I'm going to do it. If you knew the whole story, you'd understand. I can't tell because much of it is confidential."

"And the elders won't cut you any slack?"

"No, there are a few who would like to kill my career and another who stabbed me in the back."

"Wow. When this comes out in the open, the congregation will revolt and vote out the elders. This is worse than some of the lamebrained stuff the school board does."

"We're an independent church, but it's not that easy under our bylaws. And I'm not sure a new session would solve the problems."

Nathan shook his head. "They're crazy."

"You still have a job," Mike continued. "Your name didn't come up."

"But it will. You don't have to name the assassins, but if Milton Chesterfield and Barbara Harcourt are mad at you, there's no telling what they think about me."

"Miller had a dream about this situation before it happened. He saw the church on fire, only I didn't know about it."

"Then I'd better get out, too. Don't shut the door. I'll be right behind you."

"Don't rush it," Mike responded. "Living on a teacher's salary is going to put a crimp in your car payment, and I think you're doing a super job with the teenagers. Give it a chance."

Nathan gestured over his shoulder toward the door. "What was Delores's take?"

"Was she at her desk when you came in?"

"No."

"She seems supportive, but I'll have to see where she ends up. Delores is an independent thinker."

Nathan looked at Mike for a few seconds. "If I hang around for a while, what should I plan to do on Sunday?"

"Select something subject to the approval of the interim minister. I think 'Blest Be the Tie That Binds' would be a nice hymn selection."

"No," Nathan replied, shaking his head. "Since you can't tell me what to do anymore, we'll sing the 'Battle Hymn of the Republic'—with special emphasis on the grapes of wrath."

Twenty-three

DURING THE DRIVE HOME, MIKE DEBATED WHETHER TO CALL each elder individually or send a letter to the group. He decided a letter would be better. That way, no one could misinterpret his words or misquote him.

The smells of the supper left by Muriel Miller wafted through the kitchen. Mike took a couple of quick sniffs on his way to the downstairs bedroom. Peg was sitting in front of her easel, putting the finishing touches on a beach scene watercolor with a small boy scooping sand into a red plastic bucket.

"What do you think?" she asked.

"Very peaceful. If we have a girl, he can be her beach buddy."

Peg cleaned her brush and laid it on the stand. "Did you see Bobby?"

"Yes."

Mike told her what had happened in the deed room.

"I was right," Peg said. "There is good in him."

"But he wouldn't talk to me—"

"Because he's scared. That's been obvious since all this started. He likes to cut up and joke, but he's not a risk-taker like you. To Bobby and Elizabeth Lambert security is everything. Believe me, she commiserated with me when you made your decision to leave the law firm and told me she'd never let Bobby leave his job."

"Did she know you were considering a divorce?" Mike asked.

"No, I kept quiet because she would have told Bobby, and he would have blabbed to you." Peg paused. "But her comments fed into my selfishness. Bobby stepped on thin ice when he helped you."

221

"I'll keep that in mind, but if I use the minutes of Hatcher's meeting in court, it will undoubtedly cause Mr. Forrest to question Bobby."

"Then he's trusting you to protect him."

"Which he didn't do for me at the church."

Peg tilted her head to the side. "I've been thinking about that this afternoon. I think Milton Chesterfield wanted to kick you out, but Bobby came up with the sabbatical idea to stall him and sold it to the rest of the elders because everyone didn't fully support Milton. The sabbatical is designed to give you time to work things out."

Peg's theory stopped Mike in his tracks. He mulled it over for a few seconds.

"Did you talk to Bobby?" he asked.

Peg smiled slightly. "I cannot tell a lie. He called me this morning after you wouldn't talk to him at the church. He didn't mention the paper he passed along to you at the deed room, but he explained what happened with the elders. Bobby and two other elders opposed Milton's motion. Libby wasn't there, and the session was split down the middle. Bobby didn't believe he could count on Libby and suggested the sabbatical as a compromise."

"His instincts were right about Libby. She gets mad at Milton, but she would ultimately side with him, especially if that's where Barbara landed. But I don't know why Milton and the others staged a sudden revolt. Serious problems usually simmer before they boil. The desire to oust me came like a tornado out of nowhere. I still don't see why representing Sam was used as the litmus test by Milton and the others. Bobby was the only elder who seemed irritated by my continued involvement. The others seemed indifferent; no one else mentioned it to me as a problem."

"Bobby didn't offer an explanation. He just wanted us to know what happened."

"There's more to it than that. In Sam's dream, the church burned to the ground, which wouldn't happen unless something at the church was going to be totally destroyed."

"I just hope the dream is figurative, not real."

"It's not literal." Mike sniffed the air in the room. "But if we don't eat soon, our supper may be in flames."

After they finished supper, Mike pushed away his empty plate.

"No wonder Sam Miller is round enough to play Santa Claus," he said. "It would take a lot of miles behind a lawn mower to work off a meal like that."

"If you ate like this every night, you could play Santa Claus by Christmas."

"And you could be a pregnant Mrs. Claus."

Peg started toward the sink.

"Stop," Mike said. "I'll take care of the cleanup."

Peg returned to her chair. "Make sure you save the leftovers," she said. "We'll need them."

Mike cleared the table.

"After I finish in here, I'm going to write an e-mail to every member of the session, notifying them of my decision to continue defending Sam and thanking them for the sabbatical to help take care of you."

"And that's it?"

"Don't you agree?"

Peg sighed. "Yes, I just wonder how we'll feel in four months when there's no more salary."

"Maybe I can work for Sam. I cut several lawns in our neighborhood when I was growing up."

Peg stared down at the table. Mike came over and put his arm around her.

"I know this is a serious decision. But it isn't just about Sam Miller. In the back of my mind, I think God is moving us to the next stage of our journey. We didn't anticipate finding a position at Little Creek when I finished seminary in Virginia. I didn't foresee Sam Miller coming into our lives, but it's opened our eyes to spiritual things and caused us to be more honest with each other. I can't predict the outcome of our current situation; however, I believe we have no choice but to trust the Lord. During the next three months, one of my jobs is to recognize the next opportunity He's preparing for us."

"Not bad for an impromptu sermon. But don't try to stop me from complaining."

Mike picked up her left hand and kissed it. "Complain all you want, as long as you stick with me."

It only took Mike a few minutes to compose the first draft of a letter to the elders, but he spent more than half an hour revising it. The final result was more conciliatory than he'd anticipated and sounded more like a thank-you note than the defiant rejection of an unreasonable

ultimatum. He promised to support the session's decision to the congregation and offered to facilitate the transition to the interim minister. He took
the letter to Peg, who was lying on the couch in the great room watching TV
and scratching Judge's neck.

"What do you think?" he asked when she finished.

"You write like a man who doesn't easily give in to road rage."

"I don't have a problem with road rage."

"I know, and that makes you different from a lot of people. The elders
who have a conscience should feel ashamed of their duplicity when they
read this. The ones who don't care about character will consider it a sign of
weakness."

"Weak?" Mike asked. "I don't want to look weak."

"Anyone who interprets your letter as weakness doesn't know the true definition of strength." Peg reached up and patted Mike's chest. "You have a
strong heart. And not because you can pedal a bike up a mountain."

MIKE RETURNED TO THE OFFICE. HE STARED AT THE E-MAIL
before pressing the Send button. A step this significant justified a last-second
opportunity to abort if a final warning surfaced in his mind. None came, and
he launched his missive into cyberspace. He spent the rest of the evening
watching the Cincinnati bull pen barely hold on to a five-run lead.

THE FOLLOWING MORNING, MIKE RECEIVED A CALL FROM
Braxton Hodges.

"Dressler is back in town," Braxton said.

"Is he in the office?"

"Not yet and won't be for long. According to the managing editor, Dressler
has resigned his position at the paper and is moving back to Mobile."

"Do you have his home number?"

"I can get it, but you don't have to track him down. He'll be in a meeting
here at eleven o'clock, and you should be able to catch him after it's over."

"How long will the meeting last?"

"Not more than thirty minutes. I'll be in it and will make sure to stall him
if you're not here."

"Don't worry. I'll be there."

MIKE TURNED LEFT AT TRAFFIC LIGHT NUMBER FOUR AND arrived at the offices of the Barlow County newspaper. The paper was printed in Asheville and shipped to Shelton for twice-a-week delivery. The newspaper office was in a drab brown building on a side street a block from the courthouse. He parked beside Braxton Hodges's car. Glancing in the front seat of the reporter's car, Mike saw the familiar collection of fast-food bags and sandwich wrappers. Inside the building, Mike approached a young woman sitting behind a cheap wooden desk and asked for Hodges.

While he waited, Mike examined the framed front pages that covered two walls from floor to ceiling. The newspaper had been in business for more than seventy years. Headlines of major world events—news of wars, assassinations, presidential elections, and two state football championships for the local high school—were included in the historical gallery. Braxton Hodges opened a door leading to the newsroom.

"The meeting is over, and Dressler is waiting to speak with you."

Mike entered a newsroom that bore little similarity to the bustling hive of a big-city publication. No phones were ringing; the workers in view didn't seem in a hurry. News in Shelton happened at a slower pace.

"Where can I meet with him?" Mike asked.

"In the conference room. Everyone else has cleared out, but I asked him to stay. When I mentioned your name, he immediately agreed to hang around."

"Does he know why I'm here?"

"Of course not. This is an investigation. In those situations, the best information comes out when people don't know what's important."

They came around a corner to a door marked "Conference Room A." Hodges opened the door for Mike.

"I'll leave you in private," Hodges said.

Dressler stood and shook Mike's hand. The former bank officer looked tired. The conference room was only large enough for a small table surrounded by six chairs. Dressler motioned for Mike to have a seat.

"Thanks for waiting," Mike began as he sat down.

Dressler sat down across from him.

"No, thank you for coming to the hospital. Your visit enabled Marie to go in peace. It also helped me face the funeral"—Dressler paused—"and the future. You don't know the details of our problems, but losing my wife would have been a thousand times worse if we hadn't been able to come to terms with some very hurtful events in our past."

"I'm glad we could help."

"And please tell the man who came with you how much I appreciated him as well."

"I will. His name is Sam Miller."

Dressler didn't hide his surprise. "The man who embezzled money from the church?"

"Did he?" Mike responded.

"Well, I know—" Dressler stopped.

"That he didn't do anything wrong?"

Dressler leaned away from the table. "Since leaving the bank, I don't know anything about the investigation. That's in the past."

"But it occurred while you were still employed at the bank. I'm defending Mr. Miller against the criminal charges. Your name came up during the course of my investigation, and I'd like to ask you some questions."

Dressler stared at Mike for a few seconds. "Is that why you came to the hospital? To ask me questions about Sam Miller?"

"Yes," Mike admitted, "but once we arrived it became obvious God had something else in mind that was more important than my questions. Without Sam's unselfishness, none of what you thanked me for a few minutes ago would have happened. Just because an event is in the past doesn't mean it's not affecting the present and the future. Isn't that what you said?"

Dressler looked around the room.

"Are you recording this conversation?"

"No."

Dressler glanced over his shoulder at the closed door then leaned forward and lowered his voice. "I met with the representatives of the church to verify that Miller didn't have authorization to transfer funds into his account."

"Who asked you to meet with them?"

"Jack Hatcher."

"What else did Mr. Hatcher ask you to do?"

"Answering that question is not going to help Mr. Miller or me."

"Why will it hurt you?"

"I want to work in the banking business in south Alabama. I already have a black mark against me because of my termination. If I end up testifying adversely to the bank in a criminal case, it would make it more difficult for me to move on with my life. I have two grandchildren who are depending on me as the primary means of their financial support, and I need to get back to work as soon as possible."

"Why couldn't you help Sam Miller? He helped you."

Dressler looked down at the table and sighed.

"Because all I have are suspicions. If you're looking for hard evidence of improper activity by the bank, I'm not the person to give it to you."

"What are your suspicions?"

Dressler hesitated. "What have you found out in your investigation?"

"That the signature on the two checks was imprinted. Sam didn't sign them."

Dressler nodded. Mike waited.

"Your response?" Mike pressed him.

"I think you're on the right track."

"Why?"

Dressler pressed his lips tightly together. Unlike most bankers, he didn't have a face that hid its struggles. Mike watched the conflict until Dressler leaned back in his chair and spoke.

"Part of my job at the bank was to stay abreast of technological developments that could affect bank security. Hatcher approached me with questions about forgery techniques, and, at the time, I assumed someone had presented false signatures on checks negotiated at the bank. I made my own inquiry about recent irregularities and nothing turned up. A few days later, Hatcher asked me to research legitimate companies with the capability to make a printed signature appear original. He said he might want to hire an outside consultant. I gave him a few names, then authorized payment for an invoice that came across my desk a month or so later. Within a few days, I was assigned to oversee the internal investigation of the Miller transactions. When I examined the signatures on the checks, I saw they were not just similar, but identical. It was a very stupid attempt to embezzle money, but there was also the presence of sophisticated technology that didn't serve the embezzler's purpose. It didn't make sense. A smart forger would have lifted two different signatures from the same person and used them. Then, my meeting with the men from the church confirmed that Miller was an uneducated man who might have tried to steal money but wouldn't have done so in the way presented to me. I brought it up with Hatcher, and he told me not to worry about it because Miller was a 'troublemaker.'"

"What happened next?"

"Nothing. Hatcher accepted my report and instructed me to close the file."

Mike wasn't sure he was getting all the truth. He took a copy of the minutes from his briefcase and laid it on the table.

"Please read this."

Dressler put on a pair of reading glasses. The banker pressed his lips together. Mike had to force himself to breathe normally.

"How did you get this?" Dressler asked when he finished.

"Lawfully in my investigation. Were you present at this meeting?"

"No."

"Why did Hatcher assign you the task of 'handling' Miller?"

"He didn't. All I handled was the brief investigation I mentioned."

"That's not the way I read it."

"I can't explain it either unless that's what led to our initial conversation. Cohulla Creek is another matter."

"What do you know about it?"

"It's under consideration for residential development."

"How big?"

"Very big, but not yet public. Do you know what's going on there?"

"I know about the options on file at the courthouse, and the plans to obtain property from the state to build a man-made lake."

"How did you find out about the lake?" Dressler asked with raised eyebrows.

"It's hard to keep something this big quiet in Barlow County."

Dressler shrugged. "It will all come out eventually, but until that happens, my knowledge of the deal is the leverage I have against a negative reference from the bank. Hatcher and the other developers want to keep the scope of the project secret until every piece is in place."

"Is it an honest deal?"

"What do you mean?"

"How is Butch Niles involved?"

Mike watched Dressler's face closely while asking the question. He saw the banker's jaw tighten.

"Niles is the one responsible for my termination at the bank," Dressler responded through clenched teeth.

"But you were senior to him in the bank's hierarchy."

"Not at the end. He assumed control for my area of responsibility and wanted someone else in the position. Hatcher backed him, and I didn't have a chance."

Dressler hadn't answered Mike's question but continued talking.

"So I really can't give you any information that you don't already have. I'm not a lawyer, but I don't think my conversation with Hatcher about printing signatures on checks is going to help Mr. Miller."

"Probably not," Mike responded. "It's nonspecific and remote."

Dressler stood up to signal an end to the meeting. "And thanks again to you and Mr. Miller for coming to the hospital."

Not willing to retreat, Mike placed his pen on the table.

"One other question. What was the name of the company retained by Hatcher—the one that sent an invoice?"

"I don't remember."

"If you saw the name, would it come back to you?"

"Maybe."

"Where is your research?"

"It could be anywhere. I didn't open a file. I just handed the list of companies to Hatcher."

"Will you let me know if you remember the company?"

"Sure."

Mike pulled out a subpoena and handed it Dressler.

"Sorry, but I have to give this to you before you leave town," Mike said. "Otherwise, I'd have to serve you in Alabama."

Dressler glanced at the subpoena then dropped it on the table. "This will be a tremendous inconvenience, and I don't think I can help Mr. Miller."

Mike resisted the urge to point out that praying for Marie Dressler had been inconvenient, too.

"It's part of a bigger picture," he said, as casually as he could muster. "I'll let you know if the scheduling of the case changes."

"Leaving the subpoena on the table isn't an option?" Dressler asked.

"No, sir. I'll notify the court it was personally served while you were in Barlow County."

Mike obtained Dressler's contact information in Alabama and remained in the conference room after the banker left. In less than a minute, Braxton Hodges joined him.

"Well?" Hodges asked.

"*Well* is a good word to use," Mike replied with a shrug. "I have to keep digging to find any fresh water. I didn't get much from Dressler except the water I poured in to prime the pump."

"Huh?"

"He asked me what I knew, then fed it back to me with a few minor embellishments. I subpoenaed him to the trial, but I may not use him."

"What about Butch Niles and Cohulla Creek?"

Mike related the few tidbits of information. "But all that shows is the scope of the project was known within the upper echelons at the bank. That's not a big revelation. He didn't respond to my specific question about Butch Niles."

"Why would he try to protect Niles? He's the one who fired him."

"I don't know. The degree of appreciation Dressler had for our visit to the hospital only took me so far. It unlocked his wife's heart to God but wasn't a master key to the Miller case."

"What are you talking about?"

Mike smiled. "Nothing you would print in the paper, although it would be at least as interesting as the articles about alternative health remedies."

"Did you read them?"

"Absolutely, and I'm anxiously waiting for the next installment. I'm hoping you can locate a herbal truth serum that I can slip into Jack Hatcher's sweet tea at the Ashe Café. Are you hungry?"

"Sure. Let's go."

It was a short walk from the paper to the restaurant. When Mike and Hodges entered, Mike saw Bobby Lambert, Maxwell Forrest, and two other men he didn't know already seated at a back table. Bobby looked up at Mike and immediately turned away. Forrest had his back to the door.

"Sarah Ann," Mike said to the hostess on duty. "Braxton and I would like to sit in the smoking section."

"You don't smoke," Hodges said as they crossed to the far side of the restaurant. "And I quit."

"Yeah, but I don't want to be next to my former law partners."

Mike sat so he could see the rest of the room.

"What's going on with you?" Hodges observed. "You're not the one on trial."

"If you only knew," Mike responded.

The two men ordered their food.

"Tell me," Hodges asked when the waitress left.

"Off the record?"

"Sure."

Mike shook his head. "Church politics have given me a serious bite wound."

"How bad?"

"Next week I start a three-month sabbatical from Little Creek that may prove permanent."

Hodges whistled. "What did you do?"

"Other than agreeing to help Sam Miller, I'm not sure."

Hodges picked up the knife from the table and held it out like a teacher lecturing with a pointer. "I know the routine. A dynamic young minister comes to a church that then starts to grow. People get excited, and the minister believes the church is moving toward the new millennium. Behind the scenes, the old power brokers get upset and run him off."

"How do you know so much about church politics? I didn't think you went to church."

"I don't."

The waitress returned with their sweet tea.

"My father was a preacher," the reporter said after she left. "Growing up, I attended two elementary schools, one middle school, and two high schools, the last one for my senior year only—all courtesy of church politics. Can you imagine what it would be like to move to a new town for your senior year of high school?"

"No."

"But flexibility and the ability to interact with new people have helped me in the newspaper business."

"Why don't you write the religion articles? The woman who does—" Mike stopped.

"Isn't much of a writer?" Hodges replied with a shrug. "Agreed. But I can't do it and maintain journalistic objectivity. I'm still mad about some of the garbage my family had to wade through when I was growing up. Venting my personal feelings on the religion page wouldn't help us sell papers or attract advertisers."

"Where is your father now?"

"If what he preached was true, he's in heaven."

"Do you believe in his truth?"

Hodges looked at Mike and laughed.

"I believe a lot of things, but I'm not sure how many of them are true."

Mike looked up as Bobby, Forrest, and the two men with them walked to the cash register. Hodges turned in his seat.

"There go your friends."

"Do you know the other two men?" Mike asked.

"No, but that doesn't mean they're not locals."

Mike relaxed as the group left the restaurant.

"I'm beginning to feel like a conspiracy theorist," he said.

Hodges leaned forward. "The masses love a good conspiracy. I'd get a kick out of writing a series of articles about some of the conspiracies that have popped up in our nation's history. It would be interesting reading, and even though I made it clear the stories weren't true, plenty of folks would believe they were real."

"Is that how you view Christian faith?"

Hodges shook his head. "Very slick, Preacher. You turned our conversation to religion smoother than a politician about to make a promise."

Mike grinned. "It's a fair question."

"Which I'm afraid to answer."

"Afraid?"

"Because the answer could change my life here and in the hereafter if it exists."

The waitress brought their food. Without asking Hodges's permission, Mike bowed his head to pray.

"God, help Braxton fear You enough to believe in Your love. Bless this food. Amen."

He looked up. Hodges had a quizzical expression on his face.

"What did that mean?" the reporter asked.

"I'm not sure, but it covered a lot of theological ground in a few words."

Hodges took a bite of steaming mashed potatoes and gravy. "What prompted you to make the leap of faith?"

Mike returned a fried chicken drumstick to his plate. "Which one? The most recent jump into the unknown was the decision to help Sam Miller."

"The first one. For my father, that was the only one that mattered."

"It happened during my junior year in high school. I attended a weekend retreat with a buddy who went to a different church. There was an evangelistic speaker, and when he gave the invitation on Saturday night, I left my seat and walked to the front. A counselor prayed with me."

Hodges swallowed a bite of chicken. "I did that at least a dozen times from age five to fifteen, but it never worked for me. After my first trip to the altar, my father insisted every subsequent visit was simply a rededication of my life to God. I kept trying, but after a while, my rededicator wore out, and I gave up." Hodges leaned forward. "Did things really change in your life after you prayed at the retreat?"

Mike looked directly into Hodges's eyes and spoke with all the earnestness he could muster. "I haven't had a sinful thought since."

Hodges burst out laughing and didn't stop. While Mike watched, the reporter's humor caught a second wind, and he sat back in his seat, continuing to guffaw until he wiped tears from his eyes.

"I didn't know I was that funny," Mike said when the reporter calmed down.

"You're not," Hodges replied. "It was so unexpected. I thought you were going to move to the next step of your evangelistic outline. When you didn't, it caught me totally off guard."

"You don't need an outline. Given your childhood, I'm sure you know the message of the gospel."

"Yeah, when I was a kid, I had to memorize questions to ask people and the correct answers to suggest in case they didn't get the point. I never did very well with it."

"Those approaches can work, but just because it didn't connect with you doesn't mean you're a hopeless reprobate."

"My first wife might disagree."

"And she may be right except for the hopeless part. People change because God's grace is a fact, not a concept."

Hodges ate several more bites of food before he spoke. "I might come hear you preach on Sunday, especially if you promise to make me laugh."

"You're welcome to visit, but I won't be there. My sabbatical begins at sundown Friday."

"Oh yeah, sorry."

"Don't let the way the church has treated your father or me stop you from having an open mind. The longer I believe, the more convinced I am about the truth that God wants to be involved in our lives."

"I've never been able to make that connection."

Mike thought for a moment. "What did Sam Miller write in the letter he sent you?"

Hodges put down a forkful of green beans without eating it.

"He claimed my attitude toward my father had warped my view of God and that I'd violated the verse about honoring parents."

"The fifth commandment."

"Yeah, it made me mad at first until I realized he was right."

"Did he know your father?"

"No. I grew up in Tennessee. Miller is a total stranger to our family. He could have researched my history, but I doubt it."

"I'm sure you're right about that. Sam relies on what he sees in a dream or his impression of the moment. Did he offer a solution for your problem?"

"He said if I spent more time with my son, I would better understand God's love for me."

"Did you do it?"

"No. I didn't want to hassle with my ex-wife. She always throws up objections to regular visitation, and my work schedule makes it hard to stick to specific times."

"How old is your son now?"

"Sixteen. He and his mother live in Hickory. A few years ago, she married a furniture company executive who makes five times what I do."

"It might not be too late to test out Sam's theory."

The door of the restaurant opened, and Butch Niles entered. Hodges raised his hand in greeting, and the legislator headed toward their table.

"What are you going to say to him?" Mike asked.

"Just watch. Niles cultivates a good rapport with the local press."

Mike and Hodges stood up as Niles approached to shake their hands.

"Mike has been trying to convert me," Hodges said as he released Niles's hand. "He almost had me convinced, but one thing stopped me."

"What?"

"That verse in the Bible about not trusting lawyers."

Niles shook his head. "Dr. Garrison at our church says that meant some kind of religious lawyer."

"That's true," Hodges replied. "But Mike is one of those, too. Want to join us?"

Niles looked around the room. "No thanks, I'm meeting someone. Bank business."

The door opened and Troy Linden, carrying a navy blue leather briefcase, entered.

"Got to go," Niles said.

"Call me if you hear any tidbits from Raleigh," Hodges replied.

"Sure thing."

When Niles left, Mike turned to Hodges. "That's Troy Linden."

"I know. I recognize him from his mug shot from New Jersey. If I ever write a story, it will be fun showing a photo with a number beneath the picture on the front page."

"I wonder which one of them will pay for lunch."

"Troy is the one with the deep pockets. He'll make sure Butch Niles has all the mashed potatoes and gravy he can cram in his mouth."

Twenty-four

DELORES CONFRONTED MIKE AS SOON AS HE APPROACHED HER desk. "I thought you were going to wait!" she snapped. "You should have taken the advice you gave me."

"You read the e-mail to the elders?"

"Yes, and it sounded like someone else wrote it." Delores held up her hand. "And don't tell me to pray about it. I have to do something."

Mike leaned against the front of her desk. "You're a key person. If you don't react, others will follow your lead."

"I can't promise that."

"As soon as the word gets out that I'm going on sabbatical, callers with questions are going to start phoning. That will be your chance to set the tone for the whole church. If you vent your frustration, it will spread like wildfire. If you don't act upset, it may help things work out down the road."

"That's hard to do when I don't know what's going to happen." Delores eyed him suspiciously. "Have you already decided not to come back after this so-called sabbatical is over?"

Mike answered carefully. "No door is closed in my mind."

"Are you going to fight for your job?"

"I don't think that will be necessary. God is going to take care of this battle without my help."

"Please." Delores snorted. "Leave Him out of it. You'd almost convinced me."

"I'm not ordering you to keep your mouth shut. That wouldn't work anyway. Just think it over. Do you have a copy of my e-mail to the elders?"

Delores picked up a sheet of paper from her desk. "Yes."

"Except for the part about Sam Miller, you can use it to answer people's questions."

Delores didn't respond.

Mike went into his office but left the door cracked open. He waited until he saw the light on his phone blink as a call came into the church then stepped quietly to the door and listened.

"Good morning, Little Creek," Delores answered crisply.

After a few moments of silence, she asked, "Who told you that, Emma? Mike hasn't been fired. He's taking a sabbatical to be with Peg during her pregnancy. The session voted Tuesday night, and Mike accepted their offer. Here's what he said about it—" Mike returned to his desk. He didn't have confidence of total victory with Delores. Working with her was a war of many battles.

In a few minutes, she paged him.

"Braxton Hodges from the paper is on the phone."

Mike picked up the receiver. "What did I do to deserve so much attention from the press? Are you secretly working on a feature article about me?"

"That's on my list as soon as I finish a series about Confederate soldiers buried in Barlow County. Listen, do you remember the briefcase Linden brought to the restaurant?"

"No."

"My journalistic eye noticed it. It was different, kind of a dark blue color."

"Okay."

"Linden didn't leave with it. He gave it to Niles."

"I thought you weren't going to stay at the restaurant."

"I didn't, but I saw Niles walking on the sidewalk toward the bank when I went out a few minutes ago. He was carrying the briefcase, and Linden wasn't with him."

"And you think the briefcase was stuffed with money?"

"Maybe."

"Did you follow Niles into the bank and watch the teller count it?"

"Preachers aren't supposed to be sarcastic," Hodges replied. "Do you want to hear me out?"

"Yeah, go ahead."

"While Niles is walking happily down the street, someone comes up and stops him for a few moments of private conversation. I pull into a parking space and watch. Niles is nervous, looking around, glancing over his shoulder, and putting both hands on the briefcase while the man is talking to him. Even from across the street, I could see that Niles was upset. Finally, he says something I can't hear and storms off toward the bank."

"Who was he talking to?"

"Sam Miller."

"Oh no!"

Mike quickly tried to remember whether Sam had mentioned anything to him about Butch Niles. He couldn't remember anything.

"I'll check with Sam when I give him an update on the case."

"And get back to me, so I can include the exchange between them in the article I'm writing."

"Forget it. Keep researching the broken-down tombstones of Confederate soldiers."

Mike called the Miller house, but no one answered. Upon arriving home, he knew why. The familiar red pickup truck was parked in his driveway. Mike went inside. The kitchen was empty, and he didn't hear any sounds in the house. He went into the great room and found Sam sleeping in his recliner. Mike cleared his throat. Sam didn't stir. He stepped back into the kitchen.

"Peg!" he called out. "I'm home!"

"I'm in the art room!" Peg responded.

Mike returned to the great room; however, his client was still fast asleep. Mike quickly stepped over to the chair, concerned the older man might be unconscious, not merely asleep.

"Sam," he said in a normal tone of voice.

No response. He looked closer and couldn't see any sign that Sam was breathing.

"Sam!" he said louder as he shook the older man's shoulder.

Sam stirred to life. He blinked his eyes and looked up at Mike.

"Are you okay?" Mike asked.

Sam rubbed his eyes and shook his head. "This is an awesome chair. I bet you have some incredible visions while you're sitting in it."

"Not really. I use it to watch TV."

Sam leaned forward and patted the leather arms of the chair. "Well, I think it's a rocket ship to Glory. I went up so fast I could have used a seat belt. Do you want to know what I saw?"

"Not now. What did you say to Butch Niles today?"

"How do you know about that?"

"A friend saw you talking to him but didn't hear the conversation."

"Wasn't much of a conversation. Last night, I figured out he was the box of finishing nails in my dream and told him to stop doing wrong at Cohulla Creek."

"Why did you say anything to him? It's just going to antagonize the people who want to see you sent to prison."

"Do you know why they were finishing nails?"

"Are you listening to me?"

"Yep, but I'm also trying to help you understand. Finishing nails mean that Representative Niles is the one who's going to finish the deal. There is a double meaning with the nails. It sounds like his name, and he's also going to nail down the deal."

"Okay, but why talk to Niles in the first place? He's not going to change his mind."

Sam cocked his head to the side. "Are you listening to yourself?"

"Yes."

"Do you believe the Master can change people for the better?"

Mike rolled his eyes. "Yes."

"What do they have to do?"

"Repent and believe."

"How will a person know to repent if no one tells them about their sin?"

"Are you cross-examining me?"

"Only to help you understand Papa's ways better."

"Mike!" Peg called. "Are you coming?"

"Yes!" he responded.

"Go on," Sam said with a wave of his hand. "I'd like to catch another quick nap before supper."

By the time Mike left the room, Sam's eyes were closed. Peg and Muriel were in the art room.

"Sue Cavanaugh stopped by for a few minutes to check on me," Peg said. "The interim minister at the church is a retired medical missionary named Vaughn Mixon. He'll be there tomorrow."

"A courtesy call from one of the elders would have been nice," Mike replied.

"She found out about it from Libby Gorman. There won't be a general announcement until Sunday morning."

"How are you feeling?" Mike asked.

"Less bored now that Muriel is here."

Returning to the great room, they found Sam asleep in the recliner.

"Should I wake him up?" Mike asked. "He claims the chair is the seat of heavenly revelation, but I need to give him an update on the case."

"Can it wait?" Muriel responded. "When this happens, it's better not to chain him to earth."

"How long will he sleep?" Peg asked.

Muriel looked at her watch. "I'll rouse him in an hour or so and take him home for supper. After that, he'll probably be up for a while writing in his notebook and reading the Bible."

It was an odd evening. Mike, Peg, and Muriel carried on a conversation in a normal tone of voice, and Sam slept through it all. After an hour passed, Muriel rose from her seat, went over to Sam, shook his shoulder, and spoke loudly in his ear. He blinked and opened his eyes.

"You're not very good company tonight," she said. "Let's go home."

As he came fully awake, Sam turned to Mike. "If you ever decide to sell this chair, let me know."

"Is the chair that special?"

Sam smiled. "Don't fight me. Let me build your faith."

EARLY SUNDAY MORNING, MIKE'S FEET WERE ON THE FLOOR before he remembered that he didn't need to go to church. He started to lie down again, but the pain of rejection brought him awake. He looked over his shoulder at Peg, who was sleeping peacefully. With each day, his confidence in the sincerity of her desire to remain committed to the marriage grew. He couldn't imagine the pain he'd be going through if she'd decided to leave simultaneously with the trauma at the church.

Quietly leaving the room, he opened the door for Judge to go outside. It was a fine morning, and the grays of night were giving way to streaks of color in the trees and bushes that signaled the new day. Mike watched Judge trot happily around the yard in his familiar morning ritual and wished his own Sunday morning routine hadn't been so cruelly disrupted. The dog returned, and Mike directed him back to the kitchen.

"No, she's not awake," he said when the dog headed toward the art room.

Mike went into the great room and sat in his chair. He reached for his Bible, but instead of opening it, placed it in his lap and closed his eyes.

Instantly, he was in another place.

It was a barren landscape with trees so broken and disfigured they looked like old men about to topple over. The ground was various shades of sickly brown, none of which indicated any hope of future fertility. The sky was gray, the sun hidden. A few puddles of polluted water collected in what looked like shallow bomb craters that pockmarked the earth as far as he could see. An oily slime on top of the water glistened with a sickly rainbow of color. To his right rested a simple table with a spotless white tablecloth thrown over it. A plain wooden chair was pulled up to the table.

Mike sat down in the chair. Although the table was bare, he bowed his head in a silent blessing. When he opened his eyes, there was a bowl of soup before him. Mike quickly glanced around but saw no one. He dipped a spoon into the soup and tasted it. It was not easy to identify. He ate another spoonful and decided it had to be a type of bisque containing complex flavors. As the soup encountered different parts of his tongue, it interacted with each category of taste buds. It was delicious. Mike continued eating, savoring each bite until he reluctantly scooped up the last of the soup and raised it to his lips.

He woke up.

The sun was streaming in shafts into the backyard. He looked at the clock and realized it had been almost an hour since he sat down in the chair.

"What was that all about?" he spoke out loud.

Mike opened his Bible and flipped through the pages, looking for a verse in the Psalms. He heard footsteps as Peg came into the room. She sat on the edge of the chair and squeezed close to him.

"I know it's hard for you to stay home instead of going to the church," she said.

"I was depressed when I woke up, but then I came out here and had a dream."

"Tell me."

When Mike reached the part about the delicious soup, Peg interrupted.

"You could taste it? I've never had a dream involving taste."

"Yeah, it was so real I can still remember the flavors. When you're back on your feet and in the kitchen, I want you to fix it for us."

Peg smiled. "You'll have to take me with you to Dreamland so I can get the recipe."

"When I finished the soup, I woke up. Then I thought about this verse." He picked up his Bible. "Psalm 78:19: *'Can God spread a table in the desert?'* It describes exactly what I saw and experienced—a wonderful meal in a desolate place."

Shortly before 11:00 a.m. the doorbell rang. Judge barked and followed Mike to the door.

Sam and Muriel Miller stood on the front steps. Sam spoke. "Since you're a preacher without a congregation, I thought we might have church here this morning."

Mike held the door open. "Come in."

They went into the great room.

"Can I sit in your chair?" Sam asked.

"Only if you promise not to go to sleep during the sermon."

Peg joined them. She and Muriel sat on the couch. Mike brought in a chair from the dining room and placed it so that he faced the other three.

"What's going to happen during this church service?" he asked.

"You're the preacher. What's on your heart?" Sam replied.

Mike glanced at the clock.

"I want to pray for the service at Little Creek."

Sam nodded. "They can take the sheep away from the shepherd, but the shepherd's heart remains with the flock."

Mike told them the little he knew about Vaughn Mixon.

"He's a good man," Sam said.

"Do you know him?" Mike asked in surprise.

"Nope, but Papa does."

Mike looked at Peg. "I step into that hole just about every time Sam digs it."

"Let's pray," Sam said.

Peg started speaking before Mike could organize his thoughts. Her direct, commonsense approach to life came through in practical requests. Sam or Muriel interjected an occasional "Amen."

When Peg grew silent, Sam took up where she left off. He prayed in spurts, as if listening for a few moments then speaking what he heard. Mike had grown used to Sam's use of "Papa" and "Master," but was startled by the old man's knowledge of the Bible. He effortlessly quoted long passages from memory. And his knowledge wasn't limited to the New Testament. He used verses from the Old Testament, too. Apparently, Sam did more than walk mindlessly behind a mower all day. Mike felt slightly jealous; a response he knew would make Sam happy.

When Sam grew silent, Mike waited for Muriel, but she didn't say a word. After a minute or so, Mike cleared his throat to speak, but an inner restraint held him in check. Three times, he prepared to break the silence but couldn't do so. Finally, the old woman spoke. And when she did, Mike was grateful he'd waited.

"Father, let the sweetness of Your love flow over the people of the Little Creek Church. Many of them are taking the baby steps of faith. Bring them along the path with gentleness and wisdom." Her voice increased in intensity. "Protect them. Do not let the Enemy trip them up. Let the people remember the love Mike and Peg have for them and how they showed that love to them day by day."

As Muriel continued, emotion welled up in Mike. The old woman understood the heart of the Father for His children and the concern of a pastor for his flock.

The prayers of the others so beautifully communicated the need of the moment that when it was finally Mike's turn, he searched for something to add but did nothing more than provide the final "Amen."

He looked up into the eyes of the other three people in the room.

"If there was regular prayer like this for every church in America, our nation would change."

"Yep," Sam replied. "It doesn't make the evening news, but there are more praying people than you might think. I've seen the lights in the night, and they cover the whole country."

Mike looked at the clock. "I didn't prepare a sermon."

"Tell your dream," Peg said. "Sam will like it."

Mike pointed to the chair. "I took a ride on the rocket ship."

While Mike talked, Sam smiled and nodded knowingly. Mike tried to wipe the grin from the old man's face by describing in greater detail the devastation of the landscape, but nothing changed Sam's countenance. When he reached the part about the soup, Sam's face lit up. Mike stopped.

"Do you want to say something?" he asked.

"Nope."

Mike finished by reading the verse from Psalms.

"That's better than a bunch of sermons I've heard," Sam said, patting his stomach. "It's something I can carry with me when we go home. It also reminds me of a vision I had many years ago." He turned to Muriel. "Remember when we were helping that church on Mackey Road?"

"Yeah, a lot of people got saved before things turned rough."

Sam spoke to Mike and Peg. "It was during the time I met Larry Fletchall's father. His name was Victor. Back then, blacks and whites working together in the ministry didn't happen very often, but Papa showed Vic and me that we were supposed to do some meetings together. Neither of us knew much about the ministry, but Papa showed up, which is all it takes to have good church. It was a great time until a bunch of preachers, some white, some black, started telling lies about us and stirring up trouble. Some of the people working with us got sick, including Vic, who ended up in the hospital."

"Our son Matthew was little," Muriel added. "And he started having nightmares."

"Anyway, one night I had a vision. I was standing on a battlefield that looked a lot like your wilderness except there were people lying around wounded. When I saw their faces, I recognized Vic, our son, and several others. Nearby was a table, and I sat down. An angel appeared and asked me if I wanted to order soup or a salad. I thought it was a stupid question and pointed to the people who were hurt. How could I consider eating when I was in the middle of such a horrible battle? The angel repeated the question several times then I woke up. Do you know what it means?"

Mike shook his head.

"I wasn't sure either," Sam continued. "But like you, Papa reminded me of a verse. It's in Psalm 23."

Mike thought for a moment. "He prepares 'a table before me in the presence of my enemies.'"

"Yep. We may think the world is coming to an end, but Papa isn't upset. He let me know that He's in control and could offer one of His children a quiet meal even if things in life are rough. Soon after the vision, Vic got better, and Matthew was able to sleep at night. A lot of the folks who founded the Craig Valley church were saved in those meetings." Sam paused. "You know, I need to remember that one. It will help me face what's up ahead for both of us."

Peg invited Sam and Muriel to stay for lunch.

"We're eating your leftovers," she said.

"No thanks," Muriel replied. "We're going to visit a woman who lives not far from our house. I have to pick up something to take to her."

Mike walked them to the front door.

"What exactly did you say to Butch Niles when you saw him on the side-walk the other day?" he asked Sam.

"Nothing except the interpretation of the dream."

"Did you quote the poem?"

"Nope."

"Did he understand what you told him?"

"Yep. But understanding isn't the same as obeying. He got upset, but it doesn't mean he won't think about it later and do the right thing. I've seen that happen many times. Remember how long it took you to agree to help me?"

"Yeah."

"But now you know it was the right thing to do." Sam put his hand on Mike's shoulder. "And hearing what Papa is doing in your life gives me hope for what lies ahead."

After Sam and Muriel left, the phone started ringing, and Mike fielded calls from members of the congregation. He quickly learned that Bobby Lambert spoke on behalf of the elders, and Vaughn Mixon made it clear that his stay at the church was temporary. He didn't want Mike's job. Many of the people who called said they would be praying for Peg and looked forward to Mike's return. When the calls slowed, Mike went into the downstairs bedroom.

"Did you hear my side of the conversations?" he asked.

"In part. A lot of the people support you."

Mike sat on the edge of the bed. "At the session meeting, I thought my time at Little Creek was over. Now, I'm not so sure."

"We'll have to wait and see. One thing I've realized in the past weeks is that a lot of big changes can happen in a short period of time."

MIKE WOKE UP MONDAY MORNING AND FIXED BREAKFAST FOR Peg. He brought it to her in bed with a short love note placed beside her toast. Peg opened the note and read it while he waited.

"Thank you," she said.

"How are the eggs?" Mike asked. "I know you like them over easy."

Peg took a bite. "Perfect. When did you learn to do that?"

"It took six eggs to get two right. In the process, I discovered a lot about how eggs react to heat."

Peg sipped the coffee. "Where's your breakfast?"

"I ate the mistakes."

Mike sat on the bed and watched her eat. "The elders told me to care for you. Since they're the ones in charge of my life, I'd better do what they say."

Peg laughed. "That sounds interesting, but who's going to take care of you?"

"I'm self-sufficient."

"You've not been self-sufficient since you lived like a pig in college."

"We didn't live like pigs."

"I saw the kitchen at the fraternity house. But you're much more domesticated now."

"A domesticated pig instead of a wild pig?"

"That's not a fair comparison, considering how beautifully you fixed my breakfast."

"What else am I going to do today?"

Peg nibbled a bite of toast. "Keep me company."

"That will be pleasant. Anything else?"

"Work on Sam's case."

LATE IN THE AFTERNOON, MIKE TOOK A SHORT NAP IN HIS CHAIR in the great room. He'd not had any dreams as dramatic as the table in the desert, but several times he'd awakened with a thought or a phrase that he entered in his PDA. The phone rang as he rested with his eyes closed. It was Darius York.

"I called the church, and the secretary gave me your home number," York began.

"This will be the place to reach me for the time being," Mike said. "What can you tell me?"

"I've reviewed the writing sample you sent and ran a comparison on the checks. It's your man's signature on the bottom of the checks, but it's not a sophisticated imprint job."

Mike felt a sudden knot in his stomach. "What do you mean?"

"The name on the checks was stamped with a signature stamp. There isn't any smearing of the ink, but there's no doubt an old-fashioned stamp was used. Did your client use a signature stamp in his work?"

"I don't know. I'll have to ask him."

"If he had one, find out who had access to it."

"Okay. But that doesn't jive with the information obtained from a former bank officer involved in the investigation."

Mike summarized his conversation with Brian Dressler. "I was hoping for a high-tech imprint of the signature," Mike concluded. "That would have given me a better defense than the unauthorized use of a signature stamp."

"If your client is innocent, the people wanting to make him look guilty adopted a simple yet clever strategy to do so."

"Did you discover anything else?"

"The payee name and date were typed on an old IBM Selectric typewriter."

"I doubt my client owns a typewriter. He writes in notebooks."

"What does he do for a living?"

"He has a small lawncare business. No employees."

"The typewriter used to produce the checks was a business model, heavy-duty and state-of-the-art when introduced, but a dinosaur today."

"Could you identify the specific unit?"

"If I had a proper sample. The print produced by each typewriter is unique, especially after the passage of time increases eccentricities in the typeface."

"Would it be the type of machine used at a bank?"

"Absolutely."

"Do you still want to see the originals of the checks?"

"Yes. The copying process masks details that would be easier to locate if I had access to the originals."

"Could you come to Shelton to review them? The judge wouldn't let them leave the custody of the bank or the State."

"Yes."

Mike thought a moment. "Do your qualifications as an expert witness include analysis of typewriters?"

"I've performed less work with machines, but they're easier to identify. Unlike handwriting, their peculiarities are reproduced repeatedly."

"Can you send a report of your findings thus far?"

"Why?"

"So I can be sure about your opinion."

"I won't back off my assessment."

Mike felt uneasy. "I don't like to go to court without something in my hand to guide my questions."

"What more do you need?"

Mike listed several items.

"I can give that information."

"Okay."

"Do you want me to return the documents you sent me?"

"Not yet. I'll let you know as soon as possible if I find out anything about the original checks or the location of a typewriter."

MIKE HUNG UP AND CALLED MELISSA HALL. THE RECEPTIONIST paged the assistant DA, who answered the phone.

"How is your wife?" Hall asked before Mike could speak. "I heard you've taken a leave of absence from the church to take care of her."

"She's off her feet and taking it easy. It's hard because she was an everyday runner and very active."

"Are you going to ask for a continuance of the case to take care of her?"

Mike didn't answer. Judge Coberg might grant a postponement, but Mike wouldn't be completely honest in asking for one.

"That remains to be seen. When will the Miller case be on the trial calendar? I haven't received notice of trial."

"It's being worked up, but Ken has it penciled in as a backup in a week and a half. After that, there won't be a criminal court trial week for at least two months."

A two-month postponement looked very attractive. Mike made a note on his legal pad.

"If you're still pushing the case up the ladder," he said, "I need to see the original checks. I won't stipulate to the use of copies."

"I haven't received them yet."

"My expert wants to examine them prior to trial."

"That shouldn't be a problem. I'll call the bank and let you know. He can look at them here at our office. Any preliminary idea what your expert is going to say?"

Mike was so surprised by Hall's request that it caught him off guard. Modern rules of disclosure had limited the opportunity for trial by ambush in most areas of the law, but in a criminal case it was still possible to blindside the prosecution in the heat of battle.

"Uh, he's not finished his report and wants to have access to the original checks before doing so."

"I'd like to know if there are any irregularities."

Mike didn't answer. "Call me as soon as you have the checks."

Mike phoned Muriel Miller, who told him Sam never used a signature stamp or owned a typewriter. Sam's invoices, like the dreams and visions recorded in his notebooks, were all handwritten.

FRIDAY MORNING, MIKE TOOK PEG TO THE HOSPITAL FOR another ultrasound. Dr. Crawford came in shortly after the technician left.

"Everything looks good," the doctor said. "Have you had any problems?"

"The sudden shift to a sedentary lifestyle has been a shock to my system, but no bleeding or cramping pain since I came to the ER."

"What are you doing during the day?"

Peg described her routine. "And Mike's been with me all this week. The church gave him a three-month sabbatical to look after me."

"Really?" The doctor raised her eyebrows. "I didn't know churches offered family-leave time for husbands."

"It's not a FMLA request," Mike replied. "It was a decision by the church leadership."

"And I commend them for it," the doctor replied. "What's the name of your church?"

"Little Creek."

"Sounds like a good place to be." Dr. Crawford turned to Peg. "Increase the amount of walking around the house and the yard so you won't lose too much muscle tone. We want to strike a balance between avoiding stress on the baby and maintaining your own health. Your weight is good. The baby is growing fine, and the heart rate is within normal limits. Things look stable."

"Can you determine gender?" Mike asked.

"Too early for that. We may be able to tell at the next examination."

Peg patted her stomach. "Keep growing."

"How are you doing emotionally?" the doctor asked Peg. "Any depression or unusual mood swings?"

"Not too bad. Having Mike around has helped a lot."

"Bring more variety into your activities, but stop physical activity at the first sign of trouble and let me know."

"I have a case on the trial calendar in about ten days," Mike said. "Should I request a continuance to stay with Peg?"

"You're still working as a lawyer?"

"It's a pro bono case."

"How long will the trial last?"

"Could be several days depending on jury deliberation."

"That shouldn't be a problem so long as Peg has someone available on call. I'm sure you have friends who could fill in, or you could use a sitting service. Contact my office if you need a recommendation for outside help."

As they drove home from the doctor's office, Mike spoke to Peg. "I guess I can't use Dr. Crawford's recommendation as an excuse for a continuance in Sam's case."

"Do you need one?"

"There are still a lot of loose ends. Every time I pull out one string another takes its place."

They arrived home. Peg got out of the car, but Mike stayed in the driver's seat.

"Aren't you coming in?" she asked, leaning back into the car.

"I want to go to the church," he replied.

"Go," she said. "I've been impressed you haven't called or gone over there before now."

"You'll be okay?"

"Yes. I'm going to walk Judge around the yard a few times to celebrate my release from house arrest."

Twenty-five

MIKE PARKED BUT DIDN'T GO DIRECTLY TO THE CHURCH OFFICE. Leaning against his car, he let his eyes roam across the property. Every season in the hills of North Carolina offered unique beauty, but spring and fall were his favorites. Once started, spring came quickly to the mountains. The ancient trees beside the old sanctuary were in full foliage; the barren spots in the grass filled in. He listened. The explosion of birdcalls that had surrounded him a few weeks earlier during mating season had settled down to the less-ardent conversations of routine life. The creek now ambled rather than rushed, but Mike knew fresh water still bubbled to the surface of the spring.

Mike realized how much he'd tightly wound his expectations for the future around his work at the church. To end it would be painful. He'd seen the stress etched across the faces of other ministers and secretly looked down on their weakness, thinking his background as a trial lawyer inoculated him against the pressures of the pastoral ministry. The past few weeks had blown apart his confidence. He'd privately vacillated between unleashing Delores as the opening salvo of an all-out war to save his ministry and immediately resigning to avoid prolonging the pain.

He walked into the administration wing. Delores glanced up as he approached her desk.

"It's about time!" she exclaimed. "You've already cost me a steak dinner bet with Nathan."

"What do you mean?"

"I told him you would call on Monday. When that didn't happen, we did a double-or-nothing bet that you would come to the office by Wednesday.

You totally let me down, so I have to buy him a gift certificate for two to the Mountain View."

"I pretended to be on vacation," Mike replied.

"And how often did you call in the last time you went on vacation?"

"Every day. You could have picked up the phone and called me."

"That would have nixed the bet." Delores paused. "And I wanted you to have a break if you really wanted one."

"Thanks. How are you holding up?"

Delores touched a pack of cigarettes in plain view on her desk. "I've upped my nicotine intake. And don't be too hard on me," she added hurriedly. "I haven't cussed out Milton, and I've kept my mouth shut about how bad the elders treated you."

"How about Dr. Mixon?"

"He's a nice man but not near the preacher you are."

Mike stifled secret pleasure at her words. Delores continued, "But I saved you a CD of the sermon. Do you want to hear it?"

"Uh, sure." Mike took the CD. "Thanks. Any mail or phone calls I need to take care of?"

"There is a huge stack of stuff on your desk, but Bobby told me to leave it alone. The elders are meeting Saturday morning to sort through everything. I think it would be better for them to deal with it and realize how much you do."

"Any emergencies?"

"I'm taking names and numbers for people who need counseling. I think the session is going to authorize payment by the church if an individual or couple wants to go to a private counselor."

"That could cost a lot of money!"

Delores lowered her voice. "Milton put a big check in the offering plate to make everything look good."

The church treasurer and one of the deacons were the only people who knew who and how much was contributed each week. Mike purposely kept himself ignorant of the information.

"Delores, you know better than to snoop—"

"It was on top of the stack of checks, and I couldn't help seeing it. I didn't look at anything else."

"I ought to suspend you without pay for a week."

"Then I couldn't pay for Nathan's dinner. I think he's going to take Melissa Hall. She was with him again at church on Sunday."

"I'll be seeing quite a bit of her myself. The Miller case is on the trial calendar for a week from Monday. She'll be handling the prosecution."

"Good!" Delores exclaimed. "Once that's over, maybe we can get back to normal around here."

"I'm beginning to wonder if I know what normal looks like." Mike turned to leave. "Oh, one other thing. Don't you have a friend who works at the Bank of Barlow County?"

"Gloria Stinson. She's been a secretary there for years."

"Which department?"

"Different ones. She used to have her own little office, but now she's part of a clerical pool. Only the big shots have their own secretary. If she weren't so close to retirement, she'd probably quit."

"Could you ask her if the bank has any old IBM Selectric typewriters?"

"Do you want to buy one?"

Mike nodded. "Yeah, if it's the right one. Don't mention my name when you call. Because of the Miller case, I'm not the most popular person at the bank."

"Gloria can tell me. She keeps up with everything."

DELORES PHONED MIKE ON HIS CELL BEFORE HE WAS HALFWAY home.

"I talked to Gloria. She tells me they still use a couple of IBM typewriters to fill out forms that don't have templates in the computers."

"Any for sale?"

"She didn't think so, even though they rarely use them. She has one near her desk, and a lady who works in her area has the other one. She said you could find a used one at an office supply company a lot easier than trying to purchase one from the bank."

Mike slowed the car as he came to a bridge across the creek.

"Could you ask her to type a few words on each one and give it to you? I want to make sure about the font before I decide what to do."

"Sure."

Mike took a slip of paper from his pocket and slowly read a sentence provided by Darius York. "Tell her to type 'More liberty is needed in the USA for all those who love the truth.'"

"Why that?"

"Did you write down the sentence?" Mike asked without answering.

"Yes."

"And ask her to do it as soon as possible and let me know. Thanks."

Mike hung up the phone before Delores could launch another question. If Gloria properly capitalized the sentence, Mike would have the letters Darius York needed to evaluate the type on the checks.

THAT NIGHT AFTER SUPPER, MIKE AND PEG SAT IN THE GREAT room and listened to the CD of the church service at Little Creek.

"What did you think?" Mike asked after the closing hymn.

"Do you want me to compare his style to yours and tell you how much better you are in the pulpit?"

"It sounds petty when you put it that way."

Peg reached over and patted him on the hand. "You're my favorite speaker, even if you reject my sermon suggestions, but I'd like to meet Dr. Mixon and hear more stories about Africa. I think he can inspire the congregation to be less provincial and self-focused. And his prayer for us seemed sincere."

"Yeah. He came across that way when I talked to him."

"Look at it this way. We prayed with Sam and Muriel that God would bless the service at Little Creek, and He did."

"I don't want to be narrow-minded myself. I need to see Mixon more as an ally than a threat to my little kingdom."

"That sounds more mature."

Mike chuckled. "I want to be a big boy, but the little boy is still running around inside me wanting attention."

"Sometimes he's cute."

"Other times he's a selfish brat."

Peg smiled. "Don't be too hard on yourself. Many times, your little boy has been a lot less selfish than my little girl."

DELORES CAME BY THE HOUSE MONDAY MORNING AND HANDED Mike two sheets of paper. Gloria had done her job well.

"Perfect," he said. "There's nothing like the crispness of an IBM Selectric with a standard ball in place."

"What's this about?" Delores responded as she stood in the middle of the kitchen. "You're not in the market for a typewriter."

Mike looked up. "Yes, I am, but not for personal use. It has to do with the Miller case, and I can't tell you the details."

"You tricked me."

"I didn't tell you everything because I can't. I'd love to buy the typewriter if it's connected to the case. You and your friend have helped an innocent man."

"Will Gloria get into trouble?"

"Her name won't come up unless you mention it. No one will know how I got this information."

"But you might make her come to court. I know how you are when you get your mind set on something. You forget the effect it may have on other people."

"No. You trusted me, and she trusted you. I won't violate that. There is a legal way to avoid identifying her. If this works out for the case, I'll pay for both of you to go to the Mountain View."

"Okay," Delores replied in a way that didn't imply confidence. "But if something bad happens to Gloria, I'll never forgive you."

Mike drove into town and sent the sample sheets to Darius York via next-day delivery. He stopped by the district attorney's office to find out about the status of the original checks, but Melissa Hall wasn't in.

Mike phoned Braxton Hodges at the paper.

"We need to talk," the reporter said when he picked up the phone. "Are you available?"

"Yes."

"Come to my office."

Mike turned left at traffic light six and arrived at the newspaper building. Hodges took him into the same conference room where Mike had met with Brian Dressler.

"Investigative reporting is what makes my juices flow," the reporter said, leaning across the table. "Butch Niles recently went to Atlantic City where he dropped a lot of money in a weekend."

"How did you confirm it?"

"From one of the women who cleans his house. She heard Butch's wife complaining about it and mentioned it to the lady who cleans my duplex once a month. She passed the info on to me."

"That's triple hearsay," Mike replied.

"But it fits the corrupt politician model." Hodges paused. "And I have written proof."

The reporter reached into his pocket and pulled out several crumpled slips of paper.

Mike could see faint numbers printed on them.

"Receipts for chips at two different casinos," Hodges said. "The cleaning lady took them out of the trash. The total is close to $300,000."

Mike didn't touch the papers.

"Why did she take them?"

"Butch and his wife don't pay very well. I'm supplementing her income to be on the lookout for interesting information."

"You'd better be careful—"

"Don't worry," Hodges interrupted. "She knows not to take anything that hasn't been discarded."

"But still no relevance to my case."

"Maybe in a court of law, but not in the court of public opinion."

When he returned home, Mike had a voice mail from Darius York.

"I'm eighty-five percent sure we have a match on the typewriter," the former FBI agent said.

"Eighty-five percent?"

"Yes."

"I'm not sure that's high enough to help. Why can't you be more certain?"

"I'd need to see both machines and check all the letters, numbers, symbols, etc. Because it's an electric typewriter the pressure on the letters is uniform, so I have a good sample to compare with the letters on the checks. The sentence I gave you included those letters, but it takes more than a couple of significant similarities to increase the probability for a particular machine into the ninety-five-percentile range."

"I'm not sure I can obtain access to the machines."

"If you want a higher probability, that's the only way to get it. What is the status of the original checks?"

"Still waiting on the DA's office, but they have to furnish them this week. We're on the trial calendar next Monday."

"How much notice can you give me about the trial date?"

"The judge will hold a calendar call on Friday and set the preliminary schedule; however, that often changes because last-minute deals are struck over the weekend. Are there any days that don't work for you next week?"

"I'm clear but need as much notice as possible. The balance of my fee will have to be paid before I come."

Mike winced. "I'll give it to you when you review the original checks."

"Examining the checks will be helpful. It's all cumulative, and I don't want to speculate without the data to support my testimony."

"Of course not." Mike paused. "Sometimes, less is more. We may not introduce evidence about the typewriters if it lessens the impact of your opinion about the signature stamp."

Mike's confidence in the benefit he might achieve from Darius York was slipping. Jurors were skittish of experts, and if the members of the jury believed Mike was trying to hoodwink them with York's testimony, it wouldn't matter what the witness said. Mike, York, and Sam would all be considered guilty.

"That's your call," York said.

When he hung up the phone, Mike wished he could walk down the hall and ask Bobby Lambert or Maxwell Forrest what to do. One of the benefits of practicing with other lawyers was the availability of advice from peers, especially an attorney like Mr. Forrest, who had seen so much during the course of his career. Judge came into the study.

"You're a judge," Mike said as he scratched the dog's wrinkled head behind his left ear. "What do you think?"

Judge moaned slightly in appreciation for the attention.

"My sentiments exactly," Mike replied.

MIKE TURNED THE HOME OFFICE INTO A WAR ROOM. HE devoted two legal pads to each witness and jotted down ideas for direct and cross-examination. On another pad, he listed possible exhibits and the pros and cons of their use at trial. His evidence professor in law school preached one maxim that Mike totally believed—"Never do anything in a case that will hurt you more than it helps you." Lawyers had a tendency to become myopic and view all evidence in the light most favorable to their client's position. To combat this, Mike liked to mock-try cases with surrogate jurors brought in to hear the evidence and offer detailed feedback. Paying

Darius York was already stressing Mike's bank account. He couldn't afford the expense of a mock trial.

Instead, he relied on Peg.

Once he finished a series of direct examination questions, he walked from the office to the art room and read them to Peg. She listened and told him what else she would like the witness to say. Toward the end of their third session, Peg yawned several times.

"Am I boring you?" Mike asked anxiously. "A bored jury is dangerous."

"No, but I need a baby nap."

Mike looked at his watch. It was 4:00 p.m.

"I'll call the DA's office."

Melissa Hall came on the line.

"Do you have the checks?" he asked.

"No, but a courier is bringing them over from the bank early Wednesday morning."

"Where can my expert examine them?"

"At our office with a member of the staff present. Early afternoon will be fine."

"Set it at one-thirty. If that changes, I'll let you know."

Mike confirmed the appointment time with Darius York then prepared a subpoena for production of the bank's IBM typewriters at the same time and place. He'd already sent out subpoenas for Dick Bunt and Troy Linden to the states where they resided to be signed by a local clerk and served by a deputy sheriff. Their presence wasn't essential at the trial, but he hoped to tag at least one of the men. Mike filled in a number of witness subpoenas. At the law firm, he'd used a private process server to deliver local subpoenas. Without that luxury, he drove to the bank himself.

The Bank of Barlow County had an imposing gray marble facing on the front with the name of the bank chiseled in large letters across the top of the building. However, marble covered only the front. The sides and back of the block-long structure were plain red brick. Prosperity in Barlow County was often only surface-deep.

Mike entered the lobby, a large open space with a two-story ceiling. Internet banking hadn't yet dented the market in Shelton, and a row of teller stations stretched across one end of the lobby. On busy Fridays, all eight tellers would be in place ready to receive payroll checks. Late afternoon on a Monday, only two teller spots were open.

To the left of the lobby was a bull-pen area for customer service representatives and junior loan officers who handled car financing, small personal loans, and applications for residential mortgages. A vice president in a glass-walled corner office supervised the floor operations. More significant business was always sent "upstairs."

The second-floor business area could be reached by a broad staircase or an elevator. Mike took the stairs. He and Peg didn't have an account at the bank, and he'd not been to the second floor since he and the church treasurer arranged the financing for the new sanctuary at Little Creek. At the top of the stairs, there was a reception area with leather chairs and several sofas. Two women routed people to the appropriate individual or department. Mike could serve the subpoena on any bank officer. He approached the younger of the receptionists and introduced himself.

"My mother visited your church," the receptionist replied in a chipper voice. "She liked it, but she moved to Nashville to help my sister who had triplets."

"I'm glad she enjoyed the service. Is one of the bank officers available? I have something to deliver, and it won't take long."

The woman glanced down at a sheet of paper.

"Actually, Mr. Hatcher finished a meeting a few minutes ago."

Mike smiled. "That will be fine."

He watched the woman dial Jack Hatcher's office and tried to read the reaction to the news that Mike was in the building. She hung up the phone.

"He'll see you," she said. "Do I need to take you to his office?"

"No thanks. I know the way."

Jack Hatcher's office suite covered an entire corner of the building. From his desk, the president of the bank could look out large, floor-to-ceiling windows and keep an eye on Shelton. Mike opened the door to the outer office where Hatcher's personal assistant worked. The carpet in his outer office was noticeably nicer than the floor covering. The same woman had worked for the bank president for many years. She nodded in greeting to Mike.

"Good afternoon, Reverend Andrews. You can see Mr. Hatcher now."

Mike stepped into the banker's office. Hatcher rose from behind his desk and came around and shook Mike's hand.

"Good to see you. Been on any more bike rides?"

"No, I've been staying close to home."

"Have a seat," the banker said, gesturing. "What can I do for you?"

Mike opened his briefcase. "I have two subpoenas to give you."

He handed the documents to Hatcher, whose genial expression evaporated at the first glance.

"You want me to appear at Miller's trial?" he blurted out.

"Yes, sir. Along with the bank's IBM typewriters. The machines have to be delivered to the district attorney's office before one-thirty on Wednesday. Your subpoena is day-to-day next week depending on when the case is called for trial. If you provide a local contact number, I won't object to the judge allowing you to be on telephone standby."

Mike watched the muscles in Hatcher's face twitch as the banker tried to formulate a response.

"Of course, the bank wants to cooperate with the legal process, but I'm a busy man. Can't a more junior officer provide the information you need?"

"No, sir. You have unique knowledge about the facts and circumstances that makes you the only witness competent to testify."

"What are you talking about?" Hatcher's attempt to maintain his composure cracked.

"Sam Miller. That's why I'm here."

"I don't know Miller! The man embezzled money from one of our depositors. What can you ask me about beyond the records turned over to the district attorney's office? I don't know what your client told you, but if you intend on putting the bank on trial in this case, you're making a serious mistake."

Mike hesitated. "Mr. Hatcher, I appreciate your willingness to discuss this with me, but you might want to consult your lawyer."

"Don't patronize me!" Hatcher's eyes flashed.

Mike narrowed his eyes. "Would you let me finish?"

Hatcher nodded.

"I asked for access to documents generated by your internal investigation, but the information Mr. Forrest provided didn't even include what I'd already uncovered on my own. That let me know there hasn't been full disclosure, and I intend to use every legal avenue available to get to the truth. My job is to represent my client. This case has already caused me considerable personal and professional hardship, and I don't intend on backing down now."

Hatcher waved his hand to signal the end of the interview. "Then you'd better talk to Maxwell Forrest if you want anything from us."

Mike stood. "He knows my number."

Mike returned to the waiting area and thanked the young receptionist for her help.

"Is Butch Niles in the bank?" he asked.

"No."

"When do you expect him back?"

The woman looked at her computer screen. "He'll be in the office all day Wednesday."

MIKE RETURNED HOME TO A BLINKING LIGHT ON HIS ANSWERING machine. He pushed the button and listened to the familiar voice of Maxwell Forrest. The older lawyer sounded calm, but Mike knew anger boiled beneath the surface.

"Jack Hatcher notified me about the subpoenas served on him. I'll file appropriate responses with the court. Copy me on anything else you deliver to the bank or its officers." There was brief pause. "And I expect you to comply with my instructions not to have contact with anyone at the firm about this matter."

Mike made several quick notes on one of his legal pads. Powerful businessmen like Jack Hatcher were often surprisingly easy targets on the witness stand. Used to dominating meetings and browbeating underlings, they didn't adapt well to the controlled environment of the courtroom where the judge reigned supreme, and the rules of engagement allowed an attorney to dictate the topic to be discussed.

He nodded in satisfaction. Whether Hatcher was in a church pew or on a witness stand, he would be in Mike's domain. And Mike would know what to do with him.

Twenty-six

After supper, he phoned Sam Miller. "I need to go over your testimony," Mike said. "Can you come to my house tomorrow afternoon?"

"Yep," Sam replied. "But I've given my testimony so many times that I don't need to practice it. I can tell you quick what happened. I was in darkness and sin until the Master set me free and brought me into the light. I've got a longer story that I use sometimes in a church meeting—"

"I'm talking about the questions and answers in court," Mike interrupted, with a silent plea for help directed toward the ceiling. "As a criminal defendant, you don't have to testify in court, but with the evidence against you, I don't see any way around it. We need to rehearse what you'll say so you won't get sidetracked or confused in front of the jury. I'm going to write out every question and answer. We'll go over them, then Muriel can help you memorize the responses. I'm also going to write out questions I think the district attorney is going to ask and ways to answer that won't make you look guilty."

"What time? I have a couple of yards that need cutting."

"Three o'clock?"

"That should work."

Peg had taken Judge outside for a brief walk in the evening air. Mike joined her. They skirted the edge of the woods and around the side of the house.

"Do you want me to pretend that I'm Butch Niles when we go inside?" Peg asked.

"Maybe later. I've been going hard all day and need a break."

"You didn't say two sentences during supper."

Mike took her hand. "Sorry, my mind is crunching all the possibilities. With all the subpoenas going out, it's impossible to completely hide what I intend to do, and I'm still working it out myself."

"Did you serve subpoenas on the men who live out of state?"

"Hatcher didn't mention it today, so I'll need to check tomorrow."

Peg stopped while Judge sniffed the edge of an azalea bush.

"Are you concerned the bad guys might have organized-crime connections?" she asked.

"The thought crossed my mind when I found out Linden bribed a public official in New Jersey," Mike admitted. "But that happened ten years ago. I think the current deal is probably simple greed."

"Should I be worried?"

Mike looked in Peg's eyes and saw anxiety.

"It's probably the baby," she continued. "My body is telling me to be careful and protect the life I carry. I know it's nonsense, but my imagination has gone down a few scary paths while I've been lying in bed."

Mike squeezed her hand. "Try not to worry. I'm just a lawyer doing his job. We're not living in a third-world country."

"I know, and I want you to defend Sam, but don't turn this into a big crusade. Some of the questions you read to me today sounded more like a U.S. Senate hearing than the defense of a small-town criminal case."

"You should have told me."

"I am."

"That's a hard line to draw. At first glance, the evidence against Sam looks so convincing that it will take a big target to cover it up."

THE FOLLOWING DAY, MIKE DEVOTED THE ENTIRE MORNING TO Sam's testimony. He cut it up into bite-sized pieces he hoped his client could digest. During a mid-morning break, he confirmed that both Bunt and Linden had been served with subpoenas. If Mike used all the witnesses on his roster, his estimate that the case would last a day and a half would be a gross underestimate. He could already envision keeping Jack Hatcher on the stand for most of a day.

Shortly before lunch, the front doorbell chimed. Mike opened the door to a young man in a suit.

"I'm from Forrest, Lambert, and Arnold," he said. "Are you Mr. Andrews?"

"Yes."

The man handed him a thick envelope. "This is from Mr. Forrest."

Mike took the packet and closed the door. He weighed it in his hand, already suspecting what it contained.

"Who was at the door?" Peg called out from the great room.

"Someone with a present from Mr. Forrest. Do you want to open it?"

"Not unless it's addressed to me."

Mike went into the office. The envelope contained motions to quash the subpoenas for all the people he'd served except Brian Dressler, and objections to delivering any written or tangible evidence. A second batch of paperwork included motions for protective orders designed to prevent the type of broad-range fishing expedition Mike considered essential to defense of the case. A hearing on the motions was set for Thursday after the calendar call. Mike walked into the great room.

"Mr. Forrest wants me to call Sam and Brian Dressler as my only witnesses without any information from the bank or anyplace else."

"What are you going to do?"

"Keep serving subpoenas."

When he resumed work on questions and answers, Mike started humming. Returning to the battlefield, he was like a warhorse that snorts in excitement at the smell of gunpowder. He worked steadily until Sam and Muriel arrived. They went into the kitchen.

"I don't want you sitting in my recliner and leaving the planet," Mike said. "We'll set up the kitchen like a courtroom and work in there."

Peg and Judge joined them.

"The judge is here," Peg said.

Mike smiled.

"You know, animals see things people miss," Sam continued. "We had a dog named Blue that knew when angels were in the room. Sometimes, he'd stare at the corner where Muriel sat to pray and read her Bible. I asked Papa about it, and He reminded me of a verse—"

"Okay," Mike interrupted as he moved a chair to the side. "This will be the witness chair. Muriel, you'll be the jury. I want Sam to look at you while he testifies. Eye contact with the jury is very important."

"The eye is the lamp of the body," Sam replied.

"That's right. And I want the jury to see that there isn't anything criminal in you."

Peg joined Muriel in the jury box. Mike sat in a chair across from Sam.

"This isn't like TV," Mike said. "In North Carolina, the attorneys sit while asking questions unless showing evidence to the witness or the judge. As soon as you are in the witness chair, make eye contact with the jury."

Sam looked at Muriel and Peg and smiled.

"Don't smile," Mike corrected. "This isn't a time for levity."

"What?"

"Look sincere and serious."

Sam looked at the women again.

"That's good," Mike said. "The jury will be very curious about you and will pay close attention to the first minute or so you're on the witness stand."

"I'm still concerned about my dream that my enemies will be on the jury," Sam said.

"We'll be together during jury selection, and you can let me know if you spot any unfriendly faces."

"It's going to take more than man's wisdom to know what to do."

"Then ask God to give it to us so we can make the right decisions. All it takes is a couple of strong jurors in our favor to influence the whole panel. There may be twelve people on the jury, but most cases are decided by a few strong-willed individuals. You pray while I ask them questions."

"Yep."

"Raise your right hand."

Sam complied. Mike administered the oath.

"The judge will do that when we're in court."

"Like he did the other day."

"Exactly. Then I'll ask you a lot of easy questions about who you are and what you do. Let's get started."

As they worked through the background questions, Mike was pleased with the relaxed way Sam projected his responses to the pretend jury, setting a tone of truthfulness that Mike hoped would carry over to issues central to the case.

"Tell the jury about the origins of your relationship with the Craig Valley Gospel Tabernacle," Mike said.

Sam looked at Muriel and Peg. "I was involved in the beginning of the church, and although the color of our skin is different, many of the members are like sons and daughters in the faith. Over the years, I've ministered to the people on Sunday and cut the grass during the week."

"What was your relationship with the deacons?"

"Mostly good, although there have been a few who didn't agree with me about Papa's ways. That's never a happy situation, but—"

"Hold it," Mike said. "Can you stop using the words 'Papa' and 'Master' when referring to God and Jesus?"

Sam gave Mike a rueful expression. "I figured that might come up."

"I know it makes people think about God as a person who loves us and Jesus as the One who is in charge of our lives, but it's a distraction. Without an explanation, I believe it will hurt your credibility with the jury. They'll be scratching their heads trying to figure out if you're sacrilegious instead of paying attention to what's important."

"I'm not sure what that big word means, but why can't one of us give an explanation? I like the way you put it. You've got a way of speaking that would make me jealous if it wasn't a sin."

"Because you're not the apostle Paul defending his faith before King Agrippa in the book of Acts. This is an embezzlement trial in an American courtroom."

Sam looked at Muriel. "What do you think?"

"Do what Mike suggests. That's why he's helping you."

"I'll try," Sam said to Mike. "But it's such a habit with me that I might slip up."

"If you do, I'll ask a follow-up question that will let you explain."

"I'm thirsty," Sam said. "Can we stop for a drink of water?"

Peg fixed Sam and Muriel glasses of ice water then motioned for Mike to leave the kitchen. They stepped into the great room.

"What is it?" Mike asked.

"Isn't your goal to make Sam look truthful and genuine?"

"Yes, but using those words could really backfire."

"Maybe if you or I used them, but coming from Sam, it sounds as natural as can be—a man so close in his relationship with God that he calls Him by a familial name."

"It could rub someone the wrong way."

"Yes, but it might convince someone that Sam is a good-hearted man who wouldn't embezzle money from Papa's people."

Mike smiled. "That's a good phrase. I'll consider it, but let's try it my way first."

They returned to the kitchen, and Mike resumed questioning. He was pleasantly surprised by Sam's ability to provide the right information even though Mike avoided leading questions.

"How did you learn about the extra money in your bank account?"

"When I received my bank statement. I opened the envelope and almost dropped it. I showed it to my wife and called the bank that afternoon to let them know there had been a mistake. The lady I talked to was real nice and said she would look into—"

"Can't go there," Mike interrupted. "It's hearsay. Do you remember her name?"

"Nope."

"Did anyone from the bank contact you and accuse you of embezzling money?"

"Nope. I hadn't done anything wrong."

Mike looked through his notes before he continued.

"At some point, maybe here, I'll ask you about the dream and letter to Jack Hatcher. You'll probably be the last witness, so Hatcher will have testified and, based on my questions, the jury will know about the letter. I haven't written out that portion of your testimony because it will be influenced by the information received from Hatcher, Dressler, Bunt, Linden, and Niles. Add in the expert testimony of Darius York, and we may have a circus on our hands with me as chief juggler. You won't be able to explain all the balls in the air, so we'll keep it simple. You've been kept in the dark as much as anyone in the courtroom about what is really going on."

Sam nodded. "That's true, except for what Papa shows me."

Mike nodded. "You've given me a new appreciation for that truth. Anyway, you should have the same approach to the cross-examination questions from Ms. Hall."

"What do you mean?"

Mike held up the copies of the two checks. "Mr. Miller, is your bank account number printed on the bottom of these two checks?"

"Yep."

"Sam, pretend I'm Ms. Hall. You have to say 'Yes' or 'Yes, ma'am.'"

Sam smiled. "My mama would be proud of you for that one."

Mike repeated the question.

"Yes, ma'am."

"Did you have authorization to transfer $100,000 from the Craig Valley Gospel Tabernacle building fund to your account?"

"No, ma'am, and I didn't do it."

"Isn't your signature on the bottom of the checks?"

"It looks like my name, but I didn't sign the checks. Someone else did, or they used an ink stamp without asking me."

Mike glanced at Peg, who nodded. Mike raised his voice.

"Do you expect this jury to believe that Mr. Jack Hatcher, one of the most respected men in this community, is behind a conspiracy trying to frame you on this embezzlement charge?"

Sam tilted his head to the side and looked at Muriel and Peg. "Mr. Hatcher, like the rest of us, will have to answer for what he's done in this life. All I can speak about is my actions, and I didn't try to take any money from my friends at the Craig Valley church. That's been the truth from day one."

"Not bad," Mike replied. "Not bad at all. Ms. Hall may not ask that exact question, but she'll come after you at some point in the questioning. I'm impressed with your ability to think on your feet."

"I've had plenty of practice."

"When?" Mike asked in surprise.

"Walking behind that mower."

WEDNESDAY MORNING, MIKE CONFIRMED WITH THE BANK THAT Butch Niles was in the building then drove down the hill into town. When he approached the young receptionist and started to introduce himself, she cut him off.

"I know who you are."

"Good. I'd like to see Mr. Niles, please. I called a few minutes ago to make sure he was in the building."

The young woman checked her computer screen.

"He'll be in meetings all day and won't be available," she replied curtly.

Mike leaned closer to her desk. "I know you're following orders, but tell Mr. Niles that if he tries to avoid service of this subpoena, I will notify the newspaper, and a reporter will be here within the hour to find out why."

The woman's eyes grew bigger. "I'll check again."

Mike sat on the sofa while she picked up the phone and talked for a few moments. When she hung up, she motioned for Mike to return.

"Can you come back at two o'clock?"

Mike started to protest because the time would interfere with Darius York's examination of the original checks.

"That will be fine."

He left the bank and drove to the jail. The same female deputy who had questioned his status as a bona fide lawyer was on duty.

"Is Lamar Cochran in?" Mike asked.

"He's in the back. I'll see if he's available."

The chief deputy pushed open the metal door, and the two men shook hands.

"Got another case?" Cochran asked.

"No, helping Sam has become a full-time job," Mike replied. "Would you be willing to serve a couple of subpoenas at two o'clock? I'll be in a meeting at the district attorney's office and can't do it."

"I'm on duty at the jail."

Mike took out the subpoena and handed it to Cochran. "It won't take long. I need to serve Butch Niles. He's supposed to be at the bank at that time."

"What does Niles have to do with Sam's case?"

"I can't tell you details, but Sam tossed a rock into a larger pond than he imagined and disturbed the water. Some big snakes are upset."

Cochran took the subpoena. "I'll take a late lunch break and do it."

Mike handed him a second subpoena for additional records. "Give him this one for documents, too. He can be served as an officer of the bank."

MIKE WENT TO THE COURTHOUSE. HE'D CHECKED WITH THE court administrator the previous day to make sure Judge Coberg would be in his chambers in case a dispute arose about the expert's examination of the evidence. Mike walked upstairs. Two lawyers were arguing a motion in the judge's office, but the secretary reassured Mike that the judge would be back from lunch before 1:30. His preparation complete, Mike returned home. Peg's car wasn't in the driveway. Mike immediately called her cell phone.

"Are you okay?" he asked anxiously.

"Yes, but I guess you forgot my doctor's appointment this morning, so I drove myself."

"Did you remind me?"

"Last night before we went to sleep, but I'm not sure your brain had any storage space available."

"I'll be right there."

"No need. I've already seen her. Everything looks good, and she's going to let me increase my activity to include driving short distances."

"That's great, but I'm sorry I forgot."

"I look forward to getting you back after next week."

Mike hung up the phone and called Darius York, who was on his way to Shelton.

"There will be some legal sparring about the typewriters," Mike said. "The judge will be available to sort things out."

"Will the checks be available?"

"Yes."

THE ADRENALINE PUMPING THROUGH MIKE'S VEINS WOULD HAVE allowed him to skip lunch, but he forced himself to eat. Peg came in while he washed an apple.

"Can I fix you something?" he asked.

"Part of that apple would be nice."

Mike cut it in two and handed half to her. They sat at the kitchen table.

"Libby Gorman's niece was at the doctor's office," Peg said after she took a bite. "Her baby should be here in about a month."

"Did you talk to her?"

"She saw me and looked the other way when I came into the waiting room. And she and her husband don't even go to the church!"

Mike sighed. "I'm sorry."

"I didn't have anything to be ashamed about, so I sat down beside her and asked how she was doing. She mumbled something then went to the rest-room. When she came out, she sat on the opposite side of the room. It was bizarre. What could Libby have told her?"

"I can imagine a few things, but it appears the sabbatical spin isn't the only message out there."

Peg ate another bite of apple.

"People didn't like you when you were an attorney, but it was usually someone you sued."

"And some of them later hired me when they wanted to file a lawsuit. A minister is a different kind of target. Lawyers are expected to be mean. Ministers are supposed to be perfect, so any arrow of criticism can find a place to stick. I think it boils down to people feeling better about themselves if they can find something wrong with someone who is supposed to be righteous."

"That's sick."

Mike tossed his apple core across the room into the disposal side of the sink. Judge, who was lying on the floor, turned his head and watched the trajectory of the fruit.

"That's where you need to send what happened this morning. Don't carry it around. Grind it in the disposal and flush it out of your system. Otherwise, it will rot."

"Is that what you're going to do?"

Mike leaned back in his chair and laughed. "Take my own advice? That's tough to do."

MIKE WAITED FOR DARIUS YORK AT THE FRONT OF THE COURThouse. The former FBI agent was easy to spot as he walked up the sidewalk. York walked erect with his gray hair neatly trimmed, a small mustache the only departure from the TV stereotype of a government law enforcement officer. He carried a large black catalog case.

"Is everything you need in there?" Mike asked.

"Yes, so long as I have a power source."

They sat at a scarred wooden table in the courthouse library while York explained what he hoped to do with the checks and typewriters. Mike was pleased with the understandable way York described the evaluation process. Some scientifically minded people could only communicate with their peers. Mike looked at his watch. It was time to go.

They walked down the hall to the district attorney's office. Mike approached the receptionist and asked to see Melissa Hall.

"They're in the conference room," the receptionist replied.

Mike quickly tried to decide who else had decided to join them as they walked down the hall. Opening the door, his question was answered. Sitting on the opposite side of the table from Hall was Maxwell Forrest as counsel for the bank. The older lawyer nodded in Mike's direction without smiling. Mike introduced York.

"The original checks are in the file," Hall said.

Mike looked at Mr. Forrest. "And the typewriters?"

The older lawyer spoke in a measured tone. "Without conceding that any typewriters described in the subpoena are in the bank's possession, the sub-poena is subject to a motion to quash."

Mike pressed his lips together. "I'm going to Judge Coberg's chambers to ask for immediate relief. You're welcome to join me."

"The hearing on the motion is set tomorrow," Forrest replied.

"But my expert is here today."

Mike turned to Hall. "Mr. York would like to review the checks while I talk to the judge."

"Okay," Hall replied, her eyes switching back and forth between Mike and Forrest.

"Are you going to approach him ex parte?" Mr. Forrest asked Mike.

"Only if you don't show up."

Mike left the room. Once in the hallway, he slowed and listened for the sound of footsteps behind him. He cleared his throat and glanced over his shoulder. The older lawyer was closing the door of the conference room.

"I'm coming," Forrest grumbled. "But you're only going to embarrass your-self if you continue with this foolishness."

"I'm already embarrassed."

The two men walked in silence up the stairs to the judge's chambers.

"Is the judge available?" Mike asked the secretary.

The woman picked up the phone and then motioned for them to go back. Judge Coberg was sitting behind his desk. Mike took a copy of the subpoena for the typewriters and Mr. Forrest's response from his briefcase and handed them to the judge.

"The Miller case is set for trial next week, and my expert is in town to examine tangible evidence. Mr. Forrest doesn't want the bank to produce the typewriters—"

"I see," the judge interrupted. "Mr. Forrest, your response."

"There's no showing of relevance sufficient to justify the burden upon the bank to locate and produce these machines, if in fact, they exist. This case is rife with attempts to abuse the subpoena power. Mr. Andrews is using multiple subpoenas as a club to threaten and harass various officers at the bank as well as demand extensive documentation without any justification of relevancy."

"Today, we're only here about the typewriters," Mike responded. "I wouldn't be troubling the Court except for the limited opportunity between now and the time of trial for my expert witness to examine this equipment."

"What is the relevance of the machines?" the judge asked.

"I want my expert to run comparison testing."

"Comparison to what? You're going to have to give me more than generalities."

"Checks," Mike replied. "I want to determine if one of these machines was used to type the name and amount on the checks listed in the indictment."

The judge nodded. "Very well. Motion to quash is denied. Mr. Andrews, how long will your expert be in town?"

"This afternoon."

The judge turned to Forrest. "Instruct the bank to locate and deliver the items identified in the subpoena to the district attorney's office before four o'clock."

Mike and Forrest left the office in silence. They walked down the stairs together. Upon reaching the bottom, Mike expected the older lawyer to turn left and exit the courthouse in the direction of his office. Instead, he stayed beside Mike as he approached the district attorney's office.

"Aren't you going to call the bank?" Mike asked.

"Take care of your own business; I'll handle mine," Forrest answered curtly.

York and Hall were in the conference room. York had set up a scanner and microscope on the table. When they entered, he was examining one of the checks under the microscope. A legal pad beside him contained a list of notes. Forrest stepped forward and looked over York's shoulder at the notes. Mike joined him and was about to slide the pad out of the way when he saw that the writing, if not in code, was so illegible that it would have taken an archaeologist to decipher.

"What are your findings?" Forrest asked.

"Don't answer," Mike responded quickly.

York looked up from the microscope at the two men hovering behind him.

"Counsel, please allow me to do my job."

Forrest backed up. "Just curious."

Mike and Forrest sat across the table from each other, with Melissa Hall at one end and York at the other. The expert examined the checks and continued to make notes. The tension was palpable, and after a few minutes, Mike bowed his head and closed his eyes. Maxwell Forrest, like York, was doing his job, but Mike couldn't decide if the older lawyer was merely being an obstructionist or waging an all-out war. It was still impossible for him to imagine his former boss engaging in conscious criminal conduct.

"What did the judge do?" Hall's voice took Mike out of his reverie.

"Denied the motion to quash," Mike replied. "The typewriters are to be here by four o'clock."

Forrest spoke. "Mike thinks the checks were typed at the bank."

Hall's eyes opened wide in surprise. "You do?"

"I'm investigating any possible connections."

"What is the bank's position?" Hall asked.

"That this is a diversion designed to frustrate justice," Forrest replied. "Mike is an excellent lawyer, Ms. Hall, and you'd best be prepared for the unexpected when you go to court next week. Based solely on the subpoenas and potential witnesses I know about, this case could take most of the week to try."

"Is that right?" Hall asked Mike.

"Maybe." Mike shrugged.

Hall stood up. "I need to talk to Ken."

In a few minutes, the district attorney entered the room. York didn't look up from his microscope.

"Mike, can we meet with you in private?" West asked.

"Yes, as soon as we take a break to wait for delivery of some typewriters from the bank."

York looked up. "I'll be finished with the checks in about five or ten minutes."

Forrest looked at his watch. "I sent a text message to the bank. They will deliver three typewriters."

"I'll be in my office," West said, turning around. "I'll leave the door open."

Everyone resumed their positions around the table and waited. Mike opened his briefcase and began making notes on a legal pad. Fifteen minutes later, York pushed his chair away from the table.

"I'm done."

"Can he wait here for the typewriters?" Mike asked Hall.

"Yes, there's nothing scheduled for this room the rest of the afternoon."

Mike stood up and looked at Forrest.

"No communication with my witness, please."

Forrest waved his hand. "I'm just an observer on behalf of a client."

Mike followed Hall to Ken West's office. The district attorney swiveled his chair when they entered. Hall closed the door.

"What's going on with this case?" West asked.

"I'm representing my client with all the zeal I can muster," Mike replied. "You know I can't divulge my trial strategy."

"But taking up an entire week of court!" West raised his voice. "We have other business to attend to, including two aggravated assault cases against repeat felons."

Mike didn't respond.

"What if we put our plea offer back on the table?" West asked.

"Why did you withdraw it prematurely?" Mike shot back.

West rubbed his hands together. "As you can see from the other lawyer in the conference room, there is interest in Mr. Miller's case beyond the ordinary citizens of Barlow County."

"Then that should tell you something about my trial strategy. Perhaps officials at the bank know something about this case and the defendant that isn't in the skinny file in your office."

"If so, they haven't brought our office into the loop." West picked up a sheet of paper from his desk. "I have a list of the people you've subpoenaed. Most of the names are familiar to me, but who are Richard Bunt and Troy Linden?"

"Real estate developers—and that's all I'll tell you."

"Out of state?"

"That's obvious from the addresses on the subpoenas."

"Did you obtain service?"

"Yes."

West dropped the paper on his desk.

"And Ms. Hall tells me you believe the checks were typed at the bank."

"I'm exploring all options."

West sat up so quickly his chair groaned loudly in protest.

"Mike! Don't be so obtuse! If there is a fatal flaw in our case, I don't want to waste a week finding out!"

Mike kept calm. "Given the political pressure already brought to bear, it's hard for me to believe that opening my file to you is going to make these charges go away."

"Suit yourself. Ms. Hall needs trial experience, and as a preacher and lawyer you could give her a baptism of fire, but I've never been interested in prosecuting an innocent man."

Mike's eyes flashed. "Tell that to Danny Brewster's mother!"

West stared hard at Mike for a few seconds then turned to Hall.

"*State v. Miller* will definitely be the first case out of the gate on Monday morning."

Twenty-seven

WHEN MIKE RETURNED TO THE CONFERENCE ROOM, DARIUS York was alone. The expert had taken out a calculator.

"The other lawyer left right after you did."

Mike checked his watch. "Don't expect the typewriters a minute early. Let's go back to the library."

When they returned to the library, Mike checked to make sure they were alone. He sat at the table.

"What did you find?" he asked.

"The checks were signed with a stamp. Very carefully done to make it hard to spot at first glance, but once I put them under the scope, the ink pattern was obvious. If I could take a scraping of the ink, I could identify the type of pad used."

"And the stamp could have been manufactured from Miller's signature on another check?"

"Or more likely his signature card on file with the bank. If that matches the stamp, there will be no question in my mind what happened."

"Would there be collusion by the bank with the company making the stamp?"

"Not necessarily. Usually a signature on a blank sheet of paper is used, but the bank could have sent the signature card and told the company it was acting with the customer's consent."

Mike nodded. "I'll send Sam to the bank to get his signature card. Will you need to examine it under the microscope to see if it's a match?"

"That will help, although the loop on the *S* and the way he leans back the *e* in Miller are so distinctive, it should show up without magnification. When can you get the card?"

"I'll try to reach him now, and send him to the bank."

York touched his catalog case. "I scanned the checks, so they can be blown up and projected as part of a PowerPoint presentation to the jury. I've already worked up fourteen points of similarity on the checks. That puts use of the same stamp on both checks at over ninety-eight percent, but it would be helpful to create a few slides incorporating the signature card as well."

Mike flipped open his phone and dialed Sam's number. Muriel answered.

"This is Mike. Where is he?"

"In the storage shed working on one of his mowers."

"Please get him."

Mike waited, visualizing York's display. If the signature card matched the stamp, it would make it harder for Hall to argue that Sam had ordered a signature stamp. Linking the bank's typewriters to the checks would tighten the noose.

"Hello," Sam said.

Mike told him what to do.

"What if they won't give me a copy of my signature card?"

"Get the name of the person who refuses and let me know."

"Okay, I'll give it a try," Sam said with reluctance in his voice.

"Are you nervous about going to the bank?" Mike asked.

"Yep, I guess so. It's been hard not worrying even though I've tried to keep my mind on Papa and kept busy tinkering with my stuff."

"I can meet you at the bank if that helps."

"Nope, I'll head right over there."

"Then come to the courthouse. We'll be in the library. It's on the first floor."

While they waited, Mike and York worked through items to include in the presentation. The former FBI agent was what Mike called an automatic witness—swear him in and turn him on.

A few minutes before the typewriters were to be delivered, Sam came into the library. The old man looked out of place surrounded by legal books.

"Any problems at the bank?" Mike asked quickly.

"Nope." Sam handed a card to Mike. "I signed a new one, so they gave me the old one."

Mike and York ignored Sam as they leaned over the card.

"That's it!" Mike exclaimed. "It's identical to the stamp!"

York didn't immediately respond but took a magnifying glass from his case. Mike watched as York turned the card in several directions before looking up.

"You're right. I'll put it under the scope, but I think it's a match."

Mike glanced up at Sam. "Do you realize what this means?"

Sam shook his head.

Mike rapidly summarized the information York had developed, then held up the card in triumph.

"We're one step away from breaking the back of the prosecution's case. Once this comes into evidence, it opens the door for the other allegations connected with the bank to come in as relevant motivation to destroy you and your credibility."

York looked up at Sam, who was still standing near the door.

"You're an innocent man, Mr. Miller."

Sam didn't look pleased. "But you're not an innocent man, are you?"

"What do you mean?" York replied.

Sam touched his belly. "I saw bags of gold behind your eyes with writing on them in another language. The gold didn't belong to you, but you took it anyway."

Mike held out his hand. "Sam, don't be ridiculous. Mr. York is a former FBI agent. I've paid him to help us. He's doing an honest job."

"I'm not talking about this," Sam said, pointing to the information on the table.

Mike looked at York, who was staring at Sam as if the old man had grown two heads.

"Please, don't take offense," Mike said to York. "It's just part of what I've gone through representing him. Sam has dreams and sees things that aren't there."

"You didn't talk like that when I told you about Jack Hatcher and Butch Niles," Sam responded.

Mike stood up. "Sam, let's go into the hallway."

Mike grabbed Sam's arm and steered him out of the room.

"Why are you trying to sabotage our relationship with a man who is here to help you?" Mike asked furiously.

Sam tilted his head to the side. "If you'd seen those bags of gold, you wouldn't be getting mad at me. That man had better repent and make it right."

"That's not our job," Mike shot back.

"Why not?" Sam raised his voice. "Is Mr. York more important as a witness in my case or as a soul who will live forever in heaven or hell? What if he dies without meeting the Master in this life? What answer will he give when Papa looks in his face? What answer will you give for not caring enough to help him?"

Mike's head was spinning. "He doesn't want our help."

"How do you know? You hustled me out of there before we could find out."

Mike spoke in a softer tone. "I know you mean well, but you brought me into this case to defend you against a criminal charge of embezzlement. That includes finding and hiring an expert witness to testify to the truth. I've found one who is very competent and believable. Now, you're trying to take over defense of your case and destroy my hard work. If you do, there's no need for me to hang around."

"Why don't we let Mr. York decide? If he doesn't want to talk to me, I'll leave him alone. I can reveal the deeds of darkness, but conviction of sin isn't part of the job description Papa gave me. That's up to the Helper."

Mike didn't know what to do. In a few minutes, York would need to examine the typewriters.

"Okay," he said. "Let me go in alone. Wait here."

Sam folded his arms across his chest. "That's a good idea. You need to learn."

Mike felt his face flush but suppressed his anger. He reentered the library. York was sitting in his chair staring across the room.

"Does your client claim to be a psychic?" York asked when Mike shut the door behind him.

"No, I'm not sure what label he places on himself, but I've learned that I can't control what he says. This latest outburst is causing me to rethink my whole trial strategy. I'd planned on calling him as a witness, but if he suddenly starts accusing someone on the jury—"

"Can I speak to you confidentially?" York interrupted.

"Uh, yeah."

"At first, I didn't know what he was talking about, but there was an incident in my past that fits what he saw. It happened so long ago that I'd pushed it out of my mind, but it's not the sort of thing I could ever totally forget. Of course, the military statute of limitations has run out and it seems pointless—"

The door opened and Melissa Hall stuck her head inside. Mike could see Sam standing behind her.

"The typewriters are here," she said. "We're closing the office in thirty minutes."

"We'll be right there," Mike replied.

When Hall left, Mike shut the door in Sam's face and turned to York.

"Are you still willing to help?"

"Yes."

Mike breathed a sigh of relief. "Thanks for being a professional and overlooking my client's behavior."

"Don't worry about it. Let's get to the machines."

They left the library. Sam was waiting for them.

"Keep your mouth shut," Mike whispered to Sam as they walked down the hallway. "I'm smoothing things over with York."

There were three typewriters on the conference room table. Maxwell Forrest was present and accompanied by a man Mike didn't recognize but assumed worked for the bank. Melissa Hall stood off to the side. Mike watched Forrest closely eye Sam as the old man entered the room.

"Sit here," Mike motioned to Sam.

York opened his catalog case, took out a sheet of paper, and rolled it into the carriage of one of the machines. The conference room only contained a single outlet, and the cord attached to the machine wouldn't reach from the table to the outlet in the corner.

"Do you have an extension cord?" he asked Hall.

"No," she replied without hesitation.

York picked up the machine and placed it on the floor near the outlet. Plugging it in, he turned it on and methodically hit all the keys, both lowercase and uppercase, along with all the symbols. After repeating the process, he typed the exact information contained on each of the checks and repeated it as well. Finally, he typed the serial number for each machine on the bottom of the paper. While he worked, everyone in the room watched as intently as if the former FBI agent were performing brain surgery. Forrest made notes on a legal pad. Mike realized the bank was possibly retaining its own expert. The idea sent Mike quickly down the path of deciding how to respond to a battle of expert witnesses if the bank's expert was made available to the prosecution. York continued working until he finished and looked at his watch.

"That should do it with five minutes to spare," he said.

Mike turned to the man accompanying Forrest. "Your name, please?"

"Rick Post," Forrest replied.

"And his position?"

"At the moment, custodian of these typewriters."

Mike left the sarcastic remark alone. Post put the typewriters in boxes, placed them on a set of hand trucks, and rolled them out of the office. Forrest motioned for Mike to come into the hall.

"Do you have a minute?" Forrest asked.

"Yes." Mike turned to York and Sam. "Wait for me in the library. The courthouse doesn't close until five-thirty, so we have a little bit of time."

Mike and Forrest stepped into the hallway.

"Let's go into the courtroom," Forrest suggested.

The main courtroom was empty yet expectant, an arena waiting for arrival of the gladiators and the roar of the crowd. Forrest spoke.

"Mike, I've always held you in high regard as a person and a lawyer, and your move into the ministry was a great act of self-sacrifice that served as an inspiration to me. However, I know you're bound and determined to embarrass the bank and try to drag as many reputable businesspeople through the mud as you can. Whatever I have to do to defend my clients isn't meant to attack you personally. It's strictly business. I'm sorry you let yourself be lured back into the fight, but now you're here, and we're all going to get a little bloody before this is over."

"I'll stay within the rules."

"As will I, but mercy is limited to the walls of your church. When you come into this courtroom on Monday, mercy won't be a word in the dictionary."

Mike looked at the wooden floor for a few seconds before looking up and responding.

"And I sincerely hope you're not involved in what may have happened in this case."

Forrest looked Mike in the eye. "Have you ever known me to cross any ethical or moral line?"

"No, sir."

"Then we go into this with an understanding of the past, which I hope won't be violated in the future."

Forrest extended his hand, and Mike shook it. The firm grip that had greeted Mike's arrival in Shelton when he graduated from law school was noticeably weaker. They returned to the hallway and went in opposite directions.

Mike found Sam and York sitting across from each other.

"It won't be easy," York was saying.

"What now?" Mike asked.

"Nothing," York replied with a wave of his hand. "Let me set up and quickly check the typed samples. I'll do a more extensive review at home, but I can give you a preliminary opinion before I leave."

He placed enlarged copies of the two checks on the table and set up his microscope.

"Computers can do the same kind of analysis that I'm performing," York said as he prepared his equipment.

"But they can't testify under oath and give an opinion," Mike responded.

"True, but I may run them through a program on my computer to bolster the credibility of my opinion."

York placed one of the sheets of paper under the microscope and began moving it from letter to letter. In a few minutes, he removed it.

"It's not this one," he said. "The *r* and capital *M* are totally different."

He picked up another sheet and examined it, taking much longer. Mike looked at his watch. The courthouse would close in a few minutes. He really wanted an opinion before York left town.

"I think this is it," York said without raising his eye from the viewer. "I've found identifiable marks on five of the letters and two of the numbers with several more letters to analyze."

"Where would that put the percentages?"

York sat up straight. "Not sure, but by the time I finish, I should be able to convince a reasonable person that the checks were typed at the bank."

Mike broke out a smile. "It only takes one reasonable juror to stop a conviction, and a few strong ones for acquittal can usually carry the day. The signature stamp could have been explained away, but access to this typewriter is completely outside Sam's control. This is huge."

York began packing up his gear. "I'll do a thorough evaluation of the other typewriter as well and give you a call tomorrow."

"Good."

When he was finished, York stood and looked at Sam.

"Thank you, Mr. Miller."

"You're welcome, but mercy comes from Papa's heart."

After York left, Mike turned to Sam. "Mercy? What's that all about? I thought you were going to leave him alone."

Sam held up his hands in surrender. "He brought it up, and I answered him."

"What did you say?"

Sam rubbed his stomach. "I didn't think you liked the water in my well, and now you're asking for a drink the Master provided another man. What am I supposed to do with you?"

Mike shook his head. "Okay, keep it to yourself. But it's good to know there is still mercy at the courthouse."

MIKE DIDN'T REALIZE HOW TIRED HE WAS UNTIL HE'D LOOSENED his tie and deposited his briefcase in the downstairs office. Peg was in the kitchen sitting on a stool and preparing a large salad for supper.

"We're eating healthy for supper," she said. "I want our baby to like everything I'm throwing into this salad."

"Fine with me; I'll sleep soundly tonight whether my stomach is empty or full."

While they ate, Mike told her some of the events of the day. He left out Sam's warning to Darius York. He suspected Peg would be upset with him for the way he handled the situation. When he described his conversation with Forrest in the courtroom, she spoke.

"What was he trying to do? Get you to quit?"

"No, I don't think so. At first, I thought he was playing a mind game with me—a one-man good cop/bad cop routine, but now, I believe he was sincere."

"In his desire to spill your blood on the courtroom floor," Peg responded sharply.

"That part was just lawyer talk. It was the sentiment behind the words that came through in the midst of the blustering."

Peg shook her head. "Maybe I'd agree if I'd been there, but to me, he was just trying every angle to exert his will."

After supper, Mike sat in his recliner and closed his eyes. Within seconds he was in a large room without windows. The room was dark at first, but as his eyes became accustomed to the light, he could make out human shapes along the walls. Mike stood still and waited for one of the people to move or speak. Nothing happened. He waited a few more seconds then cautiously stepped toward the nearest figure. The closer he came, the more he expected a voice to challenge him, or perhaps an even more violent reaction. Two feet from the form, he slowly reached out his hand and touched it.

It was made of wax.

As Mike's eyes continued to adjust to the hazy, unnatural light, he could tell that life-size wax figures lined the walls of the room. Mike recognized the familiar forms of Maxwell Forrest, Milton Chesterfield, Braxton Hodges, along with people he'd known in the past but not seen in years. Other figures were total strangers. Some of the pedestals were empty, and he wondered whether someone had stolen the statues. Sensing a presence behind him, he quickly turned around.

And woke up.

THE FOLLOWING DAY, MIKE ARRIVED AT THE COURTHOUSE THIRTY minutes early. The fact that Judge Coberg had denied the motion about the typewriters gave him confidence that Sam's constitutional right to face his accusers would trump any privacy rights or arguments of inconvenience presented by Maxwell Forrest on behalf of the bank.

Mike entered an empty courtroom. Bowing his head, he dispatched a silent prayer thanking God for how well the case was going. When he opened his eyes, two other lawyers were entering the courtroom. In addition to motions and the call of the criminal calendar for the following week, the judge would receive guilty pleas for cases in which plea agreements had been reached. By the time Mike's watch showed nine-thirty, approximately twenty-five people and seven other lawyers, including Greg Freeman, were in the room. Maxwell Forrest wasn't one of them.

Melissa Hall was handling duties for the DA's office. She placed a large stack of files on the table without looking in Mike's direction. Several lawyers came up to her for quick discussions.

"All rise!" the deputy sheriff on duty announced.

Mike stood up as the door behind the bench opened. Judge Lancaster entered the courtroom.

"Be seated!" the deputy called out when the judge had taken his place on the bench.

Mike's heart was pounding and his mouth felt dry. William Lancaster was a rogue judge—unpredictable and, at times, capricious. Mike had experienced uneven success before him. The fiasco with Danny Brewster obliterated any positive memories.

"Court will come to order," the judge said in his slightly pinched voice.

"Judge Coberg was called out of town on a family emergency. I will be receiving pleas as well as presiding over next week's criminal trial calendar."

"Proceed," the judge said to Ms. Hall.

The young DA began calling cases. Individuals stepped forward, some with attorneys, others unrepresented. As the judge began receiving guilty pleas, Mike listened closely, not because he had any interest in the cases, but to determine if the judge was going along with the deals or rejecting them. Out of the first three cases, only one plea agreement survived intact.

Several attorneys sitting near Mike began to whisper. Mike couldn't hear their conversations but knew they were discussing whether to seek a continuance in an effort to avoid facing Judge Lancaster. The same thought crossed Mike's mind.

The requests for continuance began to flow, and Lancaster didn't seem to mind. The judge wasn't lazy, but his mood of the moment made him receptive to postponement of justice to another day. A few guilty pleas slipped through intact. When only a few people were left in the courtroom, the back door opened, and Maxwell Forrest entered. Bobby Lambert was with him. Forrest was a formidable foe, but Mike would rather face him than contend with his friend. The judge finished the first part of the calendar.

"Ms. Hall, how many cases are you placing on next week's trial calendar?"

"Seven," she responded. "First out will be *State v. Miller.*"

"I'm representing Mr. Miller," Mike said as he stood to his feet.

The judge looked at him as if noticing him for the first time. "What are you doing here?"

"I've maintained my license, Your Honor," Mike replied, "and I'm defending Mr. Miller."

"What's the charge?" the judge asked Hall.

"Felony embezzlement from a nonprofit organization. The indictment charges the defendant with embezzling in excess of $100,000 from a church."

The judge turned to Mike. "It wasn't your church, was it?"

"No, sir."

The judge grunted. "How long do you anticipate it will take to try the case?"

"One day for the State's case," Hall responded.

"Two to three days for the defense," Mike said.

The judge leaned forward. "That's virtually the whole week! Isn't there a way to get this pared down so the court can handle more than one case?"

Maxwell Forrest spoke. "Your Honor, if I could interject?"

"Go ahead."

"The primary reason for the excessive length of trial is a plethora of sub-poenas issued by Mr. Andrews to people across the entire country and his demand for voluminous records from the Bank of Barlow County. Mr. Lambert and I are here to argue several motions to quash the subpoenas."

The judge turned to Mike. "Explain what you're doing."

"We were going to argue the motions after the calendar call," Mike began.

"But I want to hear the matter now," the judge snapped, "since it may affect what I tell the rest of the lawyers on standby."

Mike cleared his throat. "Yes, sir."

Mike repeated his argument of the previous day. Every time he tried to speak in generalities, the judge interrupted with a specific question. As Mike talked about Troy Linden and Dick Bunt, he realized that Maxwell Forrest was smart enough to deduce Mike's trial strategy.

"Is Representative Niles going to claim governmental privilege?" the judge asked Forrest when the legislator's name came up.

"No, sir. The legislature is not in session next week. However, I think my client and the Court have a right to know why he's being summoned. Representative Niles was not involved in the investigation into the embezzle-ment and had no contact with the defendant."

The judge looked at Mike.

"That's not true, Your Honor. Mr. Niles and Mr. Miller had a conversation within the past two weeks."

"About the charges?"

"Not specifically. But there is a collateral connection that will be developed through the entire testimony I will present."

"What type of collateral connection?"

Mike felt his face flush. "With all due respect, to answer that question, I would have to reveal my trial strategy."

"Then you'd better decide what will convince me not to grant Mr. Forrest's motions."

Mike quickly gathered his thoughts. "The defendant possesses knowledge that may jeopardize business interests connected to Mr. Niles."

The judge narrowed his eyes. "Are you contending these witnesses engaged in a conspiracy against your client?"

"That is an issue the jury should have a right to decide."

The judge turned to Hall. Mike saw Bobby lean over to Forrest and begin whispering.

"Does the State have a position on these subpoenas?" the judge asked the assistant DA.

"Abuse of the subpoena power of the court is not constitutionally protected activity. Therefore, we concur with Mr. Forrest's arguments and hope the Court will not empower Mr. Andrews to engage in a spurious witch hunt."

"That's an interesting characterization," the judge responded dryly. "Does the term *witch hunt* apply to men as well as women?"

Everyone in the courtroom stared at Hall to see how she would respond to the overtly sexist remark. Mike saw a red tinge travel from her neck to her cheeks.

"Yes, sir," she managed.

"Court will be in a five-minute recess until I announce my decision," the judge said.

Judge Lancaster left the bench. Maxwell Forrest and Bobby came forward to talk to Melissa Hall. Greg Freeman approached Mike.

"Any predictions?" Mike asked.

"This is my first look at Judge Lancaster," the younger lawyer said, "and it's not pretty. You saw what he did to my plea bargain."

The judge had rejected the plea, forcing Freeman's client to choose between letting the judge sentence him without any guaranteed result or going to trial.

"If my case takes all week, you can bring the plea deal before Judge Coberg when he returns to the bench."

"That's what I'm counting on. Are you sure your case will take four days?"

"Yes. It always takes longer than you think." Mike motioned toward Hall, Forrest, and Bobby, who continued to talk in earnest. "They're trying to sell something to Ms. Hall right now, but I'm not sure what it is."

Mike tried to stay calm, but inside he was wrapped tight in the turmoil of suspense. The next words from the judge's mouth would dictate the scope of events for the next week and a half. A favorable ruling would allow Mike to proceed as planned; an adverse decision would force him to greatly restrict the scope of his defense. The judge returned. Instead of speaking, he wrote something on a sheet of paper in front of him.

"Motion denied," he said without glancing up. "Mr. Forrest, tell the subpoenaed witnesses you represent to be here Monday morning along with the tangible items requested by the defendant."

"Yes, sir."

"Thank you, Your Honor," Mike added.

The judge ignored him and turned to Hall. "What is the call list for the remaining cases on the trial calendar? I want everyone involved in the number two and three cases here on Monday in case there is an unforeseen delay in the Miller case."

"One other matter on the Miller case," Hall replied. "Mr. Forrest has been talking to me, and, uh . . ."

Maxwell Forrest stepped forward and continued, "Mr. Lambert and I will be filing a request to serve as special prosecutors in this case."

"That's up to the district attorney," the judge grunted. "But I'm warning all of you. Nobody is going to undermine the efficient administration of justice in my courtroom." The judge looked at Mike. "That goes double for you, Mr. Andrews."

"Yes, sir."

"I'll notify you as soon as Mr. West makes his decision," Hall said to the judge.

The judge waved his hand. "Go on. Give me the rest of your calendar."

Mike didn't hear Hall's response. His heart rate slowed as he closed his briefcase. Forrest's desire to be directly involved made sense. Never common, use of a special prosecutor occurred when the wealthy victim of a crime wanted to make sure the responsible person was convicted and hired the best trial lawyer in town to assist the State's prosecutor. Jack Hatcher and those connected to him were scared—scared enough to spend a lot of money to guarantee a guilty verdict.

WHEN MIKE TURNED ON HIS PHONE AFTER LEAVING THE COURT-room, he had a voice mail from Darius York. Mike punched in the expert's number.

"I spent the morning running comparisons on the typewriters and the checks," York said. "I'm going to blow up the individual letters on the checks and place them beside the ones from sample sheet of the typewriter used. To emphasize the uniqueness of each unit, I'll also include the letters and numbers from the other two machines. Several letters stand out strong."

"Sounds good."

"It is. The machine used is by far the most distinctive of the units. Your client is lucky."

"I'm not sure he believes in luck."

"Whatever he believes is different from anything I've ever encountered."

"You don't have to tell that to me."

"He has a strong defense. I've rarely seen this type of exculpatory evidence. I know anything can happen in court, but Mr. Miller should walk away from this with a lawsuit against someone for causing him to suffer through this ordeal."

"When can I preview your presentation?"

"I'll have it ready by the end of the day on Sunday. I'll send it to you via e-mail as a PDF attachment so you can give feedback before I drive down on Monday."

"Great. You won't testify the first day of trial. It will take all morning to pick the jury, and the State's case will fill the rest of the day. I suspect most of the evidence on behalf of the bank will take place during rebuttal. The bank president and his business partners want to use a special prosecutor to make sure their interests are protected."

"I can't blame them," York responded. "The district attorney looked younger than my granddaughter."

"This is her first felony trial. She may deliver the opening statement and handle the direct examination of the detective who interviewed Sam, but you'll be cross-examined by an experienced trial lawyer."

"It's been done before. I can hold my own. Any word on their expert?"

"No, but the State has to serve me with an amended list of witnesses if they intend to use one."

AS HE DROVE UP THE HILL TO HIS NEIGHBORHOOD, MIKE thought about the Little Creek Church. He'd been so occupied with the upcoming trial that he'd not dwelt on the shadow lands beyond the jury's verdict. Several possibilities passed through his mind in quick succession, but he squelched them. For the moment, *State v. Miller* was his past, present, and future.

Peg was in the art room working on a sketch that would be the basis for another watercolor.

"Take a look," she said.

Mike stood beside her. It was a bird's-eye view of a 1950s-era beach house with a family on the sand between the house and the ocean. Several children splashed in the surf. Mike quickly counted.

"Five kids. Whose house is it?"

"A happy family's."

Mike pointed at the scene. "The father had better get off the beach towel and back to the office."

"No. There won't be a cloud in the sky."

"I wish I could say that."

"What happened?"

Mike told her about the specter of Judge Lancaster and Maxwell Forrest's intervention.

"Was Sam there?" she asked.

"No, defendants aren't required to be there. I hope he was cutting grass somewhere."

"But wouldn't it be a good idea for him to listen, so he can tell you what God is saying about the situation and the people?"

"That's something I haven't considered. Except for yesterday, I've kept Sam isolated so he wouldn't say the wrong thing in the wrong place at the wrong time. One crazy slipup from him, and I can forget all my careful planning."

"I still think it would be a good idea."

"There won't be another opportunity. Next time up is jury selection on Monday morning." Mike paused. "I've never selected a jury for a client who believed he could uncover the secrets of another person's heart. It should be an interesting process."

MIKE SPENT THE AFTERNOON WORKING IN THE DOWNSTAIRS OFFICE. After several hours, mental fatigue began to crack his capacity to analyze and organize. He pushed away from the desk and rubbed his eyes. He stepped out of the room and found Peg lying on the couch in the great room reading a novel.

"My brain is fading, but my body needs a workout," he said. "Would you feel abandoned if I took Judge out for a romp?"

The dog, lying on the floor beside Peg, raised his head at the sound of his name.

"Go," Peg said. "Both of you need the exercise."

"Let's go," Mike said to him.

"How long will you be gone?" Peg asked.

Mike looked at the clock. "A couple of hours at the most."

Peg stretched. "Okay. I'm cooking something special for supper."

"Liver mush?"

"If that's what you want, darling."

"Surprise me."

Mike put his bike on top of his car, and Judge jumped into the backseat. He drove along a rarely used country road that ran along the valley, climbed a few ridges owned by a pulpwood company, and then became a dirt road that disappeared into the woods. The only time Mike avoided the area was during deer season. He didn't want a trigger-happy hunter mistaking the handlebars on his bike for a rack of antlers on a buck.

Parking the car at an abandoned farmhouse, Mike unloaded the bike and set a leisurely pace that wouldn't tire Judge. The dog loped along beside him with his ears gently flopping up and down and his mouth slightly open. There were a few wispy clouds in the sky, and the mountain air refreshed Mike's cheeks as it crossed his face. Within a few minutes, he'd left the stress of the day behind and settled into enjoying the world in which God had placed him.

The track turned west and he climbed the first ridge. Stopping at the top, he took a small drink of water and poured a larger serving into a plastic bowl for Judge. They'd only seen two cars and three pickups since starting the ride. Unlike drivers in town, those in the country didn't seem to resent Mike's presence and gave him a wide berth when they passed him.

He coasted down the dip between the ridges before climbing a longer, steeper ridge. Leaving the bike in a lower gear, he worked hard enough that his thighs began to burn. The harder the climb, the farther Judge's tongue began to hang out of his mouth. They reached the top and turned off the road. A hundred yards from the road was a small burned-out area caused by a fire sparked by a lightning strike. With the arrival of spring, new growth had sprouted forth since the last time Mike had been to the spot. He sat on a felled tree and shared another drink with Judge.

The clearing faced east toward Shelton. He couldn't see the town, but several roads and a few scattered houses were visible in the distance. From his vantage point, it was possible to make out the outline of the eastern edge of the paper company's property. The privately held land was a hodgepodge of fences and mixed-use fields. The tree farm had order and symmetry. Some sections were filled with bushy young saplings peeking through the soil; others contained adolescent trees bunched close together as they fought for air and light; the remaining acres had already been harvested once, but the woodsmen left some of the best trees standing so they could grow even larger. It was quiet. Tree farming was a patient endeavor, measured in decades not years. It was a good illustration for the Christian life.

"But where will I preach it?" Mike spoke into the silent air.

No answer came. Mike continued to soak in the scene. Then a thought slipped softly into his mind.

Don't preach it; live it.

Puzzled, Mike turned the words over in his mind. Before teaching others, he knew he needed to understand the truth himself. But understanding alone wasn't sufficient if inconsistent with behavior. He sensed the words went beyond to something else. He mulled them over for several minutes. Nothing satisfactory surfaced. He whistled for Judge, who was crashing through the underbrush. The dog circled around and returned to the clearing from the rear.

"Let's go," Mike said. "Supper is waiting."

Twenty-eight

PEG HAD FIXED A STEW, NOT LIVER MUSH. BOTH MIKE AND Judge licked their lips when they came into the kitchen. Mike lifted the lid of the pot on the stove.

"How did you do it so fast?"

"I cooked it yesterday. It always tastes better the second day, so I decided to make that the first day and this the second day."

"I'm not sure Judge understands you."

"All he cares about is licking the plates."

Mike and Peg sat together in the kitchen with Judge on the floor between them. The words Mike heard during his bike ride stayed with him.

"I'll clean up," Mike said when they finished eating.

He was scrubbing the pot when the phone rang. He dried his hands and answered it. It was Brian Dressler.

"I have a conflict on Monday and won't be able to make it to the trial," Dressler said.

Mike kept his voice level but firm. "You're under subpoena. It's not an optional appearance."

"I have serious personal business involving one of my grandchildren. I'll be tied up all day Monday."

Mike leaned against the kitchen counter. He didn't relish the thought of seeking a criminal contempt order against the former banker.

"Could you catch a flight and be here on Tuesday?"

"I thought the trial was on Monday."

"The first day, but the case will probably last the whole week. I didn't intend on calling you until Tuesday afternoon or Wednesday morning."

"Why is the case going to take so long? It's not that complicated."

"Your part is foundational for what follows," Mike answered cryptically. "I know you can't tie everything together, but after listening to you, the rest of my evidence will make sense to the jury."

"I haven't made my arrangements."

Mike decided to probe for another reason for Dressler's reluctance.

"Has someone from Forrest, Lambert, and Arnold contacted you?"

"No."

"How about the bank?"

There was a moment of silence. Mike knew he'd touched something.

"I spoke briefly with Hatcher."

"What did he want?"

"He was trying to find out why I'd been subpoenaed."

"What did you tell him?"

"I answered his questions but nothing more."

Mike glanced up at the ceiling. "Mr. Dressler, this could take a while if you make me drag it out of you."

"Okay, I'll get to the bottom line. They know what you're trying to do."

"That doesn't tell me much. Based on our conversation at the newspaper, I'm not sure you know what I'm doing."

"I know more than I told you in Shelton."

"How much more?"

"I'm not saying, but if you press me in court, I'm going to invoke the Fifth Amendment. I've already consulted a lawyer in Mobile."

Mike had been confident in his theory of the case, but to have it so dramatically validated by Dressler was still a shock.

"What is Hatcher saying?" he managed after a brief pause.

"I don't know. But he's scared. I could tell it over the phone. I've never heard him so nervous."

"Did he mention anything about Linden, Bunt, or Niles?"

"No, and I didn't ask. This could get ugly, and everyone is looking out for himself. I wasn't sure if he was recording the conversation, so I let him do most of the talking. With all the publicity about high-level corporate misconduct the past few years, a scandal in a place as small as Shelton could still blow up higher than the surrounding mountains."

Mike's mental wheels were turning.

"It's not my intention to make you look like a criminal. Your credibility is important to my case. What else can you tell me about the meeting with Hatcher when Sam Miller's name came up?"

"Not much. He didn't call me in until it was almost over."

Mike had caught him in a lie.

"I thought you weren't there at all."

"Oh yeah, I guess that's what I told you."

Mike waited. Once a witness started talking, it was often easier to obtain more information without prompting. Dressler spoke slowly.

"I'll verify that a meeting took place but obviously can't relate what happened before I arrived. When I came into Hatcher's office, he told me there was going to be an investigation into an embezzlement scheme by a man named Sam Miller and instructed me to meet with the victims at the appropriate time."

"Are you sure about that?"

"Yes."

"Just a minute."

Mike walked quickly into the office and found the copy of the minutes Bobby gave him in the deed room. He returned to the kitchen.

"Do you remember when this meeting took place?"

"Not the exact date."

"When did you meet with the deacons from the Craig Valley church?"

"Not long after. Maybe two or three weeks."

Mike placed the sheet of paper on the counter and stared at it while he asked his next question.

"Would it surprise you to find out that the meeting in Hatcher's office was four days prior to the date of the first check Sam allegedly wrote on the Craig Valley church account?"

"Uh-oh, I'd better back up and talk to my lawyer about this."

Mike could hear the tension in Dressler's voice.

"But you didn't have anything to do with the forging of the checks," Mike said.

"Absolutely not."

"Then you don't have anything to worry about. The wrongdoing occurred before you entered the room. Did Hatcher talk to you about the meeting?"

"No."

"Did you attend other meetings in which Miller's name came up?"

"I won't answer that. Like I said, I need to talk to my lawyer."

Dressler's refusal to respond to the last question told Mike what he needed to know. At some point, Dressler had known the charges against Sam were false.

"I should talk to your lawyer," Mike said. "Can you give me your contact information?"

Dressler had hired a female attorney from a firm with five names in it.

"Let Ms. Dortch know that I'm going to call on Monday during a break in the proceedings," Mike said.

"Okay, I'll try to find out if there is a direct number to reach her."

"Will you have your cell phone with you, so I can notify you about the court schedule?"

"Yes."

Knowing Dressler was still hiding information, Mike didn't want to hang up the phone.

"One other thing," Dressler said.

"Go ahead," Mike said, listening closely.

"I'll always appreciate what you and Mr. Miller did for Marie at the hospital. I'll go as far in my testimony as my attorney will allow."

Mike hung up the phone, went into the great room, and sat down in his chair.

"Don't go to sleep," Peg said.

"I'm not sleepy. Did you overhear my conversation with Dressler?"

"Enough to know that he hadn't told you the whole truth and nothing but the truth."

"You're right, and the truth looks more and more like the picture I'd imagined."

THE FOLLOWING DAY, MIKE WAITED ANXIOUSLY FOR MELISSA Hall to provide the names of additional witnesses who would be called by the prosecution. The State wouldn't be content to rely solely upon Detective Perkins and Jesse Lavare, the Craig Valley church deacon. As the clock ticked closer to 5:00 p.m., Mike resisted the urge to call Hall, but at 4:55 the suspense became too great. He dialed the number for the district attorney's office. He didn't want to run the risk of finding out about supplemental witnesses on Monday morning and suffer an unwarranted verbal beating from Judge Lancaster when he objected to their right to testify.

"Ms. Hall has left for the day," the receptionist replied.

"How about Ken? Is he still in the office?"

"Yes."

Mike gave his name and waited. And waited. He was about to hang up when West picked up the phone.

"Are you going to let Mr. Forrest and Bobby Lambert serve as special prosecutors in the Miller case?" he asked.

"Can't see a reason not to. It will increase the educational value of the case for Ms. Hall. Puts a bit more pressure on you, doesn't it?"

Mike ignored the dig. "I haven't received a supplemental list of witnesses."

"Ms. Hall would be the one to give that to you."

"She's not in."

"I guess she's confident enough about the case to go home early."

It was pointless talking to West.

"Do you have her home number?"

"I'll send you back to the receptionist."

Mike endured another long wait before the woman picked up the phone and gave him the number. He dialed it and a man answered. Certain he'd dialed a wrong number, Mike immediately hung up then carefully entered the correct numbers. The same male voice answered. This time it sounded familiar.

"Nathan?" Mike asked.

"Hey, Mike."

"What are you doing there?"

"Helping Melissa fix an Italian dinner. How did you track me down here?"

"I was calling her. Is she available?"

"She went to the store to pick up a couple of ingredients we needed and should be back shortly. Are you at home?"

"Yes."

"I'll let her know."

A few minutes later, Hall returned the call.

"Sorry to bother you at home," Mike began, "but I didn't receive a supplemental list of witnesses."

"I'm set, but Mr. Forrest is making the decisions about anyone else," she responded crisply. "You'll have to talk to him."

"Okay. Have a good time with Nathan. He's a fine young man."

"Don't worry. I'm not going to hurt him."

"I didn't mean to imply—," Mike began then stopped. "I'll see you Monday morning."

The phone clicked off, leaving Mike with a dead receiver. He would enjoy destroying the State's case. Melissa Hall carried a chip on her shoulder that needed to be removed. He phoned Maxwell Forrest's direct number at the office. He knew from past experience that Forrest used voice mail to screen his calls. No one answered.

MIKE SPENT SATURDAY ORGANIZING HIS OPENING STATEMENT. He knew the broad brushstrokes of the picture he wanted to paint for the jury, but it was also important to provide enough details to show he could complete his painting. Dressler's phone call made Mike less concerned about concealing information from the prosecution. If Hatcher already knew Mike had unraveled the bank's deception, it would be more important to clue the jury into what lay ahead than try to conceal it from Forrest and Hall as trial strategy. Late in the afternoon, Peg knocked on the door of the office.

"Is your brain running out of oxygen?" she asked.

"Yes, I need to come up for air." Mike rubbed his temples and leaned back in his chair. "I worked hard on my sermons, but this is ten times more intense. Trying to anticipate every possible twist of the evidence in a case like this is impossible."

Peg stepped over and kissed him on top of the head. "Won't part of it have to wait until you see what happens in court next week?"

"Yes, but I'm developing contingency plans."

"Our supper isn't subject to a contingency. Muriel and Sam are bringing it. What time should they be here?"

Mike looked at his watch. "I need at least another hour. Did you feed Judge?"

"A long time ago. His powers of concentration are focused on his food bowl."

AN HOUR LATER, MURIEL MILLER STEPPED ACROSS THE THRESHOLD and held up a large plastic bag filled with fish.

"Do you like panfried trout?" she asked. "One of Sam's customers caught a mess of fish and gave us way more than we can eat."

"I'll get the cornmeal," Peg replied.

While Muriel and Peg fixed the fish, Mike took Sam into the office.

"Would you like to hear the current version of my opening statement?" Mike asked.

"Yep, although don't expect me to criticize it."

"You mean critique?"

"That, too."

"This is an opening statement, not a closing argument," Mike said while he straightened his papers. "I have to save the yelling and armwaving for the end of the case. The judge will call me down if I get too excited."

Sam closed his eyes while Mike talked. The lack of eye contact was disconcerting, but Mike assumed it helped the older man concentrate. Mike concluded with one of the proverbs most familiar to trial lawyers.

"The prosecution has the opportunity to call its witnesses first, but keep an open mind until all the evidence is presented. Proverbs 18:17 states, *'The first to present his case seems right, till another comes forward and questions him.'* The more you hear from this witness stand, the more confident I am that, at the conclusion of the case, you will find Mr. Miller not guilty of the charge against him."

Mike waited for Sam to respond. The old man's eyes remained closed.

"Are you awake?" Mike asked after a few more silent seconds passed.

"Yep," Sam replied as his eyes blinked open. "I was trying to go ahead of you but had trouble finding the way."

"Go ahead? What do you mean?"

"Feel the spiritual air that will be in the courtroom on Monday. It's one thing to sit here in your office; it's something else when our enemies are surrounding us. What you said sounded fine for now, but I wanted to see what your words would face on Monday. Your job is to talk. Mine is to pray that your speech won't fall on ears that can't hear. I like to be ready in advance. The Master often knew what lay ahead along the road."

"Okay, but did the opening statement make sense?"

"Yep."

Mike waited. "Anything else?"

"Nope."

"I mean, how did it make you feel?"

Sam shook his head with sorrowful eyes. "Sad, very sad. But not because it isn't good. You're a fighter, and when you see something wrong, you go after it with a sword. Listening to your speech, I felt anger rising up inside me, but it wasn't wearing the Master's face."

"The injustice of it all motivates me. I don't feel bad about getting upset," Mike said.

"The Master got mad, too. But if I get angry, it will open a door for worry about Muriel that will drag me down into a pit. Papa knows how to deal with the men who have done this to me. The older I get, the more wickedness makes me cry."

"Supper's ready!" Muriel called out.

Sam managed a slight smile. "Doesn't she have the sweetest voice on earth?"

They ate in the dining room. The sight of the food on the table reminded Mike of meals his family enjoyed at his great-aunt's house when he was a child.

"Say a quick blessing, Preacher," Sam said to Mike when they were seated. "The trout is sizzling and the creamed corn hot."

The fish was delicious, and Mike had never eaten better creamed corn and cornbread muffins. But the food was flavored with the upcoming trial—the slightly bitter apprehension of an impending fear. There wasn't much table talk. When they finished, Mike helped Muriel clear the table while Sam and Peg went into the great room.

"What is Sam telling you about the case?" Mike asked when they were alone.

"Always the same thing. He's trusting in you and the Lord."

"But what does he think is going to happen?"

Muriel dipped the skillet used to cook the fish into soapy water and began washing it. "Having lived with him all these years, I've come to expect the unexpected. Predicting the future isn't my job. That's his department. Right now, I'm trying to keep my mind on my three main prayer burdens: healing for our grandniece with leukemia, health for Peg's baby, and protection for Sam."

Mike didn't ask any other questions. Trying to force Muriel Miller to analyze everything Sam dreamed, spoke, or believed wasn't fair. Her simplicity was both a protection and a strength. Instead, she focused on prayer—the most important activity of any Christian.

Twenty-nine

MONDAY MORNING MIKE AWOKE EARLY, GRABBED HIS BIKE GEAR, and slipped quietly downstairs. He'd finalized his trial preparation before going to bed Sunday night, and a brisk ride with Judge would do more to clear his mind than staring again at his notes. It was a slightly muggy morning with low mist rising from the ground. He completed two quick circuits on the hill that left Judge panting. Returning to the house, Mike greeted Peg, who was in the kitchen with fresh coffee in the pot.

"How are you?" he asked.

"A little queasy, but I have an excuse with the baby. What about you?"

"Queasy, but without a baby in my belly. I woke up this morning thinking about Danny Brewster."

"Any dreams?"

"No, just bad memories."

"This is a different case."

"I know, but there's the same pressure of representing an innocent man."

Peg came over, stood behind him, and rubbed his shoulders.

"And you've worked as hard getting ready as for any trial in your career. If preparation is the key to success, you couldn't have done more." Peg lifted her hands from his shoulders. "All you need is a cup of coffee, a shower, a prayer, and a kiss."

Mike looked up at her. "Could I have two kisses?"

Peg gave him a peck on the lips. "And you know I'll be here rooting for you. I thought about coming to the courthouse—"

"No," Mike said quickly. "I need to focus."

302

Peg rubbed his shoulder a little harder. "And I would be a distraction?"

"Yes. And seriously, Sam told me on Saturday that Muriel is going to stay at home because the arguing in the courtroom would just upset her. She'll come when it's time for the jury to deliberate. That won't happen until the end of the week."

"Maybe that's when I'll come, too."

Mike finished his coffee and went upstairs. After he shaved and showered, he stood in the doorway to their clothes closet. Peg sat on the edge of the bed.

"What are you going to wear?" she asked.

"You pick."

"The dark blue suit with a white shirt and gold tie. You never go wrong with that one. The tie complements the brown in your eyes."

Mike dressed and patted his stomach. "I bought this suit when I tried the Cramerton case. It still fits."

"It was always big."

Mike finished knotting his tie. Peg joined him, adjusted the knot, and stepped back to examine him.

"You'll be the most handsome lawyer in the courtroom," she said.

Mike smiled. "Bobby got all the girls in college. I'll settle for most persuasive lawyer."

Peg patted him on the cheek. "Before you go, I want to pray for you."

Mike bowed his head. They'd never prayed together before he left to go to court. Peg quietly expressed many of the desires of his own heart.

"And show Mike anyone in the jury pool who might be prejudiced against Sam because of his faith. Give them peace in the midst of the battle, and I ask you to comfort Muriel while she waits alone at home. Amen."

Mike opened his eyes. Peg gave him a long kiss on the lips.

"Okay," she said. "You're ready for anything."

Mike loaded his briefcase with the items needed for jury selection, his opening statement, and cross-examination of the witnesses identified by Melissa Hall, along with rough outlines of questions for the unknown witnesses he believed Maxwell Forrest would parade into the courtroom.

HE DROVE INTO TOWN AND PARKED ON THE OPPOSITE SIDE OF the courthouse from his former law firm. He didn't want to engage in any small talk with Mr. Forrest or Bobby. Sam, looking uncomfortable in a white shirt, dark pants, and blue tie, waited for him near the rear of the courtroom. Prospective jurors were finding places to sit on the benches. Mike shook Sam's hand.

"This is it," Mike said. "Are you ready?"

"I reckon," Sam replied, "but it still looks fuzzy to me."

Mike glanced toward the district attorney's table. There was no sign of Ken West or Melissa Hall.

"Did you look over the jury list?" Mike asked.

"Yep." Sam handed him two sheets of paper. "Muriel and I wrote down stuff about the people we know."

Mike glanced at the sheets in surprise. "You know all these people?"

"Several of them, but as I read the names, Papa showed me things about others I've never met."

Mike quickly read the notations beside a few of the names.

"*'Cut his brother's grass for years. Problems with daughter and blames Papa. Mulched flower beds last fall. Doctor told him without surgery his heart may not last another three years. Can't forgive uncle who took over family business and didn't pay fair price.'*" He looked up at Sam. "What am I supposed to do with this personal information?"

"Eat the meat and spit out the bones," Sam answered.

"But you're not going to try to talk to anyone—"

"Not during the trial," Sam replied. "I'm not going to make it hard for you to do your job."

Mike searched the courtroom. There was no sign of Bobby, Forrest, or any of the witnesses Mike had subpoenaed. He suspected they were congregating at Forrest, Lambert, and Arnold.

"Sit in the spectators' section until they call the case," Mike said to Sam.

Mike joined Greg Freeman and several other lawyers. As the clock moved closer to 9:00 a.m., the courtroom filled up. But without any sign of Maxwell Forrest or Bobby. Mike leaned over to Freeman.

"Have you been in the DA's office this morning?"

"Yes, I had to drop off some pleadings I filed this morning."

"Did you see Mr. Forrest or Bobby Lambert?"

"No, but they could have been in the conference room."

The side door to the prosecutor's office opened, and Melissa Hall entered.

No one joined her. Immediately thereafter, Judge Lancaster strode into the courtroom.

"All rise," the bailiff sounded out.

The judge took his seat and looked at Hall.

"Call your trial calendar," he barked.

Hall stood. Mike rose to make his response.

"*State v. Turner*," Hall said.

Mike's jaw dropped open. Greg Freeman hurriedly stood to his feet.

"Ready for the defense," the younger lawyer said.

Mike stepped toward the bench. "Your Honor, I'm here to try *State v. Miller*. I've subpoenaed multiple witnesses locally and from several other states. Last Thursday, I was assured by the district attorney's office that this would be the first case called for trial. The Court ruled on several motions to quash—"

"The indictment has been dismissed," Hall answered with a side glance at Mike. "It was a late development that wasn't confirmed until a few minutes ago."

For a moment, Mike was speechless. "Uh, was it a dismissal with prejudice?"

"This is a criminal case, Mr. Andrews," the judge answered wryly. "Voluntary dismissal prior to call of the case would allow reindictment without violating the constitutional prohibition against double jeopardy."

Mike glanced over his shoulder at Sam, who was sitting with a puzzled look on his face in the second row. Mike turned to Hall.

"But why was the indictment dismissed? There has to be a reason, and my client has the right—"

"You and Ms. Hall can chat later," the judge interjected. "The Court has business to take care of. Ms. Hall, proceed for the State."

Mike walked over to the lawyers' section and sat down. Greg Freeman and his client were already setting up shop at the defense table in preparation for jury selection. Mike motioned to Sam, who approached.

"The indictment has been dismissed," he said numbly. "We're not going to trial."

They walked up the aisle and exited the courtroom as the clerk of court began calling the names in the jury pool. No one paid any attention to Mike and Sam. When they were outside the courtroom, Mike stopped.

"What happens now?" Sam asked.

"I'm not sure. You heard my discussion with the judge. You could be reindicted, or the charges could simply go away. Maybe Mr. Forrest and Jack Hatcher told the district attorney's office to dismiss the indictment because they knew about the damaging evidence I was going to bring out in court, but that doesn't make sense. Whatever the reason, all the witnesses I subpoenaed will be free to leave, and I'm not sure if I can find and serve subpoenas on them in the future. If it turns out you're reindicted next week, this was a dirty move."

"Did you think the charges might be dropped?" Sam asked.

Mike shook his head. "No, it caught me completely off guard."

"What do I do?"

"Go home and hug Muriel, but call me if you get another visit from the sheriff's office. I'll talk to Lamar Cochran and ask him to tip me off if a warrant is issued for your arrest. I'll also notify Darius York and Brian Dressler that they won't be needed in court."

"Thanks for all you've done."

Mike shrugged. "All I did was show up."

"You know what I mean. Without all your hard work, they wouldn't have run away."

"But you could still be charged."

Sam rubbed his stomach. "I don't think so. Something inside tells me this forged check thing is over and done with."

"I hope you're right."

Sam turned to leave, then stopped and faced Mike.

"When will I see you again?" he asked.

Mike put his hand on the old man's shoulder. "Anytime you want. I might ask you for a job helping take care of Mrs. Bowen's backyard."

"Now, I can get started on the irrigation system she wants for the flower beds farthest from her house. I could use a strong back like yours to do some digging."

Sam left the courthouse. Mike lingered, still wound tight in anticipation of the trial but with no place to release his energy. He didn't share Sam's optimism about the future.

He went to his car but didn't start the engine. He could go home, but watching TV game shows on Monday morning didn't appeal to him. He had to find out what had happened to the case. Getting out of his car, he returned to the courthouse and marched into the district attorney's office.

"Is Ken available?" he asked the receptionist.

"I'll see if he's in," she replied.

Mike glanced down the hallway and saw the large form of the district attorney lumbering into his office. Mike didn't wait for clearance from the receptionist. He walked down the hall and knocked on the door.

"It's open!" West responded.

Mike stuck his head in the door. "Do you have a minute?"

West waved his hand. "Mike! Come in and have a seat. Sorry I was so short with you the other day. You did a great job for your crystal-ball-reading client. The way you hassled the bank forced them to find out what really happened."

Mystified, Mike sat across from the district attorney. "Can you give me additional details?"

"Not much, beyond the evidence implicating Brian Dressler."

"Dressler?" Mike didn't hide his shock.

West leaned forward. "Don't act surprised. You tracked him down and subpoenaed him after he was fired by the bank."

"Yes. But I also intended to question several other people."

"I know, and cast doubt on your client's guilt from as many angles as possible. Whether you use a shotgun or a rifle doesn't matter so long as you kill what you're after."

Mike sat with a blank look on his face.

West continued, "But don't look to me for an apology. With the information in our file, there's no way we could have figured out what really went down. It took the bank to unravel Dressler's modus operandi."

"What exactly was he doing?" Mike asked slowly. "I want to explain it correctly to Mr. Miller."

"You'll have to ask Maxwell Forrest for the details, but he described it as a form of internal check kiting. Dressler created a personal slush fund by shifting money between noninterest-bearing accounts that had little activity. The money didn't stay out of an account for a full business day, so it never appeared as a debit; however, Dressler could use the funds to bankroll his day-trading habit."

"The Craig Valley church building account was one of his sources?"

"Correct, and as chief of internal security at the bank, he covered his tracks. I asked Forrest if Dressler made a bad stock trade that he couldn't cover, but apparently a problem with Dressler's wife led to his downfall."

"She's dead."

"I know. Dressler was chained to his desk while running his scam. One day he left in a hurry because his wife had an emergency and didn't put all the pieces back in place. A $100,000 withdrawal showed up on the church account. Dressler had to come up with a scapegoat and targeted your client to explain the money flowing out of the account."

"How did he know my client and his connection with the church?"

"Not sure, although it was a subtle touch accusing a white man of embezzling money from a black church. Played nice on the race card in a backhanded kind of way."

"Have you seen the bank records documenting any of this?"

"No, and the bank may not do anything to Dressler because he never actually stole the money. It's all computer entries. Hatcher is considering his options, but at this point, I believe his major concern is avoiding negative publicity."

"I'd suspect as much from him," Mike answered wryly.

"Did your expert confirm that the checks allegedly signed by your client were typed at the bank?"

"Yes."

"That was a very smart move on your part. I don't think Dressler anticipated someone making the connection."

Mike stared past West's left shoulder at a street scene on the north side of the courthouse. A woman was pushing a stroller with twins along the sidewalk. Life moved on.

West continued, "You wanted to tear into Dressler, didn't you?"

Mike returned his focus to the DA. "I wanted to bring out the truth."

West chuckled. "Don't we all? There's nothing more fearsome than a capable lawyer cloaked in the zeal of a righteous cause."

"Do you know if the other witnesses I subpoenaed are in town?"

"No."

"So, can I tell Sam Miller not to worry about a reindictment?"

West waved his arms. "Absolutely. He's in the clear. The next time he'll be in front of a jury should be to prove his punitive damage claim against Dressler."

West stood to his feet. Mike joined him.

"Someone else will need to handle that case," Mike said.

West shook Mike's hand.

"I agree. Go back to your pulpit, and use your talents for the good Lord's work."

MIKE LEFT THE COURTHOUSE. CLICKING OPEN HIS BRIEFCASE, he found the phone number for Brian Dressler's lawyer in Mobile. He held a moment before a young female voice answered.

"This is Beverly Dortch."

Mike introduced himself. "I'm calling about the subpoena served on Brian Dressler."

"He's not going to honor it," Dortch said before Mike could continue. "I've filed a motion to quash it in our local court."

"On what grounds? It was personally served on your client while he was in North Carolina."

"I'll present my argument to the court."

Mike conducted a quick debate whether to communicate any of the information he'd just obtained from Ken West.

"When is the hearing on your motion?" he asked.

"Wednesday afternoon at three o'clock. If you provide a fax number, I'll send you a copy of the notice."

"I don't have a fax machine."

"You don't have a fax machine? What kind of law firm do you operate?"

Mike bit his lip. "A small one."

"Do you have access to a computer with an Internet connection?"

"Yeah, they just ran cable lines to this part of North Carolina," Mike answered sarcastically, then gave her his e-mail address. "Send me the notice, but I won't attend the hearing. Your more serious challenge will be trying to fight an extradition order if Dressler's former employer and the local district attorney decide to file criminal charges against him for illegal money transfers."

"What are you talking about?" Dortch asked sharply.

"You'll find out when it's brought up in court."

Mike clicked off the phone. Lawyers like Dortch would make a return to the ministry, even with its challenges, a pleasant prospect.

HE CALLED DARIUS YORK AND BROKE THE NEWS TO HIM.

"Your work was a key," Mike said. "The mere threat of your appearance in court scared the assistant district attorney into dropping the charges."

"Right. Tell me what really happened."

Mike summarized his conversation with Ken West.

"What do you think?" Mike asked when he finished.

"I'm not sure it's a plausible scenario. I'm not up-to-date on bank security, but there are tamperproof safeguards that would catch someone manipulating accounts in the way you described."

"I may not be explaining it properly, but at this point it doesn't really matter to Sam Miller. Getting the charges against my client dismissed is the bottom line. It's not my job to police the rest of the world."

"Give my regards to Mr. Miller," York answered. "I appreciated his honesty and insight. Tell him that I'm already taking steps to correct at least one of my past sins."

Mike cringed in regret at his efforts to squelch Sam's comments to York.

"Okay, and I'll put the balance of your fee in the mail by the end of the week."

"Forget it," York responded. "Consider it my contribution to a worthy cause."

MIKE DROVE HOME SO HE COULD DELIVER THE GOOD NEWS TO Peg. He found her sitting on the couch in the great room with a book in her hand. She glanced up in surprise when he tapped lightly on the door frame.

"It was over before it began," he said.

Mike paced back and forth across the room while he talked. Peg wiped away a tear.

"Good tears?" he asked when he saw her rub her eye.

Peg nodded. "I'm so relieved for the Millers—and for you."

"I'm still trying to find a place to land."

Peg held out her hand. "Sit beside me and let me pull you back to earth."

Mike sat on the couch. Peg put her arm on his shoulder.

"You're a great lawyer who cares about his clients."

"It's easy when you only have one."

"Quiet. And I'm not saying that because I secretly want you to go back into law practice. Your three years in the ministry have changed you for the better. Even while working long hours on Sam's case, you spent time with God—and with me. I didn't feel shut out. I think God liked it, too."

"But now what?"

"That's for you to decide."

"Will you tell me what you think?"

"Yes."

"I'll be listening." Mike took her hand and kissed it. "We have a lot of time left on the sabbatical. I could get used to being with you on a perpetual vacation."

Later that afternoon they went for a walk in the backyard and checked on their flowers.

"What are you thinking about the church?" Peg asked.

"I'll have to face it soon. The real reason for my exile has ended. The elders will know what happened by nightfall. Bobby will make sure the word gets out."

"Or you could call Delores Killian right now with the news and ask her to keep it confidential."

Mike smiled. "I've missed her."

Peg put her hand on his forehead. "Uh-oh, you're delirious. Don't make any hasty decisions until your fever breaks. Wait for the elders to contact you."

"Milton Chesterfield and Barbara Harcourt aren't going to show up kneeling on our doorstep asking for forgiveness."

Peg brushed a stray strand of hair away from her face. "A simple apology would be a good place to start. You're totally vindicated by the DA's dismissal of the charges against Sam. That's a lot stronger than a not-guilty verdict because it proves Sam was innocent from the very beginning. A cynic could always claim a jury verdict of not guilty was the result of a tricky lawyer's manipulation of the facts. No one can say that now."

"If you see a tricky lawyer in the room, kiss him."

Peg gave him a peck on the cheek. "Do you want to return to the church if it takes a power play on your part to get back in?"

Mike turned his head so he could clearly see Peg's face.

"It's not much money, but the job at the church is our security."

"While you've been preparing for the trial, I've had plenty of time to get used to the idea of a different direction. We have enough in savings—"

"To buy a few diapers."

Peg's face fell, and Mike regretted his comment.

"I'm sorry," he said. "Maybe I need to ride to the top of Jefferson's Ridge and look into the future. At the moment, you have more faith than I do."

The phone rang. Peg answered it, then put her hand over the receiver.

"It's Braxton Hodges," she whispered.

Mike took the receiver.

"Can I buy you a victory hamburger to celebrate?" the reporter asked.

Mike looked at his watch. It was almost noon.

"I'll meet you there in thirty minutes."

"CALM DOWN," HATCHER SAID TO BUTCH NILES, MOTIONING for the nervous legislator to sit down on the other side of the bank president's desk. "It's about winning the war, not a single battle. Don't blow this setback out of proportion. It's a strategic retreat. Everything is under control. I have a plan."

Thirty

MIKE CHANGED INTO CASUAL CLOTHES AND RETURNED HIS DARK
blue suit, like a coat of armor that hadn't suffered a scratch in battle, to its
place in the closet.

"What are you going to tell Hodges?" Peg asked.

"With Braxton, I always listen more than I talk. Ken West didn't ask me to
keep the information about Dressler confidential, but I'm not sure I want to
unleash a reporter on a fact-finding mission." Mike slipped a ball cap on his
head. "Do you want me to bring you back a couple of cheeseburgers and a
large order of french fries?"

"No, thanks. I'll dip a few raw carrots and uncooked broccoli spears in ranch
dressing."

Mike and Hodges arrived at Brooks at the same time and ordered their
food. The long outside table was crowded with customers.

"Let's go to the park," Hodges suggested.

A few blocks from Brooks was a public park that contained a swing set,
seesaw, and a couple of picnic tables. Both of the tables were vacant.

"How does it feel sitting here wearing a golf shirt and eating a burger with
nothing to do?" Hodges asked after they were settled.

"Surreal."

"I came to the courthouse to watch a few minutes of jury selection, and
you weren't there. I thought the world had ended, and you were snatched up
to heaven, leaving the rest of us heathens to fend for ourselves."

"You have an overactive religious imagination."

"There was a break in the proceedings, and I asked Greg Freeman what

313

happened in your case. He gave me the news that the charges against Sam Miller were dismissed. I tried to get a comment from Ms. Hall, but she brushed me off. I think she was more interested in getting ready to try her case than in talking with the media."

"It was her first felony trial. Maybe you should write about it."

Hodges shook his head. "I checked it out. The public isn't interested in a burglary case involving the employee of an auto parts store who came back after hours to steal the stuff he needed to fix up his 1957 Chevrolet. A picture of the car would be more interesting than an article about the trial. I want the inside story about the Miller case. Eat one more bite, then start at the beginning."

Mike took an extra long time to chew his food. Hodges ate two bites and looked at him impatiently.

"Come on. You can't hold out on me. Swallow your food, and open your mouth now that your lips aren't sealed by the attorney-client privilege."

"You're wrong. I can't reveal client information."

"I don't want to know what Miller told you," Hodges replied with frustration. "I want the scoop about Niles, Hatcher, the Cohulla Creek property, and the illegal payola. Don't worry. I'm not going to use your name in any article. You'll be the confidential unnamed source who refused to be identified."

"There's nothing sensational to tell. I uncovered a few bits of information, but my primary focus was proving that Sam had nothing to do with the two checks drawn on the Craig Valley church building fund account. I hired a handwriting expert, a former FBI agent, who was going to testify that the checks were typed on an old typewriter owned by the bank then signed using a signature stamp. Sam didn't own a signature stamp. The connection of the bank's typewriter to the checks broke the case open."

"That's not all," Hodges insisted. "Otherwise, you wouldn't have subpoenaed Linden, Bunt, and Dressler."

"I never nailed everything down. I wanted to expose the bank's motivation to discredit Sam, but the testimony of the others would have been based on innuendo that I'm not sure Judge Lancaster would have allowed. Judge Coberg knows about Sam's dreams and might have let me color outside the lines. Lancaster would have put a chain around my neck and forced me to try the case in a traditional manner."

"So you didn't uncover a smoking gun?"

"No. Dismissal of the charges had nothing to do with Cohulla Creek."

"That's a big letdown." Hodges sighed.

Mike sipped his drink. Hodges had helped him quite a bit with Dressler. He wanted to give him something in return.

"One thing I didn't mention to you," Mike said. "There is a memo of a meeting."

Hodges perked up as Mike summarized the contents of the memo Bobby slipped into the old deed book at the courthouse.

"Can you give me a copy of the memo?" the reporter asked. "I wouldn't use it unless I could substantiate its relationship to the overall scheme."

"Yes, I'll pass it along, but don't mention me as your source. The person who gave it to me could lose his job if my name is connected to it."

"Agreed. I found it blowing in the wind on a street corner."

DRIVING HOME, MIKE WONDERED IF HE SHOULD HAVE TOLD Hodges about his conversation with Ken West. If Dressler had framed Sam Miller, it would be a major news story, but in his gut, Mike didn't believe the former banker was the prime mover in the plot to destroy the old man. Dressler's lawyer in Mobile might be a jerk willing to file a groundless motion, but that didn't make her client guilty of anything but poor judgment in his choice of counsel.

When he arrived home, Mike turned on his computer to check his e-mail messages. Several items from the top, he spied a message line that caught his attention—"From Milton Chesterfield." Mike quickly clicked it open.

Congratulations on your successful representation of Sam Miller. The elders would like to meet with you and Mr. Miller this evening at 7:00 p.m. at the church. Unless I hear from you otherwise, we will see you then.

Mike printed the message and showed it to Peg in triumph. "Look at this! They're not only going to apologize to me, but also to Sam."

Peg took the sheet from him. "Where does it say that they're going to apologize?"

"Why else would they congratulate me and invite both of us to come?"

"It would be a major change of heart, but it's hard to imagine some of the elders humble enough to admit a mistake."

"I know, but will you let me be ridiculously optimistic for a few minutes?"

Peg smiled. "Okay. Did you call Sam?"

"Not yet. He's probably mowing a lawn."

Mike phoned Muriel, who promised to deliver Sam wearing clean clothes to the Andrewses' house in time for the two men to drive to the Little Creek Church by 7:00 p.m. Later in the afternoon, Mike received a call from Larry Fletchall, the chief deacon at the Craig Valley Gospel Tabernacle.

"I heard what happened in Sam's case," Fletchall said. "A lady from the district attorney's office called and told me charges should never have been filed. It was all a big mix-up. I can't tell you how relieved I am that Sam didn't do anything wrong."

"The system worked," Mike answered simply.

"And we'd like to celebrate. Could you be our guests at the church on Sunday?"

"Both of us?"

"Yes, along with your wives."

Mike hesitated. He didn't want to miss the opportunity for a triumphant return to Little Creek.

"Uh, not this week, but let's stay in touch. It would be an honor to attend a service."

SAM AND MURIEL ARRIVED AT 6:15 P.M. SAM'S FACE WAS SLIGHTLY RED.

"Forgot my hat and spent the whole afternoon working in the Blevinses' backyard," the old man said when Mike commented on his ruddy appearance. "They don't have a square foot of shade around that new swimming pool."

"How long do you think the meeting at the church will last?" Muriel asked.

"I'm not sure," Mike replied. "Normally, I prepare an agenda, but the only notice I received was an e-mail. If the elders want to talk about church business, I'll recommend that we do it another time. I don't want Sam waiting alone in the hallway for several hours."

Mike looked at his watch. "We don't need to leave for a few minutes. While we're together, I need to tell you why the charges against Sam were dismissed."

He related his conversation with Ken West.

"What do you think?" he asked Sam when he finished.

The old man shook his head. "I don't understand all that stuff about stocks and bank accounts. I saw darkness in Mr. Dressler's heart when we were with him and his wife at the hospital but thought it had to do with their relationship, not me."

"I know less than you do about Dressler's heart," Mike replied, "but I'm not convinced he wrote the checks and stamped them with your signature. When I called Darius York and told him what happened, he had his doubts, too."

"But are they going to leave Sam and me in peace?" Muriel asked.

"Yes," Mike said. "That's the one thing West told me we can count on. If he'd entertained thoughts of refiling criminal charges against Sam, he wouldn't have been so emphatic about why the charges were dismissed. It's over."

Muriel began to cry. Peg came over and put her arm around her. She, too, began to sniffle. Sam looked at Mike and smiled.

"We'll let you ladies be happy together," Mike said after a few moments. "We don't want to be late to church."

DRIVING OUT OF THE NEIGHBORHOOD, MIKE ASKED SAM, "WHY do you think the elders want to meet with us?"

"I don't know. I asked Papa about it during the ride over to your house, but I didn't hear anything."

They rode in silence down the hill and onto the valley road. Sam sat in the seat with his eyes closed. Several miles passed. Sam groaned slightly. A few moments later he groaned more loudly.

"Are you okay?" Mike asked.

Sam opened his eyes and grimaced. "My stomach aches. I think I put too much hot sauce on my collard greens."

"Do we need to go back to my house?"

Sam closed his eyes and didn't respond. Mike continued down the road. They neared the church.

"We're almost there," Mike said. "How do you feel?"

Sam opened his eyes and rubbed his abdomen. "My spirit is uneasy."

"I thought you ate too much hot sauce."

"No, this ache is coming from another place."

"We're here."

Mike turned into the church parking lot. The sun had just dipped below the hills in the west, but there was plenty of daylight to clearly see the property. So much had happened to Mike since he'd last been there that he saw it with fresh eyes. It felt right to return. The parking lot in front of the administration build-ing was empty. Mike looked at his watch.

"We're only five minutes early," he said. "But it's not usual for people to be late. Come inside. I'll show you where we'll meet."

Sam moaned again as he unbuckled his seat belt.

"Can you do this?" Mike asked with concern.

"Yep, but I may hold you to your promise not to let the meeting go too long."

They entered the building and went into the conference room. Mike turned on the lights.

"I'll brew a pot of coffee. If you need to use the restroom, it's down the hall on the right."

Mike returned with the water and filled the coffeepot. As it dripped down, he checked his watch. Sam sat in one of the chairs with his eyes closed.

"I'll look outside and check the parking lot," Mike said.

Dusk had darkened when he opened the door and peered out. No one had arrived, and Mike began to wonder if he'd misinterpreted the message from Milton Chesterfield. He returned to the conference room.

"I'm calling Peg."

Peg answered on the second ring. "We're alone and it's ten minutes after seven," Mike said. "Did anyone phone to cancel the meeting?"

"No."

Mike thought a second. "I didn't bring the e-mail from Milton. It's on the table in the kitchen. Please read it to me."

Mike waited then listened to Peg repeat the words he already knew were on the paper.

"It couldn't be any clearer," Mike said. "What do you think happened?"

Sam raised his hand. "Mike, I need to leave. My stomach and left arm are really hurting."

"We're coming back to the house," Mike said to Peg. "Sam is sick."

Mike closed the phone, and Sam rose unsteadily to his feet. Mike turned off the coffeepot.

"Is it your heart?" Mike asked anxiously.

"I'm either going to faint or throw up."

"Should I call an ambulance?"

Sam shook his head. "No, let's go. Muriel can put a cool rag on my head. That always makes me feel better."

During the ride home, Mike kept glancing at Sam, who sat with his eyes closed and breathing irregularly. Each time Sam didn't take a breath, Mike worried it might be the sign of a heart attack. As they drew closer to the house, Sam sighed and stretched out his hands.

"It's passing," he said. "I could feel the snake turn loose of my belly."

"Snake?"

"That's the best way I can describe it. I was getting squeezed from front to back. Thanks for praying for me."

"I did more worrying than praying."

Sam managed a slight smile. "Papa can recognize compassion no matter how it's dressed."

They turned into the driveway. Sam exited the car without difficulty and walked beside Mike into the house.

"What's wrong?" Muriel asked as soon as they stepped into the kitchen.

"I'm not sure, but it was trying to kill me. My stomach, chest, and left arm were paining real bad."

"Should you go to the emergency room?" Peg asked.

"Nope. I'm okay now."

"How can you know?" Mike asked then turned to Muriel. "Has he had spells like this in the past?"

"Never exactly like this," Sam answered. "I guess it was one of those big snakes trying to smother the life out of me. What do they call them?"

"Pythons?"

"Yep. But it's slithered back into its hole."

Mike shuddered at the image. The phone rang. Peg answered it and held it out to Mike.

"It's Bobby Lambert."

"Good," Mike said. "Now, we'll find out why the session meeting was canceled."

He picked up the phone.

"Where are you?" Bobby asked in an excited voice.

"Standing in my kitchen. Check the number; you called my house."

"But where were you thirty minutes ago?"

"At the church waiting for you and the rest of the elders to show up for a meeting. What happened?"

"A dispatcher with the fire department just called me! The old sanctuary is on fire! There are two fire trucks on the scene, but they're not going to be able to save it!"

Mike almost dropped the phone. He slumped down in one of the kitchen chairs. Putting his hand over the receiver, he whispered intently to the little group in the kitchen.

"The old sanctuary at Little Creek is on fire!"

Muriel stopped close to Sam, who put his arm around her shoulders. Mike lifted his hand from the receiver.

"What caused it?"

"He didn't tell me. Explain again why you were at the church?"

Mike felt drops of sweat trickle down inside his shirt. He spoke slowly and deliberately.

"I received an e-mail this afternoon from Milton Chesterfield that the elders wanted to meet with Sam Miller and me at the church around seven o'clock. We went to the church and waited about twenty minutes, but no one showed up so we left. I turned on the coffeepot in the conference room, but we didn't go into the old sanctuary."

"I don't know anything about a session meeting. Milton Chesterfield has been in San Francisco on vacation with his wife and won't be back in town until tomorrow."

"I have the e-mail right here."

Mike read it to Bobby.

"Check the originating address for the e-mail," Bobby said. "Are you sure it came from Milton's computer?"

Mike glanced at the top of the message.

"It lists the sender as 'user@bcsd.com.'"

"I'm sitting at my computer, and that isn't the e-mail address I have for Milton. Did you say bcsd.com?"

"Yes."

Bobby was silent for a moment. "Barlow County School District. That e-mail was sent from one of the public schools. My daughter sends notes to me at the office with that return address."

Mike panicked. "Bobby, you know I didn't have anything to do with setting fire to the church."

"Of course not."

Mike continued speaking rapidly, "I'd come to terms with the reasons for the sabbatical and hoped we could work through any problems about my leadership now that the charges against Sam have been dismissed. That's why I went to the church. I believed it would be the first step toward my return as pastor."

"That was my goal, too. But we hadn't discussed when to meet with you or if Mr. Miller would be included."

"What are you going to do now?"

"Go to the church."

"I'll meet you there."

Mike clicked off the phone.

"The e-mail was sent from one of the schools," he said to the group. "But Milton is in California and won't be home until tomorrow."

Peg looked at him with sad eyes.

"Are you sure it's a good idea to go to the church?" she asked. "If someone is trying to make it look—" She stopped.

"It will look worse if the pastor of the church doesn't show up when a major building on the property is burning to the ground. Sam and I didn't do anything wrong, and no one can prove otherwise."

Peg appealed to Sam, "Tell him not to go."

The old man shook his head. "I'm not his master. It's up to him."

"Are you going with him?" Muriel asked Sam.

"Nope. I need to get home and ask Papa what He wants me to do."

After Sam and Muriel left, Peg turned to Mike.

"I'm not sure I can handle any more of this pressure. It was hard enough suffering alongside Muriel and Sam. If the police try to claim you had something to do with—"

"They'll be wrong. I'm gone. I've got to see what's happened."

AS HE DROVE TO THE CHURCH, THE PANIC MIKE HAD FELT WHEN Bobby first mentioned the fire changed into anger. He was mad. Setting fire to a church was an act of sacrilege. He sped down the road, passing several cars against the restrictions of the yellow line.

Close to the church, he had to stop as traffic slowed to a crawl. Mike impatiently tried to peer around the corner of the road. Trees along Little Creek hid the church, but there was no mistaking the orange glow in the sky. The ancient wood in the sanctuary would burn fast and hot. Noticing that no cars were coming from the opposite direction, Mike pulled to the left, zipped past the line of cars, and pulled off the road just past the creek. Two large fire trucks and several cars were on the church property. Firefighters were spraying water onto the rear of the old sanctuary. The front portion of the building was already a charred pile of black wood.

Mike got out of the car and saw a hose stretching from one of the trucks into Little Creek. A handful of spectators had parked their cars on the opposite side of the highway to watch the activity. A firefighter approached Mike.

"Sir, please move along."

"I'm Reverend Mike Andrews, the pastor of the church," he replied. "Is there a place I can stand so I won't be in the way?"

The man pointed. "Stay close by the creek. I'll let the captain know you're here."

Mike walked along the familiar path that ran alongside the creek. He stopped near the place where the spring bubbled up from beneath the earth. One of the crews was spraying water on the roof of the administration building. Fortunately, there was no sign of fire on the adjacent structures. No one else from the congregation was present. After a few minutes, a gray-haired man in firefighting gear walked toward him.

"I'm Captain Logan," he said.

Mike introduced himself.

"There was no chance to save it," Logan said. "As you know, it was a tinderbox covered with old paint."

"Are the other buildings going to be okay?"

"Yes, the fire is contained, and we're fortunate to have the creek close by."

"Who reported the fire?"

"I'm not sure, but I suspect a motorist saw the smoke and dialed 911. We were here in less than fifteen minutes, but there was nothing we could do except keep it from getting hotter or spreading to the other buildings."

"Do you know what caused it?"

"It's a clear night, so it's either electrical or arson. Did you have any space heaters or other electrical devices in the building?"

"Nothing except the lights. It had been converted to central heating and air-conditioning years ago. We didn't use it except for special occasions."

"I assume it's insured."

"Yes."

Logan left. Mike continued to watch. He saw Bobby Lambert's car turn into the parking lot. A firefighter pointed in Mike's direction. Bobby joined him. Neither man spoke. The remaining blaze at the rear of the old sanctuary was almost out. Without the light of the fire, the darkness of night crept in except where the lights of the firefighting equipment illuminated the figures moving around the destroyed building.

"What is happening here?" Mike asked.

Bobby ran his fingers through his hair. "I don't know. Did you talk to anyone?"

"The captain came over and told me it's either electric or a set fire. Is anyone else from the church coming?"

"It was on the radio news report while I was driving out here, so I suppose people will start coming soon."

"What are you going to tell them?" Mike asked.

Bobby continued to stare straight ahead. "Nothing. Absolutely nothing."

Thirty-one

IT WAS ALMOST 3:00 A.M. WHEN MIKE CLIMBED WEARILY INTO bed. The smell of the burned building lingered in his nostrils. The responses of the church members who came to the scene and saw him beside the ruins of the old sanctuary had been heart-wrenching.

Delores Killian wept when she saw the church building of her childhood wiped off the earth. Mike put his arm around her shoulders and held her as she sobbed. He spoke to a firefighter, who retrieved a piece of the altar rail and gave it to her. Both ends of the carefully polished wood were charred black. Nathan Goode stayed by Mike's side for more than an hour. They didn't discuss Melissa Hall or Sam Miller. Most people stared at the devastation for several minutes, spoke briefly with Mike, then left. Around midnight, Bobby came over to him.

"Milton called from California. The neighbor who feeds his cat phoned him with the news. He was upset, not as seriously as Delores, but the old sanctuary was linked closely to his family."

"Did you mention the e-mail?"

"No. I told you I wouldn't bring it up."

Mike nudged the ground with the end of his shoe. "And thanks for meeting me in the deed room."

"Let's not mention that either."

"Okay."

The men stood beside each other in silence. Mike ached for the return of the lighthearted banter they had enjoyed for so many years. He turned toward Bobby.

"Will there ever be a Friday afternoon when we can play eighteen holes of golf without worrying about anything except avoiding the fairway bunkers?"

"I don't know when."

The next time Mike looked, Bobby's car wasn't there.

Mike stayed until the last firefighter left. He shook hands with every one of them and thanked them for their efforts. He drove home, sad about the destruction of the beautiful old building, apprehensive about questions he feared would come.

The doorbell rang the following morning at 6:30. Mike, wearing his pajamas, stumbled downstairs. Through the sidelight of the door, he saw a couple of men he didn't recognize. He opened the door.

"Michael Andrews?" the younger of the two men asked.

"Yes."

"I'm Hank Perkins, a detective with the sheriff's department. This is Richard Shactner, a fire scene investigator who works with Barlow and four other counties. We'd like to ask you a few questions."

The officers' sober faces confirmed the seriousness of the visit. Mike's mind raced through his options. He could refuse to talk without the presence of an attorney, which was the advice he would have given any client who called him when faced with investigative interrogation. He could show them the e-mail and fully disclose every detail of his actions the previous evening. Or he could find out as much as he could while revealing as little as possible. Even the last approach held substantial risk.

Judge bounded out of the kitchen barking. Mike grabbed him by the collar. "I'll put him in the backyard. Come in and have a seat."

He held Judge's collar as the officers followed into the great room. Peg called from the top of the stairs.

"Who's here?"

"Two men who want to talk about the fire at the church. No need for you to come down."

Mike opened the back door for Judge. He motioned for Perkins and Shactner to sit on the couch.

"What can you tell me about the fire?" Mike asked. "I spoke briefly with Captain Logan, but he didn't have much information."

Shactner spoke. "I was at the scene first thing this morning. During my initial walk-through, I could identify an accelerant pattern that ran from the front door partway down the main aisle. The burn patterns were very distinct."

Perkins added, "And we found an empty gas can in the bushes behind the new sanctuary. Did a commercial company cut the grass at the church property?"

"Yes."

"Was it Miller Lawn Care?"

Mike's mouth went dry. "No. Did the gas can belong to Sam Miller?"

"It had his company name on it."

Mike licked his lips and unsuccessfully ordered his heart to stop pounding.

"Mr. Miller cut the grass for us several weeks ago so he could submit a bid. We'd been using another service but thought he might be cheaper. He must have left the gas can when he was there."

"I know Mr. Miller was with you at the courthouse yesterday morning," Perkins continued. "Do you know what he did after he left?"

"Went to work. I believe at the Blevins residence."

"And after that?"

Mike stood up.

"Thank you for coming, but this conversation is over."

The two men remained seated. Perkins spoke. "Reverend Andrews, do you realize there will be consequences from your failure to cooperate with us?"

Mike's face flushed. "I'm not refusing to cooperate; however, you are aware that I represented Mr. Miller in a recent embezzlement case"—he paused and spoke with emphasis—"in which all charges were voluntarily dismissed by the district attorney's office. As his attorney, it would be improper for me to speculate about his activities, especially if he is the subject of a criminal investigation."

"This is part of an ongoing investigation that may or may not become criminal," Shactner said. "You're the pastor of the church, and we hoped you would assist us."

"Which I will, except to the extent that it violates the attorney-client relationship."

"Has Mr. Miller already retained you to represent him in this matter?" Perkins asked.

"The ongoing nature of the attorney-client relationship is privileged."

Perkins smiled crookedly. "Reverend Andrews. We're not just interested in Mr. Miller's activities yesterday. We also want to talk with you. Where did you go and what did you do after leaving the courthouse?"

Mike put his hands together. "That's all, gentlemen. It's time for you to leave."

Shactner stood and Perkins joined him. Mike started walking toward the door, then glanced over his shoulder to make sure they were following him. As the two men left the house, Perkins turned around on the landing and handed Mike his card.

"If you decide it's in your best interests to cooperate, please call me anytime. My cell number is on the back of the card."

Mike closed the front door and leaned against it. He looked up and saw Peg, her hair disheveled, at the top of the stairs.

"What is it?" she asked.

Mike crossed the foyer and quickly climbed to where she waited.

"The beginning of an inquisition that could make the previous charge against Sam seem like a traffic ticket. I may be implicated as well."

"What did they say?"

"Not much, except that they found one of Sam's gas cans in the bushes near the fire scene. I suggested he might have left it when he cut our grass, but I have doubts. The fake e-mail from Milton that lured us to the church; a gas can conveniently left in the bushes. I wouldn't be surprised if they don't produce an alleged witness who claims we ran from the building right before smoke started—"

Peg collapsed in Mike's arms and sobbed. He held her head close to his chest and gently rubbed her upper back while she shook in his arms. It was all he could do. Anticipating the next step of the people who wanted to destroy Sam, and now him, seemed impossible. After her body began to relax, he took a step back but still kept his hands on her upper arms.

"Will you lie down?"

Sniffling, she kept her gaze toward the floor. "I can't sleep."

"Just be still. Do you think we should contact Dr. Crawford and ask for a prescription that will help calm you down?"

"I'm not going back to bed, and there isn't a pill that can take away what I'm feeling!"

"Then come downstairs and lie on the couch. I need to phone Sam and warn him."

Mike let Judge into the house. The dog went straight to Peg and rested his head close to her hand so she could pet him without moving from the couch. Mike brought the cordless phone from the kitchen into the great room and dialed Sam's number. Muriel answered.

"I need to speak to Sam."

"It's too late. They already came and got him," Muriel said, her voice quivering. "He's been gone about ten minutes."

"Who came?"

"A deputy we didn't know took him to the jail."

"Did he ask Sam any questions?"

"No, he just told him to get in the police car."

"I'm on my way to the jail. I should be there in less than ten minutes."

Mike hung up the phone. Peg shook her head sadly.

"Is there a risk you'll be arrested, too?"

"Yes," Mike admitted.

Peg buried her face in her hands.

"I'm going to the jail to keep Sam from talking to any of the detectives. The last time he was arrested, he gave a statement that could have been interpreted as an admission of wrongdoing. I can't let that happen to him, or me."

Peg turned on her side so that she faced the back of the couch.

"Go," she said. "Leave the phone with me."

Mike touched her shoulder, which was stiff with tension. "I'll be back."

"When?"

"In a couple of hours."

Peg didn't respond. Mike stared at her back and searched for a reassuring word. None came. He turned and left.

THE EARLY MORNING TRAFFIC FLOWING INTO SHELTON seemed out of place. People shouldn't be getting up, drinking a cup of coffee, and slipping into the usual Tuesday morning routine. Mike parked in front of the jail. The familiar female deputy was on duty.

"I'd like to see Sam Miller," Mike said.

The woman hit a few keys on her computer. "He's in booking. I'll let you know when he'll be available."

Mike sat in the waiting area. The initial adrenaline rush produced by his encounter with Perkins and Shactner had faded, and he felt drained. He forced himself to begin analyzing Sam's plight, but so many possibilities rose to the surface that he couldn't begin to develop a cohesive plan. Fifteen minutes passed. He tapped on the glass. The deputy glanced up.

"Oh, you can go back now."

Mike stood in front of the metal door until he heard the click that signaled release of the lock. He pushed open the door and went to the second door where he waited again. When he passed through, he saw Sam dressed in regular clothes, sitting in a chair near the booking area. Detective Perkins approached Mike.

"I'm here to see Mr. Miller," Mike said to Perkins.

"That's fine. We just finished."

"Did you question him?" Mike asked, his voice getting louder. "I told you at my house that I was representing him!"

"That's not what he told us, and you didn't instruct me not to talk to him."

"Did he give you a statement?"

"After signing a Miranda waiver, he provided helpful details about both of your activities."

"Give me a copy of the statement."

"That will be handled by the district attorney's office. I'm sure Mr. Miller can tell you what he told me."

The detective turned and motioned for Sam to approach. Mike opened the door to the closest interview room and waited for Sam to enter.

"What did you tell him?" Mike asked as soon as the door clicked shut. "You know better than to talk to the police!"

"Nothing that they wouldn't have found out anyway," Sam replied. "We didn't do anything wrong."

"Haven't you learned anything?" Mike retorted in frustration. "Perception is as important as reality!"

Sam rubbed the top of his head. "I did plenty of sweating last night when I wrestled with the Enemy before I got the victory."

"Victory over what?"

"Fear," Sam answered simply. "It had me down, much worse than the sickness I felt when we went to the church last night. Right now, it's draped all over you."

Mike stopped. He couldn't deny the anxiety that gripped him.

"Are you saying I shouldn't be worried?"

"Ask the Master, not me."

"Please, don't lecture me."

"I'm trying to help you. Do you remember your dream about me sitting in the chair in this room? I thought about it as soon as they brought me in this morning. I think the dream was about now, not before. It's important for both of us that I stay at rest. It's easier for me since I've been through this jail once. This is your first time. That's always the hardest."

"I'm not in jail yet."

Sam looked directly in his eyes. "Do you believe they're going to let you go when we finish?"

Mike licked his lips. "I hope so."

"If they don't, what are you going to do?"

"Hire a good lawyer."

There was a knock on the interview room door. Mike opened it. Perkins stood there with a deputy beside him.

"Reverend Andrews, I'd like to see you before you leave."

"All right."

Mike shut the door. "It's too early in the morning to call a lawyer."

Sam bowed his head and began to pray. "Papa, You see inside this jail and into the hearts of all men. I don't believe Mike and I are in this place without a plan. Please show it to us so that we can do Your will. We forgive in advance the wicked men who are causing us this trouble, and help us in our time of need."

As the old man prayed, Mike began to calm down. When Sam said, "Amen," he opened his eyes.

"That helped," Mike admitted. "Except when I think about Peg. If I don't go home in a couple of hours, I'm not sure she can handle it."

Sam nodded. "Folks who are married and suffer for the Master endure four times the pain. The greatest fear I fought last night wore Muriel's face. I knew it wasn't her, but that didn't make it any easier to rebuke it. You may have to trust Papa to be there for Peg more than you will for yourself."

Mike slumped down in his chair. "How long do you think we should stay in here?"

"Until they break up our prayer meeting."

Mike looked at his watch. "Or it's time for me to call a lawyer. While we wait, tell me about your conversation with Detective Perkins."

"He asked what I did yesterday after I left the courthouse. I told him I worked at the Blevins house all afternoon then went with you to the church to meet with the elders, who didn't show up, so we left. Don't you think he would have found out about that kind of thing anyway?"

"Maybe, but they should get information on our terms, not theirs. Did you mention the e-mail from Milton Chesterfield?"

"Nope, I didn't remember his name."

"Did he tell you they found a gas can with your company's name on it near the scene of the fire?"

Sam raised his eyebrows. "I've been missing a can for a few days now. I thought I'd left it at a job in town."

"Are you sure you didn't leave it at the church when you cut the grass?"

"Nope. I've had it since then. It's only been gone since Friday or Saturday."

"Don't you see? Whoever set you up did so after realizing what I was going to bring out in your trial! That's why the embezzlement charge disappeared and a new one appeared. It's all the same."

"Same what?"

"Attempt to discredit you, and now, me. A man who would steal money from a church or burn one down shouldn't be believed if he tries to expose corruption by prominent men in the community. The only difference now is they'll try to bring me down, too. I figured out what they were doing while investigating your other case, which makes me a greater threat than you and your dreams."

There was another knock on the door immediately followed by someone opening it.

"Time's up!" a surly deputy announced. "Vacate this room."

"Is there a waiting list?" Mike asked.

Sam shook his head.

Mike followed Sam into the hallway and glanced apprehensively at the booking area.

Perkins came around the corner. "Mr. Miller, you are the subject of an ongoing investigation but may leave at this time."

"I'm not arrested?"

"No; however, you should not leave Barlow County without notifying the sheriff's office of your travel plans."

Normally, Mike would have objected to the notice requirement, but he was so glad Sam could leave that he kept his mouth shut.

The deputy grabbed Sam by the arm. "Come with me."

Mike started to follow, but Perkins stopped him.

"Reverend Andrews, please step into the booking area."

"Am I under arrest?"

"Not unless you want to confess to a crime."

Mike's eyes narrowed. "Your comments at my house made me believe you were going to try to charge me whether you had any evidence or not."

"That's not how we conduct law enforcement in Barlow County."

Mike followed the detective. The booking area contained two desks, several chairs, and a small side room for taking mug shot photos. Sitting beside one of the desks was Ken West.

"Have a seat, Mike," West said. "You got me up early this morning. Detective Perkins tells me you're reluctant to provide details of your activities after you left the courthouse yesterday."

"Those who know the system are cautious," Mike answered. "You'd be the same in my position."

"Probably right." West shifted in his chair. "However, it struck me as odd that Mr. Miller would walk away from an embezzlement charge and immediately burn down a church. Now, he tells Detective Perkins that he was with you during the relevant time period. Is that correct?"

"Yes, from approximately six-fifteen in the evening until we received a phone call at my house that the old sanctuary was on fire."

"Did the two of you go to the church?"

Mike hesitated.

"You don't have to tell me," West continued. "However, we received a 911 call from a witness who reported seeing you and Miller at the church."

"Who was the witness?"

"Didn't leave a name. The call was made from a pay phone at a convenience store about two miles from the church."

Mike leaned forward. "Ken, I'd rather not discuss what happened last night until I obtain legal counsel."

"Are you sure you want to go that far to protect Mr. Miller?"

"And myself."

West avoided Mike's eyes. "I've already begun the process of obtaining a warrant for your arrest; however, as a fellow attorney I didn't want to take that step before talking with you." He looked at Mike. "Will you provide fingerprint samples without the necessity of formal charges?"

"Why? My fingerprints would be all over Little Creek Church!"

"But not necessarily on the gas can found on the premises."

Mike couldn't remember if he'd touched one of Sam's gas cans, but he knew the sheriff's department could eventually obtain his fingerprints. If cooperation delayed an arrest and bought him a few more hours or days with Peg, it would be worth it.

"Okay," he replied.

Perkins summoned a female deputy, who expertly rolled Mike's fingerprints and pressed them on a card. While she did so, Mike glanced into the photo room and wondered how long it would be before the light flashed and his face appeared in the local paper with the caption "Local Pastor Charged with Burning Church."

Thirty-two

WHEN HE STARTED HIS CAR, MIKE ENTERTAINED THE WILD thought of packing Peg and Judge in the car, emptying his shrinking bank account, and driving as far away from Barlow County as possible. He arrived home. Peg was sitting in the kitchen waiting.

"Thank God!" she said when he walked through the door.

They embraced. Mike held her a long time, memorizing the feel of her body pressed close to his.

"How was Sam?" she asked when he released her. "Muriel called. She's torn up."

"On his way home. But the wheels of injustice are turning. I'm not sure how long it will be before arrest warrants are issued."

"Warrants?"

"For both of us. I believe everything that's happened is connected. It's all designed to keep Sam, and now me, from ruining the Cohulla Creek land deal. There is a lot of money at risk."

"Money!" Peg raised her voice. "Call Mr. Forrest and promise to keep your mouth shut! We don't care whether someone builds a bunch of houses in the middle of the woods."

"The people behind this wouldn't trust me. And there may be corruption I don't know anything about. They're probably scared of going to jail themselves."

Mike told her about the encounter with Ken West. "If they claim my fingerprints are on the gas can, I'm sure I'll be arrested."

Peg bit her lower lip. "What will I do if that happens?"

"Get me out on bond. I'm going to hire Greg Freeman to represent me before I'm arrested. I have to do as much as possible while I still have my freedom."

"Do you think you should see Bobby?"

"Why?"

"I haven't been able to get him out of my mind. If he was on the bad side of this, he wouldn't have slipped you information at the courthouse."

"Okay, but what am I supposed to ask him now?"

"To help. I can't believe he would stand by and let this happen to us if he could stop it."

"He's not close to the center of power."

"No, but I'd like you to do it for me."

Mike shrugged. "Okay, it can't hurt."

He picked up the phone. It was still too early for the receptionist at the law office to be at work, so he dialed Bobby's cell phone. The familiar voice answered.

"Are you at the office?" Mike asked.

"Yes."

"Detective Perkins and an arson investigator came to see me early this morning. Sam Miller and I are under investigation for setting fire to the church."

"No! This is crazy!" Bobby responded with such feeling that Mike was encouraged to continue.

"I'd like to meet with you."

"When?"

"As soon as possible."

There was a brief pause. "The courthouse will be open in a few minutes. Be at the library."

Mike hung up and turned to Peg. "I'm not sure where this is going with Bobby, but I'm going to meet him at the courthouse. While I'm in town, I'll slip in and talk with Greg Freeman. He's trying a case in the main courtroom, but I can catch him during a break."

"Go ahead. I'm not feeling well," Peg replied. "I'm going to lie down."

"Should I take you to the doctor?"

"No, I'll be fine if I get off my feet."

Mike reluctantly left the house. He arrived at the courthouse and went to the library. Bobby was waiting for him. Mike had a sudden urge to ask Bobby if he was going to record the conversation.

"Is this off the record?" Mike asked.

"You're the one who wanted to talk."

"I'm jumpy. Who's behind this?"

"Delores phoned me late last night claiming Miller threatened to burn down the church several weeks ago. She was going to call the sheriff's department and report it. I guess that's what she did."

Mike groaned. "It was a dream. Sam had a dream in which he saw the church on fire. It wasn't literal; it had to do with the conflict that surfaced over my involvement in his criminal case. He never expressed any anger toward the church or its leaders, and I explained that to Delores at the time."

Bobby tapped his pen against a blank legal pad. "She remembered what she wanted to. Captain Logan also phoned and asked me about the company that maintained the church grounds. They found a gas can belonging to Miller in the bushes."

"I know. They want to dust it for my fingerprints, too."

"Did you touch it?"

"I remember talking to him when he came to cut the grass, but I don't know if I picked up any of his equipment. I could have helped him load or unload stuff at other locations when I went by to see him about his case. But there must be more behind this than Delores Killian and a gas can."

"You and Miller were the last people at the church. That doesn't prove anything, but it's circumstantial enough to make a detective start sniffing the air."

Mike stood up and started pacing.

"But are there any other reasons why this is happening?" he asked.

"Not that I'm aware of."

Mike stopped and stared hard at Bobby.

"Are you sure?"

"What are you driving at?"

Bobby seemed sincere. Mike didn't know how hard to push or what to reveal. He tried a different tack.

"Why was the embezzlement charge against Miller dropped?"

"Evidence surfaced that your client didn't have anything to do with the checks."

Mike put his hands on the conference table and leaned forward.

"Did this evidence involve Brian Dressler?"

"Yes, but I can't comment on the details."

"Was there another reason why the charges against Miller suddenly evaporated?"

"No."

"Did you and Mr. Forrest talk about the dismissal?"

"Of course, but you know he just brought me in to carry his briefcase and do some research. Mike, what are you driving at? You have more immediate problems than figuring out why you won the embezzlement case without firing a shot."

"I'm just wondering if the embezzlement and arson charges are related."

"How?"

"That's what I hoped you could tell me."

"I can't," Bobby replied with obvious frustration in his voice. "I'm your friend, not your enemy. I've tried to prove that over and over during the past weeks. What do you want me to do?"

"Peg asked me to talk to you, but I'm not sure why."

"Maybe because she knows you'll ride off to battle without thinking about the consequences. You need to hire a lawyer to protect you and Peg."

Mike sat down at the table. "Will you represent me?"

"Are you serious? I'm not a criminal defense lawyer. I'm comfortable with contracts, but I've never handled anything more complicated than a traffic ticket. You don't want me."

"What about Mr. Forrest?"

"He's furious with you for pestering the bank and dragging Bunt and Linden into town just to harass them for no reason. I could talk to him, but he needs a cooling-off period before he'd consider serving as your champion. You need help now."

"I'm going to talk to Greg Freeman. He's in the middle of a trial, but I'm going to catch him during a break."

"Good. Get to him as soon as you can."

"Will you let me know if you hear anything else about the fire?"

"Yes."

Mike hesitated. "One more thing. Why did Mr. Forrest believe I subpoenaed Bunt and Linden for harassment purposes only?"

Bobby put his pen in his pocket. "Because of their ownership in the bank, of course. In the past year, they've become the two largest stockholders."

"That's what he told you?"

"Yes."

Mike stood up. "I'm heading over to the courtroom. If you won't help me, I'm going to ask Greg Freeman."

Mike ignored the crestfallen expression on Bobby's face and left the library. He slipped in the back of the courtroom. Melissa Hall was questioning a sheriff's deputy who had identified Freeman's client as the man caught leaving the auto parts store through the back door late one Saturday night.

"Was he carrying anything in his arms?" Hall asked.

"No."

Hall looked flustered. "Wasn't he carrying property from the store?"

"Objection, leading," Freeman said.

"Sustained."

"Tell us what you saw," Hall tried again.

"I saw the defendant pushing a shopping cart piled high with a set of chrome reverse mag wheels, a CD player with six speakers, and a pair of sheepskin seat covers."

Hall relaxed. The questioning went smoothly from there. When she sat down, one of the jurors raised his hand. Judge Lancaster pointed to him.

"What is it?"

"Could we take a break? I'm not feeling well."

"Ten minutes," the judge barked.

Mike walked down the aisle. Both Freeman and Hall turned around as he approached.

"Greg, can I speak with you for a minute?" Mike asked.

Freeman came around the bar into the aisle. "This was your week to star in court."

"I almost wish I could have. There's more trouble brewing. Did you hear about the fire at my church?"

"No."

"The old sanctuary at Little Creek burned down last night. Sam Miller and I are under investigation for arson."

"What?" Freeman replied so loudly that Melissa Hall turned around and stared at them.

"Yes, and I want you to represent us."

"Is there a potential conflict of interest between Miller and you?"

"No."

Freeman jerked his head toward the man sitting morosely at the defense table.

"I have to fly this plane into the side of a mountain first. My client claims his cousin broke into the store, but the police officer and an unbiased witness disagree."

"How long will the case last?"

"The prosecution should finish before lunch. I don't have any witnesses except my client. The cousin didn't want to come forward and confess. He's a repeat offender who would face a life sentence for a three-strike felony. The jury should have the case by late this afternoon. A verdict?" Freeman shrugged his shoulders.

"Okay."

"Has Miller been questioned?"

"Yes."

"What did he say?"

"I haven't seen the statement, but nothing that isn't common knowledge. I met him at the jail an hour ago and told him to keep quiet."

"Did they try to talk to you?"

"Perkins and an arson investigator named Shactner came to my house. Ken West was at the jail."

Freeman raised his eyebrows. "West came to the jail?"

"Professional courtesy. And they wanted my fingerprints to compare with those on a gas can found at the scene."

"Did you give them a card?"

"Yes, otherwise, I think I'd be calling your office from the phone outside the cell block."

"Call me late this afternoon. Unless the jury gets confused by the evidence, I should be out of here by five o'clock."

Mike left the courthouse. He wanted to be doing something, not simply waiting for the sheriff's department to act. However, he wasn't sure what to do. He drove home. Peg was in the great room lying on the couch.

"Better?" he asked.

She nodded in a way that didn't convince him. "I was nauseous right after you left. I guess it's better to face stress on an empty stomach. How did it go?"

"Nothing new from Bobby. He either doesn't know anything or is a good liar. After we met, I talked briefly with Greg Freeman and asked him to represent Sam, too."

Peg closed her eyes. Mike sat at her feet but stayed at the edge of the cushion.

"It's the inactivity I can't stand," he said. "There has to be something I can do to get to the bottom of this!"

"Maybe you're going to have to trust someone else to take care of it," Peg answered wearily. "Just like Sam did with you."

"That would be very hard for me to do."

They spent the rest of the morning at the house. Every time the phone rang, Mike jumped, but it was always a member of the church calling about the fire. No one mentioned the police investigation. Apparently, word of the day's earlier events hadn't leaked out into the community. Bobby had honored his word, and the sheriff's department hadn't issued a statement. Toward noon, the phone rang again. Mike answered it.

"Sorry to hear about the fire at your church," Braxton Hodges said. "Our photographer just showed me the pictures. Do you have a comment or two for the article?"

Mike hesitated. "Are you recording this conversation?"

"Yes, so I can quote you accurately."

"Turn off the machine. I want to come in and meet with you."

"Uh, okay, but this isn't a Brooks hamburger day. I have a two o'clock deadline to get this story into tomorrow's edition. Otherwise, it won't make it until Saturday."

"I'm on my way."

Peg lifted her head. "What are you going to tell him?" she asked. "I'm not sure it's wise to talk to a reporter."

"This is different. Trust me."

MIKE AND HODGES WENT INTO THE SPARTAN CONFERENCE ROOM where Mike met with Brian Dressler. Copies of the minutes of the Hatcher meeting and the e-mail from Milton Chesterfield were folded in Mike's pocket.

"This fire hit you hard, didn't it?" Hodges said as soon as they were alone.

"Worse than you know."

Hodges placed a blank pad on the table. "I'm listening."

"You can quote me—'*As pastor of the Little Creek Congregation, I'm saddened by the tragic loss of our historic sanctuary but believe the members of the church will pull together and go forward with the ministry God has given us to the community.'* How is that?"

"Typical. You could have given that to me over the telephone."

"From here on no notes. No recordings. This is between us and nobody else."

The reporter sat up straighter. "Mike, you have a trial lawyer's flair for the dramatic. I'm listening."

"I'm going to tell you the explanation Ken West gave for dismissal of the embezzlement charges against Sam."

Mike quickly laid out the story placing all the blame on the former banker.

"I don't believe it," Hodges responded when Mike finished. "It destroys my Pulitzer article."

Mike took out the memo of the Hatcher meeting. "Here's the memo I told you about."

The reporter read the sheet of paper then looked up. Mike continued, "At first, Dressler denied being in the meeting but last week told me Hatcher called him in to discuss Sam's embezzlement. That would have been difficult because the meeting was four days before the checks were written. Dressler either didn't remember correctly, or the plan to bring down Sam came out of the meeting. Take your pick."

"You know my preference."

"I confronted Dressler with the inconsistency when we talked on the phone. His reaction was reference to the Fifth Amendment. He's already hired a lawyer in Mobile."

Hodges leaned forward. "This is great! Hatcher must have found out that you'd gotten under their cover."

"I'm not sure. I never told anyone except Sam about the memo, but I believe the embezzlement charges went away because Hatcher didn't want me rooting around the courtroom. He may be afraid I know more than I do."

Hodges grunted. "Miller looked like an easy victim until you got involved."

Mike reached into his pocket, took out the e-mail, and placed it on the table. "It's not over. These people aren't giving up. In fact, it's worse."

When he summarized what had happened in the past twenty-four hours, Hodges's jaw dropped open.

"If you're arrested for arson, I'll have to report it," Hodges said when Mike finished.

"It will devastate Peg and ruin my career."

Hodges hesitated. "I can't stop—"

Mike interrupted. "I won't blame you for doing your job, and I'm not here to ask you to censor the news. Does anyone suspect that you're investigating Butch Niles and the Cohulla Creek development?"

"No, I haven't even mentioned it to our editor."

"Good, because you'd be at risk, too."

Hodges's eyes opened wider. "I hadn't thought about that."

"This is serious. Use caution. But don't quit. I'm already limited in what I can do."

"Do you have an estimate on the timing or any arrests?"

Mike shook his head. "No, but I was thankful when I left the jail this morning without having to call a bondsman. I'm going to hire Greg Freeman to represent me. I'll keep you in the loop of information. This fight may not be won in a courtroom."

Thirty-three

SATISFIED THAT HE'D TAKEN A POSITIVE STEP, MIKE DROVE AWAY from the newspaper office. When he arrived home, a sheriff's department car was sitting in his driveway. Taking a deep breath, Mike parked next to it and walked toward the house.

Chief Deputy Lamar Cochran, a cup of coffee in his hand, sat in the kitchen with Peg and Sam Miller. Puzzled, Mike greeted the officer.

"Hey, Lamar. Are you here to arrest me?"

"No. Sam asked me to come."

Sam spoke. "Pour yourself a cup of coffee."

"I don't really want—"

"Just do it," Peg said.

Mike obeyed and sat across from Cochran at the kitchen table.

"Now what?" Mike asked. "Are we going to play cards?"

"After I left the jail," Sam began, "I went home and lay down to rest for a few minutes. I didn't think I could sleep, but in no time I was out. I dreamed that you, me, and Lamar were sitting in your kitchen drinking coffee. We were having a nice conversation when a candle appeared over Lamar's head. That means he's going to get a good idea because we're together. I called the jail, and he agreed to meet us here."

Cochran took another sip of coffee. "I was relieved when the embezzlement charge against Sam was dismissed, and I don't believe he burned down the sanctuary at the Little Creek Church."

"He didn't," Mike responded. "We were together the whole evening. I wish you were in charge of the investigation."

"Show him the letter the elder sent you," Sam said.

Mike stared at Sam for a second. "I'm not sure that's a good idea until we talk it over with Greg Freeman. I've asked him to represent both of us, and he's agreed."

"I think we should share the letter with Lamar," Sam replied casually.

Sam made the e-mail sound as harmless as a cake recipe, and Mike could tell from the expression on her face that Peg wanted to walk out Sam's dream. He stifled his objections and went into the office and printed another copy.

"I thought it came from Milton Chesterfield," Mike said, handing it to Cochran, "but it was sent from one of the local schools. Milton was in California. Someone wanted to lure Sam and me to the church and place us on the premises close in time to the fire."

Cochran handed the e-mail back to Mike. "I know Mr. Chesterfield. My father used to work for his company. Anything else?"

"Not really."

"Tell him about your conversation with Ken West," Peg said.

Mike grudgingly obliged. When he reached the part about the 911 call from the convenience store, Cochran interrupted.

"Was it Carrington's One-Stop?"

"He didn't say, but that would be the right distance. The Burtons run a gas station two miles in the opposite direction."

"Yeah."

"There it is!" Sam said.

"What?" Mike asked.

"I saw a flash of light. I think it was coming from the candle."

"Did you see a candle?" Mike asked, not believing he was seriously asking the question.

"Nope, but what else would put out light like that?"

Mike turned to the chief deputy. "Can you tell us about your bright idea?"

Cochran shook his head. "No, but I'll keep thinking."

The radio on the deputy's belt squawked, and he pressed the Receive button.

"What's your 20?" a voice asked.

"East side of town on the ridge."

"Good. Do you know where Michael Andrews lives?"

Cochran looked at Mike as he answered, "Yes."

"Go to his house. If he's there, bring him in. The magistrate has issued a warrant for his arrest in the Little Creek Church fire."

Mike reached across the table and grasped Peg's hand.

"What about Sam Miller?" Cochran asked.

"We're sending Morris over to get him."

"No need. He's on this side of town, too."

"10-4."

"Can I have a minute with my wife?" Mike asked.

Cochran waved his hand. "Yes."

"And I need to call Muriel," Sam added.

Mike led Peg into the great room. His hand was sweating.

He spoke rapidly. "Greg Freeman is going to call as soon as he finishes his trial. Tell him I've been arrested. He'll know what to do about the bond. Ask him how much he needs as a retainer—"

Peg put her index finger on his lips and looked deeply into his eyes. "Do you love me?"

"Yes."

"That's the most important thing I need to know right now."

"Okay."

Peg continued looking directly into Mike's eyes. "Remember the look on my face if you start to worry about me." Placing his hand on her heart, she said, "And I keep hearing the same words over and over—fear not, fear not, fear not."

"Fear not."

"Right. I'll be here when you get out."

"It shouldn't be long—"

"It doesn't matter how long it is," Peg interrupted. "I'll be here."

As Mike followed Sam and Cochran from the house, Peg's words echoed in his mind and her face filled his vision. He and Sam got in the backseat of the patrol car.

"Peg's a fine woman," Sam said.

"Yes."

"And someday, what Papa has done in your marriage will be a bigger memory than the ride in this patrol car."

They rode in silence. Mike stared out the window. They passed landmarks known to him since childhood. Never before had they seemed so close, yet so far away. He could see a place but didn't have the freedom to stop the car and go there. Cochran drove to the rear of the jail where the prisoners entered through a secure entrance.

"I hope it's a short stay," Cochran said.

Mike felt a numb detachment as he returned to the booking area. Cochran left. Mike and Sam stood beside each other.

"We already have their prints," a male deputy barked. "Glamour shots only."

Mike stood on a line and stared, unsmiling, into the camera. A deputy handed him an orange jail uniform and a plastic bag for his regular clothes. Mike had left his wallet and watch at home. He changed clothes in a room no bigger than a closet. When he came out, Sam entered.

"Perkins wants them separated," the deputy said when Sam joined Mike in the open area. "Put Andrews in the holding cell and Miller in cell block A."

"Brinson, the guy who knocked the old man out the last time he was in here, is in A," a deputy said.

"Block B is two over limit."

"There's no need to put Mr. Miller in danger," Mike said, stepping in. "You could move Brinson into B."

"Your opinion about administration of the correctional facility isn't needed," the second deputy snarled.

Sam looked at Mike and shook his head. "It's okay. Papa is giving me a second chance."

The door to the holding cell closed behind Mike. He was alone. The small, dingy, white room smelled of antiseptic. There were no chairs or bed. A toilet without a seat stood in the corner. Mike sat on the floor and leaned against the wall. There was nothing he could do now but wait for others to help him. His dogged persistence and fighting spirit couldn't penetrate the walls that enclosed him. He was helpless. He closed his eyes.

And saw Peg's face.

She'd been right. The love and concern that filled her eyes were much more important than the practical information he'd frantically tried to download into her brain. He examined every detail: her slightly upturned nose, rosy cheeks, welcoming lips, and insightful eyes. Tears, not of sorrow but of gratitude for his wife's devotion, welled up and spilled down his cheeks.

Another scene from the past rose in his mind—a picnic along the Blue Ridge Parkway, not long after they married. Peg fell asleep with her head in his lap. Mike had watched her for a long time, alternating between her face and the hazy mountains in the distance. He'd always considered the picnic an idyllic time. Now, he knew it lacked depth. They'd not yet allowed God to lay the foundation upon which an enduring marriage could be built. Sam's words in the patrol car were true—the blessing on Mike and Peg's marriage was a greater reality than the other challenges they faced.

Mike normally considered enforced solitude maddening. However, instead of pacing back and forth like a caged animal, he relaxed and let his mind travel through pleasant memories. He went back to his childhood, reliving moments that bore the marks of God's grace: the Sunday school teacher who prayed with him when he was in second grade, a friend who would kneel on the ground and talk to God as if He were closer than the tree branches above their heads.

As a boy, Mike loved reading illustrated Bible stories in which he placed himself in the company of Israel's heroes. He remembered the vivid pictures and how the stories stirred him. During that formative time, a nescient faith entered his heart, a faith that matured into mountaintop experiences as an adult and altered the course of his life.

Mike didn't lodge an indictment against the Almighty. The goodness of God had been his lifelong companion. Unlike Job, he wouldn't blame heaven for the evils that marked the human condition. Other events from his life surfaced: the church retreat when he was in high school, a prayer session with Danny Brewster, a redemptive encounter with a homeless man, an afternoon when he preached with power at a food kitchen in Virginia. Time after time, hindsight revealed a plan its present concealed.

He stopped and wondered if he was losing his mind. Were these imaginary journeys the path to insanity? Like a man whose life flashes before him in the instant before death, Mike was watching an advance screening of his life's story. Why? As soon as he asked the question he knew the answer—so he could be thankful in the midst of suffering. The door to the cell opened.

"Supper time," a deputy said as he placed a tray on the floor.

"Thanks."

Mike didn't ask the time of day. He knew jail inmates ate early so the outside kitchen workers could go home. He left his food untouched. He didn't want to defile the memory of home-cooked meals until his stomach demanded it. More time passed. The deputy returned to take away the food tray.

"Could I have a Bible?" Mike asked.

The deputy didn't respond, but in a few moments the door opened and the officer placed a plain black Bible on the floor. Mike picked it up and started reading about others who had been wrongly imprisoned. Confinement, whether briefly or for years, was not an abnormal way station in the lives of saints. Old Testament prophets and New Testament apostles learned eternal lessons behind prison bars. Mike's jail had walls, not bars, but as he took time to carefully read about Joseph, Jeremiah, Daniel, Peter, Paul, and Jesus Himself, he entered into the exclusive fraternity of those who suffer imprisonment for doing good.

He put down the Bible. Ken West had called Mike a formidable adversary. Mike didn't feel formidable. The click of the electric lock on the holding cell door was an exclamation point of his personal frailty. But the recognition of his limitations enabled Mike to enter into the common denominator of those who suffer for righteousness—God's grace made perfect in human weakness. As he started reading again, liquid strength entered his spirit and hardened like concrete in the depths of his character. He looked up at the stark ceiling with gratitude. When he emerged from the cell, he had confidence that the change, no matter how small, would be permanent.

Hours passed. Mike dozed some but spent most of his time reading and thinking. He didn't try to characterize his thoughts as prayer, but nevertheless believed they were sanctified. The lights in the cell blinked on and off twice. The door opened.

A different deputy appeared. "Come out."

Mike stepped into the hallway. Even after such a short period of solitary confinement, the sight of people bustling around the booking and processing areas of the jail was a shock to his system.

"Can I keep this Bible?" he asked the deputy.

"Sure. We have stacks of them."

The deputy motioned toward the booking area.

"You can change into your street clothes. Your bail has been posted."

"What time is it?"

The deputy pointed to a clock on the wall of the booking area. It was 7:35.

"Is that evening or morning?" Mike asked.

"Morning. You're getting out too soon for breakfast. You'll have to handle that on your own."

Mike had spent almost twenty hours in the holding cell. He put on his clothes.

"What about Sam Miller?" he asked when he came out of the room.

"We're not authorized to release that information."

"I'm one of his lawyers."

The deputy stared at Mike in disbelief.

"He's right," said the female deputy who had been on duty in the waiting room when Mike came to visit Sam on previous occasions. "He's the lawyer who has been representing Miller."

"He's at the hospital. I don't know his current status."

"What happened to him?" Mike asked in alarm. "Did Brinson hit him?"

"I don't know his status."

Mike left the jail, then realized he didn't have a car parked out front waiting for him. He also didn't have a cell phone. He started walking down the street toward the Ashe Street Café where he knew he could make a call. A car pulled up beside him and slowed.

"Can I give you a ride?" a familiar voice asked.

It was Bobby Lambert. Mike got in the car. Bobby drove forward slowly.

"Do you know what happened?" Mike asked.

"Yes. I'm the one who posted your bond. I left the magistrate's office a few minutes ago to meet you, but they let you out before I arrived."

"Thanks. Did Peg call you?"

"Yes. I also talked to Greg Freeman."

"What about Sam Miller? He's at the hospital, either beat up or with heart problems."

Bobby shook his head. "I don't know anything about it. It took until morning to get everything straightened out for you. I was at the church late last night for an emergency session meeting."

Mike turned in his seat. "What happened?"

"You're out. Fired. I did my best to persuade them to wait for the truth to come out, but no one would listen to me. News of the arrest hit the street and swept you out of the church. I couldn't protect your sabbatical payments, either. I'm sorry. All ties are severed. It's over."

Mike took in the information as if listening to news about someone else.

"I know you tried," he said, facing forward. "Take me home. Then I need to go to the hospital."

As Bobby drove, Mike stared out the window at the same landscape he'd watched from the rear of Lamar Cochran's police cruiser. Things looked the same, yet different.

"Are you okay?" Bobby asked after several minutes of silence. "I mean, it's a stupid question, but you're not saying anything."

"Yeah. A night in jail can do a lot for your perspective on life."

Thirty-four

MIKE STEPPED THROUGH THE DOOR AND SAW PEG WAITING ON the other side. In a split second, the love he'd carried in his heart to the jail cell was confirmed in her eyes. They embraced and held each other as if they'd been separated for years.

"You were right," Mike whispered into her ear before another wave of emotion washed over him. "I saw your face. It was glorious."

Peg pulled away and wiped her eyes with the back of her hand.

"No, it's not. I'm a mess."

Mike touched his heart and his head.

"Not in the places that matter."

Peg leaned against his chest. They held each other again.

"Do you know what's wrong with Sam?" Mike asked.

"Not exactly. Muriel phoned from the hospital. It's his heart. He's in a regular room hooked up to a monitor."

"Did he have a heart attack?"

"She wasn't sure. The doctors were still running tests."

"Let's go see them."

While Peg got ready, Mike held Judge's head in his hands and rubbed a spot behind the dog's ears for a few moments. Even his contact with the dog seemed more vibrant than the previous day. They got in the car.

"What happened at the jail?" Peg asked. "Were you in any danger?"

"Only from whatever is wrong in me. I was alone in a small holding cell the entire time. Your face—" Mike stopped. "I can't began to describe—"

"Don't. I'm satisfied now that we're together."

DURING THE DRIVE, MIKE BROKE THE NEWS ABOUT HIS TERMI-
nation from the church. Peg listened quietly.

"I don't want to go back," she said. "I let the answering machine screen
calls while you were gone. Some of the people who left messages were almost
obscene in their hatred."

"Who—?" Mike started then stopped. "I don't want to know."

They arrived at the hospital. The cardiac care rooms were on the second floor
not far from where Marie Dressler died. Mike didn't have any problem identifying Sam's location—a deputy sheriff sat in the hallway. They approached the
deputy, and Mike introduced himself.

"I'm one of Mr. Miller's attorneys."

"Go in. Chief Deputy Cochran told me you might be coming by."

Mike and Peg entered the room. Sam had the bed inclined to a seated position. The light blue hospital gown around his neck made his blue eyes sparkle.
Muriel was sitting beside the bed. She rose and gave Peg a hug. Sam looked
surprisingly normal.

"How are you feeling?" Mike asked him.

Sam patted his stomach. "My spirit is strong, but the doctor says my heart
sent out an SOS. He and Deputy Morris want to keep me here and check
me out."

"I thought you might have gotten beat up in a fight. Did you have any
trouble with Brinson in the cell block?"

"Nope, but we have unfinished business to attend to. He showed me places
on his arms where his stepfather used to put out his cigarettes. But the real
burns are a lot deeper. The Enemy didn't want me sharing a revelation I got
for the boy and sent my heart a-fluttering. I got dizzy, and the next thing I
remember I was in an ambulance coming over here. They got me settled in,
and I had a decent night's sleep that included a dream about you. Muriel,
please hand me my notebook."

Sam held up one of his tattered notebooks. "See, Muriel brought it because
you should always be prepared for Papa to speak to you."

"I'm listening to you right now. Does that count?"

"You know there's a big difference." Sam turned the pages. "But let's see.
You were in a dark place that looked like a cave. You couldn't see anything so
you were standing real still, waiting. A little light started shining in your
right hand. I looked down, and you were holding an old black Bible. When

you held up the Bible, the light increased so you could see your way out of the cave."

"That describes it pretty well, although I'm not sure about getting out of the cave for good. I may have to go back."

"Things happen fast in dreams. Working it out can take years."

Muriel spoke. "Mr. Freeman called us here early this morning. He sounded like a nice young man. He's going to try to get Sam's bond reduced. Right now, it's a lot more than our house and land are worth."

"He'll work on it today," Mike reassured her.

They spent the rest of the morning together in the hospital room. Mike brought in breakfast from Traci's for Peg, Muriel, and himself. Sam sampled the egg substitute on his hospital tray and pronounced it as edible as the wheat straw he spread over newly planted grass seed. Toward noon, a nurse arrived to prepare Sam for additional testing.

"We'll be back tomorrow," Mike said. "Will you be here?"

"Papa told me I was going home. It may be today; it may be tomorrow."

"Don't try to outrun Deputy Morris."

"When my time to go comes, he won't be able to catch me."

Mike stared hard at Sam for a second before the nurse came between them. Mike paused at the door and handed Morris his cell phone number.

"Would you call me if he takes a turn for the worse?"

"Yeah, but I go off duty at three o'clock."

"Please pass the number along to the man covering the next shift." Mike paused. "And try to spend a little time with Sam yourself. You won't regret it."

MIKE LOOKED AT THE BLINKING LIGHT ON THE ANSWERING machine in the kitchen.

"Do I want to check our messages?" he asked Peg.

"It's up to you."

"Go into the great room and rest. I'll listen to this batch."

Mike pressed the button. The first call was from a woman who'd recently started attending the church and promised, without a hint of condemnation in her voice, to pray for him. The second was from Greg Freeman.

"Mike. Call me at the office as soon as possible."

Mike phoned the lawyer's office.

"Mr. Freeman is at the courthouse but should be back shortly."

"Is his calendar clear?"

"Yes, and I know he wanted to talk with you."

"I'll be there in a few minutes."

Mike listened to three more messages: two slanderous, one supportive. He went into the great room.

"The messages are cleared. I'm going into town to meet with Greg Freeman."

"I put the checkbook for the money market account on the counter in the kitchen. He asked me for a retainer when I talked to him about your bond."

"Did he quote an amount?"

"Yes, $10,000 for you and $10,000 for Sam."

Mike swallowed. "It's not out of line for a felony arson charge. I've charged more than that myself, but it wouldn't leave us much in the bank if we have to front Sam's retainer, too. After Greg runs through that money, I'm not sure what we'll do."

"Maybe we can become one of Sam's miracle stories."

Mike tried to push away anxiety as he drove down the hill into town. Greg Freeman's office was located on the second floor of a small office building on the opposite side of the courthouse from Forrest, Lambert, and Arnold. Mike parked on the street and walked up a flight of stairs. Freeman's name and suite number were painted in black on a glass door. Mike stepped into a reception area about the same size as the cell he'd occupied at the jail. The retainer requested would go a long way toward paying the lawyer's overhead for the rest of the year. At the sound of the door opening, a young woman came around the corner.

"Mr. Andrews?"

"Yes."

"He's waiting for you."

Mike followed her down a short hall and stepped into a plain, rectangular office with a window overlooking the courthouse square. A picture of dark-haired Greg Freeman with his wife and baby daughter prominently occupied the corner of the desk. Freeman stood and shook Mike's hand. Mike took out his checkbook and placed it on the desk.

"Thanks for working with Bobby to get me out. I'm prepared to pay the retainer for myself and Sam. Since he's not doing well, I don't want to delay moving forward on his release."

"Hold on to your money for a few more minutes," Freeman replied. "We may need to renegotiate. I went over to the courthouse and met with Ken West and Melissa Hall, who, by the way, easily won her first case at my expense yesterday."

"Hopefully, Sam and I can give you more to work with."

"It wouldn't be hard. West and Hall tossed out a couple of facts that would hurt us. First, your prints were found on the gas can taken from the scene."

"I'm not surprised. I've been around Sam while he was working several times in the past weeks."

"And the church secretary claims Miller threatened to burn down the church after you were forced out for agreeing to represent him."

Mike shook his head. "It was a dream about the church, and she has her events out of sequence."

"We'll get the details on that later. But the main purpose of the meeting at the DA's office wasn't to browbeat me into submission. Do you know Lamar Cochran?"

"Of course, the chief deputy."

"He took the initiative to contact the convenience store where the 911 call was made connecting you and Miller to the fire scene."

"Carrington's One-Stop?"

Freeman glanced down at a legal pad on his desk. "That's the place. The store has an outside surveillance camera that runs on a twenty-four-hour cycle. Cochran reached the store owner before the tape recorded over the evening of the fire. Cochran reviewed the images. The pay phone is clearly visible, and only one person made a call close in time to the fire."

"Could he identify the caller?"

Freeman paused. "Yes, it was the brother of Rob Turner, the man I represented in court yesterday. The brother's name is Vann. Cochran picked him up, and Detective Kelso is interviewing him at the jail right now."

"Will he talk?" Mike asked excitedly.

"Probably not," Freeman said, shaking his head. "He's been arrested many times and knows keeping his mouth shut is the best way to stay out of jail."

"What else did West say?"

"Nothing except that he wants your opinion about who set the fire. He respects your ability as an investigator."

Mike spoke slowly. "I have definite ideas, but I don't think Ken West wants to hear them."

"Try them out on me. I'm your lawyer."

"I haven't paid you, and after I explain everything you may want to raise your retainer."

"It would be better for me to know all the facts before we go forward."

Mike adjusted his position in the chair.

"Okay."

Freeman made notes while Mike told what he'd learned representing Sam in the embezzlement case and the events surrounding the fire.

"Do you have the date and time of the e-mail purportedly from the elder at the church?"

"Yes."

"The schools have cameras. Maybe we can check with their security as well."

Mike also summarized his conversations with Braxton Hodges.

"Do you know what Hodges is going to do next?"

"No, except keep looking through Butch Niles's trash can."

When Mike finished, Freeman stared out the window for a moment.

"Write one check for $10,000," he said. "And I'll hold it in trust for a few days while we see what develops. In the meantime, it shouldn't be too hard to get Miller's bail reduced so he can go home from the hospital instead of back to the jail."

Mike left Freeman's office. It felt good letting someone share the weight of the knowledge he'd been carrying. When he arrived home, Peg handed him a packet delivered by a local courier service. Mike opened it and took out the paperwork formalizing his dismissal from the church. The termination letter was signed by Milton Chesterfield. Mike put the documents back in the packet.

"The pink-slip letter from the church. I'll save this for a day when I think my ego is getting out of hand," he said to Peg.

"That's my job, and I don't need any help."

"Do you want to go out and celebrate my release from jail?"

"We're broke. And I'd rather not see anybody. Let's lock the doors and turn out the lights."

"Are you serious?"

Peg touched him on the cheek. "I just want to be with you and hold your hand. If I squeeze tight enough, maybe no one will be able to take you away again."

So, they spent the evening together at home. Mike's appetite returned, and

Peg fixed a full meal. After supper, they sat on the couch together while Mike told Peg what happened in the holding cell at the jail. He made it through without tears until he showed her the Bible the guard gave him.

"Your face was my encouragement and this was my light," he said, holding it up. "I think the cave is behind me."

THE FOLLOWING DAY, FREEMAN PHONED WITH NEWS THAT SAM'S bail had been reduced to an amount that would allow a property bond secured by the Millers' property.

"I plagiarized your work in the embezzlement case," Freeman said. "It saved me a lot of time."

"Glad it helped. Does Sam know about the bond?" Mike asked.

"I tried to reach him at the hospital, but no one answered in his room."

"Is he okay?"

"I assume so. I dialed the room directly."

"I'll go over there and check," Mike responded quickly.

"The paperwork for his release is waiting at the magistrate's office."

Mike told Peg the good news about the bond but not his concern about Sam's health.

"I'm going to the hospital and help them get everything in order."

MIKE COULDN'T SHAKE A SENSE OF FOREBODING AS HE DROVE TO the hospital. Etched in his mind was the stark image of Marie Dressler's empty bed. He parked in one of the clergy spots near the entrance. The elders at Little Creek might take his pulpit, but they couldn't revoke his parking permit.

He walked rapidly through the lobby and waited for the interminable elevator to descend from the second floor. When it finally opened and took him to the second floor, Mike glanced toward Sam's room. There was no sign of a uniformed deputy. Mike started running down the hall. A nurse's aide looked up in surprise as he ran past. He reached Sam's room and burst inside. When he did, a deputy whirled around with his hand on the pistol holstered in his belt.

"Hold it!" Deputy Morris commanded.

Mike stopped and held his hands in the air. In the bed behind the deputy lay Sam, dressed in regular clothes. Muriel was sitting in a chair on the opposite side of the bed.

"I thought," Mike said, breathing heavily, "something had happened to Sam."

"Things are always happening with me," Sam replied with a smile. "If nothing is happening, it's a sure sign I've drifted from the Master's path. Vic and I were having a good talk. He told me about a dream his aunt had about him and his two brothers, and I was explaining it to him."

"Okay," Mike responded as his heart slowed. "I'll step outside so you can finish talking about the dream. But I wanted you to know that your bail has been lowered, and the paperwork is ready for signature on a property bond."

Sam looked at Muriel. "I told you we would be going home."

"What did the doctors say about your heart?" Mike asked.

"It's running on six cylinders instead of eight, which explains why it knocks and pings on me sometimes. Muriel was happy to hear that I've got to watch what I eat. The oil in fried foods doesn't lubricate my blood vessels as good as I hoped it did."

"Muriel can come with me while you finish talking with Deputy Morris," Mike said then turned to the deputy. "We'll bring back the order from the magistrate approving the bond."

"He'll still need to be processed at the jail," Morris replied. "The doctors have released him, but we're still waiting on the discharge instructions."

MIKE AND MURIEL LEFT THE ROOM AND WALKED DOWN THE hall toward the elevator.

"That gave me a scare," Mike said. "Is he really going to be okay?"

"The doctor talked pretty straight to him. Sam's stubborn, but I think he heard what he said. I'll make sure he doesn't forget."

"I'm sorry I interrupted his conversation with Deputy Morris."

"Don't worry. Sam will bring it around to the right place. He's a good talker."

They descended to the main level. As they crossed the lobby, Mike turned to Muriel.

"Do you remember how hard I tried to avoid representing Sam?"

"Yes."

"Just now, I panicked because I thought something bad had happened to him."

Muriel smiled one of her wrinkled smiles. "He has a way of pulling you in, doesn't he?"

Mike nodded. "When the Lord does call him home, it will leave a big hole in Barlow County."

Thirty-five

JACK HATCHER AND BUTCH NILES SAT AT THE SMALL CONFERENCE table in the corner of the bank president's office. Hatcher had locked the door and ordered his secretary not to disturb him under any circumstances.

"Let me do the talking," Hatcher said to Niles, checking his watch.

"This is your deal," Niles responded. "I've been serving the interests of the citizens of Barlow County who want to expand the local tax base through increased development of—"

"Shut up," Hatcher barked. "Save the campaign rhetoric. The amount of money flowing into your account and where it came from is enough to interest the U.S. attorney in Asheville. Being an elected official at this point is a liability, not an asset. The federal authorities would much rather take down a politician than a businessman."

"I'm not going to be threatened," Niles shot back. "Go ahead and phone Linden."

"Fine. We'll see what he has to say."

Hatcher punched in the number on the phone in the middle of the table. A male voice answered on the second ring.

"Troy Linden."

"It's me," Hatcher said. "Niles is with me."

"Give me some good news," Linden said.

"Andrews and Miller have been arrested and charged with arson."

"Are they in jail?"

"Andrews posted bond. Miller had a heart attack and is in the hospital."

"If he dies, that would be a simpler way to take care of him." Linden paused.

"I still think it would be cleaner to get rid of both of them permanently. One phone call and Andrews will have a biking accident, and the old man won't have another dream."

"No!" Hatcher responded. "That's not what we agreed to. We're simply working the system to our mutual advantage. Niles and I are businessmen."

"Who have accepted a lot of money from Bunt and me. We're giving you a chance to take care of this once and for all. If your way doesn't work, we'll step in."

"Be patient. The deal will close in two weeks. After that it won't matter what Andrews and Miller say."

"What is the status of the legislation?" Linden asked.

Hatcher nodded at Niles, who spoke. "Coming out of committee with a favorable recommendation by the end of the week. After that, approval on the floor of the legislature is automatic."

"Andrews snooping around put pressure on us to act sooner," Hatcher said. "It would have been a recipe for disaster if we'd let him cross-examine you."

"I could handle it. Bunt is the one who worried me."

"Everything will be fine," Hatcher said confidently. "But you need to transfer the money to exercise the options within a couple of days."

"And another $50,000 for me," Niles interjected.

Hatcher waved his hand angrily at Niles. There was silence on the other end of the line.

"Disregard Niles," Hatcher said. "Did you hear what I said about the options?"

"Yeah, but there has been a change in plans. Bunt has put the brakes on more money until he knows everything is going through."

"What about the options?" Hatcher replied. "We've got to complete the purchase of the privately held land or it won't matter what happens in the legislature."

"It's time for you to assume more of the risks," Linden replied.

"I don't have that kind of money!" Hatcher protested.

"You're president of the bank. Figure it out. Bunt and I are major shareholders. We won't object if you want to use bank money."

"But there are regulators who monitor—"

"We know what you have in your personal reserve," Linden interrupted. "There's enough to exercise the options."

Hatcher ran his fingers through his hair. "But that would wipe me out. I've worked thirty years to get where I am financially."

"And this is your chance to double up. Isn't that your goal?"

"Yes." Hatcher paused. "But I'll need you and Bunt to sign an amendment to our contracts."

"Send it up. Increase your percentage by the amount you're putting in. Do the math. You'll like what you see. Call me the first of next week."

Linden broke the connection. Hatcher looked at Niles.

"You're going to fund twenty-five percent of the purchase price for the land," Hatcher said.

"I'm broke! I need the $50,000 to remain solvent!"

"The bank will loan you the money and secure it by a second mortgage on your house along with your portion of the Cohulla Creek deal."

Niles glared at Hatcher.

"You're going to pay Turner," Niles said.

"He doesn't know I exist. You handled that contact."

"With a go-between to protect me. The other $25,000 has to be paid tomorrow if we want to keep him happy and quiet."

"You're not in a position to demand anything, but I'll make sure your second mortgage is approved first thing in the morning."

Niles swore. "I don't think that crazy old man's dream justified all this expense and hassle. He stopped me on the street the other day and started spouting off a bunch of stuff. Nobody would take him seriously."

"What did you say to him?" Hatcher asked sharply.

"Nothing."

"Good. Information is power. And remember, we're not just dealing with Miller. When Andrews got involved, everything went to another level. I didn't get to where I am without taking every threat seriously."

MIKE AND PEG SPENT A QUIET SUNDAY MORNING, BUT AFTER THE church service, the calls resumed. One of the first was from Bobby Lambert.

"The church was packed," Bobby said. "But it had the feel of an inquisition more than a church service. Milton explained the real reason for the sabbatical and apologized for not terminating the church's relationship with you at that time. All the elders except me stood behind him at the front of the church. Barbara also spoke. No questions were allowed. The final announcement was the formation of a pastor search committee as soon as possible."

"What did Dr. Mixon do?"

"Made it clear that he would serve as interim only until time to visit his daughter in Peru. He's a good man, not interested in getting wrapped up in the power loop. Some of the chatter after the service wasn't favorable to the elders. There will be a lot less people there next Sunday. I'm resigning from the session effective immediately. Elizabeth and I won't be back."

The thought of an exodus of people wounded by a church fiasco grieved Mike. Some might not only leave the church, but wander from the faith altogether. After Mike hung up the phone with Bobby, another caller urged him to start a new church once he was cleared of the arson charges. Mike deflected the suggestion.

"Larry McReynolds wants me to start a new congregation," he told Peg when he hung up the phone.

"You knew that would come up."

Mike shook his head. "I can't think about that now. Maybe never."

MONDAY AFTERNOON, MIKE RECEIVED A CALL FROM BRAXTON Hodges.

"I just talked with my cleaning lady," the reporter said. "That well has been as dry as the oil stock I bought on a tip from the guy over in classified ads." Hodges paused. "Until today. Guess what she found in the trash at Butch Niles's house?"

"A winning lottery ticket."

"Something better. A copy of the letter Sam Miller sent Jack Hatcher."

Mike gripped the phone tighter. "Do you have it?"

"Not yet. I told her to carefully check for anything with Sam's name on it, and she found it in the trash can in Niles's study."

"Where is it now?"

"I'm going to get it in half an hour then bring it to the paper."

"I'll be there waiting."

Mike told Peg about the find.

"How important is the letter now?" she asked.

"Not as much," Mike admitted. "But it's the pebble that started this avalanche. It might be helpful to Freeman, if he tries to do what I did with the embezzlement charge."

MIKE SAT IN THE PARKING LOT WAITING FOR HODGES TO RETURN. The reporter parked beside him. Mike got out and greeted him.

"Do you have it?"

Hodges, unsmiling, held up a rumpled sheet of paper. "Not exactly. It's notes Niles made about the letter."

Mike took the sheet from the reporter and smoothed it on the front of his car.

Hatcher believes the letter from Sam Miller (the yardman) connects Linden, Bunt, Hatcher, and me to the purchase of the Pasley tract at Cohulla Creek. Miller threatens to go public with his accusations that he calls "deeds of darkness." (A joke???) But Hatcher is paranoid.

The rest of the sheet contained three phone numbers, and the name *Dressler* underlined twice.

"It's not dated," Mike observed. "But the last sentence has a few whiffs of a smoking gun. A persistent lawyer could question Jack Hatcher for an hour about his paranoid tendencies and how he might act on them."

"It will go in my file."

"I'd like a copy for Greg Freeman. He's going to represent Sam and me."

They went inside the newspaper office. Hodges made a copy of the notes and handed it to Mike.

"How are you doing personally?" Hodges asked in a softer tone of voice. "I know it sounds strange coming from me, but I've been praying for you and Peg. Do you think God hears the prayers of a heathen like me?"

"Keep it up. God hears everything."

MIKE DROVE TO FREEMAN'S OFFICE. THE YOUNG LAWYER WAS eating an apple at his desk.

"No time for lunch today," Freeman said.

Mike handed him the copy of the notes.

"From Hodges's spy, the lady who works for Butch Niles."

"Niles is having a busy day," Freeman responded after he read the notes. "I saw him come into the sheriff's department when I was leaving the jail after meeting with a client."

"Had he been arrested?" Mike asked, leaning forward in his chair.

"No, he went directly into the sheriff's office. The sheriff may be hitting him up for a bigger allocation for county law enforcement from the state budget." Freeman took a final bite from his apple. "I'm glad you stopped by. I needed to talk to you anyway."

Mike settled into his chair. Freeman dropped the apple core into a trash can before continuing.

"I was meeting with Rob Turner, my car parts thief, at the jail this morning. He's due to be sentenced next week, and I'm working on a list of witnesses for the hearing. In the midst of the interview, I mentioned the video of his brother Vann and its connection to the fire at the church. Rob got quiet for a moment, then asked if providing information to the sheriff's department about Vann could reduce his sentence. I told him it depended on the type of information."

"He's willing to turn on his brother?"

"Apparently. He claimed Vann had a gas can that didn't belong to him in the back of his truck a few days ago."

"With Miller Lawn Care written on the side?"

"Yes. And Vann told Rob that he had connections in Raleigh who could get Rob's sentence reduced even if the jury found him guilty. When Rob asked his brother for help, Vann told him no and now won't talk to him. What do you think I should do?"

"Talk to West," Mike replied without hesitation. "You owe that to your client who's going to be sentenced. And it will let us know if West is serious about trying to find out who really set fire to the church."

"I'll call him now."

Thirty minutes later, Mike and Freeman were sitting in the conference room in the district attorney's office. West entered along with Melissa Hall.

"Ms. Hall is going to join us," West said.

Hall's eyes narrowed when she saw Mike at the table.

"Did Kelso get any information from Vann Turner?" Freeman asked.

"It's still under investigation," Hall said.

"I'll take that as a negative," Freeman replied. "I met with Rob Turner this morning, and he's willing to provide information about his brother Vann in return for a reduced sentence."

"What kind of information?" West said. "I've been interested in getting Vann Turner off the streets for years."

Freeman glanced at Mike before answering. "Rob saw a gas can that belonged to Sam Miller in his brother's truck a couple of days before the fire. We know Vann is the one who phoned 911 to report the fire."

West turned to Hall. "Get Kelso and Perkins in here."

After Hall left the room, West looked at Mike. "When are you going to tell me what's going on?"

Freeman spoke. "If you want to talk to Mike, there needs to be an understanding of his status."

"Our conversation might change his status," West replied, "but as of right now, he's an arson suspect out on bond."

Freeman turned to Mike. "What do you want to do?"

"Ask Ken a few questions," Mike replied.

"Go ahead," the district attorney answered.

"Do you believe Brian Dressler was behind the checks with Sam Miller's signature stamp on them?"

"I haven't performed my own investigation, but the bank is in the best position to uncover what took place."

"Dressler had a hand in the checks, but he was following orders from someone else."

"Who?"

Mike put his hands in front of him on the table. "Is there anyone in Barlow County you wouldn't be willing to prosecute?"

"Not if the evidence is there."

"Jack Hatcher?"

West stared at Mike and nodded.

"Butch Niles?"

"You believe Hatcher and Niles wanted to defraud their own bank of a hundred thousand dollars?" West shook his head. "That doesn't make sense."

"But would you prosecute Niles?"

"No one is above the law."

"Even if it results in political pressure against you?"

West shifted his massive frame in the chair, making it groan. "I've been district attorney of Barlow County for almost thirty years, and I'm fully vested in the retirement program. Fear of retaliation by a local politician isn't a big issue for me anymore. But before either of those men would be charged with spitting on the sidewalk, it would have to be a case with every corner buttoned down tight."

Mike relaxed. "I wouldn't expect anything else. Once the detectives get here, I'll lay it out."

There was a knock on the door, and Perkins and Kelso, a stocky, older detective with a ring of brown hair surrounding his bald head, entered the room. Once the detectives were seated, Mike put his briefcase on the table and clicked it open.

"It all began with a dream."

When Mike finished, Kelso looked at West. "It's no secret that Niles likes to hit the high-stakes tables in Atlantic City and Las Vegas."

West turned to Mike. "It would be foolish to build a case against a state legislator solely based on the testimony of a known criminal like Vann Turner. The key will be bringing pressure against one or more of the other individuals you mentioned and see if one of them turns against his coconspirators."

Mike handed Kelso a copy of the e-mail. "Do you want to check this out?"

"Yeah, we'll get our computer guy to work on it. He's good at tracking things down."

West shook his head. "I liked it better when the high-tech stuff involved identifying blood types."

MIKE AND FREEMAN WALKED TOGETHER FROM THE COURTHOUSE.

"How do you think it went?" Freeman asked.

"Too soon to guess. They were listening, but we need something a lot more important than a meeting at the DA's office. That was a huge risk, but I think it was worth it."

"Your story was even more convincing the second time," Freeman said. "You really thought outside the box in your investigation."

They crossed the street at traffic light four.

"By the way, how did you get the memo of the Hatcher, Bunt, and Linden meeting?" Freeman asked.

Mike stepped onto the sidewalk. "You're my lawyer, but that needs to stay confidential. I don't want to jeopardize a close personal relationship."

When they reached the other side of the street, Freeman spoke. "If we let Kelso dust it, I bet Bobby Lambert's fingerprints are on it."

"If I was as smart as you claim," Mike answered, staring straight ahead. "I'd keep my mouth more tightly shut."

AT HOME, MIKE PHONED SAM AND TOLD HIM WHAT HAD happened. Peg, who was sitting on the couch reading a book, listened.

"You should have seen their faces when I started off with your dream about the hatchet, nails, and tree," Mike said. "They probably thought Greg Freeman was going to claim that I was mentally incompetent, but when we left, they were already working on a plan to follow up, using my leads."

"I wrote a letter to the Brinson boy," Sam said. "What's the best way to get it to him at the jail?"

"Did you hear what I told you?" Mike asked. "The arson case against us is unraveling."

"Yep, but if I don't get the message to Brinson, I'll be in a kind of trouble no lawyer can get me out of. Papa has a call on that boy's life, and he needs to see the way to freedom so he can follow it."

Mike sighed. "You could send it by mail to the jail, but the quickest way would be to ask Lamar Cochran to deliver it in person."

"That's a good idea. I'll catch Lamar in town tomorrow. He likes to eat breakfast at Traci's."

"But don't tell him anything—"

Mike looked down at the receiver that had gone dead in his hand. He turned to Peg.

"When Sam claimed I was going to be like him," Mike said, "I thought he meant odd and hard to understand with a box of tattered notebooks on the floor of my closet. But it's really simple. He cares about other people and what God wants to do in their lives. That's a good example for anyone to follow."

Peg took a sip of water. "Pretty soon you'll be saying 'Papa' and rubbing your belly when you have a good idea."

Mike patted his stomach. "The only idea I have right now has to do with what we're going to eat for supper."

Thirty-six

THE FOLLOWING DAY, MIKE RECEIVED A CALL FROM GREG Freeman.

"I just got off the phone with Ken West. Things are happening fast. Kelso brought Vann Turner back in for questioning and confronted him with the gas can evidence, the convenience store video, and who knows what else that he made up. Vann got scared and started shifting blame to Butch Niles."

"What kind of blame?"

"That Niles used a third party to pass money to Turner as payment for making the 911 call. I suspect Turner, acting alone or with help, is the one who set the fire and then made the call blaming it on you and Sam, but, of course, he didn't admit that. After that, West came in and raised the specter of the recidivist statute. The thought of a life sentence without parole really loosened Vann's tongue, and he identified the go-between. That guy and Niles are being brought in for interrogation."

"Niles is the kind who will roll over on someone else."

"And West called the state attorney general to notify them of the investigation."

Mike's mental wheels were turning. "The federal authorities will also want a piece of Niles, especially when Linden and Bunt are mentioned. I'm sure there's more to them than I was able to uncover."

AFTER HE HUNG UP THE PHONE, MIKE WENT INTO THE ART ROOM where Peg was finishing her third watercolor for the baby's room. A chubby little girl holding a red ball lay on a beach towel in the shade of an umbrella.

"Does that umbrella block all the UV rays?" Mike asked.

"In my picture it does."

Mike sat on the bed and told her what he'd learned from Greg Freeman.

"It was strange—like hearing information about a case I was handling for someone else," he said. "But as soon as the call ended, I realized this is about me. West wouldn't have contacted Freeman if he still harbored doubts about what I told him."

Peg looked at him anxiously. "So, are the charges against you and Sam going to be dismissed?"

"That wasn't mentioned."

"Did you ask him?"

"No," Mike replied sheepishly. "I was too interested in what he was telling me about the ongoing investigation."

Peg held out a paintbrush toward him. "Call him back or I'll paint your nose redder than that ball in the picture!"

Freeman wasn't in the office, and Mike left a message.

THAT AFTERNOON'S EDITION OF THE LOCAL NEWSPAPER CARRIED a headline in the middle of the front page announcing "Legislator Niles Questioned."

Mike quickly scanned the article for new information. Braxton Hodges reported that Niles met with Detective Kelso but revealed nothing inflammatory. In fact, the big news was simply the fact of "an ongoing investigation." Mike finished the article and phoned the reporter.

"That was the teaser article," Hodges said. "Did you see the quote I got from Niles denying any wrongdoing?"

"Yes."

"That's the setup to make him look like a massive liar when the truth comes out. The second article will bring out his gambling habits. It's all designed to make readers anticipate the next revelation."

"Who's providing you information?"

"Not you," the reporter snapped.

"Don't be touchy. You didn't wait on me. Now that I'm the client, not the lawyer, I can talk if you promise not to use my information until confirmed."

"I confirm everything."

"Are you recording me?"

There was a brief silence. "Not now."

"Good. Don't let your finger slip over to the Record button by accident."

Mike told him what he knew about the investigation.

"This is what I suspected all along," Hodges said excitedly. "What about Maxwell Forrest and Bobby Lambert?"

"I hope they're not involved."

"Don't kid me. The lawyers in these kinds of deals always know enough to be indicted as coconspirators."

"Their names didn't come up."

"What about Brian Dressler?"

"He will probably end up as a material witness once he cuts a deal."

"When will this go public?"

"When the grand jury meets. After that, Ken West will have to issue at least a brief public statement."

"I need to be ahead of him. Do you have a contact at the Attorney General's Office in Raleigh?"

"No, my political connections are paper thin. Judge Coberg is the closest I come to the power structure."

Hodges was quiet for a second. "Never mind. I know who can give me some inside information."

AT FIVE O'CLOCK, GREG FREEMAN RETURNED MIKE'S CALL.

"I forgot to ask about the charges against Sam and me," Mike said. "What's going to happen?"

"I didn't know myself until a few minutes ago. Melissa Hall phoned and told me they want to leave everything status quo until indictments are handed down against Hatcher and his crowd. Dismissal of the charges would really tip off potential defendants that they are in the DA's sights."

"But the case against Sam and me is dead."

Freeman paused. "Yes. It's over."

MIKE HUNG UP THE PHONE AND TOOK A DEEP BREATH. HE'D grown so used to the crushing weight of his circumstances that he'd forgotten what a stress-free breath of air felt like. He went into the kitchen, found Peg, and told her the good news.

She cried. Mike held her and felt the tension draining from the muscles in her back.

"It's been worse for you than me," he said. "I'm sorry."

Peg wiped her eyes. "You don't need to apologize. I just want our lives back to normal."

"Once the charges are dismissed, we won't be back to normal," he said, stroking her hair with his hand, "but we'll be able to start looking for it."

Peg lifted her chin and gave him a quick kiss. "Normal is the love I have for you. That's where I want to live for the rest of my life."

LATER, MIKE COULD HEAR PEG SINGING SOFTLY. IT HAD BEEN A long time between melodies. Peg had hung the picture of the woman who looked like Muriel Miller in the kitchen. Mike looked at it while he phoned Sam.

"Yep. I thought this thing would work itself out," the old man responded. "What are you doing tomorrow?"

"Uh, I don't have any plans."

"I'd like to visit your mountain top. I had a dream about it last night."

"Is your heart strong enough for a climb?" Mike asked in surprise.

"I saw the doctor yesterday, and he told me to increase my exercise. I've been lying about the house too much. I need some fresh air."

"Do you mind if my dog comes along?"

"Nope."

"Okay. I'll pick you up around nine in the morning."

SAM GOT IN THE CAR AND PATTED JUDGE'S HEAD THAT DRAPED OVER the seat.

"Can we stop for a cup of coffee?" the old man asked. "Muriel likes it weak, and I haven't had a stout cup since Wednesday."

"Where do you like to go?"

"The place you passed on the way to the house is fine."

At the convenience store, Mike also purchased a few snacks for the hike. Sam eyed a rack of spicy beef jerky sticks, but Mike shook his head.

"I don't want us to get in trouble with Muriel. If she finds out you ate some of those, she won't let you come outside and play in the future."

"You're right, but I can't be cut off from treats. If that happens, I'll start dreaming about the foods I can't eat, and there won't be time for Papa to show me the important stuff."

Mike paid for the snacks and coffee.

"Tell me about the dream you had about me."

"There will be time for that later."

They arrived at the parking lot for Hank's Grocery. The weather had been warm all week, and the trees on the hillsides were full of fresh green leaves primed for a busy summer of photosynthesis. Clouds streaked the sky, but they were wispy and high up. The early morning breeze had died down by the time they parked near the trailhead.

"I always tell the man who owns the grocery that I'm here," Mike said when he turned off the car.

Mike and Sam entered the store. Judge stayed in the vehicle with the window cracked open and barked in anticipation of the hike. Buzz Carrier was behind the counter. He glanced up at Mike then awkwardly looked away.

"Buzz, I know what you've heard," Mike said. "But it's not true. Soon things will start coming out in the open. Keep reading the paper before you sell the last copy, and you'll find out."

"Sorry, Mike, it was a shock to our family. I didn't know what to think."

Sam looked around the store. "You sell about everything, don't you?"

"Yes, sir, but I can't compete with the big-box outfits. They sell most items for less than what I have to pay for them."

Sam pointed to an index card covered with faded pencil writing that was taped to the wall behind the cash register.

"Did your daddy write that card?"

Buzz turned. "Yeah. It's some Bible verses about running an honest business. Did you know him?"

"Nope." Sam rubbed the top of his head. "But I don't think your daddy would be upset if you decided to sell this place and open a motorcycle shop."

Buzz's mouth dropped open. He looked at Mike.

"Did you know that's what I've been thinking about doing?"

"No," Mike replied. "I saw your motorcycle parked out front last summer, but you never mentioned opening a shop to me."

Buzz kept talking to Sam as if he'd not heard Mike. "But I didn't want to go against the family heritage. We've run this place for three generations. I wanted to get my daddy's permission to sell it when he was sick in the hospital, but he died before I got the chance."

"You're a good man, and you honored him when he was alive," Sam said. "Now, it's time to go in the direction you believe is right."

Buzz nodded his head several times then stuck out his hand to Sam.

"Thanks, I really appreciate you talking to me. What's your name?"

Mike answered. "This is Sam Miller, the other man charged with setting fire to the Little Creek Church."

For the third time, Buzz looked perplexed. "Oh, sorry about that. You fellows have a good hike. And take your time. I'll keep an eye on the car."

Sam smiled. "When you open your motorcycle business, put that card behind the cash register."

Mike and Sam left the store and walked to the car. Mike opened the door, and Judge bounded out.

"Do you have any questions?" Sam asked as they moved toward the opening in the trees that marked the beginning of the old logging road.

"Let me answer it myself," Mike replied. "Papa told you what to say to Buzz because He loves him and wants to help him. What else should I ask?"

Sam chuckled. "I'm not used to you talking this way."

"Too confusing?" Mike asked.

"Yep. Let me ponder your question while we walk."

Mike carried a small backpack and set a slow pace, but Sam didn't seem to have any problem keeping up. As they walked along, the old man began identifying the trees and plants. Mike was amazed at Sam's knowledge.

"You must learn a lot working in lawn maintenance," Mike said after Sam identified a small fern sprouting from the middle of a moss patch.

"Papa has given us a beautiful world. I enjoy finding out as much about it as I can."

They took a couple of water breaks. Sam took sips from his water bottle. Mike took out the blue plastic bowl and served Judge. At the second stop, Sam took a deeper drink.

"I'm glad this part of the trial is going to be over soon," the old man said.

Mike propped his foot on a boulder and glanced up at the approaching ridgeline.

"You mean trail."

"No, this test you and I've been going through. It's not been easy. My business is down to nothing, and worry has put wrinkles on Muriel's face in places that will be hard for her to make happy with her best smile."

"Yeah. Peg is emotionally drained, and I've been—" Mike stopped and looked at Sam. "You know, I've been stressed out, but I'm more thankful than ever. God met me in that jail cell and put a peace in my heart unlike anything I imagined existed. It's crazy, but what makes me sad now is the news about what is going to happen to Jack Hatcher, Butch Niles, and the other people who tried so hard to destroy our lives."

Sam smiled. "Papa knew what He was doing when He told me to ask you for help. Do you know why it upsets you when you hear that someone is going to be caught and judged for their sins?"

"No."

"Because Papa wants to save people. These folks deserve to be punished, but if you'd never met Jack Hatcher and ran into him in a jail cell, would you tell him about the Master?"

"I hope so."

Sam patted Mike on the shoulder. "You would. Papa is letting you know what it means to love your enemies and pray for those who persecute you. I've been praying for those men since the day I had my dream. If I ever start hating them, I'd be in jail whether the sheriff's department puts me there or not. Now, even if they all go to prison, it won't be the end of our job. The Helper wants to help them get right with the Master."

They reached the crest of the hill. A pleasant breeze greeted them.

"Now, I want my dream," Mike demanded.

Sam took a few deep breaths. "Can't I enjoy the view of the promised land for a few minutes? Think about what I said. Judge wants to show me an interesting smell."

Mike watched the old man follow the dog around the meadow. Twice, Sam bent over as if sampling a scent himself. In a few minutes, he returned.

The two men stood near the rock where God called Mike into the ministry and gazed over the valleys and hills of Barlow County.

"You know," Sam said, "a mountain top isn't just a place on earth; it's a vision Papa puts in your heart. How big a ministry does the Master have for you?"

"I don't know. Right now, it's Peg."

Sam nodded. "That's a good answer—if you also include baby Isaac."

Mike laughed.

"See, even the mention of his name makes you laugh."

"Okay, tell me the dream."

Sam was silent. They continued to gaze at the scene. When Mike finally glanced at Sam, he saw a tear running down the old man's right cheek.

"What?" Mike asked. "Was it a bad dream?"

Sam shook his head. "Nope, but the goodness of it makes me cry. I've loved the people of Barlow County for a long time. It didn't matter what church they went to or whether they went to church at all. My job was to deliver Papa's message and pray it might open someone's heart to the Master. That's what I did with your friend Buzz. In my dream, you and I were standing on a mountain top."

Sam bent over and pulled up a blade of green grass. "What do you think I did?"

Mike was silent a moment. "You offered to pray for me."

"Yep."

Speaking more rapidly, Mike continued, "But I hesitated because I was afraid God might make me do something I didn't want to do. Then I realized the essence of obeying the Lord's call was doing His will, not mine. I knelt down, and you blessed me, just like they did in the Old Testament."

"That sounds right to me, only you use fancier words. What kind of blessing do you want?"

Mike stood so he faced the old man. "To carry on your work. We'll always be different, but we can both carry Jesus's love for the people of Barlow County in our hearts."

"Yep. And that's the part that makes me cry. There's no way a human heart can contain the Master's love. It always spills out."

Mike knelt in the grass at Sam's feet. The old man put his hands on Mike's head and prayed. The words weren't eloquent, the request simple. But Mike knew in his heart it was a prayer heard in heaven that would be answered on earth. When Sam finished, Mike stood and the two men embraced.

"Anything else?" Mike asked.

"Nothing, except the rest of our lives."

As they walked down the trail, Mike felt lighter and heavier at the same time. He asked Sam about it.

"His burden is easy, and His yoke is light. You feel the burden but also know the Master's strength."

They reached the parking lot.

"Do you have anything else to say to Buzz?" Mike asked.

"Nope, but when he opens his motorcycle shop, I hope Muriel will let me get one of those things. I hear they're real cheap on gas."

Thirty-seven

WITHIN THREE MONTHS, MULTIPLE INDICTMENTS BY STATE AND federal authorities were handed down against Niles, Hatcher, and their associates. Newspapers across the nation picked up Braxton Hodges's articles about the investigation. The criminal case against Mike and Sam disappeared. Hodges inserted a brief announcement about dismissal of the charges on the bottom of the front page of the Shelton paper, but Mike declined an interview for a feature article about his role in breaking open the scandal. To Mike's relief, neither Maxwell Forrest nor Bobby Lambert were indicted.

News of Mike's vindication prompted a flurry of phone calls from people in the community and members of the Little Creek congregation who congratulated him at the news. Apparently, no one really believed he was guilty in the first place. Mike referred questions about whether he might return to the church to the elders. When Delores called and tried to download a massive amount of church gossip, Mike politely stopped her. Nathan Goode asked if he could continue to meet with Mike on a weekly basis, and they set a time on Mondays in the choir room at the high school. Mike didn't hear a word from Milton Chesterfield, Barbara Harcourt, Libby Gorman, or any other remaining members of the session.

One Tuesday morning, Mike called Greg Freeman and Bobby Lambert and invited them to meet him for lunch at the Ashe Café. Mike and Greg arrived early and sipped sweet tea until Bobby, his tie askew, came through the door.

"Sorry I'm late," Bobby said. "It's been hectic. Jack Hatcher fired Mr. Forrest yesterday afternoon and hired some big guns from Atlanta. The board of directors of the bank are bringing in outside counsel in an effort to distance themselves from anyone in Shelton. All our bank files have to be boxed up for delivery to the new attorneys."

"How is Mr. Forrest doing?" Mike asked.

"He's aged five years in five weeks. It wouldn't surprise me if he retired by the end of the year and spent most of his time at his house on the beach."

Their waitress arrived, and the three men ordered their food.

"Did Mr. Forrest call you?" Bobby asked Mike after the waitress left.

"No."

"I told him he owed you an apology. He gave a grunt that I interpreted as agreement, but I could be wrong."

"I'm glad the authorities didn't try to drag you into the investigation," Mike replied.

Bobby gave Mike a grateful look. "I can't give details, but until you started your investigation, I didn't have a clue the Cohulla Creek development was anything except a business deal the parties wanted to keep confidential. You were way ahead of me on the underlying facts."

Mike sipped his tea. "I've been doing more investigation on a different piece of property. Did you know Bob Allen is going to sell his building near traffic light five?"

Greg shook his head. Bobby's face registered surprise.

"How did you hear about it?" Bobby asked. "I thought that was totally under wraps."

"A source."

"It's a nice piece of real estate," Greg said. "Do you know how much he wants for it?"

Mike squeezed a second lemon wedge into his tea.

"I had an interesting dream two nights ago," he said. "Do you want to hear it?"

The other two men nodded.

Mike stirred his tea. "In the dream, I was driving past the courthouse. When I came to the corner where Mr. Allen's building sits, I looked to the left and saw our three names written over the main entrance." Mike stopped and gave a sheepish grin. "Uh, that's it."

"We'd started a law firm?" Greg asked.

"I assume so. The sign said 'Attorneys at Law.'"

Greg turned to Bobby. "What do you think?"

"I'm not sure what to think," Bobby answered, glancing warily at Mike.

"It sounds like an interesting idea to me," Greg continued excitedly, "but Bobby is the one with the big-time practice. He would have the most to lose."

"True," Mike said, looking at Bobby. "If you strike out on your own, you'll miss the chance to take over Forrest, Lambert, and Arnold."

"That may not be an option," Bobby replied. "Mr. Forrest would want a lot of money for a buyout, and I'm not sure Arnold is going to hang around."

Greg turned to Mike. "But what about you? Aren't you going to find another job as pastor of a church?"

"I've found it," Mike answered.

"Where?" Bobby asked.

Mike swept his right hand across the table. "From one end of the county to the other. I may serve a congregation for a while, but as a lawyer, I can reach a lot of people who might never set foot in a church."

"Is Peg on board with this?" Bobby asked.

"Yes, we talked about it yesterday. After she and I talked, I made notes about organization of the firm that included a start-up budget." Mike took a sheet of paper from his pocket. "If the three of us join together, I'll help Greg develop as the primary litigator, and I could ease the demands of your business practice."

"You always worked efficiently," Bobby said, inspecting the numbers on the sheet of paper. "It's an intriguing idea. I'd like to think it over and discuss it with Elizabeth. She's fed up with what's happened at the office and would be happy if I left tomorrow."

"I'm tired of practicing alone," Greg said.

The waitress brought their food.

"In the dream, whose name appeared first?" Bobby asked after Mike prayed a blessing for the meal.

Mike laughed. "Do you really want to know?"

"Yeah, even though it sounds petty bringing it up after you've prayed."

"It was Lambert, Andrews, and Freeman. I don't want to create an image of primary responsibility for the firm, especially since I'll also be doing ministry work."

"That suits me," Greg said. "Since I'm still new to the law, it would feel strange with my name ahead of yours."

"And $300,000 is a fair price for that property," Mike said between bites. "It will probably require another $150,000 to equip it as a law office, but once that's done, it will be an appreciating asset."

"How did you know the price?" Bobby asked, putting down his fork. "I didn't even dictate a memo to the file about my discussion with Mr. Allen."

"It was in the dream."

Bobby shook his head. "From now on, I'm going to have to watch my thoughts around you."

Mike grinned. "Absolutely. My supervision of your soul will go to the next level."

It was the first week of December, and snow began falling when Mike and Peg pulled into the driveway of their house. Peg rested her hand on her protruding abdomen. Sunday morning services at the Craig Valley Gospel Tabernacle didn't end until early afternoon. Mike had preached for more than an hour.

"I'm going to miss it," he said. "It's been a great four months, but I'm glad they found a permanent pastor."

"If you hadn't quit talking, I was worried I might have our baby in one of the pews."

"You know, it's difficult to stop when people keep yelling for you to keep preaching."

Peg winced. "Mike, let Judge out of the house for a minute while I get my suitcase. I think it's time to go to the hospital."

Mike rolled a clear plastic bassinette with a blue ribbon taped to the top and "Andrews—Boy" written on a card into the hallway where Sam and Muriel waited. Muriel's smile lit up every crevice in her face. Mike proudly picked up the baby.

"He's beautiful," Muriel said, stroking the infant's cheek. "How's Peg?"

"Resting, but she wants to see you. I'll take the baby to the nursery."

Muriel slipped past the men into the hospital room. Sam stayed with Mike.

"What do you think we named him?" Mike asked the old man.

"Isaac."

"You're half right. His full name is Samuel Isaac Andrews."

Sam leaned over and gently kissed the top of Samuel Isaac's head. "Yep. That will work. I wrote something about him in my notebook last night. I'll show you later."

Acknowledgments

I WOULD NEVER HAVE BECOME A NOVELIST IF MY WIFE, KATHY, hadn't told me a divine dream in 1995. Thank you for your faith and courage.

In writing this story, I received superb editorial help from Ami McConnell, senior editor at Thomas Nelson Fiction, and Traci Depree, tracidepree.com.

Reading Group Guide

1. What do you think about Sam's dreams? Do you believe that they were messages from God? Have you ever had such a dream?

2. What does God the Father mean to you? What is the significance of the name "Papa"?

3. In chapter 8 Sam says, "The right word in the wrong time is as bad as the wrong word in the right time." Do you agree?

4. Peg mentions that church members rarely reach out to help them. What needs might a pastor and his family have? Are there ways that you could minister to your church leaders and their families?

5. What contributed to the distance in Peg and Mike's marriage? What steps did each of them take that allowed them to reconnect?

6. Sam and Muriel take their roles as mentors to Mike and Peg very seriously. How do they care for them? Do you have a special person in your life who is a mentor to you?

7. How do you feel about the way Mike's church leaders handled their disagreements? Have you had an experience of conflict or distrust in the church? Compare and contrast how Mike's leaders conducted their meetings with Sam's church leaders.

8. Did Peg do the right thing when she told Mike about her past struggle with wanting to leave him?

9. Mike says, "The memory of a wrong isn't stronger than the grace to forgive and go on." Do you believe that is true?

10. Mike and Sam went to the hospital to talk to Dressler about Sam's case, but instead they ministered to him and his dying wife. Can you recall a time that you thought you were headed to do one thing, but God had different plans?

11. Have you ever written anyone a particularly special letter? Ever written a stranger? How would you respond if you received a letter like Sam's?

12. Which one of the dreams described had the most impact on you?

13. Which character did you identify with the most? Why?

14. The story deals with deeds done in darkness. Have you ever done something you knew was wrong and then God shed His light on it so you could repent and restore fellowship with Him?

15. What was the significance of the mountain top throughout the story? How did the author use the mountain top to develop the characters and their relationships with each other?

16. Did you relate to Mike's encounter with God during his night in jail? Do you agree with his conclusions about the role of suffering in a person's life?

17. In the end, Mike decides to return to practicing law. What do you think of that decision?

A poignant tale of innocence and courage
in the tradition of *Huckleberry Finn* and
To Kill a Mockingbird.

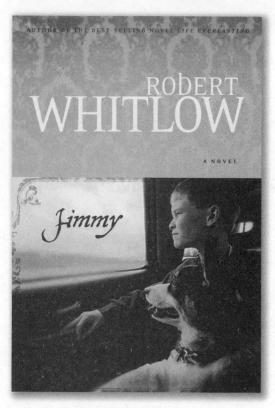

Experience *Jimmy*,
a story that will leave you forever changed.

– *One* –

The defense calls James Lee Mitchell III to the witness stand."

Hearing his name, Jimmy looked up in surprise. For once, it sounded like Daddy was proud of him. Mama leaned close to his ear.

"Go ahead. All you have to do is tell what you heard, just like we practiced this morning at the kitchen table. Your daddy is counting on you."

"But Mama—"

"Mr. Mitchell, are you intending to call your son as a witness in this case?" the judge asked.

Mr. Laney jumped to his feet. His freckled, round face flushed bright red, and his voice rose in protest.

"Your Honor, I discussed this with Mr. Mitchell as soon as I received his list of potential witnesses. This is highly improper. His son is mentally limited and not able to provide competent testimony. Parading him in front of the jury is inflammatory, prejudicial, and inherently unreliable!"

Tall, with light brown hair and dark, piercing eyes, Daddy responded smoothly.

"Judge Robinson, I believe the district attorney misstates the legal standard for competency to testify in the state of Georgia. It is whether a witness understands the nature of a judicial oath. Age and intelligence are not the final arbiters of the capacity to offer probative testimony. That determination rests with the Court, and I'm prepared to lay the foundation necessary for this witness to testify. The fact that he's my son is irrelevant."

Mr. Robinson removed the pen clenched between his teeth and peered over the edge of the bench at Jimmy. The young boy stared back through thick glasses held in place by large ears. Jimmy shared the same hair color as his father, but his eyes, like those of his birth mother, were pale blue. Average in height for a sixth grader at Piney Grove Elementary School, Jimmy ran his finger inside the collar of his shirt and pulled at the tie around his neck.

"How old is he?" the judge asked.

"Twelve, but he'll be thirteen in a few weeks," Daddy replied.

"His chronological age is not an indicator of his mental capacity," Mr. Laney responded quickly. "We're not dealing with a normal—"

"Gentlemen," the judge interrupted. "We'll take up the competency determination outside the presence of the jury. Bailiff, escort the jurors to the jury room."

Jimmy watched as the people sitting in chairs on the other side of his daddy left the courtroom. One black-haired woman wearing a cobalt-blue dress looked at him and smiled.

Pointing in her direction, he whispered to Mama, "Does that lady in the blue dress know me?"

"That's Mrs. Murdock. She's a teacher at the high school."

"I hope I'm in her class when I go to high school. She looks nice. What does she teach?"

"She teaches English."

"Oh," Jimmy said, disappointed. "I already know English."

As soon as the last person left and the bailiff closed the door, Mr. Robinson spoke.

"Mr. Mitchell, proceed with your evidence as to the competency of this young man to testify."

Jimmy watched Daddy pick up a legal pad and turn to a new page.

"Admittedly, Your Honor, Jimmy is mentally limited. However, that doesn't automatically eliminate his capability to offer testimony with probative value in this case."

"What kind of testimony?" Mr. Laney asked. "The defendant is charged with felony possession and intent to distribute over two pounds of cocaine. To bring in an impressionable child who can be manipulated in an effort to distract the jury—"

"Don't jump ahead, Mr. Laney," the judge interrupted. "That goes to the weight assigned to his testimony, not the competency issue. We're going to take everything in proper order, and you'll have ample opportunity to raise your objections."

Mr. Laney, his face still red, sat. Jimmy poked his mama's arm.

"Is Mr. Laney mad at Daddy?"

"Not really. They'll still play golf on Saturday, but he doesn't want you to tell what you heard."

"Why not?"

"He's doing his job."

That didn't make sense, but Jimmy could tell that Mama didn't want to talk. He looked at the man sitting at the table beside Daddy. His name was Jake Garner, and Daddy was his lawyer. Garner had long black hair and a very realistic drawing of a blue-and-red snake on his arm. The tail began at the man's elbow and coiled around his arm before disappearing under his shirt. Jimmy stared at the drawing and wished Jake would roll up his sleeve so he could see the snake's head. Jimmy wasn't afraid of snakes; he'd seen several while walking in the woods with Grandpa. He knew not to pet them or pick them up.

"Mama," he said in a whisper. "Will that drawing of a snake on Jake's arm wash off in the shower?"

"No," she answered. "It's a tattoo. It's permanent."

Jimmy thought a moment. "Could I get a tattoo of Buster on my arm?"

"No. Hush."

Mama turned toward Daddy. Jimmy scooted back against the wooden bench and sat on his hands. He'd never talked to Jake Garner and didn't know about cocaine. But he knew what he'd heard Sheriff Brinson say to Detective Milligan.

Daddy kept talking. "Before asking Jimmy any questions, I thought it would be beneficial to offer expert-opinion testimony from a psychologist who has evaluated him. I'd prefer that both the jury and the Court hear this testimony."

The judge shook his head. "That's not necessary, Mr. Mitchell. Whether this young man is competent to testify is for me to decide. Proceed."

Daddy stepped back. "Perhaps you'll reconsider after you hear what the psychologist has to say. The defense calls Dr. Susan Paris to the stand."

Jimmy hadn't seen the psychologist with blond hair and bright red fingernails slip into the courtroom. He turned around and saw her sitting beside Sheriff Brinson.

When Jimmy first met Dr. Paris, he was shy around her, but after she fixed vanilla wafers with peanut butter on them, they'd gotten along fine. She gave him a test at the beginning of each school year. Jimmy's friend Max told him that tests should be given at the end of the school year to find out what a student learned, not in September to find out what had been forgotten over the summer. But Jimmy didn't argue with Dr. Paris. Eating perfectly prepared vanilla wafers with peanut butter was a small price to pay for having to fill in little circles with a number-two pencil.

Dr. Paris walked to the witness stand. When she passed Jimmy, he glanced down at her hands. Her fingernails were so red they looked wet. She took the witness stand and raised her hand. She looked calm and pretty.

"I do," she said after the judge asked her a question with God's name at the end of it.

The psychologist reached into her purse, and Jimmy entertained a hopeful thought that she'd brought some vanilla wafers into the courtroom. But all she did was take out a tissue.

"Please state your name," Daddy said.

"Dr. Susan Elaine Paris."

"What is your profession?"

"I work part-time as a school psychologist for the Cattaloochie County Board of Education and maintain a private practice focused on children and adolescents here in Piney Grove."

"Please outline your educational and professional qualifications."

"I received a BS in psychology from the University of Virginia, and I earned a master's and doctorate in clinical psychology from Vanderbilt University."

"Are you licensed to practice child and adolescent psychology in the state of Georgia?"

"Yes."

"How long have you been licensed?"

"Five years."

Daddy paused. "Your Honor, we tender Dr. Paris as an expert in the field of child psychology."

"No objection," Mr. Laney said.

"Proceed," the judge said.

"Dr. Paris, have you had the opportunity to evaluate my son, Jimmy Mitchell?"

"Yes, as part of my regular duties for the school system, I give Jimmy a battery of tests each fall to determine his status and help formulate an educational plan for the teachers working with him. I also have access to the evaluations conducted by Dr. Kittle, my predecessor."

Jimmy had forgotten Dr. Kittle's name. She had white hair and didn't paint her fingernails at all. Jimmy leaned close to Mama.

"What happened to Dr. Kittle?" he whispered.

"She retired and moved to the beach."

Jimmy liked the beach but not the ocean. Even small waves terrified him.

"Can you summarize Jimmy's general mental status?" Daddy asked.

"Yes. He has below-average general intellectual functioning with deficits in adaptive capability. Age-appropriate IQ testing has consistently revealed a verbal, performance, and full-scale IQ in the 68 to 70 range. An IQ score less than 59 indicates a severe deficit. Over 70 is dull-normal. Thus, Jimmy is in between mental retardation and the dull-normal category."

Jimmy squirmed in his seat. He didn't understand everything the psychologist was saying, but he recognized the word *retardation*. Mean people used that word when they talked about him.

"Where is he placed within the school system?" Daddy asked.

"Jimmy does not have any abnormal behavioral problems and, pursuant to the school board's inclusion policy, is integrated into a regular classroom. His teachers utilize nonstandard testing to monitor his progress, and I review the results on a monthly basis."

"What can you tell the Court about Jimmy's current level of intellectual functioning?"

"Once Jimmy grasps a concept, he is capable of retaining it. However, he faces a formidable challenge in appropriately applying what he's learned. The educational process can be frustrating to him, but he maintains a good attitude and has shown adequate progress."

Mr. Laney stood. "Your Honor, this is a criminal trial, not a parent-teacher conference."

"Move along, Mr. Mitchell," the judge said.

"Yes, sir."

"Why did Daddy say 'yes, sir'?" Jimmy whispered to Mama. "Mr. Robinson doesn't look as old as Grandpa."

"But he's the judge."

Daddy looked down at the legal pad in his right hand. "Dr. Paris, given the results of your testing, and based upon your three years of professional interaction with Jimmy, do you have an opinion whether he has the capacity to know the importance of telling the truth?"

"Yes, I do."

"What is your opinion?"

"I believe it is a concept he understands. One of the primary points I emphasize in testing a student is the need to answer every question truthfully. Some psychological tests incorporate inquiries that reveal whether a child is being consistent in his or her responses. Jimmy is uniformly forthright and honest, even if the truth casts him in a negative light. He does not exhibit an inclination to manipulate his answers and try to fool the test."

"What is she saying about me?" Jimmy asked.

Mama patted him on the leg. "That you're a good boy who tries to do his best and tells the truth."

"Will Jimmy understand the language of a judicial oath?" Daddy asked.

"If it is explained to him in the right way. He believes in God and will tell the truth because he believes it is a sin to lie. In fact, I think he understands what it means to be a false witness. We discussed the concept recently when he told me that his mother was teaching him the Ten Commandments."

"Will I have to say them?" Jimmy asked Mama, touching the ends of his fingers. "I can do it with you in my room, but I'd be afraid in front of all these people."

"Not today."

Daddy stepped closer to Dr. Paris. "What can you tell Judge Robinson about Jimmy's memory?"

Dr. Paris sat up straighter and looked up at the judge. "When he works hard, Jimmy can memorize rote information. The Ten Commandments are an example. However, there is another side to his memory that is, at times, remarkable. He will occasionally remind me of a phrase or sentence I said months or even years ago. I've discussed this unusual ability with members of the school staff, and others have noticed the same capability."

"Objection," Mr. Laney said. "The opinions of other teachers would be hearsay."

Daddy responded, "She's been qualified as an expert and can rely on statistical data to support her opinion."

"I don't hear her claiming to have collected statistical data, but I'll allow her to state her opinion and give it the weight I deem appropriate," the judge said.

Daddy spoke. "If Jimmy told you the substance of a conversation he'd overheard, would you believe him?"

"Generally, yes."

"That's all from Dr. Paris."

"Mr. Laney, you may cross-examine the witness," the judge said.

A few stubborn strands of reddish hair clung to the top of Mr. Laney's head. His face no longer appeared flushed.

"Dr. Paris, are you aware that Jimmy is in the courtroom?"

"Of course. I saw him on the front bench with his mother."

"Does his presence have any effect on your testimony?"

"No. He doesn't understand the terminology I'm using. He knows he's a special boy."

Jimmy sat up so he could pay attention. He'd lived almost thirteen years with the word *special* hanging around his neck. Teachers told him that being special was good, and even though he knew he could get in trouble for disagreeing with his teachers, Jimmy thought they were wrong. He'd been special all his life, and it had created a lot of problems for him, especially at school. Being special meant being different from other children, and differences brought persecution and loneliness.

However, when Mama told Jimmy he was special, the word took on another meaning. Coming from her mouth, the word wrapped around him like a hug. Mama couldn't have children of her own, so Jimmy was the one and only object of her love. She chose him when she married Daddy, and from that day forward, Jimmy enjoyed unique status in his family as a very special boy.

Mr. Laney spoke. "Dr. Paris, are you claiming that Jimmy Mitchell has a photographic memory for everything spoken in his presence?"

"Photographic memory relates to visual images. Jimmy's ability is auditory."

The side of Mr. Laney's neck flashed red all the way to the top of his left ear.

"Dr. Paris, if you want to engage in a semantic—"

"But I know what you mean," Dr. Paris continued calmly. "Jimmy can't recall everything he hears. In fact, his memory of conversations appears somewhat random. All I can say is that he sometimes has a parrotlike ability to repeat what he's heard, including words he can't define."

"Does he understand the significance of what he's repeating?"

"Only if it falls within his level of current cognitive functioning. His world is expanding, but at a much slower rate than for a typical child."

"Does he remember the information verbatim?"

"I can't answer that because I've never had the opportunity to quantify it in a reliable way, but in my experience the substance of what he remembers is accurate."

Mr. Laney turned toward the judge.

"Your Honor, the defense is trying to tout this boy as a human court reporter. This is exactly the type of prejudicial activity I warned the Court about before the jury left the courtroom. You have a handicapped young man who will play on the jurors' sympathies when they need to be focusing on the hard evidence in the case."

"Are you finished with your questions?" the judge asked.

"Uh, no sir."

"Then save your argument for later."